Praise for Kate Williams

'Brilliant – a passionate and poignant story of a glittering family on the precipice of a vanished world. Spellbinding, gripping and beautiful – a must-read'
Lisa Hilton

'An all-encompassing, sweeping epic. It's a book to get immersed in for hours at a time … a wonderful achievement'
Katherine Webb

'A wonderful evocation of a family torn apart by war, packed with drama and written with a sensitive warmth and fantastic historical insight'
Imogen Robertson

'Kate Williams paints a spellbinding portrait of a family clinging on desperately to their privileged way of life'
Good Housekeeping

'A beautifully conjured family saga. Fans of *Downton Abbey* will love it'
Alison Weir

'Richly detailed, light of foot, Williams tantalises with loose ends and disturbs with shocking shadows'
Independent

'This terrific saga comes with a fascinating twist …Williams has a gift for showing how great movements in history affect the lives of people caught up in them'
Kate Saunders, *The Times*

'Williams has a sharp eye for the contradictions and mysteries of human nature and a vivid turn of phrase … she uses her historian's knowledge to brilliant effect'
Daily Mail

'Shades of *Downton*, with a dash of *Atonement*'
Tatler

'Williams draws expertly on mysterious, flawed characters coming of age in a displaced world in this gripping period novel… A haunting piece of historical fiction'
The Lady

'Her insight into the aftermath of the First World War and shattered society shines out of every pa ˉ powerful family saga'
Sunday Mirror

'Gripping from the first pa   l. Following the journey of Celia, whos   World War, it combines suspense with history an   .. It's a must-read'
Grazia

The HOUSE *of* SHADOWS

KATE WILLIAMS

ORION

First published in Great Britain in 2018 by Orion Books,
an imprint of The Orion Publishing Group Ltd
Carmelite House, 50 Victoria Embankment
London EC4Y ODZ

An Hachette UK Company

1 3 5 7 9 10 8 6 4 2

A CIP catalogue record for this book is
available from the British Library.

ISBN (Hardback) 978 1 4091 3995 9
ISBN (Export Trade Paperback) 978 1 4091 3994 2

Typeset at The Spartan Press Ltd
Lymington, Hants

Printed and bound in Great Britain by Clays Ltd,
Elcograf S.p.A.

MIX
Paper from
responsible sources
FSC® C104740

www.orionbooks.co.uk

Also by Kate Williams

FICTION:

The Pleasures of Men
The Storms of War
The Edge of the Fall

NON-FICTION:

England's Mistress: The Infamous Life of Emma Hamilton
Becoming Queen
Josephine: Desire, Ambition, Napoleon
Young Elizabeth: The Making of Our Queen
Rival Queens: Elizabeth I and Mary

'We're explorers,' he whispered, reaching for Lily's thin hand. And so they were, passing deep into unfamiliar land, looking for dragons, treasure, except they weren't looking for things but freedom. Pulling the branches aside and entering the forest they had been so consistently forbidden. *Don't go there. Promise me.* He could almost feel the blueish light burn his cheeks, fluttering like flame on a stove.

He'd thought she would be afraid. As they passed over a branch, she let go of his hand and then she was moving forward, her dark hair swinging down her back.

'Come on,' she said. He followed her, even though inside he was crying out. *Let me go first.* She was going on, jumping over the knotty branches on the floor, as if it was a game. *It's not a game!* The whole wood was silent now. You couldn't hear the noises they'd left behind, the adults, drinking and talking and laughing in the warm late summer air even though it wasn't funny, none of it was ever funny. They lied, pretended, didn't live for the truth. He and Lily would never be like them, not ever.

He caught his ankle on a branch, almost fell. The damp ground dipped towards a stream, fast running, faster than it should be for September. The dashing water filled his head. He'd drawn a map but he hadn't put in a stream. He couldn't think where it had begun, it would have to start in the Stoneythorpe garden, but there was only that stagnant pond in the place where he and Lily had sat and made their dreams – until the adults had come in and everything had been spoiled. He thought of his mother, holding tight to him in those early days, telling him she'd never leave him.

His heart lurched and he threw his mind into the rushing dark water, staring at it until the thought of his mother went away.

'We have to jump,' said Lily. 'Come on.'

A few years ago, they'd played explorer games. Arctic, Africa, India. It had to be the Arctic first, he said. Start at the top. They fought polar bears, skipped over icebergs, chased the woolly mammoths. The worlds had been divided by the stream and when they grew weary of one, they were supposed to leap to another. Lily would always mark out the stream in the garden. 'Jump,' she said, already weary of polar bears, keen for new beasts, capturing lions in Africa or wrestling snakes. He didn't want to, he wanted to stay where they were. 'We haven't finished!'

'Yes, we have. Come on.'

And so he did, leaving the world unfinished behind him, waiting for them to return.

Lily leapt over the stream. She waited on the other side, hands on hips. 'Why are you so *slow?*'

That pierced his soul. He stared at her, dark figure against the tangled branches on the other side. The trees were like strands of a woman's hair. Lily had pulled her hair down as they had run together and now he wanted to beg her: Put it back! Tie it up before it gets tangled in the hair of the tree and girl and tree become one.

He took a step, felt his foot slide in the mud. He grasped at a branch. I don't want to fall, he wanted to say. Lily was already turning away.

He'd jumped over a million streams, surely. He'd jumped into the sea, swimming ponds, a river or two. His mind filled with his aunt, who'd fallen from the cliff and died on the rocks. But why did his mind do that? If he fell in, he'd only get wet. Aunt Louisa had died, looking at the sea. Uncle Arthur had held out his hands to catch her but he couldn't stop her fall.

He shook the thought away. They were leaving all that behind, all the secrets and boxes full of letters and all that talking but no one ever telling the truth.

He landed in the mud on the other side, reached out and held tight to Lily.

'Finally!' she said, shaking off his hand. 'Let's go.'

Now they were together. They could never be parted. He moved forward and his foot caught. He looked down at the spiral of small vines and pulled it free.

He had been in charge of the planning. Weeks of hiding from the adults, writing lists in his room. He drew a map and hid it under her bookshelf. Every day, one of them would steal some type of foodstuff from the pantry, a box of something, a packet of sugar, a tin of meat, food that wouldn't spoil. They took sheets and blankets from the cupboard, packed them up into his bag, along with other things they really needed, like toothpaste and soap, their notebooks.

They'd spend the first night in the woods, so that no one would find them, and then head towards the road, where they'd find someone to take them in a car along the way. No one would guess his real age, they'd think he was quite grown, not eleven at all. He would draw and she'd write stories for money – and then they could travel, live in France, Italy, places by the sea. They wouldn't be like the others, bowed down by work and home and money, never seeing what really mattered.

They'd stolen from their grandmother. One day, she'd beckoned him into the room where she lay on the pile of pillows. He didn't much like her room, the air hung heavy, full of scent that smelt of forced flowers. On all the sides of the room were vases, of wobbly, wavy, marbled glass, pale colours, pink, mauve, turquoise, green, with cut lips like fancy tulips.

'No one likes my vases,' she said to him. 'They say they're ugly. My mother said they were ugly, even then. Do you think so?'

'I think they are nice,' he said. 'And you like them, that's all that matters.'

Verena lay back, smiled. 'I knew you'd understand.' She held out a finger, heavy with its gold ring and sharp-shaved jewel. 'Come here.'

He went closer, into the jungle leaves of scent, the pink silk cushions.

'Closer.' She pointed at the floor and he knelt.

He was by her bed now. The scent was cloying, like cotton wool in his nose. He held his breath.

'It's all money,' hissed Verena. The sound rushed around his ear like when you hold a seashell to it. 'Money! They all laugh at those vases but they're full of money. All my money. That's where it is.'

She fell back against the pillows, as if exhausted by the effort. 'And when I die you shall have all of it. Don't forget. Come here and take it.'

'Thank you.'

'You deserve it. You deserve everything.'

He'd stayed kneeling, not sure what to do. And then he looked up and her eyes were closed. He'd crept backwards then, so she didn't notice, out, the scent clinging to his hair and eyes.

And then he'd gone in and taken it. All of it. When she was asleep, he'd swept it into his hands and however wrong he'd felt, it hadn't stopped him.

Lily too had stolen. She'd taken all the money from the box that her mother kept under the bed – a whole twenty pounds.

'I'll go back,' Lily said. 'One day. Explain she didn't really need the money like we do. She won't mind.'

Would Verena feel the same? He didn't know.

'Come closer,' she said. 'We need to go deeper!' The thicket was dense around them, close on their shoulders.

'I wrote on the map we should go around. Not through.'

She shook her head. Her black eyes glittered against her bright cheeks and he wanted to touch her hand, the two of them against the world. Even though he was plain and childish next to her. He felt he could never reach her.

'You never know what we might find.'

'Aren't you afraid?'

'I have you! Why would I be afraid? I'll go first.' She ducked her head, moved forwards. He watched her.

And then there was a sound. A branch cracked. A bird fluttered, flew to the sky. There was someone there. Someone behind them. Michael swung around. The shadows skittered away. Mice, voles maybe.

He turned back for Lily.

He cried out, reached forward, looked frantically. Nothing.

The air was closing around where her shape had been. He reached out to stop it but it was no good. Too late.

Lily had gone.

PART ONE

ONE

———

Manhattan, January 1929

New York shone. The sharp brightness of it gleamed on your face, behind you when you weren't looking, loomed high over you and glittered down at your head. Even in wintry January, it was alive. Celia had never seen anything like it. London felt low and scrubby in comparison. She could hardly believe she was actually there. It didn't look real, false high buildings, shimmering windows and people rushing along the sidewalk, the roads full of cars. The whole place was always being rebuilt, she thought. She sometimes went out in the street and did nothing but stare above her head at the buildings, new great masses of apartments and offices and hotels being constructed. The city was all energy, building, talking, hurrying, making anew. The whole of America full of things bright and improved, not like the old world. And underneath all the new buildings, the glass and stone, was a different world, where you could buy the alcohol that was banned, dance hard and fast to music that beat in your mind.

They'd stepped off the chill boat into the freezing port to make their fortune ten days before, taken eye-wateringly expensive rooms in the Plaza on Central Park, they'd had appointments – three, four, five a day, hour-long meetings in large, dark-panelled, overheated rooms, with men, dozens of them, tall, dark, pale, thin, fat, all of them in grey suits, expensive shoes, their faces and bodies saying 'money', even if their mouths never did. Celia stared at them as Arthur talked – for no one expected her to speak – not a woman. But she was there to help him – for getting the Americans to invest in Winter Meats was their last chance. And Arthur said she looked the part. 'We're selling the family,' he said. 'Stoneythorpe and the English country home. And you look exactly it, nice family girl, English rose.'

Not true, of course. She was half-German, full of dark secrets she could never tell. And Stoneythorpe was falling down, the great Jacobean house Rudolf had bought them when they were rich, before the war. He'd dreamt of being lord of the manor – and now they were desperate, dependent on Americans to give them money. Their time in America had to succeed.

Looking at Arthur, it made you think he'd be kind: handsome, a chiselled face, tall and broad in his suit, moving with that easy grace that made people want to look at him, men and women. Arthur and Emmeline had got all the looks. Celia had the fair hair and large eyes, like them, but she didn't have their smooth shell. Her skin seemed to have been designed to hide nothing, flaming with cold, heat, embarrassment, love. Her hair was fine and she didn't have Arthur's clean movement, but legs and arms too long, like a bird, and often when she looked in the mirror, she had a startled look in her eyes. At what, she didn't know. But she doubted that it charmed the bankers in the same way as Arthur's face did. He looked like he was always about to host a party.

'My sister,' he said, introducing her, and they all shook her hand politely, offered her a drink, sometimes told her their names. Otherwise, she sat there, tried to listen to what they said. She tried – but, really, as it was today, at Messrs Morgan and Co. on Fifty-Second Street, her mind was elsewhere. It grew and flew, high up out of the room, up past the windows into the cloudy sky – so high that it hovered above America, and there, looking down, it saw Michael, spotted her son's little, seven-year-old face, outside a house somewhere, captured him and flew him up, back to New York and the dark panelled room, where Celia was waiting for him. She took him in her arms and held him for ever. She filled his room with toys and they built a life together.

When he said, 'Why did you give me away?', she told the truth, said she'd been put to sleep and he'd been taken from her, spirited away because her mother, Verena, didn't want the blot of an illegitimate child. She'd sent him to America, believed all the advertising that life was better there – and Celia had never known where he was, didn't even know he was alive – until her father, Rudolf, started talking after Arthur's trial. 'I'll keep you forever.'

But she didn't promise to tell him the whole truth. When he asked, 'Who was my father?', she'd tell him he was a soldier. *Father unknown*. 'You don't need a father,' she'd say to him. 'We have each other.'

But, instead, she sat there, her body present, mind far away, until the meeting ended and the younger men came to show them to the stairs and the way out into the street. 'That went well,' Arthur said. 'Didn't you think?'

She nodded, but he barely needed a response, went leaping off into his own ideas, talked of how well they'd do, how Winter Meats would take over America, what it would be like to watch investors falling like ninepins, if they could just get one bank to start things off.

Everyone was busy. Shiny, icy cars – so many shiny cars queued in the roads, their bright fenders pushing into each other like a line of impatient school children. Carriages waited on the streets near Central Park, the Upper East Side, but by the shops and the theatres and town, it was all cars. Business, business! And money. So much money – women flashed by in furs, men in the new suits, double-breasted, pinstriped, loose around the waist, their shoes sharper on your eyes than the sun.

When they'd arrived, Celia had realised that she and Arthur weren't dressed correctly, that their English clothes were outdated, but she'd had no chance to visit a shop, only to stare in windows that were sometimes so highly glazed that they reflected nothing back at you but light. Their days had been all meetings, cool men with piles of papers in dark panelled rooms, talking numbers, zeros, tens, thousands, customers, products, sales.

She could see the truth. The men in the banks were polite – but they would give them nothing. How naive they had been! They had come over thinking that Winter Meats would be wildly successful, seized upon by America, factories bursting to make their pies. Coming to America was their last chance to save the family, for if they failed, then the business would crash, they'd have to sell the house and they would have nothing. Their parents near destitute, nothing for her sister, Emmeline, and her children, Lily and Albert, still so young. And their brother Michael, dead in the war, and Louisa, who fell from a cliff when she was happy – they would be left alone in the churchyard and all of their history would be forgotten.

Celia knew she had to do it. Arthur was growing angry, blaming the new fad – lady vegetarians and their fretting over baby lambs. He was impatient with the men in the banks, and that wouldn't get them anywhere. And she had a plan. She would go to one of the grand new stores, find the floor where they sold the food. She imagined it not looking like a shop back home, but a wondrous museum of things – with space, surely, for Winter Meats. She'd work out exactly how their pies and meats would fit in and then the men would listen.

She crossed over the road and fell in behind two small boys walking together. They were shabbily dressed, without an adult. Some of those they passed swerved to avoid them, thinking they were pickpockets, she supposed. She moved closer. They must be so cold without coats. The larger would be about the same age as Michael now, maybe a little older. He was talking animatedly to the other one, a thin child with gingerish hair. She longed to step nearer still, hear what he was saying. She always wondered what children talked about, especially those around Michael's age. She found herself following children, searching for him in their faces, staring until their mothers hurried them away, casting suspicious glances at her over their shoulders.

The two boys drew ahead and she hurried to catch up with them. She wanted to reach out her hand for them. She grew closer, forgetting the department store now.

The boys paused at the edge of the road. The older one put his arm round the younger. He must be afraid of the road, great roaring cars hurtling past them, buses, men dodging in between, carrying crates of bricks, parcels, deliveries. She wanted to hold their hands, help them over. She was just about to touch the elder's shoulder, tell him there was a better place to cross further down, ask them if they didn't have scarves when they pitched off into the road. Two cars flew past before she could move out – and then she saw them.

They were still walking forward, holding hands.

A black car was coming towards them. The driver couldn't see them. Things were winding around her, the cars, the people. Someone behind her was talking. Celia's eyes blurred. She couldn't see. Only the two of them holding hands. People were still passing, not understanding.

What if he were Michael? He could be.

She had to save them.

Celia threw herself forward and it felt to her as if she were jumping further than she ever could, halfway across the road, as if a car had thrown her forward. She grasped the children with a strength that felt like it was someone else's and pulled all three of them back. Then they were lying there in the freezing road, in front of the car, and the cold sun was burning her eyes. People were crowding around her, so many that she could see nothing but clothes. All the cars had stopped and she could hear horns beeping behind. 'Move on!'

'There's been an accident!' a man shouted.

'Are you all right, Miss?' One was trying to help her up.

'Don't move her! She might be injured!'

She gazed up into a woman's face, matronly, dark hair. Her head hurt so much. 'The children.' The driver she had jumped in front of was out of his car, head between his legs. The front of his car shone bright silver.

A man who looked like a fireman leant over her. 'All right, Miss. We'll take over from here.'

'Well, they can't be hers,' said a voice. 'Look like pickpockets to me.'

Celia tried to speak the word, 'No,' but her voice wouldn't move.

'We need a doctor. Is anyone a doctor?' The word rippled around the crowd. Doctor. Doctor. She heard it in the back of her lost mind. A man was leaning over her, feeling her forehead and her wrist. His hands were on her sides. 'Where does it hurt, Miss?'

'My head,' she managed. He touched it. She lifted her eyes, tried to see the children. The elder boy was sitting up, drinking from a tin cup. A woman had her arm around him. The other one was still lying on the floor.

The doctor looked again. 'I think she is fine. No broken bones.' He gestured to the woman and they both helped her up. She leant against him, wanting to fall again, feeling as if she was made from a ball of wool. 'They're not yours? That was a brave thing you did. Foolish, some might say.'

The words were lost. Her face hurt. She nodded.

'You could have died, don't you see that? You should go to the hospital.'

She felt a strength rise in her, pulled it up to speak. 'They would have died. That car would have killed them.'

She leant against him. 'Don't fall,' he said.

She looked at the children, tried to reach out her hand to the eldest. The youngest was sitting up now, looking around. Of course, neither of them was Michael. One was too old, the other too young.

'They're fine,' the doctor said. 'You took the weight of the landing. They'll be running around in a minute.'

'Oh of course they will,' said a woman behind him. 'Off robbing more like. Turn out their pockets and they'll likely have stolen something.'

She heard people nodding, agreeing. She looked around. The crowd was changing. Nobody was dead and their emotions had been wound up for nothing – they had to put them somewhere. The accents, thick and unfamiliar, wrapped around her.

'Turn out their pockets!'

'Easy enough to see why they were running.'

One of the men had hold of the older boy. Another one was seizing the younger.

'Stop it!' She pulled loose of the doctor holding her arm. 'Leave them alone. Why don't you search my bag!' She looked down and saw it on the floor. 'There! Search that bag! Maybe I was a pickpocket. Just because they're poor doesn't mean they did wrong.'

'What is she saying?' said a man. 'Is she some sort of tourist?'

'If you want to search anyone, you search me!' Her head didn't hurt any more. She was so determined on shouting that it took up her whole body. 'You check *my* bag!' She stamped her foot. And then she looked over to the boys and nodded. The elder one seized the younger and they began to edge away.

'You look at my bag!' she cried. 'You search me!'

The man who had been complaining reluctantly picked up her bag. A woman pushed through and said, 'A lady should do this!' and started pulling out the things with enthusiasm, purse, mirror, throwing them into the hands of the man next to her. Celia's pencil clattered to the floor. Celia stared hard at them, resisting her desire to look away.

And then she glanced to the side – and the boys had gone.

The doctor followed her line of vision. 'Look!'

A man shouted, a woman screamed. 'Find a policeman!'

And then they were all flustering about the boys, saying they were criminals. She picked up her bag and limped across the road, leaving them behind. She walked past a shoe shop, dragged herself around the next corner and then leant against the wall. The boys weren't there. Of course they weren't. They'd run far away. She'd lost them.

She felt a tear slip down her cheek. She'd never see them again, not in this great city of thousands.

Probably, on these roads, it happened every day, children fell and were injured in front of cars. Those great, terrifying cars. 'It's wrong,' she said. A man walking past raised his eyebrow and she looked away.

She breathed deeply. Her hands were bloodied, her face was probably scratched, her dress was torn. She wasn't in a fit state to go to the department store. They might not even let her in.

But she had no choice. This was her only spare time. They had meetings with men in banks all day tomorrow. She reached up, straightened her hat, scrubbed her hands on her dress, walked forwards. She made a bargain with God. *Because I saved those boys, please let somebody save Michael. Make them keep him safe.* Someone, somewhere, must leap out for him, just as she had for them.

She passed Lord and Taylor and Bloomingdale's, then to Bergdorf-Goodman's, through the great gold-tipped doors as the doorman held them open for her and the heat blazed on her face. The perfume hall opened out to her, giant bottles that looked like they could barely be real, beautiful women with bright lipstick holding out presents. There was so much gold. And probably frankincense and myrrh as well, the whole lot.

She smiled politely at the women wielding glass bottles – who were themselves so polite, they didn't flinch at her, when she was dirty and probably even had blood on her face. She asked for directions to the powder room and saw that her face was even worse than she'd thought, sooty smears around her eyes, grazes on her chin and her forehead. She dabbed at her face and hands. The dirt on her gown would have to be left as it was. She sailed out, holding herself high, pretending to be her mother in the old days, before her world got old and sad.

'Food Hall, please.'

She walked down the stairs, holding the golden bannister, passing women who looked like housekeepers and office girls looking for lunch. She stepped into the hall and the place dazzled her eyes, bright piles of boxes, a great mountain of perfect red apples, glowing like a leftover Christmas tree, towers of fruit cakes arranged on tables, glistening dried fruit, dates and figs in tree-like stacks, a beautiful array of chocolates that you couldn't dare to touch. She walked in further, as if into a forest of beautiful arrangements – and saw heaps of vegetables, the meat counter, a whole cabinet full of cream puddings, chocolate eclairs and little sponges topped with strawberries, horns made of pastry, tiny chocolate cakes. She trailed a finger across the glass front. The food in New York was more brilliant than that in London. Most of the cakes she'd never even seen before, large glistening chocolate-covered things, round doughnuts glossy with pink and red icing. Meringues were stacked so high in windows that she wondered if anyone ever got to the bottom of the pile.

So much food. So many people wanting it. An office girl pushed in front of her and bought a chocolate eclair, packed up by the man behind the counter into a pristine white box.

The girl smiled, briefly, a flash of lipstick, bobbed hair under the smart hat.

'Excuse me,' she said in a thick Brooklyn accent. 'In a rush.'

Celia nodded. Her mind turned and then flew back to the boat over, a fleeting memory she had all but forgotten. She had been sitting on the deck when a group of girls had sat down nearby, not one over twenty-five. They were giggling and talking at the same time. Something about the face of one, the curve of the mouth, the cheekbone, was like the office girl with the eclair.

The boat had been full of girls. 'What are they all here for?' she'd asked one of the officers who had got talking to Arthur at dinner. He and Arthur had been laughing, calling them the ship of girls. 'They're like the ones going out to India last century, would-be wives,' he'd said.

'They're all going over to work. The shopgirls of New York are coming from England. Hundreds of them. Wouldn't you?' he shrugged. 'You're young, no men at home?'

'We're all going over to make our fortune.' Arthur grinned. 'Them and us.' He wrinkled his mouth. 'Not everyone can succeed.'

Celia had stared at the group of girls. *The shopgirls of New York.* They were talking non-stop, smiling, met on the boat, but now they'd maybe even take rooms together, always remember each other. The one who made them all laugh, they'd exchange Christmas cards with her and her husband and children, a memory of the old days.

'In New York, we'll have a restaurant under our flat so we never have to cook,' one was saying.

'We won't even need a kitchen. We'll never stay in.' The taller blonde was laughing. 'My ma spends her life in the kitchen. No fear I will be like that.'

The smaller blonde tossed her hair. 'And how will you eat? You can't afford restaurants every day on a shopgirl's salary.'

'My Prince will come. Or I will invent a way to replace meals with some sort of pill. Buy a pill, then you've had a meal.'

'No! I like eating!'

'But not *cooking*.'

'What if your Prince is hungry?'

'Then he can cook for me!'

Celia looked around the Food Hall. There was something in it. All these girls, shopgirls, office girls, waitresses, clerks. *Not wanting to cook.*

She had briefly been one of those office girls, living in a flat after she'd had Michael, when she thought he was dead, worked as a secretary, handed all her money to spiritualists and fortune tellers to contact him. What had they eaten? She tried to remember. She had shared rooms near Baker Street that had a tiny kitchen, but they'd never turned the oven on for fear of how much it would have smoked the flat. Not that Celia really knew how to cook. Tom had mocked her when they'd been children, saying she'd never made a cup of tea.

The girls she had lived with ate at Lyons' tea houses and picked at cake, a full meal only rarely, if they'd been paid. There must be thousands of girls like them, in London and New York, not cooking, not dining out, living off scraps of cake and strong tea.

And then she thought: it wasn't about serving up great stacks of meat to cooks in large houses like Stoneythorpe, it was about the modern girl in a flat and what she might buy for herself.

Living alone. That's the future. She thought back to herself: what would she like to have eaten? She imagined vegetable pies, other foods in jars, soup, a lot of soup. And puddings, so many puddings, chocolate cakes, jam sponge, jam tarts, biscuits of chocolate and jam, delicate ones. Could you put a mousse in a jar? Meringues? Her father had served canned meat – but it was mere fuel, nothing attractive and New York didn't want it. Her jars would be beautiful, things that women would buy because they had to have them.

She stood there and her mind flashed with new ideas, food for flappers, lovingly cooked by her in a kitchen in New York. Or overseen by her, since she couldn't cook. She'd have cooks to help her, other women chopping and making sauces, creaming butter, kneading shortbread. Her heart soared, her mind flew across the shop, creating displays, imagining satisfied girls leaving with baskets of food in jars, the excellence of the future cancelling out the misery of the past.

She cast her mind back to the time that she thought they had Stoneythorpe forever, in those last days before the war. She'd been fifteen, Emmeline had been about to marry Sir Hugh, Michael was back from Cambridge with his friend, Jonathan. In the days, she'd been riding with Tom and thought they'd stay friends forever. Instead, everything around her changed – Michael ran off to war with Tom, Emmeline eloped with her tutor, Mr Samuel Janus, Rudolf was taken away and interned, Verena let the house crumble around her. Celia couldn't bear it, so had lied about her age and drove ambulances in France, cradled her friend Shep when she died in the bombing, kept going until the news came to her about Michael's death. And then Tom – whom she loved, had thought she would always be with, because they'd loved each other as children – told her that wasn't how he saw it at all, that he would never love her and so she had to find a life without him.

Now she imagined great stacks of glass jars, luminous, boxes filled with rustling silver paper. She put the memories that made her cry out at night into the glass pile, the towers of fruits and jams and chocolates. Wrapped up in the beautiful glass, they would be safe, unable to hurt. She'd find Michael and create a business her family could be proud of – and then they could all live together in Stoneythorpe, mended, back to its own glory, and there would be money for Emmeline, Lily and Albert, so they could have a proper home of their own, and even though Michael and Louisa were dead, the rest of them would live and little Michael would carry their dreams forward.

Celia walked back towards Central Park, the wind slewing grey across the streets, her mind whirling with ideas. They'd start with a small kitchen, just a few women in Brooklyn busy weighing and stirring and baking. Then they would expand out, build factories, take the jars to shops all over the country. They'd go to California in the sun, then the prairie land of the Midwest, Kansas, Ohio, all the way right to the very edge, Michigan, Montana. Boxes and boxes of jars on the trains, criss-crossing America, taking the food to the modern girls so they could keep working, dancing, do what they liked.

In the boardroom, Arthur was standing at the front, talking to a table of men in suits. He went through the list of facts and figures, talked about the company's heritage, the excellent taste. He came to the end and stood expectantly. Celia hurt for him.

'We've heard all this kind of thing before,' drawled one. 'Nothing new.'

The man sitting at the head of the table nodded. 'Mr Witt, you seem like a good guy. So let me be honest with you. We don't need the British coming here telling us how to make meat. We have plenty of meat in America. We're looking to invest in something new. American customers are searching for novelty. We're straight talkers at Broad and Brothers. The truth is that there's no market for this.'

Celia looked from the man to Arthur. Her brother was almost falling against the wall.

Celia leapt up. 'I have something.'

The man – Mr Broad, she supposed – raised an eyebrow. Then he moved to stand. The others followed him.

'Wait!' Celia hurried to the front. 'Just listen. Please! I have something. I know.'

And so she started talking and conjured for them the piles of glowing jars, the modern girl dancing at cafés with no time to cook, bread and pies in jars and cans, cakes they could take away. She didn't stop. She didn't look in their eyes to see if they were bored, she just kept going. Something in her said, *This is your last chance.* It was different this time. She had the girl in her mind, going into the store. She talked and talked, about the girls in their flats who were never going to be like their mothers, the trains crossing America full of jars and tins, the girls buying dozens of them at a time.

'It's the flapper girls,' she said. 'So far, everybody has been trying to sell them make-up and films and clothes. But what about *food*? The modern girl has to eat!'

She stopped, breathless, excited as if she'd been running. The dark clock in the corner ticked.

The man at the head of the table nodded.

'Miss – Witt, is it, too? Well, Miss Witt…' He paused. He looked at her. The time in the room stood still. The air fell around her, tiny pieces of dust. Then he raised an eyebrow. 'I think there just might be something in this.' He smiled. 'I do believe you have struck on something here.'

And so the others broke in, began nodding and agreeing.

She looked over their heads and smiled at Arthur. He gave a smile back, just about.

TWO

Manhattan, January 1929

'*Psst.*'

Celia looked up but couldn't see anything, drew her coat closer around her. She lit the match by the moon and tried to light the cigarette. The thing smoked. She breathed in, started coughing. The smoke was up her nose, at the back of her throat, her eyes were watering. She wished she'd brought water with her, coughed violently again. She was sitting at the back of the hotel, on the dustbins. It was the only place she could think. She looked around for the source of the noise, but it was all bricks and darkness. She must have been imagining things.

'You need to breathe it in,' said a voice.

She looked up, both sides, could see nothing.

'I'm up here,' said a small voice. Brooklyn accent. Probably a boy.

'Who are you?'

'You know!'

'Where are you?'

'I said, up here!' There was a shuffle and a boy jumped down from the dustbins. His clothes were ragged, the ginger curls around his face needed cutting. He tugged back his hair, and grinned.

'It's you!' The smaller child she had rescued from the car. 'Is it really you?'

'Of course it's me!' He grinned. 'Why are you trying to smoke that thing?'

Close up, she saw the freckles dotted over his tanned nose and cheeks. His brown eyes were bright under tiny eyebrows. He almost crackled with energy in the cold.

She looked at it ruefully. 'I thought I might enjoy it. I can't understand why anyone would. It's horrible.'

'You just have to get used to it, I reckon. Practice!'

She raised her eyebrows. 'You shouldn't know. You're a child. Anyway, what are you doing here? It's too cold for you to be out. Where's your brother?'

'Oh, he wasn't my brother. Just a friend. Well, sort of a friend. Anyway, he's gone. I think he went off North.' He scraped his hand through his red hair.

'He's gone? You don't know where. And what about you?' Her head was spinning. 'How old are you?'

'I'm not sure. People have tried to guess. Maybe eleven? Twelve? Can I have one of those?' He pointed at the cigarette.

'I think you're a bit young.'

'Oh, come on, miss. Anyway, I can show you how to do it.'

He probably smoked to forget he was hungry. She couldn't not give him one. 'Here you are,' she said, passing it over. 'I have a match as well. But you know you shouldn't. Aren't you worried about fire? It's not safe.'

He lit it, experienced, and breathed in. 'See this is how you do it, miss. Breathe it right down then blow it out.'

He looked even younger than twelve to her, but that was maybe because he was so small and thin. 'How long have you been smoking?'

'Oh, for years!'

'And you live on the streets?'

He shrugged airily. 'All kinds of places. Now, miss, to business. Lots of people wouldn't try to help children like us. So I'm grateful. I came to see what I could do for you.'

'What's your name?'

'Red,' he said. 'The hair, you see. And you?'

'Celia.' She held out her hand to him and he shook it solemnly.

'But how did you know where to find me? Do you live around here?'

He shook his head. 'Oh no. I live all over. At the top, these days. I followed you, of course!'

'You followed me?'

'You bet! After you saved us from the car, I wanted to know where you were, in case I could ever help you.'

'I looked for you after the accident,' she said. 'You know you should have a coat.'

'Oh, yes, we saw you looking. But you didn't do it well. You fine people. You wouldn't see what was going on, right under your nose.'

'Well, that's probably true enough.'

'We hid behind the wall and then we followed you. You do a lot of wandering round shops, miss, don't you? Looking at all that food and not buying. John said you were maybe mad in the head but I said maybe that's what they do in wherever it is you come from. You lost ladies,' he said, shaking his head affectionately.

She had to smile. 'Listen, have you eaten tonight? Today even?'

'I had a spot of bread. I don't need much, you know, miss.'

'We need to get you more than that.' Perhaps she could get some food from the hotel kitchens. 'What about I bring you a coat?'

'No thanks, miss. They slow you down. I don't get cold. But I wouldn't say no to food. I can't now. I've got business. Tomorrow, though?'

'I'm supposed to be working tomorrow.'

'Oh, work. You don't need to do that. You're rich, if you live in a hotel. Actually, I might have things to do. I'll come back when I can.'

'I don't have my purse with me. But if you wait here, I can go and get it and give you some money.'

He waved his hand. 'I don't need money, miss. We live our own way.'

'I might as well give you these then. Perhaps you can trade them.' She passed over the cigarettes and the matches.

He stowed them in his pocket. 'Not your thing anyway, are they, miss?'

'Probably not.'

'I'd better go. Things to do.'

'See you – when?

'Maybe tomorrow. Or maybe next week!' He hopped back onto the dustbin. 'If I'm not too busy.'

'If you're not too busy. Do you want to walk out with me?'

'I don't walk, Miss! Not on the pavements. Well, not often, anyway. I was when you saw me but usually I'm not down there. That's for you ground people. You never see us.'

'Where are you, then?'

He waved up at the roof. 'I'm there. I go along there!'

'Over the roofs?'

'You should look up there, sometime, Miss. You'd be surprised.'

She grinned at him. 'I think I would. Listen, are you sure you don't need any money?'

He shook his head, patted his pocket. 'These are better. See you, Miss!' He turned on his heel and jumped off the bin onto the wall, climbed the pipe swiftly and was on the roof. She gazed up to see his shadow but there were only blurred shapes lit by the moon. She stared up again, tried to see. Maybe there was a whole tribe of lost boys up there. Running over the roofs, looking down on her and the other adults shuffling around like ants. She gathered her coat around her and walked back to the hotel, wondering where he'd sleep.

Celia often thought of how Emmeline would like the shops, the excited bustle, the plenitude. Her sister was the sort of beautiful person that the shops were there to serve. Sometimes she missed her sister and little Lily and Albert so much that she thought she was bursting. She'd be walking along next to Arthur and see something to point out to Lily and realise that she wasn't there. The children would be changing every day and she couldn't see it. She thought too of Euan, born just before Arthur's trial, who had been weak and died before he'd even got to a year. They'd had a sad little funeral at a church off Russell Square – Emmeline's husband Mr Janus refused to let him be buried in the church next to Stoneythorpe. Emmeline had been broken, and Mr Janus had thrown himself into work. Celia's heart had smashed for

Emmeline, too, but deep inside she had felt anger towards Rudolf and Verena and their pity for Emmeline. *You made me feel the same grief and it was all a lie,* she wanted to say. They'd told her Michael was dead when he was alive. The feeling scalded her – and she was glad to be away from home. Her parents had sent Michael from her, sent him to America and told her he was dead, all for the good of the family, they said. And now here she was in New York, near to him she hoped – but she might never find him again.

She wrote to Emmeline but not her parents. Emmeline had written her one letter – which crossed hers, she supposed. She'd said that Mr Janus had been acting oddly, talking about travelling to Spain. Celia didn't pay too much attention. Mr Janus was always having crazes, fresh ways to change the world. Otherwise, there was little from Stoneythorpe. Rudolf's brother, Heinrich, and his wife Lotte, the children Hilde and Johann, wrote sometimes – they had little money, and life in Germany was hard. Celia blushed reading about them – her visit just after the war, their dream she would marry Johann. They'd laid so much hope in her. The terrible meeting between Tom and Heinrich. Tom had expected the older man to want to see him because he was his father, but Heinrich wanted to forget it, the indiscretion with the maid employed by his brother, and Tom was all pain at being rejected by his father. Then came the night with Tom by the lake in Baden – and everything was changed.

Celia had tried to tell Arthur about Emmeline's letter, the few bits of news. But he wasn't interested. 'You can write the letters,' he'd said. 'That's women's work. I prefer just to go back and surprise them.'

So in the evenings, she had written letters. There wasn't much else to do. Arthur often went down to the bar and he wanted to drink alone. Although alcohol was supposed to be banned, it was easy enough to get it to drink in your room at the Plaza. You could often drink it in the restaurant too – they said the champagne was lemonade. He'd spent the last of their money on the Plaza. 'We have to have the right address!' he'd said. It was a handsome room, the size of the parlour in Stoneythorpe, with a big bed she could lose herself in, a sofa and even a dark wood desk with gold painting on the edges. The carpet was so thick that she had even lain on it, to test it out. There were dark wood panels on the wall, so you could never hear a thing from the neighbouring rooms, all entirely silent. It felt anonymous to her, so she'd strewn it with her things, books, notebooks, shawls, like a bird stuffing its nest with favourite twigs. She looked out onto Central Park and there was a balcony to stand on – dark wrought iron. Sometimes, at night, Celia stood on it and gazed out at New York glittering below her. She wondered if anyone could see her, a shadowed lone woman, looking down. Arthur had an even bigger room – for doing business in, he said.

'No one here cares that we're German,' Arthur said to Celia. 'They can't tell. Here we're just English.'

He was right, Celia thought. She wasn't half-German, half-English, she was British, European even, and no one questioned more. Americans didn't care that Germans like them had been the enemy in the last war, that their father had been put in an internment camp, the rest of them reviled.

'What about Louisa's money?' she had asked, cautiously, one night.

Arthur shrugged. 'You wouldn't begrudge me that, would you, Celia?'

She supposed he had spent it all. And it was true, how could she criticise him? Not after he'd been wrongly accused of her murder, imprisoned, trialled. If it hadn't been for their lawyer, Mr Bird, and his patient checking of the words of the witnesses, Arthur might be in prison still, or even worse, sentenced to hang. He had been Louisa's husband and so what was left of her wealth was his, as it should be. And yet, still, her heart lurched when they went to restaurants and Arthur said, 'Have what you like!', and when she looked at her giant hotel room, gazing over Central Park.

And she and Arthur had spent money. The room, the food, new suits they had bought from the department store. Hers was a bright blue, cost more money than she could imagine. As he said, though, they had to look the part. Magazines called her the modern woman: single, with money, educated, travelled. But she felt none of these things; instead, shy, out of place in America that was so confident, so new. American women were so shiny clean: spotless dresses, scrubbed skin and white teeth – how did they get them so white? And she was twenty-nine and all the fashion was to be nineteen, twenty. Her skin was a little thinner around the edges of her blue eyes and her hair was still just about golden, but parts of it growing darker. She saw the New York girls passing her, hurrying off to work or lunch or meeting friends – colourful coats, short skirts, heeled shoes, bright hair that moved as they walked, full lipsticked mouths.

But, she told herself, who cared about looks? She wasn't in America to find a husband. She'd come here to find Michael. She stared at herself in the mirror, wondering which features of hers he had, whether he had her eyes or Rudolf's, or Tom's – or those of someone else, far back in all of their history, someone they had never seen.

On the second day there, she'd been walking Fifth Avenue, studying her map, when she saw a toy shop. Lily and Albert had begged every Christmas to go to look at the windows in Harrods, just to gaze at the toys. There was a shop nearby in Bloomsbury that sold handsome dolls Lily adored. She couldn't imagine what the twins would think of toy shops in New York. The one Celia saw, beckoning to her past the dress shops, was huge. The gigantic windows were piled high with soft toys, cloth ponies, bears, dogs, dolls, a multi-coloured rainbow of plush bodies, faces with sewn-on eyes. Who could ever want so many? She walked through the gold swing door into the first room, smiling staff dressed in black and white. There was an elephant the size of a pony and a bear at the front almost five foot high. They must be for a rich sultan's child, a prince.

Just as she came in, she saw a tiny model farm in the corner. Wooden sheep and cows were dotted around the buildings, tiny hens pecked at the ground, ponies nibbled on hay in a pen. At the front was the farmer carrying a pail, his wife in a red-and-white-checked dress and an apple-cheeked boy and girl were playing by a tree. She bought it in a moment, knowing she had to have it.

'It's a present, madam?' the man at the counter asked.

She nodded. 'For my son.' She revelled in saying the word, ignored the drift of his eye to her naked ring finger. She took her prize back, her great blue-wrapped present, hid it in the bottom of the wardrobe.

Arthur asked her to come to the bar with him, where he drank glass after glass of golden liquid.

'Maybe you've hit on the answer,' he said, slurring his voice. 'The modern girl who can't cook, wants pretty things in jars.'

'They seem to like it,' she said, cautiously.

'Well, clever you! You got it in the end. Their little golden girl. They're going to lend you money for your idea. And then where does that leave me?' He drummed his hands on the top of the bar.

'But—'

'Where does that leave Winter Meats? The business that keeps us all afloat? If we can't sell in America, we are lost.'

'But – maybe—'

'Have you forgotten? I was in prison. I almost went to *hang*.'

Arthur's trial catapulted into her mind, her brother's pale face as he stood in the box, watching the proceedings, gazing as the barristers argued back and forth about whether he was a bad husband, a bad man, if he'd killed Louisa in Margate because he'd never loved her, wanted her money. And they had all been wrong, and now he was innocent, free.

She swallowed. Arthur had nearly died. She was selfish. She gazed at him, and her heart turned. There was no need to remind him of the truth – that the banks said Winter Meats had no future in America.

'Well, when I receive the money for Flapper Foods, or whatever we're going to call it, then maybe we can do something with it.

I could lend you the money for one factory and then you could borrow on that?'

He smiled broadly. 'Would you? Would you really?'

He was family. She had to help him. And what did those banking men know anyway? The answer danced in her head. They looked at the figures. She shook it away.

He put his arms around her, held her close. 'I knew I could rely on you! What about tomorrow?'

Celia shook her head. 'I want to go to the agency tomorrow.'

'What agency?'

'The adoption agency. Where Michael was sent.' He'd known that her reason in coming in the first place was to find Michael. It had been at the dinner held at the Ritz to celebrate Arthur's freedom that the whole story had come out. She had told her family, told Arthur that she was coming to find Michael and he'd nodded, agreed. Now – she saw in his face – he thought differently.

'You're never going to find him, you know,' he said. 'They won't give you the address, even if they have it. Not unless you give them millions. And you don't have millions.'

She felt as if he'd slapped her. 'I'll tell them the truth. I will tell them that he was taken from me.'

'Don't you think all girls say that?' He shrugged. *I didn't mean it! I've changed my mind!*

'It's the truth. Mama took him from me. It was a criminal act.'

'So call the police. But you can bet this agency won't give you a thing.'

'Of course I can't call the police. It was years ago.'

Probably, if she called the police, they would agree with Verena. *It was the best thing for the boy. A loving family. Not brought up with the shame and stigma of illegitimacy.* The whole of society would agree.

'Well, that's it then. You'll never find the boy. He's gone. Get a new life, a husband and have babies.'

'I only want him.'

He shrugged. 'Take it from me. Time is running out. You're a pretty woman, but you're not getting any younger. You need to find yourself a man before you lose your looks.'

'I'm not listening to this any more.' She stood up.

'You know it's the truth. Don't you? Don't look like that. If you ask me, you're just using this whole Michael thing as an excuse. "Oh, poor Celia. Searching for her little boy!" If you can tell the world you are searching for your child... then you can avoid meeting a new man.'

'Arthur. No more.' She started to walk away.

'Selfish. That's what it is.'

She spun around. 'Selfish? Selfish to search for my child who was taken from me?'

'Yes. You have duties to your family. You need to find a husband to make our fortune.'

'Me? What are you talking about?'

'Yes, you. Emmeline is married and even if he died tomorrow, who'd have her? She's like wet washing, always fussing over those children. I've done my bit, I had my rich wife and there aren't that many to go around. So it's up to you. Marry well.'

Every word burned.

'I'm going, Arthur. We'll make our fortune the honest way, through business, rather than me hunting out a rich husband.'

Arthur narrowed his eyes. 'That's you, Celia. Live as a spinster, mourning a child who died long ago.'

'What?'

'He's probably dead.'

'No. No.'

'Look at the facts. He was weak when you gave birth to him, everyone agrees. Then sent off to London to a baby home where so many of them die. And then the sea journey that even made you sick. He died on the way over here, I wager.'

She bent over. She wanted to crouch, as if he'd punched her. 'They would have told Mama.'

'Of course they wouldn't. She signed him away. He wasn't anything to do with them any more. And even if they did, do you think she'd have told you?'

'What?'

'She'd never tell you. You'd never forgive her. Far easier for her to let you go on this wild goose chase, let you always be hoping. Let you blame yourself if you couldn't find him. But if he'd died, you'd hate her. But I say he died at sea. Too weak.'

She held her head. 'No. He's alive. I know he is.'

'You delude yourself.'

She couldn't listen any longer. She fled from the room, found herself in the lobby but that was too full of people, too much. She hurtled out of the front door of the hotel, into the New York street. She flung herself against the wall. Her legs wouldn't move. She put her face up to the sky, the grey, overcast sky, dark with buildings, all of them ready for another day of people making money. Then she began to cry, weeping great, soaking tears, even though she tried to force them back because she knew how ridiculous she'd look, sobbing in the middle of the street. She stuffed her hand in her mouth not to cry out loud, but she couldn't help it. Arthur and his words dug hard into her soul. *Dead. Your fault.* She tried to clutch to the old imagining, the dappled, sunlit dream of Michael and she together, but it was faint, indistinct. She had to go to the adoption agency, and find out the truth.

THREE

Manhattan, February 1929

'Please,' said Celia. 'Please.'

'I'm sorry, Miss Witt. It is really quite impossible. There is nothing we can do.'

Miss Bellenden was talking but Celia didn't want to hear the words. She was sitting upright behind the pristine desk, pictures of landscapes behind her. 'New Lives, New Hope', read the sign over her head.

'We have to think of the children,' she said. 'You cannot just come in and out of their lives.'

Miss Bellenden was tall, thin, official-looking. Her grey hair was piled on top of her head, as it would have been in the Victorian era, as if she was not letting the new age in. It moved as she talked, side to side. Maybe she would relent, have mercy on her. Celia told her that she had come all the way from England to America, just to find him. It was better for Michael that he was with her. She was thinking of his best interests! He would be happiest with her. She was his mother.

The name of the agency gave her hope. Bluebells were beautiful things, growing in sunny forests in May like fairy spells; they meant happiness, *children running through them.*

The woman carried on. 'You signed for our sister agency in London to take the baby. When you did so, you gave away all your rights. You cannot come back on a whim.'

The chair was too small, rickety. It was probably weak because so many girls had sat in it, weeping, begging, rocking back and forth. *I didn't mean it. I want him back.*

It was because of shame that Rudolf and Verena had taken

33

him away after birth. She said she'd never forgive them. But after Arthur's trial for murder, she'd forced herself to feel compassion. They had lost their niece, Louisa, nearly lost a son – a second son, since Michael had died in the war. The family had been splashed across the papers, hated, discussed as degenerate Germans, Arthur as a cruel chaser after money, such terrible lies. She'd reminded herself that one day they would die and she would be alone. And although she was still filled with pain, she told herself that if she found him again – and surely she would – then so much would be forgotten. Her heart told her she was half a person without him, and he couldn't be whole either.

When she'd made the appointment, she'd said she was a girl hoping to give up her child for a better life in the country. And then, when she arrived, she'd told Miss Bellenden the truth. The woman hadn't seemed too surprised. Celia supposed she had women like her every day, weeping in her office.

Let me have him.

Seven years ago, her body wracked with pain, the monster of it riding her as she held on to the bed at Stoneythorpe. The nurses taking the baby from her as he needed medicine. Then she woke up after being sedated – and they told her he was dead. So she'd believed – until Mrs Stabatsky the medium told her he was alive, not through hearing his spirit voice but because she showed her the whole episode barely made sense. And then, after Arthur's trial, her father had shouted out, 'You need to go America.' Because Michael was alive and he was there.

Miss Bellenden put her chin on her hand. Her hair fell even more alarmingly to the side. 'Miss Witt. If I could only tell you how many young women I have in here. They say – too – that they never signed, or if they did, they didn't understand what they were doing. Our forms are perfectly clear. And what we do here is give children a better life.'

'I've only just found out he was here. I would have come straight away if I'd known.' Celia leant over. 'Please, Miss Bellenden, can you just tell me he's healthy.'

'All information is strictly confidential now. Please understand, Miss Witt.'

Celia looked at the clock. She'd been in this tiny, white office, piled high with files, for twenty minutes. Miss Bellenden had said the same things over and over, was beginning to cast glances at the clock herself. Celia guessed she only had a few more minutes.

'But I'm his mother.'

'You chose to sign away your rights. You cannot change your mind.'

'But I never agreed to send him away. Like I said, my family did it without my knowledge.' She stared around the room, desperately looking at the walls, the paintings of mountains, the peeling paint, trying to cling on to it. Her eyes darted across the curtains, clenching her hands to hold a little of the air of the room, trying to keep it. Somewhere on the bookshelves was a file and in it were details about Michael. She could only be feet away from it. And yet, she couldn't find it. She gripped her hands again.

'That couldn't be the case, I'm afraid, Miss Witt. We always have the mother present. You said you were ill after the birth. Is it possible you have forgotten signing?'

'Of course not.'

Miss Bellenden sighed, put on her glasses, reached into a drawer and pulled out a brown cardboard file. There was the file! That was it. It looked to have a whole sheaf of papers in it. Miss Bellenden covered the front with her hand but it was too late. Celia had seen the writing. *Michael Witt.*

He was alive. He was real.

Celia wanted to reach up, grab the woman and seize the file off her. Michael's file. His life.

'Let me see. Miss Witt, it says here – very clearly – that you were in attendance at the meeting. You agreed to hand over your child. My colleague in London discussed this with you and you said you understood. There is no note here that you looked particularly ill, just a little exhausted, which is to be expected for a lady who has just delivered a baby.'

Celia stared at her. 'But that's not true. I wasn't there!'

Miss Bellenden put down the file. 'Miss Witt, I see little worth in continuing this conversation. You signed away your child. As I said, I see a lot of young ladies in here. What they – and you – must remember is that the child has a better life. He no longer has the stigma of being illegitimate. He is part of a family.'

shook away her words. 'So he is still alive then. That's what you mean.'

Mrs Bellenden shook her head. 'I told you, Miss Witt. I cannot give you any of this confidential information. You are fortunate that I have even entertained you here at all, after your false representation of why you came. Now, if you will forgive me. I have other people to see.'

Celia gazed at the file on the desk. Two feet. So close. All she had to do was bend down. She stretched her fingers. Miss Bellenden was old, weaker. She could seize it. It was so near. She stretched out her fingers. Miss Bellenden saw her, snapped the file shut and pushed it onto the shelf.

'The interview is over, Miss Witt,'

Celia stood there, two sides of her pulling, one half of her sympathy for Miss Bellenden, sticking to the rules, the other half longing to throw her aside, grasp the file, run with it.

'Please,' she said. 'Please give it to me.'

Miss Bellenden shook her head. 'I will call for the police. The interview is over.' She drew herself up. 'I will call for the police.'

Celia backed away, slowly, looking at Miss Bellenden, hoping for one word, one gesture that might suggest that they could talk more, a chink she could edge through, talk to her, find her humanity. Miss Bellenden turned away, adjusted her hair.

'Good day, Miss Witt.'

'I understand,' said Celia. She smiled. She had to smile. She had to try to make the woman like her, to see that she was really someone respectable. Miss Bellenden was looking down at her papers. *Give it to me!*

Celia turned for the door. She paused. Miss Bellenden did not look up. She pulled it open, burst out through the waiting room, into the street beyond, desperate to breathe.

Celia looked around her, then turned, pacing towards the hotel, feet hitting the ground hard, walking, thinking. She wouldn't tell Arthur. Not yet. But she needed to tell someone. She needed *someone* to help her through, as Miss Bellenden wasn't going to let her go any further. She put her head in her hands. The world in front of her eyes flamed red.

FOUR

'Hello.' A woman's voice. 'I saw you go into Bellenden's, didn't I? Yes I know they call it Bluebells, but she calls the shots.'

Celia was leaning against the wall, a few doors down from Bluebell's. She'd been trying not to faint. She opened her eyes and a small woman with short black hair and a mauve hat was standing in front of her, very close. Her eyes lifted when Celia looked at her and the hope was one Celia recognised.

'I saw you. What did you think? She's a dragon, isn't she? From the way you look now, I guess you were trying to find your kid, right?'

'It was Mama,' she said. 'She'd told them I'd signed him over. I don't know how. Maybe she paid them a lot of money.'

'Well, maybe. Or maybe she had someone pretend to be you. Paid an actress or something.'

Celia stared at the girl. 'Really? They'd do that?'

She nodded. 'You bet they would.' She had a pretty, rather moon-shaped face, a heavy oval, a great smile, large dark eyes, inviting. She had a soft, laughing voice, and a look about her face that she was keen to be surprised, amazed. Her body was small, like a dancer's. She was beautiful really. In another life, Celia thought, she'd like to be her friend.

'Listen!' said the girl. 'Let's walk together. I'm Violet, by the way.'

Celia knew she shouldn't really, knew she was better going back to the hotel to work on plans for the business and trying to think of some legal way to get Michael, with lawyers and letters. But something about Violet's eyes, entrancing, pulled her in, and so she nodded and, in a minute, they were side by side and anyone looking at them would have thought they had been friends forever.

Violet, she told Celia, worked in the Primrose ladies' store on Fifth Avenue, specialising in gloves. She said she'd been engaged and thought she was safe – then her fiancé died and she was pregnant. She'd hid it at work with scarves and the rest – lucky it had been winter – and no one suspected her because they all thought she was such a good girl. Celia thought that she wasn't lying. Celia didn't think she'd really know how to lie.

'It's only mother and me,' she said. 'Without my wage, we'd starve.' Her mother was ill, delicate, sometimes couldn't get out of bed. Violet did everything for her – came home from a long day in the shop and cooked and cleaned, brushed her hair, remade her bed, read to her, stroked her forehead until she slept. 'She needs me,' Violet said.

So when she fell pregnant, what could she do? She'd tried not to think about it as she'd grown bigger, prayed to God to bring her a solution. But He didn't. 'He couldn't hear me,' she said. 'I prayed to him but He couldn't hear me. I'd hoped that mother might get well and be able to look after the baby. But even if she could, the neighbours would have talked and I would have lost my job.'

She had the little girl at home, pulling on a rag for the pain, her mother fretting from the bed. A little girl. She called her Hope. She took the child to Bluebells. 'I wept all the way. But I believed everything they said in the literature that it is a better life for a child. They'll live happily ever after in the country. I wanted to help her. I thought, what sort of life does she have with me, shushed and secret in our one-room apartment?'

'And now you want her back?'

'I don't know. I want to know she's happy. I want to know that the people she is with love her as much as I did. Do.'

'I know she's happy,' said Celia, not sure she was convincing. Because if she didn't believe that Michael was happy with his family, why would little Hope be any different?

'Why did you end up getting pregnant then? You look like a clever enough girl.'

Celia shrugged. 'I didn't think straight.' That was true enough, for she didn't, she hadn't, that night in Baden with Tom, eight years ago. She'd met him by chance there – she was with her cousins and her aunt and uncle and he was there after finishing business. He'd been pleased to see her and that had thrilled her soul. He'd told her that there couldn't ever be anything between them, that there never had been really. *I was the servant*, he said and the painful undertow of it all hit her. He had never had any choice, stuck in the house, imprisoned really, he hadn't truly wanted to spend hours riding with her or playing games. But it hadn't been like that, she was sure! They had really been friends. No matter what he said. When he had told her that he believed Rudolf was his father, she had been shocked. He'd said it was because she was disgusted by him, would never want someone so poor in her family. And when she tried to explain, it didn't come out right, it was because her father wasn't *like* that, he'd always been loyal to her mother.

And then she had realised, through working back, the dates of visits, what she'd been told – his father had to be Heinrich, her uncle. Tom had been furious with her. He wanted it to be Rudolf, had admired him so. He had said he would never speak to her again. And in Baden, when she'd sent him to Heinrich, it had been terrible. Her aunt had screamed and the whole restaurant had stared and Tom ran from there, her following after him. They'd drunk wine that night, and then in the cold grass near to the lake, he'd turned to her – and she'd thought, yes. No more talking. Just the two of them, close together, one of them really, and nothing else mattered. But afterwards, he'd been shocked that she had been a virgin and she had felt shame, ran away.

'I couldn't tell him. I told my family it was a soldier.' They still thought it.

'Was he married?'

She shook her head. 'No. He just didn't love me.'

'But he'd manage to do whatever with you? That was *fine*.'

'It wasn't like that.'

'Oh, it was. Men do what they want. And we have to deal with it.'

'That's not always true.' But then, Rudolf had always told her mother what to do, and then Arthur, ordering Louisa around. But Tom hadn't been like that. Nor had Jonathan. The name rang in her head like a small stone dropping into water. *Jonathan.*

Violet clutched her hands. 'I need to go to the store now. But we must help each other. We need to get your Michael back and find Hope. See she's happy.'

'How do we do it?'

She smiled. 'We'll do it together! I'll meet you back here in a week.' She turned and dashed down the street. Celia watched her go, a tiny, mauve-clad whirlwind. She didn't know how. But they'd succeed together.

FIVE

Manhattan, February 1929

Whatever she did, wherever she walked, her mind returned to Bluebells. She went to see a solicitor and he told her that Michael had been signed away and she could not have him back. She took out the farm set from the bottom of her wardrobe, touched the miniature animals, perfectly carved, imagined handing them to her son. She put a horse into her pocket and told herself she would keep it there until she could give it to him.

At the end of each day, she went out to the back of the hotel, hoping to see the boy, Red, again. No luck. She had to fill the week until she saw Violet. The banks had offered her enough for her to start up a small kitchen. If she made a success of the business, she told herself, she might gain a position, a status in America that could win Michael back. Every morning, she scribbled up the figures, conjured pictures of glittering tins and jars, and finally she had nearly a hundred pages of plans. Supplies, transport, labour, packaging. She found a comfort in methodically working through it all. Tom's voice came to her, from their childhood. 'You couldn't even boil a kettle for tea!'

Well, she'd show him. Not that he was watching, she reminded herself. But still. She showed Arthur the ideas she had written out.

'The puddings seem quite English,' she said, doubtfully.

'Do you think it's not too filling?' said Arthur. 'The girls I used to know never used to eat a thing.'

'Plenty of girls eat. Especially working girls.'

Jars like theirs would make Violet's life so much easier. Instead of having to shop after work, then cook for Mother and clean, she'd be able to buy a few jars and then just go home to heat them up. And maybe, once Flapper Foods was established, Violet would come and work for them.

She carried on writing down the recipes, rough guesses of ingredients. 'You have to put in a bit extra,' she said to Arthur. 'I think. That way people think they are getting something special. Onions and leeks in the macaroni cheese. Little bits of chocolate in the cake.'

'What about an advertising campaign?'

'A what?'

'We need an advertising campaign, Celia. Something to show the world what we've done. We can't just hope that girls will happen to see the things in a shop.'

He was right. She had seen all sorts of advertisements since she'd been in New York. Beautiful, white-teethed ladies in summer dresses smiling out of billboards, holding raisins or ice cream or gesturing at new apartments in Florida.

'We need a modern girl,' Celia pondered, 'as a model.' She had to be a girl like one of those on the ship. Short hair, not too much powder and lipstick, a smile.

'What about a competition to find her?' said Arthur. 'Everyone could send in photos. Then we could get a lot of publicity.'

'That's an excellent idea. The Flapper Foods Girl!'

They conjured ideas: the competition, how they'd advertise it, newspapers across the land, how the competition would be on the radio news, talked about everywhere. How could it fail? They took their dinner in Celia's room, the waiter coming up with trays of food and a note he said was for Celia. She put it aside, too busy thinking about their ideas, supposing it was probably something about the laundry. They kept on writing. Finally, at ten, they agreed they had everything.

'Tomorrow,' he said. 'We will take it to the bank tomorrow.'

Arthur kissed her goodnight and she felt flooded with affection for him. As she fell into bed, exhausted, she remembered the note.

She lay there for a moment and swung herself out of bed. She wouldn't have time to deal with it tomorrow, as it was an early start.

She picked it up from her desk and opened it.

Telephone Message: Mr Jonathan Corrigan Telephoned from Connecticut.

Then an address. A phone number.

Celia stared at it, blood beating hard at her face. He must have called home to Stoneythorpe and they'd told him she was here.

Jonathan. She had all but forgotten him. When he'd said goodbye after the trial had ended, he'd told her to come and see him. 'You'd like America,' he'd said. 'People can do whatever they want. It's not like England where they're always trying to hold you back.'

They'd been in a restaurant near King's Cross station, windows steamy with the breath of dozens of travellers hurrying in and out, the sort of place that would have been full of soldiers in the war. Handsome, tanned, confident, American Jonathan, making the English people around him look shabby. Everything she'd said sounded shy and stiff. When the trial had been adjourned, when she'd gone back with him to his hotel and she'd tried to forget that Arthur might be found guilty and hanged, and to remember her brother Michael, who had been with Jonathan at Cambridge before the war, when they were young, on the brink of possessing the world. She and Jonathan had held tight to each other, forgotten it all. Perhaps they could be free together. But then, in the restaurant, her world had been stopped by the news she'd just heard from her father – that her child was alive and had been sent to America. After that, nothing anyone said had any meaning at all.

She had smiled at him, barely making her voice heard over the hubbub. 'I'll come,' she said, telling him it was for the business, for she'd never mentioned her son to him. 'I promise.'

And yet she'd arrived and hadn't contacted him. All her thoughts had been about her child. But he was Michael's best friend from university. Her link to her brother's past.

She looked at the clock on the wall. Half past ten. Quite late. But there wouldn't be time tomorrow. She had to do it now. She dressed hurriedly, putting her gown over her nightgown, pulling on stockings and shoes, hurried down to the concierge. She thought she saw Arthur just through the door in the hall, sitting at the bar. Drinking. She shuffled behind a pillar.

'I need to return a phone call,' she said to the concierge. He was her favourite – Alberto – a small man, fifty or so, grey hair, round, trustworthy face. She was glad it was him, not the tall dark-haired one who made her feel nervous. 'Please could you dial through to Connecticut for me?' She blushed even asking it. She held out the paper and the address.

Alberto nodded. 'I'll try the operator, madam. When do you wish to place the call?'

'Now, please.'

He raised an eyebrow. 'It's late.'

And he was right, of course, the hotel lobby was full of well-dressed people leaving after dinner. The evening was over.

'It's important. I must do it now.'

She waited by the desk as he walked away. The dark-haired one came to stand in his place. She stared at the people going past, a handsome man and a woman who looked like they were pretending not to be lovers. She gazed out at them. She might brush past people who had seen Michael – and she'd never know.

'Madam?' The voice came through the fog of faces in her mind. 'The call is connecting.' The tall concierge gestured her towards the door behind him.

Alberto held out the receiver. 'I have the house here for you.'

She reached out, tentatively. She'd never used a telephone, not really. They'd had one in Stoneythorpe, but she'd only lifted it to hear the sound, speak down it to the crackle. At the few office jobs she'd had, she'd never been senior enough to answer the telephone. It sat, polished and handsome, on the head secretary's

45

desk, treasured. She asked the reed-thin voice in the receiver for Jonathan, gave her name.

'Hello, Celia.' Jonathan's voice was incredulous, she could hear that even over the crackling of the line. 'Is it you? How are you? Are you really in America?'

She breathed. She should have told him she was coming. She had been caught up in Michael. 'I'm sorry,' she said.

'How long have you been here?' He was telephone-distorted, slower and deeper than he normally was. He sounded older.

'Quite a bit of time. I – I came with my brother...' The line was flinging crackles into the air, burning. 'I did mean to tell you,' she began.

'We promised that if you came to America – I, I could have helped you. It's my home. Why are you even staying in the Plaza? The service is bad.'

Celia thought of Alberto, helping her with the telephone. 'They are very nice.'

'I've dreamed of you coming,' he said. 'I'd meet you at the boat, take you to your hotel.'

'I'm sorry.' Her mind had been caught up in finding her lost child. She couldn't tell Jonathan about it. She flushed hot, red, ashamed. How she had hurt him. But then, if he had always been there, she might not have been able to look for Michael. Arthur wasn't curious, she could carry on a whole secret life without him even noticing. But Jonathan would have cared, asked questions.

'Could we meet?' she asked. 'Are you coming to New York?'

'You're probably too busy,' he said.

She listened to the line flame. 'I am not busy. Please.' The sound of his voice pulled hard on her heart. He was kind, generous.

Jonathan sighed. 'How long are you here for?'

'I'm not sure. It's up to Arthur and how the business goes.' *Until I find Michael*, she didn't say, but that was the truth.

'So we have time, then. I'll call and let you know.'

'When?'

'When I can.'

'I wish we could meet!'

'Do you remember that time when I saw you in the garden at your house? You were so young.'

The memory made her blush more. How different things had been then, before the war. So simple. Everything had seemed so straightforward, as if love and family and the bonds they had together would last forever, and Celia would always be safe within their branches, never having to hold the tree up herself.

He was still speaking, as if he hadn't heard her. 'The light was coming through you. You came over with your sister and the light was behind you, flowing through your hair.'

We've grown up, she wanted to say. She'd been in her dell, at the bottom of the garden, and she felt that her future was in front of her, that she was on the verge of reaching out, touching it and then everything would glitter, shift and change and the world would never be the same again. She looked back on herself, incredulous about the selfishness of youth, simple, wishful. She'd thought all the change would begin and end with her, that all the others would stay the same. As if the point of her life was discovering herself and the years would be taking her through doors, and behind one waited her own self, predestined, certain.

His tone grew clipped. 'I don't know. What's the point of holding on to the past? None of us are the same any more. Why pretend?'

'Yes, we are! Inside we are!' They had to be. Otherwise, all of her brother was lost, if the parts of them that had known him before the war were gone.

'I don't know, Celia. Listen, I'll telephone you another time. Perhaps in a few weeks when you say you're free. Or whenever it is.'

'I'm sorry I waited.'

'Me too. It's getting late. Goodbye, Celia.'

He put the phone down and she listened to the breaking line hiss. If he picked it up again, she'd still be there. She willed him to. Nothing happened. She put down her receiver on the table, still burning. She gazed at it again, then put it back on the hook.

She wanted to race up to see Jonathan this minute, beg his forgiveness. But what if he turned her away, or was angry with her for her presumption? What if she made things worse? She rushed upstairs and scribbled a letter, would post it the next day.

SIX

Manhattan, February 1929

Celia couldn't sleep. Even the street lights scored into her mind. She gave up, dressed quickly and walked downstairs for some air. She sat at the back of the hotel, wishing that she might see Red.

'Hello, Miss,' came a voice from above her. 'How have you been?' She looked up and saw Red peering down at her.

'I was wondering if I'd see you again.'

'I've seen you a lot. You don't go out much, do you, Miss?'

'If I knew when you were coming, I'd have some food for you. I have some money upstairs.'

He shook his head. 'I don't want money. I want to repay the favour. You saved me. So I should do something for you.'

She hesitated. It was too much, impossible. He was only a child. But she had no one else to ask. 'There is something I need. I don't think you could get it for me.'

'I can get anything. Try me.'

She couldn't ask him. Telling him her problems would be a burden to him. But then. Someone had given him up too.

'I lost my little boy. He's only a few years younger than you. My parents gave him away when he was just a baby. I need an address for my little boy. It's in an office.'

'That one you went to and were talking to that lady in purple outside?'

'You followed me there.'

'Of course, Miss.'

'Well, there's a file in there that I need. It's a piece of cardboard with papers in. And I need another file for a friend of mine.'

'And you want me to take them for you?'

49

'Could you do that?'

'I can try, Miss. We could definitely get in. The thing is – I can't read so I wouldn't know the right files.'

'I'll come with you.'

He shook his head. 'No, Miss. No one sees us. Everyone notices you. Give me the names and I'll ask the others. We must know someone who can read.'

She fished her notebook from her purse and wrote down the names. 'Could you match them up, perhaps?' But if they were in alphabetical order, even that was no use.

'Maybe,' he said, doubtfully.

'Let me come with you.'

He shook his head. 'You'll get us arrested. We'll find a way. Must go, Miss.' He swung himself up, disappeared.

She didn't want to wait a week. Next morning, she rose and took a cab to the Primrose ladies' store. She needed to see Violet, her gentle smile, her pretty oval face. She wouldn't go near her counter. She'd just stand and watch nearby. And Violet might guess what she was thinking: that they were closer than they'd ever been.

The Primrose department store was laid out like all the rest. The glove counter was near to Hats and not far from Scarves, on the ground floor. Violet wasn't by Gloves – it was two smart-looking girls and a stern woman of fifty or so. Celia stationed herself by Scarves, easier to be unobtrusive there, she thought. She told the girl behind the counter that she was merely looking.

'Here on holiday, madam?' she asked politely.

Celia shook her head. 'I live here.'

She was on her third scarf (all such wild colours, who would buy them?) when Violet finally came out. She must have been down to the stockroom because she was carrying a heavy box. Celia's heart leapt.

'Oh, finally,' said one of the smart-looking girls, the taller one with dark hair. 'Here you are, *finally*.'

'Sorry,' said Violet. 'I couldn't find the box.'

'You can never find the box, can you? You can never find

anything. I don't know why Miss Adams sends you there. Except I do – it's because you make so many mistakes with the customers. Unless it's a handsome man, of course.'

Violet continued to lay out the gloves. Celia felt as if she was swelling with fury.

'And you're not even pretty. Miss Adams? Don't you think? Miss Betts is not even pretty.'

Violet didn't answer again, busied herself with a display.

'When did you last make a sale, Miss Betts?' The smart girl, the blonde one, was joining in. 'Tell us.'

Violet's head was bowed. Her hands fluttered over the pink gloves on the display case. She didn't look up. Celia remembered school, a girl who was cruel to the younger ones, how they'd used to flatten themselves against the wall. You thought you had to hide yourself from bullies. But that only made them come out more. But how could she tell Violet that?

She couldn't stop herself. She marched over.

'I'd like to look at some evening gloves, please?' she said. The smart girls were standing upright, all smiles now. 'And I'd like this lady to show me.'

Violet's face was pure shock. She mouthed something at Celia but Celia didn't know what.

'Well, get to it, Miss Betts,' said the stern woman. 'Evening gloves.' Violet flushed red and Celia felt guilty.

Violet brought out tray after tray of gloves. They were all rather ugly, Celia thought, thin material, not much quality, but she expressed interest, asked Violet her advice.

The smart girls tried to intervene and Celia ignored them. She turned to Violet, looked at her only. The other girls hung back, stood resentfully behind the counter.

By the third set of gloves, Violet was no longer red and mumbling. She was smiling, expansive. She recommended gloves and textures and Celia pretended to be fascinated. Net flowers and silken fingers, bead embroidery, tiny pieces of glitter, white, pale blue, cream. She asked Violet to put aside three of the most expensive, elaborate ones – what on earth was she going to do with those?

'Yes, madam,' said Violet, nodding.

Violet rang them all up perfectly – ridiculously expensive – and Celia took them in a bundle.

'Thank you, Miss,' she said. She turned to Miss Adams. 'I must say, I really must compliment you on your staff's excellent service! The levels of service are practically *European!*' She gave Violet a beaming smile. 'I shall be sure to come again.'

The smart girls stood holding the counter as if they were being buffeted by winds.

Celia took the parcels under her arm and set off towards the door. She had taken a risk. She knew she had. But it had been worth it, every moment of it. As she headed to the hotel, she passed an old woman begging on the street.

'Have these,' she said. 'Sell them on the market.'

She hurried on, leaving the old woman taking the evening gloves out of the paper, net and silk and flowers fluttering.

She still held the list of prices in her hand. At the bottom, in Violet's handwriting:

You shouldn't have come. But thank you.

When Flapper Foods was a real business, she'd employ Violet. And they'd both have their children back.

Eventually, Red came once more. She was ready for him with chocolate and cigarettes; she'd waited every night. 'I have what you want,' he said. 'One of the boys could read.' He passed over a hefty paper bag. They'd taken the whole files. Miss Bellenden would surely realise. What if she called the police?

'Can you take them back after we've seen what we need?'

He shook his head. 'Don't think so, Miss. It was close.'

'Did you break in?'

'I wouldn't ask, Miss. I won't go back. None of us will. We nearly got caught.'

Her mind rang with the panic he must have felt and she felt filled with guilt. 'I'm sorry.'

'Don't apologise! We enjoy it. But it took Sun a long time to read the names and the bells were ringing. We thought they'd catch us.'

She stared down at the brown cardboard files. Michael De Witt. Hope Pennington.

'Thank you,' she said. She'd have to hope that Miss Bellenden would think she'd lost them herself, or even if she guessed what had happened, would never admit it.

'Don't go back there, Miss. Better not raise any suspicions.'

'No, I won't. When will you come back?'

'In a night or two, maybe. There's a lot of business at the moment.' She watched him bounce away into the night, while she held tight to the papers.

She stared at Michael's file, back in the hotel room. She was almost afraid to open it. She kept staring, took a breath, put her hands on the pale card. A signature that wasn't hers. Birth certificate. Age. Address. The light from the lamp slipped through her fingers, broke into a thousand stars.

'Twenty-two Upper Eighty-Seventh Street'. Michael's home. *New York.* He lived there. Not so far from her. She might have even walked near it, on the odd walk she had taken to Central Park. She might have passed him. She'd thought of him on a farm Upstate, picking apples, helping with the crops. Not in some great apartment in a new building on the Upper East Side. Perhaps his family was poor, was in service. But something in her told her that they were rich.

He had a home, an address. He probably had a new name. The truth of it all hit her, hard. If she went to him, she might bring such discord into his life. He might be happy, in Upper Eighty-Seventh Street.

Was she being selfish? Wanting to take him from people who loved him. Maybe she should only observe him from afar, check he was happy, not go further, come back when he was an adult.

She closed the file, her heart on fire.

SEVEN

Manhattan, February 1929

The next day, Celia walked to the department store, but Violet wasn't there. Thinking she was on a break or an errand, Celia waited outside, her hands growing painful with cold. Ready to give up, she ventured back inside. The stern woman, Miss Adams, had shooed her away, but one of the other girls had come forward when the others weren't looking, slipped her Violet's address. 'I think she needs someone to look out for her, Miss,' the girl had said.

She found a cab and the driver headed north quickly. He let her out at a ramshackle house, the roofs built across, windows falling in. Celia knocked at the door. A pale woman in a dirty flowered apron opened the door, one child clutching at her side, another behind her legs. She looked as though she was always tired, as if all she could tell you was that she was tired, great purple smudges under her eyes.

'I'm looking for Violet,' Celia said.

The woman raised her eyebrows, gazing at Celia's hat and bag. 'Upstairs.' She pulled open the door and Celia squeezed past her and the children. 'Second staircase on the right.'

Celia balanced her way up the rickety staircase, watching where she put her feet. The wood was splintered, cracked, broken across the sections. Children were standing in the corridors, men leaning, a couple smoking. There were doors everywhere, names on doors. It must have once been two great houses and now the rooms that had been bedrooms, grand salons, were housing whole families. She walked across the corridor and came to a door. Betts. Violet

54

and her mother. She leant against the door frame, listened, heard low voices talking.

Celia knocked on the door. There was silence behind it. Quickly shuffling feet. She knocked again and stood back. No response.

'Violet? It's Celia.'

She approached the door again. Then it opened, just a small crack. Violet's eye peered out.

'What are you doing here?'

'I came to see you.'

Violet sighed. 'Well, you'd better come in. Quickly.' Her pretty face so sad now, the moon lost all its light. There were broken veins on her cheeks as if she'd been ill.

Celia looked around, took in the low bed, older woman lying seemingly asleep under a lace coverlet, the walls broken and splintered like the stairs. There were a few pictures, scraps of material to decorate, empty bottles of what must have been hair stuff arranged on the shelves. There was a worn-looking table and a rickety chair.

Violet stood back, against the wall, face pale. 'We have to keep our voices down,' she said. 'Mother's sick.' She shook her head. 'Why did you come?'

'I have something. I think I have Hope's address.'

'How?'

'Never mind. But I do.' She handed over the file. 'Now I can help you find Hope. We could do it together.'

Violet shook her head, pushed the file back at her. 'I don't know why you're here. I don't know how you got this and I don't want to know! If you stole this, do you realise what this could do to me? Mother and I could lose everything. But I suppose you didn't care. I'm the kind of girl who'd be a servant to you. Don't you expect everyone to be your servant?'

'No!' Celia tried to move forwards but her legs were locked, cramped. 'I don't want anybody to be my servant. I – well – we had so much in common. We had both lost a child. I thought—'

'You rich people, you're all the same.'

'All?'

Then something struck her. 'Your fiancé. He didn't die, did he?' The words they said in the shop. *Unless it's a handsome man of course.*

Violet looked away. 'Don't talk to me.'

'It was a rich man. He left you.' Celia's legs released but she didn't move forward. 'Why didn't you tell me?'

Violet shook her head. 'I was stupid. Wrong. He said he loved me. Of course he did. I thought he'd rescue us. What stupidity. Still, I wonder every day if he's written me a letter. And I wonder if he might come to the shop and find me. Save me from all this.'

Celia had thought of the same. Tom appearing, saying he loved her after all.

Violet shrugged. 'And what do I get instead? You. You following me round. Stealing things for me.'

'We won't get found out. I promise.'

Violet closed her eyes. 'Your sort makes promises.'

'Why aren't you at the shop anymore? I went to find you there.'

She shrugged. 'Got above myself, they said. And so they asked me to leave. And that's when I understood that I had to keep away from you. You see, people like you remind me of what people like me can't have. I thought of myself as your friend and all the rest of it. How wrong I was.'

'They were horrible to you at that job. And I'm not like him. I want to help us.' She and Violet had talked so happily that day they'd met. It couldn't just go.

And then, even though it didn't seem the right time, she couldn't stop herself; Celia started talking of her dream. 'I wanted you to come to work for us. You're so good with figures. The business will need someone to deal with the accounts. We need you to help us.'

Violet shook her head. 'You need to go. Mother will wake up soon.'

Celia's head swam. 'But Violet. It would be a good job. Proper money.'

'He made me promises too. If mother was awake, she would say – better to do honest work.'

The sick woman on the bed stirred. 'Violet?'

'Go back to sleep, Mother.' Violet shot Celia a furious glare, hurried over to the sick woman, tried to soothe her.

Celia watched her, thoughts turned in on herself. She tried to see it from Violet's point of view. If they both got arrested for the stolen files, no doubt the courts would be harder on Violet. She watched her try to soothe her mother back to sleep.

But the woman was sitting up now. Gazing at Celia. 'Who are you?'

'She's no one, Mother. She's looking for one of the neighbours.'

The woman wasn't old, maybe late forties or so. She didn't even look so ill. She was just lying there, under her crochet blanket, making Violet work so hard, earning, cooking, cleaning. No wonder she had believed that man and all his promises.

Celia moved over. 'I hear you're ill,' she said. 'I'm sorry. What exactly is wrong with you?'

'Celia!' said Violet. 'Why can't you just go?'

The woman reached out her hand. 'I just feel so tired. Tired all the time.'

Celia moved towards her. 'I could send a doctor. When did you last see one?'

'Not for years. They're too expensive.'

'You need to go.' Violet picked her bag up off the floor.

'She needs to see a doctor.'

'We don't need your help. Do we, Mother? We don't need you.'

'Please,' she said. 'Take the file.' Violet shook her head and then she was pushing her towards the door, stronger than she looked. The door was opened and closed and Celia was outside. A wide-eyed child sat on the stairs, fiddling with a doll.

Celia leant against the wall, then took a piece of her notebook from her bag, scribbled her hotel address on it and pushed it through the door with the file. *In case you change your mind.*

She meant to travel back to the hotel. But she couldn't bear it, staring at the empty walls. She thought of the address she'd taken from the file, crammed in her purse. She could go there. She could just see where he lived. Then she'd act on it, later, when she felt sure Miss Bellenden had not gone to the police.

Celia got out at Lexington and changed trains to go north. She'd head up to the Upper East Side and find the apartment building. She'd look. She wouldn't do anything else. She'd just see that he was safe.

EIGHT

Manhattan, February 1929

Celia jumped out at the subway and walked up, heart beating hard against her blouse. She turned a corner, walked through a small green space dotted with plants and up in front of a large, red-stone building. She stood outside, gazed up at the spotless windows.

She walked to the other side of the road, tried to work out which window was Michael's. 'Come to me!' she wanted to cry. 'I'm here.' After half an hour or so, a well-dressed man walked out of the building. Two maids came next. A tradesman with boxes knocked at the door and what looked like a concierge in uniform let him in.

The door, opening, closing. She could pretend again – say she was a maid – but how far would she get? She could try saying that she was Michael's new governess, say she had come for an interview, but surely they'd check.

Perhaps she could just tell the truth. Go in and say she was his mother. But they would tell her she was wrong – and how could she prove it? And what if Miss Bellenden had told the family about the break-in? Then she would be exposed and perhaps bring Violet and Red down with her. But there had been nothing in the newspapers and she felt sure that Miss Bellenden would want to keep such a thing quiet.

She couldn't steal him away. All she could do was see if they might take pity on her. Maybe let her see him, just once. Tell him about her when he was grown up. She stepped forward and pressed the bell.

The concierge answered. 'I'm here to see Number 22. I have an appointment.' She gave her name, the real one, trying to sound confident. She had to hope that her English voice, the fine upbringing that Verena had planned, destroyed by the war, would be something to let her through.

The concierge nodded. 'I will ring up.' He went to his office, picked up a phone, returned and told her to enter the elevator. She sat on the bench as he stepped in with her. The metal grille closed across, he whirled the handle and they were going up. She couldn't turn back now.

He let her out at a grand, dark-wood door. A maid dressed in black and white stood there. Her eyes were sharp, would surely see through Celia in an instant.

'The name is Miss Witt. I have an appointment,' she said. 'With the – er – Mistress.'

The woman nodded. She drew back, let Celia past. Luck, pure luck. Perhaps the lady of the house was often receiving people without telling the maid. 'She should be back in about ten minutes,' she said. 'Please wait here.'

The maid ushered Celia through the hall full of dark oil paintings. She opened the door to a cool room with great windows that Celia could just see looked out onto Central Park. There were fine sofas, a grand piano, beautiful rugs. There was nothing for a child, no toys, just handsome furniture, all pristine surfaces. She thought with a pang of Stoneythorpe's old, shabby curtains and rugs, splintered sofa legs, nothing they could afford to repair. Michael's life here was completely different. He had money.

Then it struck her: if he was here.

Perhaps they had moved.

But, surely, people who lived in a place like this would pass on their address. They wouldn't just disappear in the middle of the night like they might in other parts of the city. She sat down on the sofa and tried to still her beating mind. The apartment was entirely silent, muffled by carpets and rugs, no sound of the traffic outside. But still, perhaps she might hear a child. Please. She begged. Michael. Come to me.

She heard the front door open, conversation with the maid. Steps in the hallway. The door swung open and a finely dressed woman, arrayed in navy-blue silk, walked through, the maid behind her. Celia stood up hastily, then thought that might have been a mistake. The maid closed the door and they were in the room together, airless and cold.

'Do we have an appointment, Miss Witt, is it? I don't remember it.' Her tone was not unfriendly. Perhaps, Celia supposed, if you were a very rich woman in New York, you met all sorts of people who might attend you, never needed to remember them.

She could offer her the chance of investing in Winter Meats. That would seem legitimate. She could say she'd read about her in the newspapers and thought she might be interested. She almost opened her mouth that way, let the words flow out. But she didn't. Couldn't. The truth was pushing at her.

'Do you have a child, Madam?'

The woman looked confused. 'We have four.'

'A young boy. Seven. Seven and a half, exactly.'

'Yes. Sebastian. Is this about him?'

He's not Sebastian, Celia wanted to cry. 'I'm sorry if this sounds shocking to you, Mrs—'

'Mrs Whetstone.'

'I'm sorry if this sounds shocking to you. But what did the agency – the Bluebells agency – what did they tell you when you adopted the child? Sebastian.'

The woman's face turned cold. 'We didn't adopt him. He's ours.'

'That is not what the agency told me.' The lie came easily to her. 'You adopted him.' She was betting that Miss Bellenden hadn't contacted the clients. That she'd kept it secret.

The woman took a step back towards the door. 'We did not.'

'I'm sorry if this is a great surprise. But they told you lies. I expect they said the mother was unmarried, ruined. But he was mine and he was taken from me. I hired a private detective. He found it all out for me.'

'This is madness.' She stepped back again.

'Don't go! It's the truth. I just wanted to talk to you.'

The woman reached for a bell on the table by the door and

rang it hard. 'Merden,' she shouted. 'Get Edward. This person is leaving.'

'I just wanted you to hear the truth.'

'You are here for money. You are here for blackmail. Well let me tell you, it will never happen. Mr Whetstone receives such threats often, as a wealthy man, and we speak directly to the police. If you don't go, I will call them now.' The maid appeared at the door with a burly man in a suit.

'Make her go, please. You should never have let her in, Merden. I blame you for this.'

The burly man advanced. 'You don't need to force me,' said Celia. 'I will walk out. Don't send the maid away. It was my fault.'

'How dare you tell me what to do? You are a criminal, Madam. You must leave immediately.' Merden stood there, her face frozen.

Edward seized her arm and started propelling her forward. 'You don't need to,' she said. But he was pushing her on and there was no point protesting. 'Just let me do one thing,' she said. 'Please. I left my notebook.'

He must have pitied her, let her dart back to get it from the chair. Then in a moment she had picked it up, was scribbling on the paper, tore it off and left it on the table.

'My address,' she said. 'If you reconsider it. I am at the Plaza Hotel.'

Mrs Whetstone looked at it, then her, eyes all disgust. 'This is disgraceful. You are disgraceful. Remove her from my house, Edward.' She hurried from the room, her skirts flouncing behind her.

He pushed her forward.

'I'm sorry,' she said to Merden. 'I didn't know this would happen.'

Edward moved her out of the door, into the hall, past the paintings, to the lift in the hall. 'Will she be fired?'

He looked at her and she saw something like pity in his eyes. 'No. She knows too much about the family. But don't come here again, Miss.'

'Just tell me, please. Is Sebastian happy?'

Edward stared at her, sizing her up. He shook his head. 'No. He should stand up for himself more.' He raised his voice. 'Now, I don't know who you are or why you came, but we'll never see you again. I have friends who are much quicker to anger than I.'

He pressed the button and the elevator and the concierge appeared. 'I'm sorry about Merden,' she said. 'I didn't mean to get her in trouble.' She opened her purse and took out a note.

Edward shook his head. 'You don't need to worry. Like I said, the lady will never let Merden go. She's been here too long.' He ushered her into the lift.

She sat against the wood wall of the elevator. Michael was back there in the apartment. Called Sebastian. She had been so close to him. But in her quest to find him, she had got Merden into trouble. Her heart overflowed with guilt.

Outside the building, she stood against the wall, buried her face in the bricks. Mrs Whetstone would never see her. Women like her didn't look out of the window. She was probably tearing up the address right at that minute. She spun the day over and over in her head, how she might have done it differently, approaching Mr Whetstone first. But he would have probably sent her away too, whatever she'd said. *He should stand up for himself.* She needed to think. Her thoughts were too much, rising, threatening to engulf her. She needed to be out of the New York streets, sitting quietly in her room. She hailed a cab, clambered in, closed her eyes as it bumped her to the hotel.

'There you are!' Arthur's voice. She turned and he was behind her in the lobby. 'I've been looking for you. Where have you been?'

'I went—' But already he wasn't listening, he caught her arm and started talking.

'I've been to the bank. They love everything. They said we need to launch the competition now. And what they said is that they think you should be the face of the competition. You will advertise the Flapper Foods Girl.'

'Me? What do they mean? I can't do that.'

'Yes, you can. You will inspire all the girls across the country to send in their pictures to become our Flapper Foods Girl.'

'But this can't be possible. I'm not a flapper! There are a hundred girls on the street who'd be better than me!' And I'm exhausted and all I want is my son back, she thought. If Mrs Whetstone loved Michael, then yes, she should leave him. But if the family hated him, she needed to save him. But how? She couldn't just take him. He would be terrified and he might even protest anyway. Just because they didn't love him – he might still love *them*.

'But we don't want some girl off the street. We want you. It's your idea. You will be the face of the competition. That's what they said at the bank. Businesses like ours need faces.'

'I'm too old.' She thought of Edward's face as he'd said, 'No.'

'You look twenty-one.'

He was excited, all talk. It could save them. Her parents could live and die in the house they loved. Emmeline wouldn't be destitute. They could guard Michael's and Louisa's ghosts, be near them. Flapper Foods would rescue them all.

'I don't know,' she said. 'Let me think about it.'

'But we don't have time to spare. We need to strike while the iron's hot.' He stopped at the top of the stairs. 'Listen, Celia. I've been looking after the business for years now, and I've never seen anyone as excited as this. We have the chance to make it. We can succeed! I don't want it to slip through our fingers.'

He was right. They were so close. But Michael was locked up in a tower and she didn't know how to get to him.

NINE

Manhattan, February 1929

'Just turn to the right!' Celia tipped her head up and moved as the photographer said. The lady who had come to do the make-up jumped forward to brush back her hair. They'd cut it to make her look the part.

She doubted she could see a lawyer again, since she'd had no right to find out the address and by all accounts had signed him away. And even if she could prove she hadn't – she knew that any judge would believe it in the better interests of a child to stay with a rich family like the Whetstones, rather than an unmarried woman like her. The Whetstones probably knew all the judges!

She'd sat in the salon as the woman picked and plucked at her hair, talking on about young girls today. She'd tried not to look in the mirror, watching her hair shorn away. Bobs suited girls with sharp chins, cheekbones that came out as if they always had shadow on their faces. She suspected that short hair would make her eyes and cheeks look even more round.

Arthur had found a dressmaker with two gowns, pale green for summer, red for winter. They were exquisite, lace edged, just past the knee, delicate fabric in the green, fine wool in the red.

So she stood there with her new hair, unfamiliar make-up over her face, so much of it that she felt her skin was almost suffocated, smiling for the photographer. Arthur couldn't stop talking.

'You know, Celia, I never thought you would have the answer to all our problems. Little Celia saving us all.'

He jumped forward in a photograph break. 'But are you happy? This is what I want to know. Are you happy?'

She almost started. Michael. The Whetstones. Jonathan. Violet.

She opened her mouth. But then he started talking again, on and on about how he was lonely now and needed a wife; where could they meet anyone when they only knew each other? He hoped that one of the bankers might have a sister or a friend. The words came tumbling out, so fast. She was glad she hadn't spoken. He wasn't really interested – he had only been asking so he could talk. Don't forget Louisa, she wanted to say. But it was over two years since she died.

She smiled for the photograph, wishing she could make everything stop, but things just kept moving on and there was nothing you could do to stop them, time was taking them all and everything that had happened yesterday was already gone. Back in her room, she unwrapped the toy farm at the bottom of her wardrobe and cried.

The days proceeded. Celia tried to fill them. She attempted to telephone Jonathan, to tell him she was sorry, but each time she was told by a sharp-sounding man that he wasn't at home. Red didn't come even though she waited outside with cigarettes and chocolate every night. Sometimes she worried that he had been caught by the police but she scoured the newspapers every morning and there was no mention of the break-in at Bluebells. She supposed that they'd kept it secret, not wanting their clients to know. Violet didn't write. Mrs Whetstone didn't write either – but at least she hadn't contacted the police and sent them to the hotel. Or if she had, they were biding their time. She tried to throw herself into work. She bought cookbooks from the bookshops and wrote up ideas for foods, wrote plans, stood in grocers' shops surveying flour, sugar, bought samples of meat in the butchers' and fish from the fishmongers'. They advertised for a cook to try out the recipes for them. She added up numbers, went to the studio where they were drawing and painting pictures of her to be advertisements, put on her best dress and sat with Arthur through bankers' meetings. Twice she did what she promised herself she would not do and went to Upper Eighty-Seventh Street and looked up at the windows. Sometimes she told herself that she saw a shadow, but she couldn't tell if it was anything more than a trick of the light.

An agent, Mr Martinez, found a few restaurants for sale that he judged to have big enough kitchens for food preparation and cooking. She chose the first one she saw – a long, light kitchen in Brooklyn. She imagined it full of women making cakes, puddings, pickling fruit, rolling pastry for pies.

So this was her vision – eight girls and maybe a man or two working in the kitchens, baking, cooking. She thought of Mrs Bell in the old kitchen at Stoneythorpe, the warm steam coming from the oven, gathering pieces of biscuit dough from the table. It was all gone now – they had no money for a cook, so the ladies from the village Rudolf and Verena could manage to pay brought in ready-cooked food from the bakery. The Flapper Foods kitchen would be like the old Stoneythorpe kitchen, but bigger. And Celia wouldn't be like the rest, paying the lowest wages, sacking people when they were ill. They would have a good wage, a high wage, maybe as much as a man, and she'd pay when they got ill and give them some days of holiday. They'd set a new standard and soon all businesses would be like Flapper Foods. She told Arthur her plan and amazingly, he agreed.

'You and your high ideals. But if things start to drop and we need to cut wages – we'll have to? Do you agree?'

It seemed a fair compromise. She nodded, vowing that if it came to it, she wouldn't give in.

TEN

Connecticut, March 1929

'I've come to see Jonathan. Mr Corrigan, I mean.'

The man on the step, the butler she presumed, raised an eyebrow. 'He is at home. But he didn't tell me he was expecting anyone.'

Celia smiled. 'Might you tell him I'm here? It's Celia de Witt.'

'Will he know who you are, Madam?'

Arthur had gone to see Mr Martinez and she'd said she'd stay behind and go through the applications of the cooks. But walking past the telephone where she'd spoken to Jonathan struck at her heart. She rushed to her room, hunted through her address book for Jonathan's address, caught a cab to the station, crossing her fingers that he would be there, taken another cab up a long drive past trees that looked as if they had been growing there for two hundred years.

Celia recognised his sharp voice from the man who answered the telephone. Her hope sank. He would never let her through.

And then he nodded. 'I will ask him. You can wait in the hall, Madam.'

The butler ushered her into a marble hall with a grand gold clock on a marble table. After fifteen minutes in which she tried her best not to look around, not to touch the clock because who knew who was watching (Red had taught her that), the butler returned to usher her into a beautiful library. She gazed out of the window at the grounds full of sheep, touched the wooden globe on a stand, looked at the books on the shelves. She stared at them behind the glass fronts of the bookcases. She tried to open a door, but it was locked. She traced her hand over the smooth glass.

Lucky Jonathan living here, this beautiful parkland, the library full of books. His lucky wife to be mistress of all this.

The door opened. Jonathan stood there, against the frame.

'Celia,' he said. He didn't move forward. He hadn't changed. Still radiating health, blond hair, ruddy face, tall and broad, wide almond brown eyes, everything about him shooting energy and a heart strong enough to bear them all. He was wearing clothes for golfing, she supposed, casual.

She smiled at him. Her heart warmed, sent the fire up to her face. 'Your family have a beautiful house.'

'You look different. You've had your hair cut.' She wondered what she really did look like to him, her skin flaming red from the New York cold and the late nights, her hair dried out.

'Oh, yes.' She held her hand up to her fringe. 'Arthur – we – we have this idea for a business. Who knows if it will work.' She was gabbling, she knew, but she couldn't stop herself. Everything was coming rushing back – dancing together in the Ritz in wartime after he'd seen her in the street, his arms around her. Then that night before the trial when they had held each other close, and she had felt not just that he was rescuing her from it all, because he was, he was, but that she was rescuing him, too.

He took a step forwards. Then he stopped, leant against the bookcase. 'Celia—'

She had to get in first. 'I'm sorry I said the wrong thing on the telephone. I should have told you I was coming. It was all such a rush, Arthur was coming, I came too, and—'

'You didn't think about me.'

'No – I...' She stopped. It was true. She hadn't really thought about him. Her mind had been full of Michael. 'I'm—'

'I've told myself that I need to stop this,' he said, looking at the globe. 'It's been going on too long.'

Celia gazed at him, watched his hand on the globe. And then she was flung back, so hard it almost made her breathless, to fifteen years before, 1914, when she'd first met Jonathan. Michael had brought him home from Cambridge. They sat on the lawn and talked about boats and people she didn't know. She'd been awkward, not really popular at school, always running away at home to be with Tom or hide in her dell, seek out her imaginary friends. Michael and Jonathan had seemed impossibly grown up, the promise of what she might have if she studied, went to Cambridge too, jumped with both feet into the world. And here she was, nearly thirty, having never jumped at all. The one thing that she did do – spend the night with Tom – had only tied her even more strongly to Stoneythorpe and her parents.

Jonathan had shone with promise then. Michael, too. But Michael had died without dignity and Jonathan did everything instead: joined the Air Force, finished his degree at Yale, lived in a house that was whole and handsome, not like crumbling Stoneythorpe, the castle in *Sleeping Beauty*, falling to bits, covered in moss, while everyone slept inside.

He'd kissed her, the night the war broke out, out on the lawn, and her body had coursed with shock. The ornamental garden Verena had been so preoccupied with, the false canal, the fountain, the perfectly symmetrical flower beds, and beyond it the garden billowed up, overgrown rose bushes and hedges, flowers so inter-woven you didn't know where one ended and another began. The garden Verena had hoped would be the seat of culture, refined behaviour. Instead, Jonathan and she, Emmeline with her tutor and Arthur and Louisa walking. A place of secrets.

'I'll always remember it, you running out of the door, your hair loose from its plait. Michael laughed and said you'd come back. You didn't. Then later, after I'd greeted your parents and your sister, Michael and I came to look for you. It was my idea, you know. But he said he knew where you would be. We walked down to the bottom of the garden and there was a cut in the hedge. We looked in – saw a small pond with a willow tree. You were sitting on a stone. We came through. I wasn't sure – I thought we might be invading. But Michael said you wouldn't mind. He called you and you wouldn't come. He laughed and said you had to. But you shouted back that you were staying there and you weren't moving. I looked at you sitting there, and your hair was so bright. It was as if you were all light.' He looked up, gazed at her.

Jonathan spun the globe, hard and fast, bitter. 'So long ago. Of course you were so young. But I said to myself: that's it. The light was flowing from you. It was a *sign*, that's what I saw. And then the war came and Michael left and what reason was there for me to stay? With everything that was happening to you, I was just making it worse.'

She remembered. Sir Hugh breaking off the engagement with Emmeline. Suddenly they were Germans. And then in the garden, the lit end of Jonathan's cigarette burning as he swooped down. *Little German fräulein.*

'I know it was wrong of me to kiss you. I shouldn't have. If it hadn't been for the war – I thought I might never see you again. I tried to write all through the war, but the words wouldn't come – and anyway, I knew I'd have to wait. Then I saw you in London – and—'

'I know,' Celia said, her head bowed. 'I remember every moment.'

'The world turned,' he said. 'You were an adult, then, driving your ambulance. We went for tea, we danced. I asked you to marry me. And then Burlington turned up and told you everything.'

You would think there were enough Fritzers killing off our chaps without the Brits doing the same to our own men.

Jonathan had bundled her out and she'd begged him, forced him to tell her. Michael was ill, he'd said. He couldn't go over the trench. His legs wouldn't take him.

They make the officer stand in front of his men. Each of his men has a gun. Then they are told to shoot.

It had all been a lie. Michael hadn't died bravely, as they'd been told. An officer in charge had known him at Cambridge and covered it up 'for the family'. He'd been shot as a coward.

I hate you! She'd stood in the street and shouted at Jonathan. *I hate you! How could you not have told me!* Then she'd fainted and woken up in her bed in Emmeline's flat, her sister scolding her.

'You didn't say this at the Ritz. You'd said you'd liked me at Stoneythorpe. You hadn't said you'd loved me.'

Jonathan looked back at the globe. 'Well, I'm telling you now. It's true. I thought it would only frighten you away. Anyway, I thought I'd lost you. I came back here. I tried other women. Nice women, pretty women. But I thought of you. I read of the trial and I came back for you.'

Celia blushed hard.

'We were together that night. You and me. I thought that – despite everything that had happened to you, I was helping you.'

'You were!'

'And then you forgot me.'

She felt tears at the back of her eyes, tried to push them back. 'I'm sorry. But with Arthur being freed and the rush and I…' She broke off. If she went any further, she'd have to tell him about Michael, him being taken from her and he'd ask, but whose was it? He'd think badly of her, going with him and another man before marriage. He might think she'd been with dozens. Or he might tell her, as she always expected people to do, to leave Michael where he was. Say that he was better off in a real family. She blushed, miserably.

She wanted to say, 'You can't love me! I have a son! What makes you want to love when I already have a child?' Jonathan's wife, the mistress of all this, would have to be pure. She should tell him the truth. At least he might understand why she'd been so distracted. But then, maybe he'd say, why didn't you tell me before? He'd be disappointed in her. The tears were billowing at her eyes.

'I can't explain,' she said. 'But I promise, there is something important. I can't tell you.' Everything was rushing through her head now: the war, Michael's death, his few belongings sent back to be buried, later her nightly imaginings of Michael's end, shot by his fellow men. Shot by *Tom*. No matter what he'd said, that he hadn't wanted it to happen, that he had no choice – he had fired shots forward, along with the other men, and her brother had died. Maybe he'd shot him. She couldn't blame Tom – he'd had no choice – but how could she love him after that? It wasn't possible.

'You're in love with someone else.'

She jerked her head. 'No!'

'Celia, don't say that. You're trying to make me feel better. But you're not free for me. I can see that.'

It's not a man, she wanted to say. It's my child!

'Would it have made a difference? If I'd said before, *I loved you since the moment I saw you*. You were thinking about your family, just as you're always thinking of your family – that brother who was never worthy of you. He pushed Louisa, didn't he?'

'No! They found him innocent.' The barrister, Mr Bird's words at the end of the trial came back to her. He'd questioned the witness who said he'd seen Arthur push her. 'Are you saying you cannot be sure?' He'd taken his assistant, Miss Sillen, to the spot, reproduced the distance in the court. It was too far for anyone to see clearly – and Mr Bird was proving them wrong. 'He is no murderer and there has clearly been no crime.' The men of the press rushing to file the story.

'No, Jonathan. Arthur and Louisa had walked to the edge. They stepped out too far. And Louisa fell. It was a terrible accident.'

'I was watching in court. A clever lawyer proved him innocent. But you can't tell me – Oh, anyway.' Jonathan shook his head. 'You're – how old? – thirty? And you're still obsessed by your family. Perhaps there isn't another man. Perhaps it's just *them*.'

Celia looked at his finger, on top of the globe, tracing out the lines of a country. 'Jonathan—' But she couldn't speak. She tried hard to bite down the tears. 'I had a—' She stopped.

'You know,' Jonathan said then, taking a step towards her, 'I always thought you looked exactly the same, still that runaway girl. Even at the trial. But now, we're all older. You've changed.'

Celia stepped back towards the window. He was right, she knew. Her face wasn't the same. In the same time, Jonathan had only grown more handsome – his healthy, tanned face, pale hair. He looked even taller. She was about to nod – and then a streak of anger ran through her.

'People grow older. Women do! I like it. I'm independent now. Arthur and I are making a business and it's my idea. I don't want to be eighteen any more.'

Jonathan shook his head. 'Sorry, Celia. I didn't mean it like that. You're still beautiful. You still look like that girl. I was just – I was just trying to get free of you. I was just trying to tell myself that I don't love you any more. I have to. My father wants me to marry. He introduces me to girls of good family all the time. The country club, the sailing club. All the rest of it. But it isn't honest to marry if you're in love with someone else, is it?'

'I don't know.' *Yes*, she'd said to him, that night in London, pretending that Tom didn't exist. 'Maybe everyone is. A bit.' Perhaps love was always mixed, traces of other people you'd been in love with, a cocktail, like the ones the flappers drank.

He wasn't listening to her. 'I was doing well, getting free of you. And then you turn up in New York. I think – well, here she is, perhaps we can begin. But then I find you've been here for ages and I know you are here because you want something.'

'No. I just – I just want to be friends again.'

'That's not true. Why did you really come to America? Was your man an American soldier and you've come here for him?'

Her head whirled. She was on the edge, her feet either side of the fall. She could do one of two things. She could throw herself forwards, tell him she loved him, too, that it had all been a misunderstanding, that she wanted to try together. When she was sure, she'd tell him about Michael and he would be kind to her, say it was in the past – and he was right, it would be, since Mrs Whetstone would never let her have him. Or she could tell him the truth now and the whole house of cards might come tumbling over her.

She felt the air speed past her. Time waited.

'I had a baby. After the war. I came here to look for him.'

'A what? A baby?' He stared at her and then he began to stammer something.

She shook her head. 'Not yours.' How much easier if it had been. Jonathan would never have allowed his child to be taken away. He'd have got solicitors and policemen, the full force of his money and power.

'Whose was it?' She saw his mind working. 'When?'

'After the war.'

'So, after we met in London, went out. But before the trial.'

She nodded, miserably. She hadn't told him there had been a

man before. They had been so caught up talking about the trial, it had seemed such a big thing, so much bigger than anything else, nothing else seemed to matter.

'Who was the father?'

She couldn't get the words out. 'I don't know. It was after the war.'

'Did he take advantage of you?' Jonathan's voice was softer. She wanted to catch it, hold on to it, the tone of a man who cared. She wanted to agree with him, so the softness didn't stop. But she had to tell the truth.

'No. I probably persuaded him.'

Jonathan raised his eyebrows. 'You didn't tell me before. I suppose your family don't know either.'

She shook her head. 'They know. I had him. They gave him away, told me he'd died.' She should stop there; she could see it in his face. But she rushed on. 'When I found out it was a lie, I tracked him down in America, I tried to see him but they sent me away. I've lost him forever.'

There was silence. Jonathan looked at the globe.

'And this man. You aren't trying to find him?'

'He never loved me. He would never want me.'

'But you don't love him?'

She couldn't speak. She couldn't tell him the whole truth, tell him it was Tom.

He gazed back at the globe. 'So you adore your family, who took your son from you. You forgive them. And you maybe love this man who deserted you. But not me.'

'I'm sorry. I did. I do! I just. I'm confused. My mind was caught up in finding Michael. I should have telephoned you. If only I could turn back the clock.'

'You called him Michael?'

She saw his face change and she thought he too was remembering her brother, young with him at Cambridge, before the war. He shook his head. 'How we miss him.' And then his eyes were cool once more.

'And you're here with Arthur. After helping him dodge his—'

'He didn't do it!'

He shrugged. 'Whatever the truth is. Anyway, you should go. Before my father returns. I'll ask them to call you a cab.'

'Will I see you again?'

'I don't know. I need to think. This – I didn't expect any of it.'

'You think less of me for having a child.'

'No! I'm not that sort of man. Or I thought I wasn't. Those men who take as many girls as they want but expect their wives to be pure are hypocrites.'

'I'll be at the hotel. If you want to write.'

'Celia. I need time to think.'

She stood still, watched him as he left the room. She stared at the back of the door. She couldn't move. She was like a broken plate after you'd balanced all the pieces together – and then, if you moved it a tiny spot, they'd all fall and shatter and nothing would be left.

INTERLUDE

Lily had decided what the answer was. She needed a friend. All girls her age had friends. After all, she was nearly ten now! In every book she read, little girls had friends. They told each other secrets, wrote letters to each other, it was the *two of us against the world*. They spent hours together. And she had no one. Albert wasn't interested in her, he only wanted to make trains and engines and read books about them. It was strange how people called them 'the twins' as if they were two parts of the same person, when Albert and she seemed so very different!

It was typical of Mama to not understand. She'd never have any friends and if Lily ever asked, Mama just said she didn't want any. She said her family and Papa were enough. Papa, of course, before he went away, used to have dozens of friends, always coming over to talk, all day, all night. That was going too far. She wasn't going to be a girl who had too many friends so that she could never go to sleep.

She just wanted *one* friend. One little girl. At night, she lay awake and dreamt about her. She called her all sorts of names: Jenny, Sarah, Ruby, Rose. She had their story entirely worked out. She would meet her in the square where she and Albert were sent to run around and get their exercise while Emmeline watched from above. Usually, the square was deserted, but this time, there would be a little girl there, alone too. And they'd look at each other shyly, walk towards each other. They'd talk. And then every day, they'd meet up. She'd give Ruby a bracelet made of beads that she'd taken from one of Mama's broken necklaces (she had so many broken necklaces. She should really throw them away, you could never fix them now and they were years old). Ruby smiled and then next day bought her a card that she'd coloured and made herself, a pin-and-red heart with flowers around it.

Best friends forever.

She clutched the soft purple cat that Papa had made for her, trying to show how even men could sew. It had tiny holes in the mouth so the stuffing escaped. She loved it, though, even though it was worn, made her wishes on its gentle cloth face.

She said it to Papa, but he wasn't really listening. 'I have to have a best friend! Maybe if I went to school?' A proper school with other girls, rather than the boring room in Mrs Kinle's house where she and Albert learnt history and wrote out sentences that never started with And or But.

'School is repressive,' he said. 'It teaches children to obey, be factory cogs in the wheel.'

Mama said that female friends were a waste of time. 'Mine all stopped being friends with me when the war broke out and everyone said we were German.'

They didn't understand. But Mama once had friends. And if you didn't have a best friend, then you had no one to practice being in love on and *you would never have a husband.*

Lily didn't care what her parents thought. She was going to find a friend. She had to save herself.

ELEVEN

Manhattan, April 1929

Red bit into one of the apples. 'Why are you interested in that rich house up near the park?' After a week of waiting, he had finally come. She'd asked him if he'd heard that there had been any report to the police of the break-in and he said he thought not. He barely even seemed to remember it. He had a new pullover another boy had grown too big for, red and yellow with holes on the shoulder. It suited him, made him look like a small, bright elf.

'What?'

'That rich house near the park. Why do you stand outside?'

Celia shook her head. 'I can't hide anything, can I?'

'I just wondered what you were looking for. Do they owe you money?'

'That's where my little boy is.' She shook her head. 'The address you found. I'm looking for something I can't ever have.'

'I can get it for you, Miss. I got the files, didn't I? I can get *anything* for you.' He took a huge bite of the apple. 'You don't know what I can do.'

'I told the woman that he had been mine. I only wanted to see him.'

He nodded, chewed on the apple. 'So let's go and get him for you.'

'No, no. We can't do that. It would be a crime. We can't kidnap him. He's theirs. I just want to see him. And how can you do that?'

It was ridiculous, placing her faith in a child. He couldn't help her. He had enough problems, surely.

'I just want to see him. That's all I want.'

He patted his head. 'I'll be back when I can.' He picked up the bag of food. 'Any more smokers?' he tried.

He raised his eyebrows and jumped up onto the bin lid.

She watched his legs disappear upwards and then he was gone.

Two nights later, he was back.

'I told you I'd find an answer! We've worked out how to get onto his house and through his window.' He wagged his finger. 'One of us – Jamie – he got in through another window and managed to get round and get the key for your little boy's. He has opened it up so we can push through. But it's only time before they find out and lock it again. So we need to move fast.'

'We?'

He blew out smoke. 'You're coming with me! Tonight. You need to climb through that window, Miss!'

'Climb through the window? But I can't.'

'Yes you can. You ladies! Then you can see him and talk to him, well you'll have to wake him up first. We'll stand guard.'

'I can't go into his room in the middle of the night! He'll be afraid.'

'Jamie said you should just say you're an angel or something. Then the parents won't know.'

'Say I am an angel?' Her mind was reeling. 'I—'

He put down the cigarette she'd given him. 'Don't you like our answer, Miss?' His face looked hurt. 'We've been working it out.'

Her heart rushed. 'No – no. I like it! I just worry that – we'll get caught. We all might. And you've found me the address. You don't need to do more.'

He blew out more smoke. 'Oh no, Miss. The decision is made now. We are helping you. No going back.' He patted her hand. 'None of you ground people has ever done anything kind for us, you know. They just shoo us away, usually. Come on, Miss, no more talking. Let's go. I'll see you there.'

And then she was in a cab to Upper Eighty-Seventh Street ready to meet him there. She clambered out and waited. It was only ten minutes or so before she heard a whistle and looked up to see Red surrounded by five or six shadowy figures, little boys too. In a moment, they were clambering down the side of the building, jumping next to her. 'Hello, Miss,' hissed Red. 'This is Jamie.' He waved at a bigger boy. 'And the rest I'll tell you later. Come on! They're all asleep.'

She followed them. 'I can't climb up there,' she said, flatly. 'I just can't.'

'Easy,' said Red. 'Easy measy. Just follow me. There's a staircase at the back.'

They walked around and then she was at the back of the house and being pushed up to get onto an iron flight of stairs. She clambered up, watched Red pulling himself up onto the window ledges above her. When she got to the top, he reached down for her. 'I can't climb on the ledges,' she hissed, but already Jamie was pushing her up and she was balancing on someone's iron balcony; then Red was tugging her hand and she was being pulled up, feet flailing onto another. *Don't look down.*

'Up there,' hissed Red. She gazed up, and one storey above was a window, slightly open. He nodded. 'There you go.' She hoped he was right, was too dizzy to count.

He jumped up ahead of her and perched on the sill. She heard the traffic behind her, the sound of someone drunkenly shouting maybe a few streets along. She could never get her feet on such a narrow piece of wood. It was impossible.

'You won't fall,' whispered Jamie behind her, as if reading her mind. 'We'll catch you.'

'I don't know.'

'Go on,' whispered another boy. 'We can't wait around.' And so she had to. She had to push herself up and try somehow to manoeuvre her foot onto the ledge, as Jamie pushed her from behind and Red held her hands on the ledge to steady her. He reached across, nimbly, caught her and hauled her up by the waist. It felt strange to have the child's hands on her, holding her close on the ledge. He was bearing her weight, she couldn't help it, felt too dizzy to hold herself up. The curtains were closed, she couldn't see in and yet behind that window was Michael. Or Sebastian. He was there. 'You've got the right window, yes?' she hissed.

'Hope so.'

If they hadn't, she hoped they would burst in on a maid or a store room – rather than Mrs Whetstone.

He shuffled her along, opened the window to his side, pulled it out. 'Through you go. Lucky you're not fat, Miss.'

He pulled her hand and she bent and ducked and balanced herself and then she was pushing through thick material and putting one leg down on the other side of the window. The ledge was hard on the back of her legs as she put down the other foot.

A room, darkened. Not large – it might be a maid's room. Her eyes adjusted to the lack of light. Shadowy shapes, a chest of drawers, a chair. Not much else. Any toys must be all packed away. She looked across to the single bed. There was a figure under the covers, hunched up in a ball. It had to be him. Michael. She moved across the room, tiptoeing, reached the bed. The figure didn't stir. She bent down, her hand hovering over the covers. And then the figure sighed, turned onto his back and she looked at his face. Pale skin, long eyelashes, round cheeks, dark hair over his forehead. Small nose, large forehead. She had imagined him, thought of his face so many times. She'd searched for him in the faces of different children. He hadn't looked like this – not quite. She'd imagined him blonder, more ruddy, thick hair. His was fine, looked as if it would feel shiny if you even touched it, his skin looked delicate too, would go red with wind, rain, show up embarrassment, emotion. Skin like hers. He was biting his lip in his sleep, small white teeth. He sighed. He looked so tranquil. She could hardly bear to wake him. And what if she did and she scared him? He might scream – he surely *would* scream. And then he'd wake everybody.

She wished she could just sit by him, watch him sleep. She'd engrave the contours of his face onto her mind. She'd never forget him. She'd come back every night, sit by him until morning. But she couldn't, of course not, she couldn't ask Red to spend every night helping her – he had business to attend to, whatever that was. It would be impossible to get into the window without him.

She knelt by his side, reached her hand out for his forehead. She extended a finger, touched. His eyelids fluttered a little. She put the fingertip on his forehead, warm to the touch, fine as she had thought. *Hold yourself back.* She wanted to seize him up, never let him go. 'Michael,' she whispered. He didn't stir.

'I love you,' she whispered. Maybe he would hear it in his dreams.

She couldn't pretend to be an angel. Ridiculous. Angels didn't wear navy day dresses and sensible boots. You couldn't touch them and feel flesh. She reached for his hand on the coverlet. The fingers clenched back, lightly, as if they were truly holding hands and her soul soared. He knew her. Even in his dreams, he knew her. He let go of her hand, turned over.

She couldn't wake him. It would be too much for him. She turned, gazed around the room. No toys, as she had thought. No toys on the bed, not even a bear, so fashionable because boys could have them as well as girls. It could be anybody's room, she thought, nothing there to indicate it was a child's. *Is he happy?* Her words to Edward by the Whetstones' elevator filled her soul with dread.

There was a shuffle, a movement. She turned back.

And then he was turning over again and his arms moved, his hands up in the air. He was breathing faster, harder. He was beginning to sigh. He was moving, tossing, then crying out. 'Stop it!' She turned to him, couldn't stop herself, put her arms around him. She held him close. He cried. 'Sssh. Don't cry. You're safe. Don't cry.' His warm body against hers, his hair under her hands. She held him close. Her child. She wanted to call him by name, held herself back. His blue pyjamas were threadbare, nails unkempt but all of him was true. He was *real*. She stroked his hair. He was still mostly asleep, his eyes fluttering. She willed him to wake. To see her. Her soul catapulted, afraid again that he would wake up and scream. She rocked him, back and forth. *Don't cry.* Although it was she who wanted to cry, weep for all those days missing, the days and nights she would have done this for him, when he was ill or sad, toothache or nightmares.

'Do you have many nightmares?' she whispered.

And then his eyes opened and he looked up. Her heart skipped. She froze.

He blinked, opened his mouth. She felt her hands on him grow slack. Her heart filled with dread.

He blinked again. 'Who are you?'

She wasn't an angel. Of course she wasn't an angel. Her heart, blood was beating as she held him close. She gazed down into his beautiful brown eyes. Not her eyes. Maybe Tom's. She couldn't bear to think about it. They were beautiful, whatever they were, whosever they were.

'I'm—' she stopped.

'Are you a new maid?' His voice. Once she had heard him speak, *how could she ever leave him?* His voice was curiously high, clear, a little like Michael's had been when they were children.

'Yes! Yes I am. I'm the new maid.'

'Oh.' He settled back into her arms, close to her. Their warmth, the two bodies. They might be one. *I am your mother*, she willed through, wouldn't say it.

He sat away again, opened his eyes. 'Is your room up here?'

Was he on the same floor as the maids? 'Er. Yes.'

'You must be very new. You know you're not supposed to come in to me when I'm crying or having a nightmare.'

Jamie's voice at the window. 'Miss. We need to go.' But she couldn't.

She didn't think he'd heard it. She squeezed him close. 'I think children should be held.'

'Well, Mother says it's fine for my brothers and sisters to be held. They're strong. But I'm weak and I need to learn. The first time I cried all night. But I've got used to it now.' He was sitting up, talkative now. 'I wish I had a doll or something but mother says they make me weak too.'

'And the others?'

'Well, they're different. They're naturally strong!'

'Ah.' Her heart was swelling, blood rising.

'Miss!'

There was a step outside the door. 'Sebastian?' A woman's voice. She looked at him in panic. He pointed to the area under the bed and she scrambled down, slid herself under, pushed to the side near the wall. She saw feet visible through the gap at the bottom of the door.

'Shouting in your sleep again? What is wrong with you?' Mercifully, they stopped and didn't come in.

Then Jamie was in the room and he was grasping her. 'We need to go. Now!'

She reached behind to Michael. 'Come with us!' He looked at her in shock. 'Please.'

He was staring at the child behind her, his face terrified. 'Who are they?'

'My friends. Come with us.'

He began to back away from her. 'Who are you?'

The fear on his face broke her heart. 'Please, we want to help you,' she said.

'Come with us. I promise we'll look after you. They aren't kind to you here, are they?'

'No.' But she saw it in his face. It was all he knew.

He shook his head. 'I can't. I live here.' She couldn't lift him, even if he'd wanted to let her. Her heart was wrenching. Quickly, she took the toy horse from her pocket and thrust it into his hand. He clutched it, barely looking, staring into her eyes.

'Please! Please come.'

He wouldn't. He couldn't. He loved them. Probably despite everything, no matter what they did to him, he loved them. The woman was shouting for someone else to come up. Michael's face was terrified. Jamie grasped her and she scrambled out. 'I'll come back!' she said. And then Jamie was pulling her out and she was running down the staircase and they were all hurtling along the street.

TWELVE

Manhattan, April 1929

How could she have been so stupid? She had put him in such danger. He could be beaten, punished. All because of her. Back at the hotel, she'd given Red the food she had and all the money in her purse.

A feeling seized her, washed over her, emotions pulling at her. 'Come and live with me. I'm not like the others. I can look after you. You can even go off wandering if you like. I won't stop you. I won't make you do anything. I just – it's not safe out here. Someone could kill you. Bring Jamie too, if you like.'

Red reached down, patted her hand. 'That's very kind of you, Miss,' he said, indulgent. 'But we like things this way. We know you're different. But other adults might make you send us to school and all the rest of it.'

'But what if you get ill? And it's dangerous here.'

He grinned through a mouthful of chocolate. 'Why don't you come and live with us? You're a good climber. We could teach you. Once you've lived outside, you'll never go back.'

'I can't.'

'Like I said. Adults are afraid.'

It was true. 'Wait. I have something in my room. I bought it for Michael – but – I'd like you to have it. It's a toy farm.'

He shrugged, looked pleased. 'I've never had a toy.'

She hurried inside, ran upstairs, took the farm out of the wardrobe, took it back down, wrapped in a shawl. Red opened it up, looked quizzical.

'What do we do with this?'

'You play with it.'

He cocked his head. 'I don't think we'd have time for that.'

'At least – take a few animals. Please. For me.'

'If you like, Miss.' He picked over, selected horses, pigs and the farm dog, lifted them up high, inspected them. 'These are swell.'

'Please take them. And the money. And if you ever need me – here's my home address, if I'm not here, you can write to England. Or ask your friend who can write. If you're ever in trouble, I can help.'

He grinned. 'We never get in trouble. That's for you adults! I'll take it though. Maybe I'll learn to read one of these days.' He tapped his head. 'I'll see you again, Miss. I can almost guarantee it.' He scratched his nose. 'Fate. That's what this is. It's fate. I might tap on your room one day. You'd better watch out!'

'Would you go and check on my little boy, from time to time? And maybe tell me? Or don't tell me. Just see he's all right?'

'I'll do it. I'll see what I can do.'

'Thank you. Come down. Please.' He clambered down from the bin and she hugged him hard. He wriggled out, laughed. 'Must run! Goodbye, Miss!' And then he was gone.

That night her mind was restless, visions of Michael, cruelly beaten, crying out for help. How wrong she had been. She'd ruined things for him and made his life worse, perhaps nearly unbearable – all from her own desires. Or perhaps seeing her, being held by her, the offer of friendship, of coming with them had been a help. At least he knew that someone liked him, wanted him.

But still, she thought. She should have left him alone.

She turned her head into her pillow. How could it hurt so much? And this wasn't like death, the pain she'd felt at the loss of her brother. This wasn't wartime, it was peace. She wept for him, for everything, for her own love for him and because it was hopeless, there was nothing she could do.

*

The next three days were busy with Flapper Foods, looking at advertising, the arrangements for the kitchen, looking over the lists for suppliers. Celia threw herself into it so Arthur wouldn't suspect the anguish inside. The photographs were being made up into advertisements. They interviewed six cooks and chose a Miss Salm, who had trained at a cookery school in New Jersey and was working in a department store restaurant – but had so many ideas for her own recipes that Celia fell in love with her on the spot.

'Once you've been here a month or so and we have the recipes, you might start recruiting the under-cooks. We need six or so to help you, I think.'

She had three orders – from Macy's and Bloomingdale's and Bergdorf's – as soon as they were ready, they wanted a display of cans and jars. Mr Goodman had been first and once she had told the rest that Bergdorf's had agreed, all the others wanted the same. Four more were considering the numbers.

She checked at the desk for messages – from Jonathan, Violet, even from her family. Nothing. She didn't allow herself to hope for anything from the Whetstones. She wondered after Albert and Lily, Lily particularly, missed her sweet smile, laughter. She wrote to her sister, asking if Mr Janus had stopped talking about Spain, and saying how well Arthur was doing. She even wrote to her parents at last. *We both like New York*, she said. The words felt stiff and hard. She couldn't help it. She couldn't help but blame them for Michael's cruel situation. She longed to go to Miss Bellenden and shout, 'Look what you have done! You said he'd be in a happy place. Loved. Wanted! That you shouldn't disturb him because he was settled. But you gave him to these cruel people.'

Why had they taken him if they hated him so much? Maybe they had thought they couldn't have children and when they did, preferred their own. Or he didn't turn out as they thought. She didn't know. But she prayed and she wished and she begged any god she could think of, even though she knew it wouldn't do any good.

The burgeoning business couldn't fill the void inside her. After a week, Celia went to the local church. 'I'm here for a few months,' she said to the weary-looking priest, Father Crisp, after finding him in his office. 'Maybe longer. I want to help. I wonder if I might help with children.' He relented, eventually, sent her off to the Sunday school attached to the orphanage, where a Miss Breadker told her to start cutting up triangles of blue for the children to use to make pictures of the Virgin Mary. When they finally let her play with the children, she was immediately struck by one little boy, Ethan, red-haired, big blue eyes, about eight or so, she thought. Their heads were bowed. Except him. He gave her a giant smile and winked – boldly. She almost jumped. He was skinny like the rest of them, but unlike them, he was sparking with energy, his limbs fizzing. He couldn't sit still, always jiggling his leg or wiggling his hand. She smiled at him and he grinned back. When she went around to help them cut out paper, he gave her another great smile. 'Where are you from, Miss? My family are from Ireland. Have you ever been?'

'Not yet.'

'If you go, will you take me?'

Miss Breadker looked on disapprovingly.

'They've got pixies in the hills.'

'Ethan!' Miss Breadker looked positively shocked.

'If I plan a visit, I'll let you know,' Celia whispered into his ear.

Miss Breadker had told her that the children's names weren't their own, they were re-named when they arrived at the orphan- age. 'New name, new life,' she said. Celia wondered if Ethan or any of them might know their real name – whether they kept it at the back of their minds, to hold on to, return to. Or whether it meant nothing to them, just another word given to them by parents who had died, left them, not cared enough, just another of the many names they might have, along the way.

Michael stayed hidden in her heart, waiting for her – and when she came out of the door of the orphanage, he came back to the fore and she could think of nothing but him.

*

Over the next days and weeks and months, Celia tried to devote herself to Flapper Foods. Miss Salm and the cooks she had hired created the recipes, and Celia costed each of them. She and Miss Salm spent two days trying to perfect the tying of the red bow at the front of each jar, throwing away yards of ribbon after they'd tried and failed to get the bow exactly correct. They created a whole range – six savoury, six sweet – and packaged them up into the jars. Celia bought a new suit and took them to show to the bankers. They smiled and nodded and signed off more money. The third bank even brought out forbidden champagne to share. She sipped at the yellow liquid, honeyed, sweet, felt the bubbles dance down her throat. She interviewed companies about creating packaging, looked at designs for labels, debated whether they should feature flapper girls or hats or flowers. They made final plans for the advertising and the competition. On one walk back from the kitchen, after a particularly rewarding day in which all the biscuits in the latest recipe had been perfect, she looked up at the New York skyline and thought, Why not do more? Why spend so much time on charming Macy's and Bergdorf's when she could simply have her own shop?

She went for another meeting with the bankers two days later, sketched out her plans. She conjured visions of starting with a small food shop in an exclusive part of town. A grand opening with actresses smiling and girls dancing. Then stores across America. Chicago. Los Angeles. Detroit. The man in charge nodded.

'Quite so, Miss Witt. The female shopper is the engine of our modern economy. If Flapper Foods does well, after six months, we will invest in a store.'

Celia's mind circled the business all day and at night she dreamt of shelves and jars and shop windows and the Flapper Foods Girl up in lights.

She advertised for salesgirls, interviewed ten and chose two, Betty and Mary-Anne. Betty was pretty, dark hair, red lips, pale skin, a fast-talking Snow White from Brooklyn, had sold furniture from a warehouse before, loved food, was fun and young and could be a flapper girl herself. She told Celia that she never let a sale get away. Mary-Anne was fair, taller, quieter, from Connecticut, just moved to New York, had been to teacher-training college and worked in a dress shop in New Haven. She was the type to send to the subtler stores, because she seemed quiet, but once she began talking, she didn't stop, she wove you in and her eyes were so bright and engaged, you just wanted to agree and buy anything she offered. Celia took them to meet Miss Salm, go over the products and they packed up two cases, sample jars, tied with bows, a few boxes, jars of puddings and stew. They would start with the New York shops and then move out of Manhattan, to the stores in Brooklyn and Queens, and then past into New Jersey and Connecticut. Celia gave them the money to buy three new suits and hats, agreed the salary, said she'd go with them to the biggest stores like Bergdorf's and Macy's – but all the others would be soft clay in their perfect hands. Once they'd sold into a few shops, she'd advertise again and they could interview the next girls, to see who they'd most like to work with them.

Outside of the business, she continued at the orphanage Sunday school and tried not to favour Ethan too much, although she did give him extra sweets, found herself listening to his readings for longer than the others. She read the newspapers in the hotel lobby and scoured them first for news of the break-in at Bellenden's and then for news from Europe, although there didn't seem to be much. Every day was a fight not to walk up to the Whetstones' house.

'We need to do more with our money,' Arthur said to her, on the way back to the hotel. He grasped her hand. 'After all our work. We're making a lot now.' He had accompanied her to see Miss Salm, talked to Betty and Mary-Anne. Her happiness dropped a little, watching him smile at Betty and listen to her talk – then she chastised herself as a poor sister. He was just friendly to women, nothing more.

'We haven't got much of it. Not yet.' They had paid for everything so far – but the big tranches would come when they needed to go into proper production, hire factories and dozens of girls. 'Once we have some more orders, then we'll have more money.' Her mind was dizzied, sometimes, by the amounts they needed, bags and bags of sugar, hundreds of chickens, great piles of potatoes, as if they were feeding a king and his giant Tudor court.

Arthur put his arm through hers. 'But don't you think it's a waste, just leaving it in the bank?'

Having his arm so close to her was comforting. 'How do you mean?'

'Property. All the money's in Florida. It's a gold mine there. If we don't invest now, we're missing our chance.' And Arthur conjured up Florida as they walked along, money there for the taking, houses and land so cheap, it would double, triple in price within a year or so. America was on fire and Florida was the burning coal, pure energy, pure money. Florida was the place that bred money, created money, where there were dollars on the sun-baked trees, falling from the ever-blue sky. He talked and talked and she was swept up in it, all his words, the girls on the billboards in swimsuits smiling with their bright teeth, the houses reflecting the white light of the sun.

'Well, maybe,' she found herself saying. Because why would you want to miss out? You couldn't fail to make money! There didn't seem to be much interest in Winter Meats any more and the banks wouldn't fund it. This could be Arthur's new focus. 'Maybe we could pledge some of the money.'

Arthur caught her up in his arms. 'My brilliant sister!' he said. 'I knew you'd have the right idea!'

It was America. Investing in America. It was the land of the future.

And then Arthur caught hold of a lamppost and swung himself around it. Celia laughed, smiling. Her old Arthur back again.

'I think we should go to a ball!'

'A what?'

She hadn't been out in the evening since that night after his trial. The night where they'd been sitting around a table in the

Ritz and Rudolf had started talking about America. Then she'd understood about Michael.

'I didn't just come here to make a business. I came here to find a wife.'

Of course. He'd talked about it before, but she had put it out of her mind. Blood rushed to her head with Jonathan's words, murder, Louisa. She pushed them away. It had been an accident. Arthur deserved happiness like anybody else.

'I don't think a ball is really me.'

'Come on, sister. Imagine you're in a book, one of those ones you're always reading. Just see yourself as regarding it all with the eye of an observer. I want to meet a pleasant girl, someone I can talk to. And I've read there's a Vanderbilt girl who is free.'

'Oh excellent.'

'Look, it would do you good to get out. You're sitting here, thinking about that child and you'll never find him.'

'No.'

'So it's a yes, then.' He caught her up, drew her to him. 'Thank you, Sis! You won't regret it.'

'Just once!' she said. 'That's all.' She didn't want him to marry. Louisa seemed like yesterday.

'Splendid! I'll pay for the gown. Will you be ready enough for tomorrow night?'

'Tomorrow night?'

'No time like the present! Buy whatever you want.' He laughed, jumped towards a door.

'I'll need days!' she called, trying to laugh. But he'd gone, the door closed behind him.

'Is this the set of a play?' Celia whispered to Arthur. 'It doesn't look real.' They were walking up the stairs to the ball, through palm trees in pots on the stairs, strung with what looked like diamonds. The chandelier glittered above them. They'd arrived in a cab at the door of the great brownstone house on the park to see dozens of people queueing at the door in front of them; ladies in fur stoles and long, glittering cloaks, gentlemen in white tie.

Celia watched the women kiss each other and chatter ahead, all of them like jewels, rubies, amethysts, emeralds jostling together on a crown. A few had ankle-length gowns but most were long, trailing nearly to the feet, you'd almost think you were in pre-war times – until they turned around and you saw the bodices were cut very low or so close that they couldn't possibly be wearing a corset or even any underwear at all. Celia's dark-green dress was calf length – the dressmaker had told her it was all the fashion. But she was completely wrong, she knew it while she watched the women-jewels wait to glide in the door, hand their stoles to the waiting servants in the hall.

'Don't twitch, Celia,' Arthur said, as they walked up the stairs. 'People can see.'

He was right, she was being excessively nervous. After all, she wasn't going to dance. She wasn't looking for a husband, on show, proving herself to a dragon-like mamma. She was accompanying Arthur, she'd sit quietly with all the chaperones, enjoy the music. The only thing she had to do was not stand out. And since her dress was darker and plainer than everyone else's – and far too informal, she had no jewels and her hair was thin and looked barely styled, even though she'd spent three hours at the hair-dresser – she was hardly rivalling anyone for fashion. She would watch the others, sitting in the background. Arthur had been clever, said the right thing to her: she liked the idea of being an observer, watching, keeping the secrets.

'You never had a coming out ball, did you? I suppose you never wanted one.'

'I suppose I didn't.' She'd never had the choice, of course, the war had come and by the time it was over, no one wanted coming out balls. There were no men, for a start.

'Father could have set you one up. After the war. It seems rather a rum deal you missed out. Surely he could have found the money.' Celia remembered Emmeline's; watching the guests arrive from her position at the top of the stairs, too young to go. Laughing young men, beautiful girls. Her sister the handsomest of them all. She'd watched her dancing with Sir Hugh, her eyes shining.

'You forget, Arthur. Everyone hated us then. The village wouldn't even come to our summer party. Who'd come to a ball for a *German*?'

They passed a giant arrangement of flowers, the perfume so strong that it almost knocked Celia back. 'Now come along, Celia. Smile.'

Celia did so, a bright, painted smile, and faced the ballroom. She felt as if she was looking at a great body of water, a wave of colour, blue, red, green gowns, all coming forth for her. A thousand people, it seemed, pretty women, tall men, dancing, waltzing, giant arrangements of flowers, waiters with trays of delicate glasses, giant silver bowls of drink, a table of cakes and biscuits and enough space for the fine meal to come later. 'Isn't it lovely?' said Arthur, and in a moment, he was gone. Celia gazed around, dizzily, and saw a row of older women sitting straight backed against the far wall. She started over there, dodging dancing couples, waiters and young men who already looked drunk. There was a spare chair at the end of the row. She smiled at the woman next to it and got a quizzical look in return. She sat down, carefully, steadied her head, looked up. Everyone seemed to know each other, all caught up in dancing and celebrating, kissing and talking. She watched a young couple just in front of her, dancing, gazing into each other's eyes.

The women next to her had begun to talk. Another woman, tall and rather plump, came over and stood as they continued the conversation. She threw Celia glances. Then Celia realised that they were all looking at her. She was in the way, not welcome. She stood up and the woman hastily took her chair, without smiling. They bent their heads together. She stood there against the wall, alone. She couldn't even see Arthur. But of course, she said to herself, of course – these people have known each other from childhood. It takes time to be accepted.

She leant against the wall, watched the dancing. Circling,

swirling, dancing, hundreds and hundreds of them. She wondered how Arthur would even discover who the really rich ones were.

'Do you mind?' said the woman who had taken her place. Celia looked back. 'I said, do you mind?'

They were all staring at her now. Celia looked back, unsure.

'I said, do you mind? We're trying to talk here.'

Five faces, beautifully coiffed, necks hung with diamonds, all looking at her with hostility. Celia shrank back. 'I'm sorry,' she began. But then she thought better of it. Why should she apologise? She turned her back and walked away from them, into the dancers. But as she did so, she realised she had no idea where to go. The other wall had a line of sitting women. They probably wouldn't want her either. The only women standing were those near the table, waiting to be asked to dance, pausing between waltzes. Everywhere else she saw men, lounging by the table of food, clustering by the bowls of punch. Or, at least, she supposed it was drink. The police would never come and raid somewhere like this – she supposed it counted as drinking at home. She stood and watched, but no women came to collect a glassful.

She had nowhere to stand, no one to talk to. She stepped forward – and as she did so, a dancing couple moved forwards and hit into her. She fell with them, a tangle of legs and arms, the girl's skirt on the floor. 'What the hell do you think you're doing?' said the man, furiously. *I'm hurt too*, Celia wanted to cry. The man gathered the girl up, delighted, Celia supposed, to look like a rescuer. The couples were stepping and dancing around them. 'You've ruined the whole dance,' he said. 'Look!' Celia lifted her eyes and saw all the couples staring at her as they circled. Someone laughed.

'Oh, Emmanuel,' the young woman breathed, clutching his chest, tears glimmering on her perfect, delicate cheek. 'I think I've hurt my ankle.'

'I'm talking to you,' Emmanuel said to Celia. 'What the hell do you think you're doing?'

Celia was about to answer. The words were there, waiting in her mouth. And then the room was turning and shooting and there were a thousand gowns whirling, people looking, waiters standing, faces, eyes gazing. She couldn't bear it. She pushed through the dancers, a crowd of men, new couples coming through the door, ignoring the shouts, the gasps. She flung out of the light onto the stairs, shoved through the couples coming up, threw herself past the flower arrangement, dived down the stairs and through the last block – a group of men in deep conversation by the door. There were laughs and shouts of 'Stop running, girl!' She ignored them, jumped out into the cool air. The clusters of manservants and drivers leaning by the cars stared at her in shock. She turned away from them, picked up her gown again and began running down Fifth Avenue.

Celia burst into the hotel, her hair falling around her face, her bodice stuck to her with perspiration. She meant to scurry through the lobby as quickly as she could, dive into her room. Three or four couples walking through the lobby stared at her.

'Miss Witt.' It was Frederick, the dark-haired concierge, calling to her across the hall.

'I feel rather unwell, Frederick. I really must go to bed.'

'There's someone waiting for you, Miss Witt. He was very insistent that I tell you he was here. He's in the restaurant.'

'For me? This late? It must be some mistake.'

'He was very insistent, as I say, Miss. The minute you got in, we must tell you that he was here. He is a Mr Crogan.'

'I don't know any Mr Crogan.' But the couples were staring at her. 'All right, Frederick. I'll see him.'

He ushered her to the restaurant. The lights were still on. He opened the door – and Jonathan stood up.

'Celia,' he said. There was a half-drunk cup of coffee in front of him. There was a flurry of a breeze as Frederick left, closed the door behind him.

She gazed at Jonathan, feeling the sweat on her bodice cool uncomfortably on her skin. She felt painfully self-conscious, untidy, no coat, emerald dress covered in street dirt. She held her hand up to her straggled hair. 'I went to a ball,' she said. She meant to say that she felt ill, had to leave – but then she looked at his face and couldn't lie. 'I hated it. I bumped into someone and they shouted at me. So I ran away.'

Jonathan gave a small smile. 'Still running away.' His face was swollen, his eyes red.

'How … are you?' She couldn't think. His last words rang in her mind. She had resigned herself to never seeing him again.

He stood up. 'I had to see you. I thought it would be easier if I told you I wouldn't see you again. But it wasn't. I couldn't stop thinking about you.'

She looked at him, the expanse of restaurant behind him. Her mind was muddled, on fire. She tried to speak. The words wouldn't come.

'I was unfair to you, Celia. I wish you'd contacted me. I was hurt. But I can't let pride stop me. Like you say. We were friends.'

'But – I—' She couldn't say it. The words were lost, somewhere in the back of her mind.

'I'll help you, if you still want me to. To find this child, I mean. If you'll accept my help. I understand that you must have been thinking about him. And I think of how hard it must have been to have lost him. You should have told me before. I could have – well, we could have talked about it.'

She leant her hands on the chair. Her head was dizzy.

'I think I've lost him for good.' But perhaps Jonathan could help, had another idea.

'Sorry, Celia. This is probably too much to take in. I don't mean to cause you even more pain. I just had to see you. I'll go. I've made things difficult for you. I can see that.'

He started to walk. As he passed her, she grasped his hand. She felt it, the rough whorls of the fingers.

'Don't go,' she said. 'Stay.'

His eyes were on fire, his face sparked gold.

He tightened his grasp on her hand, suggested they walk out, get some air, and she agreed. They'd walked out into the street, his arm in hers. Frederick had looked oddly at her but she'd ignored him. He's my cousin, she was ready to say, but he didn't ask.

'I'm sorry I didn't ring you up.'

The city was going to sleep around them, cab drivers on their way home, men sweeping the pavements, workers from the diners setting off home to Queens or Brooklyn.

'I spoke out of anger. I didn't mean what I said.'

She nodded.

'Let's be friends again,' he said. 'Can you forgive me?'

'Of course,' she said. 'There's nothing to forgive.'

They had been so out of time, the one wanting to forgive the other when the other didn't want to forgive, and it was almost amazing they had managed to coincide, rather than go on for years, back and forth.

'You look thoughtful.'

'I expect I'll be in a lot of trouble with Arthur. I rather wrecked his ball.'

'Him.' Jonathan held her arm tightly. 'You need to stay away from him.'

'He's my brother! He wanted to make an impression at the ball. He's trying to find a rich wife.' She was trying to put it out of her mind, how they had clasped each other before Arthur's trial, in his hotel room, holding on to each other as if they had been shipwrecked.

Jonathan's body sharpened, she could feel it. He straightened up. 'A rich wife?'

'He's aiming high. Probably one of the girls you know in New York.' She couldn't help that stab.

'Celia. You can't let him—'

'Lower your voice!' she hissed. 'Anyway, stop it. I know what you think. I'm not listening to this. He was innocent. It was a terrible accident.'

Jonathan snorted.

'And you know more than the judge, do you?' She turned to face him, feeling her eyes blazing. 'How dare you!' she hissed, still keeping her voice down. 'He's my brother. Michael's brother. How can you treat us this way?'

Jonathan looked at the street. He came towards her. 'I'm sorry, Celia. Forget I said it. You love your brother, of course you do.'

'And you know nothing about it.' Her voice was rising, but she didn't care.

'I was at the trial. Don't you remember?'

She kept on. 'You're all the same. You made your decision. Don't you think Arthur's suffered enough? He lost his wife. People suspected him of killing her. You wouldn't say it to his face, would you? You wouldn't dare.'

Jonathan put out his hand. 'I'm sorry, Celia. Let's not – look.'

'No one dares! They all whisper behind his back at home. So it's no wonder he has to come here. At least people here can see him properly.'

The door beside them whisked open. A man poked his bald head out. 'Do you *mind*? I'll report you to the police for noise.'

Jonathan grabbed Celia's hand. He pulled her as he began to run and the two of them hurtled down the street. She started laughing despite herself as they turned the corner, breathless. Then he was laughing too, and she pulled him along and they were back at the entrance of the hotel. She stood with her back to it and laughed. He stood there, across from her, leant on the wall.

'Poor man,' she said. 'I'm in trouble. With him. With Arthur. And the hotel, probably, for wandering off with strange men. Maybe they'll tell me to leave. I've been here long enough.'

Jonathan shrugged. 'Not if you keep paying the bills.'

She smiled.

'I'm sorry I said that about Arthur. I know it upsets you.'

'But you believe it?'

He shook his head. 'Let's not discuss it. We've come this far. I don't want to argue. Let's forget it.' He held out his hand. 'We've lost so much. Let's be friends.' She felt his hand around hers. 'Are we friends?'

'Of course!'

And they were then, her heart flooded with warmth for him, her friend in New York. And they held tight to each other and it was love and forgiveness, and all the rest of it was forgotten, deep in the ground, intertwined with all the deaths and the memories. His arm around her, they stood, quietly.

THIRTEEN

Manhattan, April 1929

'I can't hear you!' She was dancing to music she'd never heard before. Jonathan had taken her to a café, the tables so close that she could barely squeeze in to sit down. The people were all around them, the women in bright colours like butterflies, all of them laughing and talking as if they had never known unhappiness in their lives.

For the last two weeks, she'd seen him nearly every day. He said he was in town for the month and had plenty of free time outside of discussions about the business with his father's manager, Mr Galss, and they'd fallen into the habit of meeting up most evenings and in the daytime too. She'd shown him the kitchen in Brooklyn, taken out the recipe descriptions, discussed the art-work on the advertising. He'd had clear ideas, useful suggestions. Jonathan took an interest, said how fascinated he was, told her that they were really onto something!

He introduced her to Mr Galss, a tall man with thick glasses and a grey suit that never seemed to crease. Mr Galss set up a meeting with a lawyer, who'd acted for the family before and she told a story fudging how she'd got Michael's address. The lawyer looked at her over his papers and Celia thought he probably didn't believe her, or at least knew there was more to it than she gave, said that she didn't have much chance of getting Michael back, but he would look into it. Jonathan took her on walks about the park, but only in the afternoon, in case anyone thought ill, he said. That made her laugh – who was here to mind about her reputation? But he insisted, courtly, protective.

He'd gone with her the first time she'd met Arthur after she'd fled the ball, at lunch at the hotel. She'd rushed into an apology.

'You can't apologise enough for that, Celia. You behaved badly.'

'I'm sorry.' The words stuck in her throat.

Arthur raised his eyebrow. 'Not that you care. I danced with a Vanderbilt girl. They're a very rich family. I have an invitation to visit next week. I told her mother that you were ill.'

So it had continued, through the meal. By the time the apple pie had arrived, Arthur relented and they changed the subject. 'What are you doing here, anyway?' he asked Jonathan, as he poured cream over the pastry.

'I came to see Celia. And business. I've been looking at invest-ments. What's your opinion?'

That was clever. Arthur started talking about the property funds. There was no point investing in Miami any more – that was all done. But Florida. Everything was in Florida! The whole place was just one giant money-making machine.

Jonathan agreed with him. They started talking about money, hundreds, thousands, piles of it, just flowing out of Florida.

'It can't fail,' Arthur was saying. 'If I put in all our money, it still couldn't fail.'

'I agree. Mr Galss is so cautious. He won't let our family. I envy you. It's such an opportunity.'

'You're right. I'm going to do it. We're going to be rich!'

They held up their glasses and drank to it. 'To a hotel in Florida! To apartments! To the sun!'

Celia thought of them all, sitting somewhere on a beach, great hotels and houses going up behind them. Was it so easy to get rich? Celia gazed down at her drink. Why did everyone want to be rich? And then she reminded herself that someone like Violet would tell her that it was important – that otherwise you would be poor, and think about money even more. Violet would say that it was fine for Celia to be romantic about it – she'd never gone hungry.

In the days after, Jonathan and Arthur didn't get on so well. When they met up with Arthur, Jonathan was cool, sometimes even argumentative. 'I was pleasant to him for your sake,' Jonathan said. 'Once is enough.' Arthur talked about the business and Jonathan looked blankly at the table. Celia felt for Arthur, trying to tell Jonathan about his latest meeting and Jonathan looking so bored.

Jonathan shrugged when she challenged him. 'He's untrustworthy. Celia, try to look past loyalty. Your love for your family was always one of your most endearing qualities. But Arthur is untruthful and cruel at best, a—'

'Stop it!'

'A murderer at worst. You shouldn't trust him. And especially not with the business! You have really come up with an excellent idea here, Celia. It could make a lot of money.'

'I'm not listening to these lies. I'm not!' But something in her was cold, as if a thick liquid was pouring around it. 'Stop saying these things!' She stood up and Jonathan followed her, touched her arm. 'Look, Celia, I care about you! I worry that he'll take it all from you, all the money, all the credit.'

She sat down, heavy against the seat. 'He wouldn't.'

'How do you know? Has he asked you to sign anything?'

'He's talked of it. I put some papers he gave me in my room. I don't like signing anything I haven't read properly.'

'I'll wager he is trying to take the business.'

'No, he's not! And anyway, even if he did, what does it matter? It's for all of us. The business is to make all our lives successful! To give money to mother and father, to rescue them, Emmeline, Stoneythorpe.'

'And you think that's what Arthur wants?'

'Of course!' But yet again, that cold, thick stuff curling around her heart. What if Jonathan was right?

'But why do it at all for that house? It's only a house. It's not even that appealing. It's an ugly old place.'

'No, it's not. Just because it doesn't look like New York and isn't all shiny! It's just different.' Stoneythorpe, the ivy tangling around it, the turreted walls and the roof sloping down over the top windows. Built for a friend of Elizabeth I, still there, unchanging.

'No, Celia. It's too big and it's falling apart. Well, it was when I saw it. God knows what shape it is in now.'

She looked down, fingered the drink, one of those New York juice cocktails that the waiter would secretly drop another spot in. 'But it's all the history, memories. I grew up there. And – it's their home. My parents'. They're too old to move now.'

'Too old? I don't buy that. They weren't too old to lie to you.'

She shook her head, not wanting to listen.

'If you're going to make money, then use it for your future. Try and get your son. Give it to your sister, the poor woman needs some luck. But your parents deserve nothing. Look at you! Your heart is broken. And that's what they did to you.'

'I'd have done anything to shield their reputation, if they'd asked. I could have gone off and had the baby in secret, brought him up in London and no one would have known. I could have kept it secret.'

'Look, Celia, I'm not saying they don't have reason. How Germans were treated, are treated. But they lied to you repeatedly – and still you'll do anything for them. I don't understand it.'

'Of course I'm angry with them! I can't write to them anything but pleasantries. When my heart aches for Michael, I blame them. I scream at them in the middle of the night. But what's the point? They did it. They said they were sorry and I have to try to forgive them. I have to hope that I'll get him back and so it will be like it always should have been.'

'Apart from the fact that you've missed nearly eight years of his life.'

She bowed her head again. 'Yes.'

'And if you don't get him back?'

And this time, what she had been withholding, the tears pushing at the back of her eyes, came forwards. One dripped and fell into her glass, dissolving in the dark liquid. She watched it, then another. 'I'll wait until he is eighteen. And I'll make sure he can be proud of me in the meantime, with the business and everything I do. One day, we will be together.'

He clenched her hand. 'I upset you.'

She shook her head. 'I was thinking some of it. Maybe you're right about the house. But it would break their hearts. They're my parents.'

He patted her hand. 'I know. I'm sorry.'

If they stayed away from talking too much about her parents and Arthur, they were almost constantly contented. She had forgotten how easy it was to be with another person. They talked, laughed, sometimes sat quietly. He introduced her to some of his friends from Yale at the club, saying she was a friend from England. They were pleasant-enough men, responsible, building family businesses to earn well.

She kept trying to confide in him her secrets: Mrs Bellenden's, Arthur's final words, Michael's real father. She longed to tell him – but the words wouldn't come. She'd written to Violet and received no reply – and when she went to Primrose's, a new girl was in her place, being spoken to maliciously by the smart girls again.

So she sat there in restaurants and cafés and bars, feeling like two people. The one was smiling, laughing at their jokes, talking about the business and everything from New York politics to the other people in the place. The other was keeping secrets, of love and death and deception. She couldn't reconcile both sides. She wondered if it would be too much to ask to see if he could too.

And then when they were both tired and Celia's head was confused over the accounts and she'd had enough, she said, 'Let's go somewhere different to dance. Somewhere we can listen to music. Somewhere small.' She lowered her voice. 'I wish we could have something to drink.' The red wine that Arthur stowed in his room, refused to give to her. The punch at the ball surrounded by the men.

'Oh!' he said. 'I see. I had some at home.' He walked along. 'I don't know New York well enough. Let me think. Someone told me about a place. I wonder if it's still open.'

'We could try it.'

'I don't know, Celia. They can be dangerous. Sometimes the police are called.'

'Well, then we can run away! It's ridiculous that you can't buy drink here, anyway. I think it's that they just don't want poor people to drink. At home, Lloyd George said that drink was the enemy in the war, but he didn't mean in the House. All the MPs were drinking. Rich men can ruin themselves through drink too.'

'That's true. Listen, I can remember somewhere. It's on West 49th. Let's get a cab.' He held out his arm, a car stopped and he helped her in. 'Number 50, please.'

When they got out the street was quiet. 'It's not really Number 50. Or at least I don't think it is. These places keep moving.' He set off towards a door, knocked hard. A face peered out of a small shutter.

'My friend Robert Vertstein recommended we come here. For an evening.'

The man moved back and opened the door. There was a dark passageway. 'Come in,' he said. The noise of music and people flooded up the stairs towards them, shouting, women laughing, trumpet music.

The man pressed another button. 'We have a system of four alerts,' he said. 'The last one drops all the bottles in the cellar so it looks like everybody is sitting around drinking tea.'

Celia followed Jonathan down the stairs and into a room not three times the size of her room at the Plaza. The crush of people and voices was like two arms, holding out to her. She couldn't distinguish them, bodies whirling, hair, skirts swinging, shoes tapping. The band was on a stage, four black men in suits, two trumpets, one double bass and a drummer who was using what looked like a brush on his cymbal. They were playing fast, energy spilling out of them, the music flooding and circling around the room. The couples – some not even couples, women dancing with women, men with men – were throwing themselves into it, so much that you couldn't see them, not as they had been, normal people, walking down Fifth Avenue, going for a drink, working. They were all dance.

'Do you want a drink?' Jonathan was shouting in her ear.

She nodded. 'I'll come with you.'

'How do you get it?' Jonathan asked the barman as they shuffled forward.

'They get it over the border. Who knows how. I once heard that it comes in egg boxes. They inject the eggs and put it in the shells.' The man handed over two glasses. 'Whisky. Our best tonight.'

She drank, quickly. 'Strong stuff,' said Jonathan.

They stood, watching the dancers whirl.

'You know, they said this jazz music would never catch on. But they look like they're never going to stop,' he said.

She nodded. The music was taking her over, too. 'I don't know how to do this dance.' She'd never paid much attention to dance lessons at school, and every dance she'd ever been to since had been simple stuff. The awful people at the ball with Arthur hadn't even been dancing, not compared to this. They'd just been stepping around each other.

Jonathan nodded. 'Nor me. Maybe we should try it.'

And then the band paused. A woman in a purple dress stood up in front and the brushing cymbals and the trumpets started again. Jonathan seized Celia's hand and in a moment they were in, deep in the throng. Jonathan had her arm and the rhythm was throwing them, back and forth, nothing else mattered but the music, beating above their heads, whirling them together as if they were one person. He shouted something in her ear, she couldn't hear, smiled, it didn't matter. They kept dancing.

'Do you like the music?' he shouted across to her, as they walked to the side for a pause. She nodded and smiled, because really she didn't want to talk, she wanted to watch the dancers whirling past, dancing, not stopping, skirts flying, feet off the floor like they were flying too. She didn't want to use words or think or any of it, just wanted to hear the music, feel it in her soul. He raised his glass to her, she took hers, drank it quickly, felt the liquor go to her head, fast, but it didn't matter, because it didn't matter what her head did, she just wanted to dance. She stood up and seized his hand and back they went, deep in the music that made you forget everything. She felt that anything was possible. She could do anything. Jonathan could get Michael back for her. The three of them would live together as a family.

When they stood back at the bar, he was talking to her. 'It's like I said, Celia. You had so much when I first saw you. But ever since, what fun have you had? Working to support your family, now here looking for your son, again spending all your time trying to earn money for your parents and the rest. Is that enough?'

'But I'm alive, aren't I? Michael died. Shep died. They all died. I'm here. Isn't that enough?' Her brother died in France and millions of others had died, and they both had life. Even dancing seemed wrong when there were so many men buried in the soil, who would never feel anything again.

He shook his head. 'There are thousands of girls out there who lost their brothers, more. And they're still grasping at happiness. Look, Celia, don't take this the wrong way. But don't you want to do something for yourself?'

'The business is for myself!'

'I think you need to travel. See some more places. More of America.'

'Maybe.' He was right. The Celia of five years ago would have leapt at the chance. 'I've never been to California.' The magazines she'd looked at, the smart girl in the swimsuit, palm trees over her head.

And the music started again and they were dancing. They were dancing through New York, again in the secret club where the music flew through her body.

On the way back, he started talking about the night of the ball, how he hadn't been sure whether to come to New York.

'I'm glad you did.' She realised how much she liked his voice. It was deep and reassuring, close up.

'If you hadn't run away, I would have had to wait for hours. And maybe you might have been swept off your feet by some railroad magnate – and by the time you'd arrived home, you'd be entirely in love with him.'

Celia smiled, tried to laugh. Jonathan was kind, gentle, funny – and fond of her. But Michael was always at the front of her mind, cutting hard into every thought, her loss of him, her failure to get him back, always thinking of what she might have exposed him to at the Whetstones', how she might have made things worse for him, for surely the woman had been shouting for men to come to chastise him or beat him. Every day, things sparked in her, toys in a window, little boys who were Michael's age. Yet, she told herself, it didn't matter how many times she replayed it. She had to face the truth. Michael was gone. She had to live without him.

She tried to talk, couldn't get the words out. There was too much to say.

He held her hand. 'When I was younger, I used to question things a lot,' he said. 'Before the war. Now I just feel—'

'I know.'

'I don't know where to start.'

He closed his hand around hers. 'Don't try. We don't need to talk.'

Michael buried, somewhere in France. They didn't know where. His grave in Stoneythorpe marked him, but he wasn't there.

'We're alive,' he said. 'Aren't we?'

And they wouldn't be, forever. Not many more years at all, really, maybe thirty or forty or fifty, no more. And by the end, they'd be too old, like Rudolf and Verena, fighting daily private battles with pain and ailments. *I promise you*, she said to Michael in her mind. *We will be together*. And then another voice, even stronger, said to her *You've lost him. You'll never see him again*. She fought it back.

She turned to him. 'Yes.'

And then every blood cell, every bone, pounding, she turned and caught his hand and they began to run together, hurtling up the road like the night when they first met, past slick cars and smart people and delivery men and maids and running made them all cross, all of them. And they were free, running not to get away but because they could, they were alive, and others weren't, they were under their feet, and if they didn't run now, they might never. She clasped his arm and they ran and ran, dodging people, old men clucking in anger, jumping past cars, they were alive and young and they would live forever. Jonathan was whirling her and smiling and her mind was laughing and he talked and she didn't want it to stop.

FOURTEEN

Manhattan, August 1929

In August, people left New York and Celia felt as if she had the city to herself, wandering up and down to Miss Salm in Brooklyn to try the latest recipe, readjust, talk about seasoning, discuss the flavours. The artwork was ready for the advertising – they'd made her eyes rather too big but the artist said they had to, that this was what people expected to see. She sketched out how they'd create displays in the department stores, went to meetings about the figures with the bankers, made plans and spent her free time with Jonathan, talking of travel, plans, walking through New York, admiring shops. The whole, great city, which had seemed so odd, cold, unfriendly, opened itself up to her like the sun and she said, 'Oh!' and 'I see!' because it was the New York that everyone had been talking about, expanisve, beautiful, sharp-edged with expectations.

She missed Lily, Albert and Emmeline, wrote to Emmeline, who filled her in with what news there was – the house was still crumbling, Verena low-spirited, Mr Janus was out all the time for meetings, still talking about Spain. Albert and Lily were happy enough. Winter Meats was struggling on at home under Mr Pemberton, their family lawyer who they'd asked to take over in the interim. Celia tried to read between the lines, see the real truth but she found nothing. Emmeline asked after Michael and Celia wrote that she thought she knew where he might be. There was no reply from Rudolf and Verena to Celia's letter asking them to lay out the circumstances of Michael's adoption. The Whetstones wrote back to the lawyer Mr Galss had found to say that Celia must never contact them again. Celia walked past their house a few times, looked up, saw nothing. At night, she took out the brown cardboard file and looked at the words, as if by gazing at them, she could be closer to Michael himself. She knew it was dangerous to have kept it, that even though it seemed as if Miss Bellenden hadn't reported the break-in, she might change her mind and do so – and if the police investigated, the file was evidence. But she couldn't help it.

On a too hot Wednesday, she and Jonathan were walking down the street, on the way to see Miss Salm in Brooklyn and she saw a woman in front, with her familiar walk and dark hair. Celia hurtled after her, seized her arm. 'Violet!' She flung herself forward. 'Violet!'

The woman turned. It was Violet, older, thinner, sadder.

Celia clasped her hands. 'I've missed you! I've been hoping to see you, I even checked at the shop in case you went back.' Violet was wearing her usual blue dress but it looked thin, ragged. Her cheeks were hollow and her eyes were yellow at the edges. 'Where are you going? Can I come with you?' Jonathan stood aside, watching.

Violet shook her head. 'I have to go.'

'I'll come with you.'

'Please don't.'

'How is your mother? Have you seen Hope?'

Violet shook her head.

'I'm not well.' She began to waver on her feet.

Jonathan stepped forward. 'Let me help. You should sit down.' There was a bench to the side. He tried to steer her towards it. Violet shook her head.

'We could help you,' Celia stammered. And her heart struck with the thought of Michael crying out and she thought: perhaps Violet shouldn't find Hope. Because if the child was suffering, then what good was it to know? Violet would have even less chance of getting Hope than Celia had – for she'd been right, the law was more forgiving to rich women. But then, surely it was worth it, just to see her daughter. Just to know she was alive.

'I've told you. I don't want your help.' Violet turned around and

Celia noticed that one leg was dragging slightly. 'I have to go.' She probably had never looked at the file and never would.

Celia persisted. 'Please take some money!' But Violet shook her off, carried on.

'She won't take anything from me,' she said to Jonathan, watching after her. 'It means nothing to me, this money, but she won't take it.'

'She doesn't want charity.'

'It's not charity. We were friends!'

Jonathan shrugged. 'Not any more.'

'I suppose not.' She had been naive: her brightest, most golden dreams of she and Violet finding their children together, taking them to the park, rescuing them, being free, were ridiculous of course, but surely there had been *something* in them.

'Maybe you could go and talk to her,' she said, impetuously. 'Take her some money.'

'I don't think she'd welcome me either.'

'But she might let you in the first time. And then you could just give her the money and go.'

'You can't solve everything with money, Celia.'

'But you can solve a lot! They're so poor.'

'I will try.' He looked at her quizzically. 'Although there's a lot you're not telling me, isn't there?'

She looked away.

'I can't tell you,' she said.

'You don't have to.'

'Too many of other people's secrets.'

'I can wait. Or never.'

They sat for a while, then got up and walked on.

Three days later, Jonathan went to see Violet. He came back, saying he'd given her the money, that she wouldn't talk much but asked him questions and so did her mother, who didn't look so unwell as all that, he thought. He said he'd try again in a few months. 'Give her time to think.' Celia held his hand, grateful that he didn't ask why Violet meant so much, just did it for her, without asking.

The business carried on. Celia and Miss Salm carefully assembled the sets of sixty jars and cans for Bergdorf's and the other two big department stores, working until eleven every night, decorating jam jar lids, tying bows around the fronts. They hired a cab and delivered them, with Jonathan's help to carry them in, and then assembled them in the Food Hall, decorating the top of the pyramid with little sprays of paper flowers that Miss Salm's sister had made. Celia stood back and looked at the display in Bergdorf's and wished that Rudolf and Verena had been there too. It looked so beautiful.

'I think this looks marvellous,' said Mr Goodman, coming behind her. She jumped, surprised. 'Very attractive.'

And once they were in Bergdorf's and a few others – well, everything began. She put on smart gowns that she bought newly from Bergdorf's and Macy's and she and her sales girls went to the offices of other stores to talk about Flapper Foods. She smiled a lot to men in suits, with Arthur and sometimes Jonathan behind her (she did better with Jonathan, she thought, perhaps because he was American, too). They tested out different ways of keeping the food fresh in the jar – and even talked of buying a canning factory to send things all over America.

They all came, one after the other, dominoes, all the shops. 'Yes, Miss Witt, please do, we would take one thousand dollars, thank you, and do you have anything else?' Jonathan or Arthur would mention that other shops were interested and so the buying men would ask for more – 'I'll take it all!' one said. They all asked to be the exclusive retailer but Jonathan thought it was best not to agree to it – because if the store changed its mind and didn't like the foods any more, then where would you go? They were dizzied by all the interest, like a girl with a dozen lovers. 'Enjoy it,' Jonathan said. 'You must enjoy it while it lasts.' She tried but every day was a panic of hurrying between meetings, saying the right things and smiling. The shops bought from her, resulting in pages and pages of figures and numbers, the promise of boxes and boxes of stews and soups, cakes tied with bows, biscuits and even the bread rolls in a jar, bought it all up, promised her sums of money she could hardly comprehend. She rushed, rushed, dashed between places. She went to help at the school on Sundays but, otherwise, her mind was all hurry. It meant she didn't think about Michael.

By late September, they were all exhausted. Celia's eyes were permanently watering from lack of sleep, Arthur couldn't shake off a cold and Jonathan's back ached, nearly always. The products were flying off the shelves (most popular – chocolate pudding, sausage rolls, cheese scones, chicken à l'orange) and they had hired another kitchen, ten more cooks and three more deliverymen. Sometimes Bergdorf's or Macy's would telephone Miss Salm and demand another twenty jars – within the hour.

'We need to take a holiday,' Jonathan said. 'We've all been working too hard. You've been working too hard. We decided on California, we should go.'

She was loathe to, there seemed so much to do. But he was right, she knew. And they'd talked of the holiday, the palm trees and the oranges and the beaches.

'I'll stay here,' Arthur said, when they told him about it. 'I'm too tired even to travel. I'll stay and sneeze in the hotel room until I can't sneeze any more.' He'd been quiet of late, Celia thought, sometimes going off to meetings that he didn't tell them about. They'd knock on his door and he wasn't there. Jonathan had been walking up to his club and he'd seen Arthur go into a bank. Celia supposed he was finally investing that money he'd talked about – and he was right of course! That was where the money was now, hotels in Florida or Hawaii, sets of flats. There were advertisements for it everywhere. She had given him over half of the money he asked for, but he said that was fine, he could borrow the rest against Winter Meats.

'Unless you see something you want to buy in California,' he said, because that was where they were going, Los Angeles, the home of the movie stars and beauty and sunshine. She was going to see America.

*

She and Jonathan went by rail all the way to Los Angeles, sleeping on the train for two nights, and he took her to a hotel on the Boulevard which had a balcony. She and Jonathan stood there and looked down on the city – and it seemed like all the lights and beauty of it were just spread out for her.

Jonathan knew people and so they went to a great movie set, a giant sign under palm trees and inside the floor was covered with cables and dozens of people were watching a beautiful girl in a red swimsuit dive into a tank against a painted backdrop of the French Riviera. She dived, came out, three women in black dried her hair, and then she dived again. Then the director shouted, 'That's the one,' and the women in black hurried forward with robes for her. 'Come along now, Miss Grilt, let's get you warm.' And they ushered her away like a queen. Celia watched her go – and all of the glitter fell out of the picture, as it was only men in overalls cleaning up the water and moving the backdrop as the director and some other men pored over a script.

That night, Jonathan poured her more wine from a bottle disguised as apple juice and no one seemed to notice. She drank it because the words and the wine went together and her heart had broken out from her body and it was flying over the hotel, high above the autumn night city.

'I love you,' she said.

'Do you really?' Jonathan replied. 'Do you really love me?' His face was as if it had opened, she thought.

'Yes,' she said. 'Yes I do.' But then, she thought of what she'd done, not telephoning, getting Red to steal for her, breaking into Michael's room and probably exposing him to more ill treatment from the Whetstones. 'I'm not good enough for you. I'm not.' She was too damaged, like Verena's broken vase.

'Don't say those words again. You're Celia. You're – you're – I can't find the words.' He smiled. And then he took her hand and she moved towards him and they were holding on to each other, as if everything around them was shipwrecked and they were the only ones not drowning.

*

On the next day, they walked down to the beach and he was holding her hand. 'Celia,' he said, talking through the bright mist in her head. 'Celia, there's something I wanted to ask you.'

And she turned to him and said, 'Yes. I'll say yes to whatever it is.'

'You don't know what it is.' He held her hands. 'Will you marry me?'

'Yes,' and they were in each other's arms and she knew she wanted to say yes to everything from now on, because now was the beginning and Jonathan had the future in his hands.

FIFTEEN

Manhattan, October 1929

Two weeks later, they were on a train back to New York. 'We need to speak to Arthur,' Jonathan had said.

She would have married Jonathan there and then in the hotel, but Jonathan was talking about the ceremony and speaking to his father. He said he had a family ring that he'd like her to try. She nodded – but she supposed it must be a great diamond. She'd rather have something small, a simple stone. She shrank at the thought of it, such scrutiny.

'Couldn't we just run away and do it?' she asked. 'We could find somewhere to marry us quickly.' Arthur would want a big occasion too, it would help him with the Vanderbilt girl.

Jonathan shook his head. 'How would that look, Celia? Really.'

She dreamt of it, just the two of them, free and high above the city as they had been, not talking about ceremonies and money and who they should invite.

Penn Station was packed with people, even busier than it normally was. They were crowding around the newspaper kiosk next to the platform. Jonathan held her hand and pulled her through – and the other kiosks were even busier. 'We must have missed something while we were away,' said Jonathan. 'Perhaps someone's resigned.'

Out in the street, the buses were crowded and people were hurrying around again. There was no getting a taxi, so they started to walk, pushing through throngs of people.

'What's happened?' Celia said. 'There must have been something.'

They passed a group banging on the door of an office. And

then a woman weeping on a corner. A group of men in suits were arguing and one looked as if he was going to break into a fight. They looked around for a newspaper boy, but each one was shouting, 'Nothing left.'

Jonathan touched a passing man's arm. 'What's going on?'

'Wall Street,' he gasped. 'Sell everything. Sell!'

'What is he talking about?' Celia said.

'Stock. But it's riding high. Mine was worth thousands before I left.'

She nodded. 'They said it would stay high forever. Permanent plateau, that's what Arthur said.'

He looked around. 'Still no taxis. Come on, let's walk. To the Stock Exchange.'

They started walking along, heading south to Wall Street. He was gripping Celia's arm. She watched people flooding past them, women weeping, some men arguing. Others were sitting on the roadside, head in hands. She believed it now. Something terrible had happened.

They couldn't get close to the Stock Exchange. It was crowded with people shouting. They were begging people – anyone – to sell for them.

'They should close the market,' Jonathan said, staring at the crowd. 'This is terrifying.'

'They couldn't,' said the man next to him. 'They couldn't get them out. We wouldn't let them.'

'Have you seen a newspaper?'

'Sold out hours ago. Have to wait until this evening. If we're lucky.'

'How did this start?'

He shook his head. 'It just began, they say. Out of nowhere.'

'We've been in California,' Jonathan said. 'They have no idea there.'

'They don't have any idea anywhere. The President was on the radio,' a man burst in next to him. 'He said business was strong. What does he know?'

'We have to get in,' said Jonathan. 'I need to sell.'

'You and everybody else. Big business comes first.'

'What about Arthur?' Celia said, suddenly struck. 'He bought more at the last minute, do you remember? That property fund for the hotels in Hawaii and houses in California.'

'I was just thinking that. He borrowed a lot. He took money from your accounts at Flapper Foods, yes?'

'I know.' We encouraged him, she didn't say. Because it wasn't Jonathan's fault, not really, everybody had agreed on how it was the thing to do. Everybody was buying. 'Now we're all selling.' That night at the table, clinking their glasses. *It can't fail!* Arthur had said. *If I put in all our money, it still couldn't fail!*

She looked at the people surging forward. 'It's carnage here.'

'This is dreadful,' Jonathan was saying. He pulled her away, wouldn't let go of her hand until they had moved on a couple of blocks. They ran, not thinking, to the hotel.

Arthur was sitting there, in the lounge. People were hurtling around him. He sat, staring straight ahead.

Celia shook him. 'Arthur! Arthur, we're here.'

He looked to the side, down. He didn't see her. 'Everything,' he said. 'We've lost everything.'

SIXTEEN

London, November 1929

Emmeline felt as if she'd said the same words too many times. *Don't. It's not safe.*

'Please don't go to Spain,' she said. 'There are hundreds of men out there. Why does it have to be you?'

'I've told you. It's bigger than just me. We were put on earth to change things.'

Samuel was always so patient when answering her, so reasonable. It made her want to scream, throw herself on the floor, anything to get a reaction. 'Why don't you care about us?'

'I do care. But this is important.' He patted her shoulder. 'You'll be fine. You always are.'

'The children need you. I need you.' He told her not to talk about Euan, that it had been two years now and she should forget. She tried. But it made her treasure her time with her children, try and seize every scrap of their time. It seemed so wrong that he'd want to leave them all behind.

He grinned. 'I'll be back before you know.'

'To go somewhere else again.'

'Maybe. Look, Emmeline, the Crash has liberated us. It's going to mean the end of the system as we know it. We can free ourselves from the banks. They've all gone. We can make a new world without them. Free of money. But this country is cowardly. We always choose the Establishment. I have to go to Spain. Forces are rising there. The military will be put out of power soon by the people. That country will show the rest what to do.'

She put her head in her hands. She couldn't stop him.

'You go and stay with your parents while I am away,' he said. 'We'll give up the flat.'

'Don't go,' she said. 'Please.'

'I have to go. It's our chance, Emmie. Maybe our last chance.'

It reminded her of the early spring three years ago, 1926, so filled with possibilities. The flat had been busier than ever with visitors, meetings going on after Emmeline and the twins had been bundled off into bed. Lily and Albert slept while she lay there, listening to the voices rise and fall. When Samuel came to bed, finally, at two or three in the morning, she tried to speak to him, ask him what was going on but he told her he was too tired. She read the newspapers instead, poring over them, read the pamphlets handed out on the streets by men who looked like Samuel. They were going to strike to support the miners. It was time to throw off the tentacles of businessmen and politicians, who were rich because they kept so many in poverty. They would show the country how much they depended on the workers, bring it to its knees.

She felt as if she'd been spinning and the world wouldn't right itself. Everything was out of her grasp. She bought a magazine, cut out the pictures of sitting rooms, plush sofas, cushions, comfortable chairs.

The people came in and out, made plans. Emmeline opened the door to them, made tea and sandwiches. They were all hope and optimism. They had been promised so much for fighting in the war. Now they were going to take it, whether those in power liked it or not.

Things got so fervent that Samuel barely slept. He lived the cause, all the time. At the end of April, the baby Princess Elizabeth was born. Samuel said what was coming would be the end of the Royal Family, too – they would have to live like the rest of the people. Samuel banned mention of the new baby – but Emmeline brought home a newspaper for Lily. 'If she's going to be ordinary like the rest of us, there's no problem is there?'

He shrugged. 'You have a point.'

Emmeline and Lily read the article together: the little Princess, visits from King George and Queen Mary.

'She'll only be royal for a week or two. Maybe a month,' said Emmeline. 'What Papa is planning will change everything. She'll be so ordinary, she might even move next door to us!'

Lily was delighted with the idea, imagined pushing the new Princess around in her pram.

'You'd have to call her Elizabeth,' said Emmeline. 'That would be the new way.'

The planning intensified. She had never seen her husband so animated, so caught up, so genuinely excited. He said they were standing on the brink of it, just about to jump.

And then – what happened? A strange sort of doubt started to creep in. Reports that men were losing their nerve. The government bringing out middle-class men and women to staff the railways. The army were going to come out too. And then the worst blow. The head of the unions said that not all workers could go out. They said *only some*, because they feared revolution.

The day came. Samuel went out and didn't return. Emmeline kept the children inside in case the law broke down, but ran out to buy a newspaper. The transport stopped. But nothing much else. Over the next few days, buses started to run with volunteers. The army protected lorries so that they could get to Hyde Park with food. Samuel still didn't come back.

Then nearly a week after the strike began, she woke up, walked into the sitting room and found him on the sofa.

'We've failed,' he said. 'The unions have given in. They can't even get the government to promise strikers will get their jobs back.' Tears ran down his face as he talked. 'This is the end. We could have done it, made a change. Now we've lost everything.'

She tried to comfort him, sat down beside him, held his hand. He wouldn't listen. 'It's all gone,' he said. 'They've won. We can't fight again.'

No one came for discussions that night. He lay on the sofa, staring at the ceiling, refusing to eat. Deep down she was grateful. Grateful that it hadn't worked, that the government had won. Now she had her husband back.

*

How naive she'd been. To think she'd thought that was the end of it all. He'd been in what she supposed was shock for weeks, not really speaking, barely eating. Then he'd started working as a tutor once more. She hugged herself at the possibility – just a possibility – that he was going to behave *normally*. He was going about his days like some sort of machine – but she hoped, no *knew*, he would go back to his old self, the man she'd fallen in love with.

When he started taking an interest in Spain she had become so saddened by her broken husband that she welcomed it, his talk about politics and the change of system in Spain.

Then came the Crash and he was suddenly truly alive once more, the old Samuel, bursting with hope and possibility for the future. He talked of a new society, free of money. Exchange rather than markets. She worried about Arthur and Celia in New York, her parents' house – but didn't tell him because he would say it was better for them – for the whole world – to lose all their money and then begin again.

Men came over to their house once more, talking endlessly into the night. She lay in bed listening to them come and go. Albert was still preoccupied by his trains but Lily was growing more interested in the conversations. She'd become fond of one of the younger men, who seemed happy enough to chat to her. He explained to her the point of their discussions, talked about Karl Marx and communism. Emmeline had to smile to see Lily looking so serious, pretending she understood.

At night, she'd crawl into bed with Emmeline and whisper her questions.

'What do Papa and his friends want to do?'

Emmeline held her close. 'They want to get rid of money. They want it so that there's no money in the world.'

Lily thought. 'But where would they put it? Where would they put all the money? In a big hole?'

'I don't know. That's a good question. Maybe they'd melt it all down and do something useful with it.'

'But what would we do without money?' Against Mr Janus's

orders, Emmeline had been teaching Lily a little about money. The teacher at the school where she and Albert went in the mornings had told her that Lily was a little behind in mathematics, so Emmeline had been using coins for simple sums.

'But how would you buy anything?'

'Well, Papa says that we don't always need to buy so many things. They tell us we do, but we don't really. So we'd start by buying less. And then, well maybe we'd exchange or give each other presents. Papa thinks that money is wrong. It ruins our mind.'

Was she disloyal, always saying, *Papa thinks*? Shouldn't she say, *I think*? He was probably right about money. It did trap people – and what good had it done for their family?

SEVENTEEN

Manhattan, November 1929

'It hasn't changed anything, you know,' Jonathan was saying. 'We'll still get married. It just won't be quite such a big ceremony.' She'd tried on the ring – a very large diamond from his family collection and it was too big. 'I'd prefer something smaller,' she'd said, but Jonathan had looked so hurt that she'd relented, said they should get the gold resized to fit her finger and she loved it really.

Jonathan's family hadn't lost as much as they'd thought. They'd kept so much in land that it really only meant twenty per cent or so. His father's manager, Mr Galss, had said he saw something odd coming and changed a lot of the stock to gold in September – just in case, he said.

'We were fortunate,' Jonathan said, sheepishly. 'I wasn't paying attention. I was – er – distracted. Lucky Mr Galss saw prices dropping and wondered if the tide was changing. I do remember he tried to tell me. But I didn't believe him.'

'Clever man.'

Because Jonathan had been distracted by her, of course, and how dreadful it would be if he'd lost all his money because he was trying to spend time with her. She already blamed herself enough for Arthur. She knew that thousands, hundreds of thousands across the country had made the same mistake, but perhaps if she'd made the effort to research – or even to think *of course this can't last.*

'He did try to stop Arthur, while we were away. But Arthur wouldn't listen.'

'I wouldn't have done either,' Celia said, meaning to be loyal. 'The money seemed like it would never end.'

'I blame the newspapers,' said Mr Galss, when he came up for lunch. 'Telling the ordinary man to buy stocks. What did they think was going to happen? Investment should be for professionals.' He sighed and rubbed at his thick glasses. He talked about Jonathan's money and how much he had. He asked Celia about hers.

'I have the banks'. Not much of my own. But the banks are happy to lend to us, still. They think we're a good bet. And Arthur must have something. He had so much money after Louisa died. He can't have invested it all.'

It had been a week now since that awful Monday. Surprisingly, Flapper Foods was holding steady, sales were still quite good. One of the managers in Bergdorf's had told Betty that people had stopped buying clothes, toys, furniture, everything – but the one thing they were still buying was food. And women, especially, since they weren't having the enjoyment of buying clothes, wanted to treat themselves to pretty food. The orders were staying the same – and Miss Salm was considering hiring another cook.

'They'll start to ask to pay less soon,' said Mr Galss. 'I would say. Take the orders while you can.'

Mr Galss said that she was lucky to keep the favour of the banks but she needed to drop the wages if they were to survive. 'Everyone else is doing it,' he said. 'It's imperative. You need to show the banks you are making savings. And the workers would prefer to have a job paying less than no job at all because you can't pay the bills, Miss Witt.'

'But we can. We can make different savings.' She wouldn't do it.

'What? Ingredients are more expensive. Inflation.'

'We'll find another way. Rent somewhere cheaper if we have to.'

Mr Galss raised his eyebrows. 'Indeed.'

She promised Miss Salm and all the workers that they wouldn't drop the wages. The girls lined up and were meant to shake her hand but then the one at the front hugged her and they all did.

'All the other businesses are laying off,' said Miss Salm, on the way down. 'Thank the Lord you're not like them.'

'No,' she said, fighting off Mr Galss's words. 'No, we're not.' But she knew Miss Salm wanted more of a promise, couldn't get the words out. In the cab back, the tears pricked at the back of her eyes.

They couldn't persuade Arthur out of his room. Stocks were still falling. The newspapers screamed the headlines, politicians counselled calm, no one went to restaurants and half of the hotel was empty. Every bank they passed was crowded with people trying to take out their money. Jonathan had taken his. But Arthur said there was nothing left – he'd put it all into stocks. He'd said that on the first day – and now he wouldn't speak.

Luckily Mr Galss had told Arthur to get out two thousand dollars, just last week, in cash. So he had money to live on – pay the hotel, buy what they needed. Celia hadn't telegraphed or written home about it. She didn't know what to say. It would only worry them more – and Emmeline's letters about Mr Janus had been growing more and more fretful. And – she said to herself – perhaps the money news would change for the better. Everyone said markets were always swaying around. Maybe they would go back up. Hopefully, the American business would soar back and her parents would never have to know.

Celia worried about Violet, alone with her mother. If food got even a little more expensive, as the newspapers said it would, how would they survive? She sent some money to Violet, pretending it was anonymous, but she must have guessed because it came back to the hotel.

Reverend Crisp was distracted, afraid, worried there would be no more donations. She feared for the orphanage. A wild feeling possessed her.

'I wonder, Father, about the children's future. Ethan. I hope to make a life for myself here ...' Ethan's twinkling smile, the way he clutched her hand when she had to go.

Reverend Crisp looked sad. 'Oh, now Miss Witt. You know the rules. I didn't think you were one of those ladies. These children must go to proper godly families in the Catholic faith. You know that.'

'I could give him a home. I'm getting married,' she persevered, knowing she shouldn't.

'He has a home. He lives here, in the faith and if we let him go, it will be to a home in the faith. Father and mother. Really, Miss Witt. Perhaps we will have to stop the classes altogether.'

'Please! No!' she begged him. He relented a little. 'But you have clearly got too fond of the boy. It isn't good for him – or you.' The next week, she was sent to make cards with the girls. She walked back to the hotel and the covers of the newspapers burned into her mind. Central Park was full of little houses and tents now, people who'd lost their homes in New York and had set up home in the park. The churches went out there with bowls of soup. One of the concierges had said they'd seen a man taking and roasting a Central Park sheep.

'We need to make progress with the wedding,' Jonathan said that night, at dinner in the empty hotel restaurant. 'How about December? Then we can go over and have a celebration in London and be there for Christmas.'

It seemed wrong to talk about weddings when the whole world was falling apart. If she had a wedding, would Violet come? She wished she could ask her to be bridesmaid, but Violet would never accept. She would have Jonathan's sisters and cousins instead. She nodded, listened to his ideas.

The shops opened doors for them, begged them in, shops that she felt sure would have been too busy for her a month ago. Ladies in black suits showed her fabrics, tried tacked-up dresses against her, talked about flowers and veils. Jonathan took her on a tour of New York hotels to look at their dining rooms. 'I thought you said *small*,' she hissed to Jonathan, after one manager had shown them a room the size of a church. He gestured at her, helplessly. It was hard not to let the managers show them their best rooms, their eyes shining with desperation, a wild need for someone, anyone, to sample their wonderful food, flower arrangements, impeccable service.

'I can't bear to see it,' she said after one terrible afternoon when the manager had practically begged them to throw the wedding there.

Jonathan shook his head. 'We shouldn't stop ourselves. We need to put money into the economy. Even the President said it.' They decided on the small dining room in the Tower Ballroom – and Celia felt pained with guilt at all the other places that wanted them. She knew she should be dreaming of herself in a slender white gown, embroidered veil, holding flowers, but couldn't do it.

Two days later, she went up to Brooklyn and found Miss Salm in tears. There had been a spillage of water and all the flour and sugar was ruined. The girls were arguing over whose fault it was. She and Miss Salm cleared it up, then passed over the money for more, tried to settle the arguments. The girls were angry, resentful.

'They are afraid that they will lose their job even though you said they wouldn't,' Miss Salm said. Celia looked into her dark eyes and knew that she felt the same.

She found a taxi and fell into it. She was so exhausted by the day. She just wanted to lie down in her bedroom and not talk. If Jonathan was there, trying to discuss the wedding, she'd tell him she had an awful headache and say she had to lie down.

She walked into the lobby – and her heart stopped. Mrs Whetstone and a heavyset man with pale eyes who was probably her husband were sitting there on one of the sofas. With Michael. The air around her curved and disappeared. She clutched her hands. They were looking ahead, not at her. She moved towards them.

'Hello.' Mrs Whetstone looked oddly smaller, nothing like she had done in their house.

She stared at them. She couldn't speak. Mr Whetstone stood up. 'I don't believe we have met. Miss Witt?'

She nodded. Michael was looking older already, his hair grown now, flopping over his collar, trousers patched at the knees. He looked so handsome, his dark eyes against his brown skin, the eyelashes even longer. She wanted to run over to him, seize him in her arms. She stood there, gazing at them all.

'Would you like to go somewhere quieter?' She gestured towards the restaurant. 'We could go and sit in there.'

He shook his head. 'No point wasting time. Listen, Miss Witt. We're having problems. We have loans. The bank are calling them in.'

'You need some money?' She thought of the Whetstones' beautiful apartment block, thick red walls, high windows.

'We need more than that. We need a miracle.'

Michael was looking at his feet.

'So what I wanted to say was – how much?'

'How much what?' Celia was confused.

'How much to give him to you?'

The hotel lobby, the desk, wavered and fell. The air pieced around her into tiny specks. 'Give me?'

'You want him. We don't need an extra mouth. But we're not giving him away for free.'

She stared at Michael. He sat quietly, hands in his lap. He could clearly *hear*.

She stepped forward. 'I don't know what to say. I'd give anything, do anything to have him back.' She looked at Michael, staring at his feet and her soul lurched. 'If that's what he wants, of course.' A picture of him in his room, terrified, the woman shouting through the door, calling men – to do what, beat him? – flashed into her mind. 'Are you sure? He's your son, too, on paper.'

Her heart wrenched as she said it.

Mr Whetstone shook his head. His face was stony. 'You can have him. There's nothing to talk about. It's yes or no.' She gazed at him – and then he broke away. 'Sebastian,' he said, gesturing at him. 'Go and walk around.'

The boy stood up, head bowed. Celia watched him go. She swallowed. 'I was wrong to come to your home, Mr Whetstone.' Despite her actions that night she'd broken in, surely it was not right to take Michael from them so abruptly. They'd lost everything.

Mr Whetstone rolled his eyes. 'You don't understand, Miss Witt. We don't want him. We can't afford him. You can have him. If you don't take him, my wife says she's giving him to a home.'

'But—' Celia looked at Michael's back, painfully vulnerable. He was bending to look at something on the floor. 'You said...'

'We took on an orphan. But he's never worked. He's always been bad. You can have him. Everybody's doing it.'

'What?'

'Sending back their orphans. Charity begins at home.' He shook his head. 'You know, Miss, a lot of things fell into place when my wife told me about you. When we took him on as a baby that agency told us he was from good stock, that he'd be the boy for us. But he was never good at applying himself, always off dreaming, never right. And then you turn up – this wafty, dreamy person – and you were entirely him. He wasn't from proper stock at all, he was from you, and whatever man you found. He doesn't fit in with us. Either you take him or we send him to a home.'

Celia stared at his angry, resentful face, clenched hands.

'Yes or no.'

Her heart opened up and flew to the sky. She held tight to it, as if it were a balloon. 'Yes. Yes, of course. If he'll come.' *My son. Michael.*

'Ten thousand.'

'What?'

'We've lost everything. That's the deal, him for ten thousand dollars.'

'I'll find it.'

'How soon can you get it?'

'You want *cash*?'

He nodded.

'This isn't right!'

'It's up to you. Money or child.'

'I don't even have ten thousand dollars.'

'You'll find it. You're staying in this hotel aren't you?'

'But I don't have cash. Everything we make goes back into the business.'

'Not my problem. Pay or don't get him.'

'I'll need to talk to people. But I'll go and speak to Michael – Sebastian – first.'

She walked towards her son, carefully, putting her feet forward as if she was playing that old game – *don't step on the cracks. Don't fall down a crack. Get to the other side.* She knew they were staring at her, on the concierge desk, she ignored them, kept moving forward. *Don't step on the cracks.*

She stood next to him. He was still looking at something on the floor. She put her hand out for his back – then drew it away again. Then she reached out and touched him.

'Sebastian.'

He turned around. She wanted to gather him into her arms, pull him towards her and dash upstairs with him. She held back, looked at his eyes. Why were words so *useless*? 'How are you?' she said, feeling how hopeless they were as she said them.

'You're the maid,' he said. 'I saw you.'

'I'm not the maid. I'm sorry I came into your room. I just had to see you.'

His face crossed with confusion, questions. 'My parents don't want me any more.'

Her heart broke. 'I know. I'm sorry. But *I* do. I've always wanted you. I want you more than anything. I promise.'

He stared at the floor. 'Did they ever love me?'

'Yes. I'm sure they did.'

'They were always angry with me. And Mama told the servants to beat me. It's because I wasn't their son, that's what Papa told me on the way.'

'I'm sorry.'

'I never knew. I thought I was their son. But I'm not.'

She held his hands tighter. 'I'm sorry they've been cruel to you. It's all over now.'

He was still reluctant. 'Who were those other people with you? The boys who came into my room.'

'They were helping me. I wanted you, you see. So much.' And it all flashed into her mind, the night, the shouts, the fear.

'Why?' he said. 'Why did you want me?'

She took a breath. 'Because I'm your mother.' She said it and it was just the two of them, no one around them. The people in the hotel, the Whetstones, none of them were there. She said the words and his face flamed with confusion.

'You're my mother?'

'Your father told you that you weren't their child. That's because you're mine. I'm your mother. You were taken from me when you were just born. And given to the Whetstones. They didn't know you were stolen, of course. But I wanted to get you back.'

He said nothing. The whirl of the hotel crashed around. She made herself wait.

He stared. 'Sometimes I dreamt of another mother. A kind one.' A single tear ran down his face and she reached for his hand. 'Why did you take so long to find me?'

'They told me you were dead. When I heard you were alive, I looked everywhere for you.' She reached out and gathered him in her arms. After a minute, he was hugging her back and her heart was on fire.

Tears were pouring down her face and dropping onto his. She couldn't believe it. She felt him clutch to her and she never wanted to let him go. She never would. 'I love you,' she said. 'I've always loved you.' His body so close to hers, touching his hair, his face. 'We'll always be together,' she said. 'I'm here for you now.'

Mr Whetstone's voice. He had walked up to them while she was holding Michael. 'I'll take him with me now. You can have him when we have the money.'

Celia's heart gripped.

'No. You know where I live. You'll leave him here and I'll get the money for you. I won't let you take him away!' She stared Mr Whetstone down.

'Like I said, no money, no child.' Michael was weeping beside her.

'If you take him away, like he is some sort of used toy... Well, no deal!' She knew she was in the stronger position. She knew she might even argue down the money. But she couldn't bear to bargain. Not over Michael. She drew herself up. 'You'll leave him here with me!'

She could see him think, uncertain. 'Agreed, then. I'll come back tomorrow,' he said. 'To get what we discussed.'

Celia nodded. 'Where are his things? Where are Michael's things?'

'Sebastian doesn't have much. What he has can be thrown away. We've spent enough on him. You can buy him what he needs.'

Celia gazed at him. 'Why do you hate him so much? What did he ever do to you?'

Whetstone paused. Then he put his face closer. 'It was all his fault. Everything that went wrong with our family went wrong after him. He was like an evil spirit. My wife – she changed. The children changed. I said we just need to get rid of him and then we'll be back to normal.'

'He's a child. He's so gentle. He wouldn't hurt anyone!'

'Dumb insolence. That's what he did. Dumb insolence. I told my wife to give him back but we couldn't as everybody thought he was ours.'

'You were cruel to him.'

Mr Whetstone tossed his head. 'You'll have to watch him! If you pay, that is. Otherwise I take him back.' He turned and walked away.

Celia stood there, in the hotel lobby, with her son in her arms. He was hers, her blood. She felt a strange fear as if she'd been given a china child, and even the slightest wrong movement might break him. She stroked his hair, his forehead.

She couldn't believe it. The thing she had longed for, desired for so long, was here, given to her. She had thought it would never happen. And now it had and it was almost too much to understand. There was so much to tell him, she didn't know where to start.

She had no idea how to get the money. If she went and asked the bank for it all, they might refuse her. She had to pay, though, make herself free of them. But she didn't know how.

'They didn't want me,' he said. 'They never loved me. They loved their other children. Not me.'

She held him tighter. 'I'm sorry,' she said. 'It was your home. We'll make a new home together.'

She didn't know how to make Michael's hurt go away.

'I got hit for so many things,' he said. 'Talking too loud, waking up, crying, looking the wrong way.'

'That's over now. I won't hit you. Never. Most parents don't, or at least only when the child has been very naughty.'

'Oh.' She could see him thinking it over. 'I wish I'd gone with you then,' he said. 'In the days after, I was watching for you. I wish I'd gone. I thought I'd missed my chance.'

'I'm here now. It's all better now.' She added his name. Sebastian. She'd tell him about his true name later.

'I'm hungry,' he said. 'There was nothing to eat today. For me, I mean. They had things. I came last.'

'Do you like ice cream?'

He nodded. The ice cream shop window she'd stared through before, envying all the happy children, the counter piled high with bowls of the stuff, pale colours, pink, green, yellow. 'I know just the place!' And she caught his hand and he didn't pull away and they hurried together to the shop where she said, 'You can have anything, anything you like!' And he stood there, gazing at all the pictures of the different types of ice cream, the glittering bowls, triangle wafers and cherries on top, chocolate sauce.

He turned to her. 'How did you come into my room?'

'I broke into your house. Like a burglar. It was very wrong of me but I wanted to see you.' People were pushing past them. She drew him close to her.

'I kept watching, I wished you'd come back.' He was buried in her chest now, nearly crying. 'Why didn't you come back?'

Her heart broke. 'I couldn't. I didn't want to get you into trouble.'

'I waited for you. I looked out of the window and I waited.'

'I'm here now.'

'And you're my mother?' He was testing out the words. 'You'll never send me back?'

'Never. Never. We'll always be together now. I promise.' Her heart broke at the thought of him watching for her from the window.

'They gave me to you for money.'

'I know. I'm sorry. It's because they knew how much I loved you. They knew I'd do anything for you.'

'Tell me about when I was a baby.'

She didn't have much, told him about the early days. 'And I called you Michael,' she said, nervous of how it would be received.

'Well, I shall be Michael, then. I've always hated Sebastian.'

She hugged him hard. 'Do you think you can forget – how they were? Do you think you can try? We have a new life now.'

He nodded. 'I'll try.' Then he whispered, 'I don't know which ice cream to choose.'

Celia hugged him and whispered back. 'Just choose any one. And then we'll come back tomorrow and have another one.'

'Another one?'

'Yes, tomorrow. We'll come back tomorrow and have a different one. Or you could always have the same one if you like.'

He nodded solemnly, eyes great and round. 'Anything I like?'

'Anything.'

He held out his hand and pointed to a picture of a big sundae in a curved glass. 'That one.'

The man behind the counter made the ice cream carefully, handed out two spoons. 'Would you like to share with your mother, young man?'

Mother. That's what she was. She watched him eat it, ate a little of the cream and the chocolate sauce. She told him about her home, Stoneythorpe. He talked a little about the Whetstones and her heart pierced for him. How cruel they had been. She could see the loss in his face, the pools of his eyes, as he looked around nervously, his hands twitching, wanted to reach out, cover it all with love. But she had to let him talk through the Whetstones, listen to every time they were cruel to him or hit him.

He reached the bottom of the ice cream and was scraping for the last scraps of vanilla.

'I'll never leave you, you know,' she said. 'You were taken from me. I'll never let it happen again.'

He looked up quickly and back down again.

'I mean it,' she said. 'Whatever happens.' *I'm your mother now*, she wanted to say, worried it might be too much for him. Then with a flush of guilt she remembered Jonathan, how would he feel now Michael was real. Surely Jonathan would help her sort out the money. She'd marry him, be grateful. They'd be a family.

After the ice cream, she took Michael to buy some clothes in Bergdorf's, the one she had haunted, once upon a time, staring at the toys, thinking of her son. The shop was quiet, the assistant pleased to see them. He fitted Michael up for a suit, talking about his own son all the time. 'There,' he said. 'Doesn't he look handsome!'

Celia smiled. 'Yes, he does.'

'Would you like to wear them now?' the man asked.

Celia looked at Michael. He shook his head.

'One last thing.' And they went to the toy department and she said he could pick out anything he wanted – and he chose a small brown bear with a red ribbon around his neck.

'I shall call him Harvey,' he said. 'I will carry him.'

'Come on,' she said. 'Let's go home.' Now he was with her, she'd have to find somewhere proper for them to live. She supposed she'd have to rent an apartment.

She burned for Violet, yearning for Hope. She was lucky, so lucky, and because of money. Violet could never have found ten thousand dollars.

She held tight to Michael's arm, walking back. He clutched the bear. Her *son*. She wanted to pepper him with questions, about what he liked and didn't like, try to get back all the years that had gone. But he was gazing around him, staring at the buildings.

'I couldn't believe New York when I first came,' she said. 'I felt like an ant. You wouldn't think you could get things so high, don't you think?'

'They look like they hit the clouds. I didn't go out of the apartment much.'

'Well now you shall. Maybe we can even go and see the clouds one day.'

He nodded, craning upwards to see.

'I'm here with my brother you know, Arthur, you'll meet him. He'll love you. He doesn't have children.' And then she was talking, telling him all about her childhood, about Stoneythorpe and Emmeline and Arthur. She hesitated – then she told him about Michael and how he had died in the war. 'He was brave,' she said. 'He died bravely. And then I called you after him.'

'I like Michael. I am going to keep it.'

She wouldn't tell him the whole truth about her brother, not yet. But what she had said was true. He had died bravely. It was just that they hadn't understood him at the end. She talked a little about the war for her, trying to make it sound like an adventure, driving fast with men in the back, hurrying to hospital, playing cards at the end of it all with the other girls. Not the horrors of the men screaming, Shep dying on the road, hit by a bomb.

She stopped herself, talked about Stoneythorpe, Verena and Rudolf again. Emmeline and Lily and Albert living there too, when Mr Janus left for Spain. He'd have a friend to play with.

'Grandma. Grandpa.' He tried out the words.

'Lily and Albert are so much fun. And only three years older than you. They'll be so excited to meet you.' She thought that he might even get on a little better with Lily than Albert – she was a little delicate, dreamy. She conjured them together, playing in the Stoneythorpe garden, being imaginary explorers. 'You'll have so much fun,' she said. She talked about her life, her childhood, her world. She told him about everything except Tom. She told him a little about Jonathan, the engagement. She could see his mind was reeling, so much information, so much change.

Back in the hotel room, Celia took out the model farm from the wardrobe, laid it out on the carpet, wondering where Red and his animals were. Then she listened to her son making the remaining animals talk to each other. Harvey was sitting solemnly at his side and could barely believe she had him with her, that they had found each other and now they could begin their lives.

EIGHTEEN

Manhattan, November 1929

That evening, after Celia had tucked Michael into her bed with his bear, Harvey – realising that she'd forgotten to buy him pyjamas or a toothbrush or even a storybook – she sat with him, smoothed his hair until he slept. She wanted to sit in the chair and watch him – but she had to find Arthur. She took off her shoes, stepped noiselessly out of the room, into the corridor. She hurried to the stairs – and Jonathan was standing there.

'Oh!'

She had forgotten. She had been supposed to meet him.

'I came to your room,' he said. 'I was about to knock on the door. But I think you were talking to someone.'

She laughed. 'You're jealous?'

'Well, I am if you're talking to someone in your room! And it wasn't Arthur, you don't speak to him that kindly! Who was it?'

She moved towards him, held his hands. 'It was Michael.'

'Who's Michael?'

'You know.' She was weeping, tears at her eyes, she knew it. 'Michael.'

'Your son?'

She nodded. 'Michael's here.'

He gazed at her. 'How? What happened?'

'Come in,' she said. 'We'll just have to be quiet.' She opened the door, closed it behind him. Jonathan looked across at the sleeping child, the eiderdowns piled up on his bed.

'His father brought him here. They've – lost their money – they need more. They said I could have him for ten thousand dollars.'

'Have him?'

'If I got them ten thousand dollars. I have to find it. I have money in my accounts but it's due to the bank. I'm supposed to give it back if I don't make Flapper Foods work. It's not mine, not really. But I have to. Do you think they could tell the police?'

'I imagine they'd have other, bigger loans to chase at the moment.' Jonathan took her hand. 'When do you need it by?'

'Mr Whetstone's coming tomorrow to get it.'

'Otherwise he takes the child back?'

'He does.'

He shook his head. 'What sort of people do that? I'll give it to you. Don't worry. You have to have it.'

She blinked. 'What?'

'I can get it for you. Tomorrow.'

'Thank you! Thank you. I will pay you back, I promise. You must come and meet him. You'll love him.'

'But we need to make sure they'll never come back to get more from you.'

'They wouldn't.'

'You don't know that. They might. I'll ask Mr Galss to draw up a contract. That's it. We don't want to see them again.'

'Legally, they're his parents.'

'Celia. Don't be so honourable. They tried to sell him. There are parents all over the country who can barely afford to feed their children, but they're not *selling* them. These two aren't even poor, not really. They're greedy. I'll ask Mr Galss to deal with it. You don't need to see them again.'

'They're expecting me.'

'Mr Galss won't take any nonsense. They can't come back for more.'

'I'll pay you back.' She would. She'd make sure of it.

'Later. You might need that money for yourself.'

'What do you mean?'

He looked away. 'You two wanted to make money in two ways, yes? Your business. And investing money. Arthur's money.'

She didn't have to nod. He knew the answer. The billboard girls in the swimsuits were turning away, crushing the oranges under foot, their bright white smiles dimming as they moved into the darkness.

'Arthur was wrong when he said he had nothing. It's less than nothing. I saw Mr Galss today. Arthur doesn't understand.'

'Doesn't understand what?'

'Mr Galss had a letter from the bank. Or, the last of the banks. Arthur had borrowed from four to put into the property funds. Did you know?'

'No.'

'He borrowed against Louisa's money, which he'd invested. He also borrowed against Flapper Foods.'

No. She'd promised her workers that their jobs were safe. She'd promised herself that Flapper Foods would rescue Stoneythorpe. She'd told herself so much. She'd been sure. At her school, Winterbourne, their year had been dominated by a beautiful girl, Eloisa, half Russian, darkly glamorous, cool in her passions. Celia walked past and Eloisa laughed behind her hands at her. The girls on the California billboards were all Eloisa, mocking them with their beautiful, perfect faces. They had reached out their hands to them, offered friendship, love, happiness – and now they were taking it all away.

She clutched his arm. 'We've lost everything?'

'I don't know. I think so. I'm sorry. But – Celia, you have me!'

'Does Arthur know?'

'Mr Galss said he was going to try to talk to him. But he probably does, I imagine, Celia. That's why he won't see anyone.'

'I'll see him. I'll tell him it's not his fault! I understand.'

'What do you mean?'

'You were praising those funds too! He wasn't the only one.'

Jonathan's face clouded. 'Don't blame me! He wanted to. He could have put just a little in. And certainly not borrowed against your business. He had no right.'

'I'll tell him. I can make the money back. Flapper Foods will survive! I will make it so! I'll tell him about Michael, too. He'll be so pleased.'

'Celia, I don't think so. I think—' But she was opening the door, running down the corridor and up the stairs, hurrying towards Arthur's room. She banged at the door. 'Arthur! It's me!' There was no answer.

'He's probably not even there,' Jonathan said, catching her up. 'Look Celia, he'll be fine.'

She leant against the door. 'I should be with Michael. He might wake up.'

'That's true. Let me take you back.'

He took her arm and they walked to her room. Inside, Michael was still sleeping, turned over onto his back. She stroked his hair.

'He looks like you,' Jonathan whispered.

She smiled. 'Why don't you stay a while? He's asleep. We can talk.'

'If you don't mind.' He sat down.

'What will I tell the workers?' she said.

'Don't tell them he borrowed money. Just say that you are pushing through the difficult times. As long as you pay their wages, they won't care.'

But did she? Did she have the money to pay the wages? Her heart dropped.

Jonathan put his arm around her as she talked. 'Things will right themselves,' he said. 'We're just having a dip. Business will start again. Your business. That's what Mr Galss was trying to tell Arthur.'

'Trying to tell?'

'Arthur was a little upset. He wasn't really listening. I'm sure he'll be calmer tomorrow.'

She'd thought the money and the good fortune would go on forever. She'd borrowed and spent, told everyone how well it was going, she'd danced with Jonathan and laughed as they whirled to the music – and she'd thought they could dance, keep dancing and the music would never stop. She hadn't seen a thing, not really.

*

She woke, still on the sofa, having slept in her clothes. Michael was stirring. She'd sent Jonathan away when she woke earlier at four o'clock or so. 'We'll come and find you,' she'd said, as she pushed him sleepily out of the door.

'How did you sleep?' she asked Michael.

'Pretty well.'

He sat up in bed. He looked so small, surrounded by the heaps of covers. It struck her that she should find him a school. Then, once he had structure – children liked structure, she'd read – they would be more comfortable with each other. She looked at his big eyes, wondered if he felt fear that he didn't know what they were going to be doing.

'Let's get some pyjamas today,' she said. 'And then I thought we might go to the park again. And the ice cream store. I've got a friend I'd like you to meet.'

She sat down on his bed. 'How about you and I have a few days enjoying ourselves? Then maybe I can find a place to live – my brother might come too. You could even go to school. Would you like that?'

He shook his head. 'No.'

'Why not? You don't like school?'

He looked down at his hands.

'I learnt at home. They said I should never go to school because they'd be mean to me there, I was such a dunce.'

How she hated them.

'Well, they were wrong. You're not a dunce. But you can learn at home if you like. I think you might like school, though. And if you don't like the school, we'll take you out and we'll find you another.'

But then what? Were they all going to rent a townhouse together, she, Jonathan and Michael? Jonathan had always said that after they were married, they'd take a house on Washington Square or similar and divide their time between it and the country. He said that his father would like that best. But now – what?

They dressed, shyly, turning their backs on each other. Michael wore his old clothes – she didn't ask him why. Of course he clung to what he remembered.

Being with Michael was like cleaning a window in smog – each time she managed to clear a little gap and see through it to his heart, it would fog up again and she'd have to find the right bit once more, keep rubbing and rubbing. Of course, she knew, she'd never expected him to suddenly fall into her arms and talk. He was in shock, everything had turned – and no one had ever encouraged him to talk anyway. The Whetstones had taken him in, then had their own children, preferred them. The only reason they hadn't given him up was due to how they might look to society, she supposed. When he spoke of what they had said to him, done to him, it made her heart stop. She held him tight, walked next to him, followed his eyes when he looked up at a bird in the tree or down at a bug in the park. She would go at his pace, wait for when he wanted to talk. He told her about his two elder sisters, who were kind to him but even when they were back from school, their parents kept them away from him. He asked if they might see the girls but Celia knew the Whetstones would never agree. She said they could try, or if not, write a letter. He missed the servants too, he said – Edward, who would slip him biscuits and Merden who was kind when no one was looking. Merden had told him he was always the child indoors, watching from the window while the others went out: skating, to cafés, to the zoo. 'I'll write to ask,' said Celia about a meeting. And then he began to cry.

'Why did they just want to get rid of me? I tried to be good.' She took him in her arms. 'I don't mean it against you. But why did they?' She could only hold him, tell him they were wrong.

In the afternoon they met with Jonathan. He shook Michael's hand solemnly and she was ashamed of the wash of relief she felt – someone else to talk to Michael, another man. They wandered down to look at the ducks.

'Mr Galss has spoken to them,' he said. 'He's got the agreement from them.'

Michael was kneeling down, with the remains of some bread Jonathan had brought, throwing it into the pond. Harvey was clutched under his arm. He took the bear everywhere with him now, even into the bathroom.

'Why would you ever give him up? How could they have been so cruel?' *He should stand up for himself.* Edward's words in her mind.

'Some people are.'

'Should I give them an address when we leave? I'd rather not.'

'They won't care. They want – *need* money. And ten thousand – well, I had to ask my father hard. I can't give it again if they come back in the future. And they might, Celia. They might try to break Mr Galss' agreement.'

'It all feels so wrong.'

'Celia, they don't need to know how he is. They gave him up. They didn't want him. They're glad to get rid of him. We've given them enough.'

He was right. She watched the ducks swim up to her son. 'I wish I could think of what to say. To get through to him. He's been hurt so much.'

'You will. It will happen when he wants. You're his mother, don't forget that.'

She breathed, readied herself. 'We come as a package now,' she said. 'The two of us. He comes with me.'

The air shone between them. He could go. He might say, *yes, well, maybe we should rethink.*

'Of course. I know that. I always knew that might happen.'

'So, we'll all live together?'

'Of course. How could you think anything different?'

He pulled her towards him and she leant on his chest. She could feel the tears pricking at her eyes. *How could you?* she wanted to ask. *How can you love me so?*

After wandering around the park, then to the ice cream shop, they walked to the hotel. 'Come on, sport,' said Jonathan. 'Let's go to a restaurant. Eat potato fries.'

In the days that followed, she felt pure gratitude towards Jonathan. He found fun places to go – museums, parks, a car showroom,

Grand Central Station to watch the trains go in and out. They bought books at the bookstore that he'd read as a child. 'This one is the best,' he said to Michael, who held it in his hand all day. He seemed to know just what was right. A man in the shop suggested the zoo, but Jonathan thought Michael wouldn't like to see the animals in cages. They played sticks in the park and made patterns out of stones under trees.

Sometimes Celia felt a pang of jealousy, envy at how Jonathan knew exactly what to do. But she knew it was only because he had once been a small boy too. She watched them kicking a ball, Jonathan laughing as Michael shot it past him, and it led to her thinking about the children she might have with Jonathan – a little boy and a little girl, running down the stairs in the old house in Washington Square, dashing into the garden, out into the sun.

NINETEEN

Manhattan, November 1929

A week passed and Celia still hadn't seen Arthur. She'd knocked, left notes. He left her a reply at the reception saying he was busy. She hadn't telegraphed home. She meant to tell them that she'd found Michael – but then she changed her mind. Everything was too precious, unbelievable. Her mother and father might say something to spoil it. So she'd hug the secret to herself – and take him home to meet them. Emmeline had written in misery that Mr Janus had gone to Spain, and that seemed to be enough for them all to bear. She decided not to worry them about the Crash and tell them that Arthur had invested in those funds. The market would improve and everything would get better. It would all be forgotten. She went to the Sunday school, where Father Crisp said that many more children were being left at the door and they had no time to direct volunteers. Her soul cut for Ethan.

'Tell him I said goodbye,' she said.

'I shall tell all the children.'

She passed him an envelope, money she'd asked Jonathan for. He nodded, pulled the door shut.

In her heart, her wildest heart, she'd thought about taking Ethan so that he and Michael could be brothers. But Father Crisp had been right. She'd known the rules. She walked home past stores with flimsy Christmas decorations in the windows. Who on earth would buy Christmas presents at the moment? Her vision of the modern woman, stocking up on jams and jellies for Christmas, not possible now. But they still needed to eat, to survive, and some of them had the money for it, scurrying to the food counters and ignoring all the other more expensive goods that filled aisles empty of customers.

But if the shops were deserted, the streets were full of people, men wearing placards looking for work, their wives following behind with children. The newspapers talked on about failing banks, mechanisms, money. She went to a meeting of a charitable organisation she saw advertised in the newspaper and they discussed setting up stalls in the street where people could get soup for free. The woman in charge seemed exhausted by all of it. 'There are too many!' she said, at the end, when Celia tried to ask her a question. 'Too many!'

Mr Galss said that they should sell off the stock of Flapper Foods and pay back Arthur's loan. She refused. The banks didn't want their money back right away. They had been so clear, so secure. 'It would be such a waste to stop now,' she said. 'Everything would be ruined. We're still getting in big orders, making sales. We're expanding!'

Mr Galss shook his head. 'I would get out now,' he said. 'Get rid of that kitchen while you still can and sell the rest. Then they can't come for you for Arthur's loans against the business.'

'You won't need to worry about running the business,' said Jonathan. 'Not when you're my wife.'

That made her even more determined. She shook her head. 'I have to see it work!'

She wanted to speak to her brother. 'I want to tell Arthur. I wanted to tell him about Michael in person but I'll have to write – he still won't see me.' And then her mind cleared. 'We'll ask Mr Galss. He has meetings with Arthur. We'll ask when one is and go at the beginning and tell him.'

'I suppose so. He can't be having a very easy time of it.'

She saw the doubt in his face but ignored it. 'When he finds out about Michael, he'll be so pleased. It will lift his spirits.'

They left a note for Mr Galss, asking him to come and see Celia in her room that evening at six thirty. On the dot of the half hour, he knocked.

'I wanted to talk to you about my son,' she said to Mr Galss, ushering him in. 'I wanted to tell Arthur the news that I've found him.'

Mr Galss took off his glasses and held out his hand. 'Hello, young man.'

'Say hello, Michael.' The child smiled, extended his hand for Mr Galss to shake.

He nodded politely.

'So we're terribly keen to see Arthur and talk to him. He'd be thrilled to meet his nephew. I just wanted to tell him in person.'

Mr Galss sat down. 'With all the losses, he's very upset.'

'Michael will cheer him up.' And he would. Just the sight of Michael, the child that everybody – even he – had thought was dead. It would encourage him, a success gained. Michael putting his hand in his, hugging him as an uncle.

He sighed. 'Perhaps, Miss Witt. I can't tell.' But she was sure. Arthur never gave up. He bore things, even though he sometimes pretended not to care. It was only money. They'd get it back. They were selling more jars every day, the salesgirls were taking more around New York and they would get there – bit by bit! And then the economy would improve – and the modern woman would want to buy Flapper Foods across the country.

'So I wondered if I could come to the beginning of one of your meetings. I'd just speak to him quickly. Where do you meet?'

'We meet in his room, Miss Witt.'

'In his room? But I've knocked on the door so many times!'

'I doubt he's answering. As I said, he's rather distressed at present.' Mr Galss sighed. 'I'm afraid he's said he will only speak to me.'

'So if you knocked on the door now and said it was you, then he'd open the door?'

Mr Galss sighed, nodded.

She firmed her voice. 'Well, let's do that.'

He shook his head. 'Arthur trusts me to follow what we agreed.'

'But I'm his *sister*. And this is his nephew.' She was going to sort this out, make Arthur look to the future again.

'I could go too,' said Michael.

Celia ruffled his hair. 'I'll tell him first. Then I'm sure, the first thing he'll want to do is to rush to you and meet you.'

Mr Galss gazed at Michael, sitting on the floor, laying out his farmyard animals with the assistance of Harvey. 'Very well. It can't do any harm, I suppose.'

'You'll be all right on your own, won't you?' Celia asked Michael. 'You can play.'

He nodded happily. 'Then I'll meet my uncle.' They closed the door on him in Celia's room, leaving him already deep in his imaginary world.

At her brother's door, Mr Galss knocked. 'It's me, Arthur.'

There was no response.

'Are you there?' He turned to Celia and Jonathan. 'Perhaps he's gone out.' He looked relieved.

Then Arthur's voice, thin, breaking up. 'Is that you, Reginald?'

'Yes. And I – have someone with me.'

'Who?'

She put her mouth close to the door. 'It's me, Arthur! I came to see you. I've got something to tell you.'

'I'm busy.'

They'd run around Stoneythorpe together, him always ahead. His room at the top of the house was filled with his treasures. She was never allowed in. But they'd been children then. 'I'm not going until you see me! Why are you avoiding me?'

'Go back to your own room, Celia.' He was only inches away. If she were a witch, she could have reached her hand through to touch his, join fingers.

'No! I want to see you. I have to see you! You have to let me in.'

'We can come back,' Jonathan touched her hand.

She heard steps, to and fro behind the door. 'Arthur?'

'Why are you always trying to see me? Why can't you leave me alone? I don't want to see you.' His voice muffled by the heavy wood of the door.

'Look, Arthur, I know about everything, about the money. It doesn't matter. We don't need money. We'll manage.'

'You think that's right?'

'Of course. Listen, if you just let me in. Then we can talk. Please.'

There was silence. Celia waited. 'Let's go,' said Jonathan. 'We'll come back when he wants to see us.'

'That might be a good idea,' said Mr Galss. 'I'll try and talk to him.'

Celia stood closer to the door, pressed herself against it. Then she heard hands on the doorknob. She turned to Jonathan to smile – but the door was open and Arthur was standing there, staring at them all. His hair was awry, his eyes dark and wild.

'You wanted to see me?' he said. 'Come in, then!'

She edged towards him. 'Not you!' he hissed at Jonathan, and then he turned to Mr Galss. 'Not either of you. If she wants to see – then she should!'

He slammed the door behind her, his face pale, his eyes confused, maybe even crazed. The room was freezing, dark around him, smelt strong and musty as if he hadn't let the cleaners in for weeks. She could see that the bed was unmade, piles of clothes on the floor. He seized her hand and pulled her forwards – so close to him, she smelt him too, dirty, unwashed, a sickness about him. Arthur, who was always so fastidious.

'Arthur, I'm sorry. I know we've lost—'

'You don't know anything. You don't know anything at all.'

'I know that I love you. I know that you're my brother.'

'Words! Women's words. Don't you think I've heard enough?'

She breathed deeply. 'Look, Arthur, everyone's in the same boat. Everyone's lost money. We just have to pick ourselves up and try again. Things go up and down. We'll be up again once more, just you see.'

'*Just you see,*' he mocked, waving his hand effeminately. '*Things go up and down.*' She saw herself through his eyes – stupid. He had buried his face in the curtain now, had his back to her.

'I've been out there, working. I know we can do it.'

He shook his head. 'Just go away.'

'Arthur. There was something I wanted to tell you.'

'Nothing you say could interest me.'

'I've found Michael! I found my son.'

Arthur turned his face to her. 'Oh, did you?'

She nodded, ignored the bitterness in his voice and smiled. 'It's wonderful!'

'And how are we supposed to support another mouth to feed? Celia, you have to get down from your dream world. We have nothing! Absolutely nothing. I can't even pay for this room any more, my money ran out yesterday. We should be on the streets.'

'I have the business. That is still here!'

'That's too late! Who will buy that stuff now? No one has a job. It's dead, Celia. Why can't you see?'

'I don't agree. We've put in so much. The banks trust us. We still have each other. We can go back home and be with Papa and Mama.'

'*We have each other*!' There he was, cruelly imitating her again. 'Celia, you're so naive, it makes me sick.' He buried his face back into the curtain. 'There's no getting through to you.'

She stood quietly, took a step towards him. 'Why don't you try?' she said, gently. 'Tell me. Talk to me about it. We can find a solution.'

He roared and this time his face was on fire. 'Don't come near me!' he shouted. She fell back, afraid. 'You can't solve anything! You're the problem! You and your idiotic words, your stupid ideas. You've been nothing but a burden since we got here. You've ruined everything. And then you come here and expect me to congratulate you because you've found your bastard? Get away from me.'

She stared. She'd listened to him – but then 'bastard' turned the knife. 'How can you say that?'

'It's the truth, Celia.'

'Money's made you cruel.'

'You live without money then.'

'I will. We don't need to stay in a hotel like this. We don't *need* these things.'

Arthur lifted his head. She thought he was coming to her. He was going to turn around, talk to her properly. He paused. She waited. Then he started to roar again. He threw his head back and roared, like a child.

'Stop it!' The noise filled her mind, deafening. 'Stop it!' He carried on. Surely he'd stop, surely he'd cough, and his voice would fade. 'Stop it!' He wasn't looking at her, wasn't even hearing. He was staring at the ceiling, still shouting. Someone was knocking at the door, then Jonathan's voice came. 'Celia? What's going on in there?'

'Please, Arthur.'

He threw back his head again – and this time he was laughing. He was laughing, cruel, painful peals of laughter. 'Please!' he shouted. 'Oh please!'

He turned, backed against the curtain. 'I did it all for money! Everything. And now I've lost it.'

'You'll get it back. Stop this now.'

'Come here.'

Her heart was touched with fear. She told her legs to go forward, around the bed. They wouldn't move.

'I said, come here now.'

She clutched herself. He was her brother. She had to go to him. She edged along the bed, around the end. She was a few feet away from him. He jumped forward, seized her, and then he was swinging her around, through the curtain, and then they were standing on the tiny balcony over the street below.

'Arthur! You're holding me too tight!' He clutched her harder. Fear was sparking around her heart.

He pushed her forwards, her hips thrust hard into the iron of the balcony. She wanted to cry out in pain – did not. This wasn't Arthur any more, not her brother, not the man she loved. This was someone else, a man possessed and angry.

'Look down there,' he said. 'Look at all those people.' She'd gazed out of her window enough times, down at the people walking around. And now it made her afraid. The people below were tiny figures walking up and down. The dizziness seized her mind and she closed her eyes. 'Arthur—'

His mouth was close to her ear now, not whispering, for that would be too kind, but speaking quietly, cruelly. 'Don't you ever want to look down, little sister? Don't you wonder what it might be like?'

The world was spooling apart in front of her. Everything was breaking. His hands clutched her waist, his body pressed into hers – and there were thoughts bleeding in her mind that she didn't want to hear. *Stop it! Please.* She tried to move to the side, just a little, but he was holding her too hard. It was as if she was shored in iron: she couldn't move. 'Arthur—' *Please let me go. I'm your sister.* Louisa at the edge. *No!*

'Times like this really tell you the truth,' he said. 'You see the truth of everything, when you're on the brink. You understand what's important.'

'Please let me go.' But she whispered it, the wind swallowed her words. She was too afraid to shout.

'And you say that money isn't important. But what if you'd given everything in your life up for money? What if you'd done – the darkest act for money? And now you had lost it all?'

'What darkest act?' The words were out before she could stop them, because she didn't want to know, she really didn't, she wanted never to know.

He hugged her waist tightly. 'I was here with Louisa. On the cliff. I said, *Would you not like to see further?* She didn't want to. I said, go further. And she did – because she loved me.'

'Stop it. I don't want to hear any more.'

'Ah, but I want to tell it. Because then you'll understand why I don't want to talk and why all your words are useless. Because I killed her for her money – and now I've lost it all.'

'You didn't. I don't believe it.' Louisa's body crumpled at the bottom of the cliff. The trial, Arthur standing there, Mr Bird talking in court about how the couple couldn't see a thing, how they had been wrong to say that Arthur had pushed her. The dinner at the Ritz after Arthur went free, holding up their glasses. *To freedom!* Louisa's dresses, packed up and taken to Stoneythorpe, pink, green, gold, her evening bags piled on top. Her ring. 'Arthur—'

He pushed into her again so she was almost bending over the balcony.

'Please let me go. We can talk.'

'Oh, don't lie, Celia. You don't love me any more. How could anyone? I killed my wife for money – and then I threw all the money away. What was the point?'

Words ran through her head. *Arthur. Don't kill me.* She didn't want to say them, make it real by saying them. She was going to have to find some way of getting free. She couldn't fight him off, he had her pinned so tight. He pushed her again and they swayed together. She gazed at the people dizzily. They were looming at her. *Look up,* she begged. If they looked up and saw her, surely they'd send someone to rescue her. *Help me.*

'Please, Arthur. You have to let me go. Whatever you've done, it's in the past. You need to let go of me. We can help you.'

'Let go of you?'

'Yes. Please let me back into the room.'

'But I love this game. I want to get to the edge. I want to touch it. Why won't any of you come with me?'

'I don't like it.'

'You're just like Louisa.'

And then the idea came into her mind. 'But you're not at the edge. I am.'

He laughed, hard ringing laughter. 'I am at the edge. I'm always at the edge.'

'Show me.'

And then they were scuffling and he was at the front and she was behind him. She was flung back into the room, breathless. He stood against the balcony iron, back to the air.

'Show you? Here I am. Now what shall I do?'

'Come back.'

'Do you love me, sister?'

'Of course I love you. Please come back.'

'What do you think it would feel like to fall? You're dropping through the air, grabbing at it. But at the same time, you're flying. Free. Entirely free.'

'I don't—'

But he wasn't talking to her any more. He eased himself up

so he was sitting on the rail of the balcony. 'You'd be flying. And then, the moment before you hit the ground, how would that be? You'd see the truth then, wouldn't you? I bet Louisa saw it.'

Her whole body revolted at the idea of going back onto the balcony, taking his hand, trying to bring him back into the room. But she had to. She had to help him. She stepped forward, cautiously. He laughed again. He jumped back down from the railing and her heart swelled with relief.

'Come with me,' she said.

'Never.' He swung one leg, then another over the rail, so he was standing on the stone edge of the balcony, on the tips of his toes, holding the iron. 'You have nothing I want.'

She flung herself forward. 'Arthur!' She grabbed for his hand – but he pulled away, laughed again. 'See you!' Then he smiled, closed his eyes. He leant back. She screamed as his arms and legs wavered, desperately, his hands clawing. 'Arthur!' She grasped the rail. And then the noise of all the traffic horns and people and market boys shouting stopped as she heard a blow of body on stone – and she knew she had lost him.

TWENTY

Manhattan, December 1929

'I have to go back,' she said to Jonathan. 'I need to take Arthur home.'

The past week had been a miserable flurry of police, interviews, arrangements. The police wanted Arthur buried in New York – as did Mr Galss – but Celia was adamant. 'I'm taking him to Stoneythorpe. That's where he belongs.' They'd bury him in the graveyard of the church, next to Michael, where plots waited for all of them. She'd written to her parents to tell them and say she would bring him with her. It had been almost unbearable to write the letter.

'You won't come back.'

'I promise I will.' Jonathan and Mr Galss had taken care of so much. The hotel wanted them to leave after such a scandal, but Jonathan had persuaded the manager to let them stay for just a little while, at increased cost. He had taken Michael out to feed the ducks and eat ice cream when Celia was so captured by sickness and guilt that she could only lie in the dark and feel hatred for the world. He had tried to talk to her, make her feel better. At night, the darkness overwhelmed her and she couldn't be alone. He sat by her, held her.

'Don't leave me,' she said then. 'Don't leave me alone.'

She couldn't stop talking, telling him things. 'I tried to save my own skin,' she said. 'I thought he was going to make me jump. I made him change around. I was just trying to save myself. And he died.'

'You did the right thing.' They were whispering, as Michael was asleep – the only time they could really talk. She didn't tell him about what he'd said about Louisa. She couldn't.

'I pushed him to do it.'

'No, you didn't. It was going to happen eventually, don't you see? He was in a bad way. Mr Galss knew it, but thought he was improving. Galss said that a lot of men are in a bad way. Arthur just couldn't cope with the losses. He—'

Jonathan stopped himself. Celia guessed what he wanted to say. *Lots of businessmen have become suicides.* There were names reported every day, a list on the inner page of the newspaper. Celia had read that the newspapers had agreed to put the names on the inner page in case people were brought too low by seeing them on the front. She had agreed with the decision. But now she wanted Arthur blazing out of the front page, with a picture of him, a memory of his life. He'd just been a name in a list – an interesting note that an Englishman had thrown himself out of the Plaza Hotel.

'I don't think it was just the losses.'

'Of course, he'd had hard times. You all have. He lost his wife.' Celia nodded. Alone, late at night, she told herself that he was unbalanced when he said he'd killed Louisa. He was saying wild, mad things, thrown out in anger, not true. But something edging towards her heart told her that they were, that they'd all been wrong. Arthur had told the truth – and Louisa had died at his hand. That was the secret eating him, making him so terrifying, so dark in the final moments. Then the ivy furled up to her and tightened its grip on her soul and she had to stop herself from thinking, stop thinking at all.

'I can't stand it,' she said, and Jonathan stroked her forehead.

'I know,' he said.

But it wasn't just what she'd seen, it was the weight of all the knowledge, everything she had to keep from her family – Tom shooting Michael, Arthur killing Louisa.

'I wish someone could save me,' she said. 'From having to feel.'

'I'll save you.' She knew he'd say that. It wasn't what she meant.

'But you have Michael now. You have to be strong for him. He needs you.'

'I know.'

'Just pretend you're strong for him. That will be enough. And in time it will come.'

'I don't think I can. Not all the time.'

'Of course you can. I'll help you.'

That night she was restless, and woke when the men came for the dustbins. The bottles and leftover food from all the dinners, the paper she wrote on and threw into the bin. She couldn't imagine where it all went to. Things that people had once wanted. The soldiers had left their things in the trenches, bullets, bits of clothing, books, even guns. She'd read that in some places – not the ones full of tourists clutching their guidebooks – the grass had just grown over all the metal and the guns and you'd never know, now, that they were there.

They were falling on her, like snow.

There was no point fighting. The police and the authorities won, said that all they could allow Celia to do was have Arthur cremated, then take the ashes back home. A few days later, they had a funeral at a chapel near the park with Mr Galss, Miss Salm and the girls, Jonathan and a kind man who Mr Galss had invited, knew Arthur from the banks. He mopped his forehead, held his hand out for Celia's. Michael stayed behind with Mr Galss's sister, a teacher's wife from New Jersey who came down for the day to take him to Central Park. The minister looked exhausted, mispronounced Arthur's name, hurried through the words. That afternoon, the undertaker came to the hotel and handed Celia a dirty-looking jar. She sent a telegram to her parents. They hadn't answered her letter, too broken she supposed.

She put the urn on her desk in the bedroom, then waited for Jonathan to bring Michael back from the trip with Mr Galss's sister. Michael was tired and happy, fell asleep almost as soon as they had tucked him up in bed.

She whispered to Jonathan, all the same. 'I have to go. Arthur needs to be home. I need to see my mother.'

'I'll come with you.'

She shook her head. He would make it easier – she imagined him helping her on the boat, talking to people about the arrangements, looking after Michael. But then. 'I should do it alone.'

'I insist. I have to help you. You're my fiancée.'

'Look, it's not for very long. I just need to take him back. I need to do it alone. I owe my family. I owe him.'

'That's just making things difficult for yourself.'

'Maybe I want them to be that way. If you came, you'd make everything easy. I have to try.'

'What's wrong with easy?'

She shook her head. 'Look, Jonathan. I won't be long. I promise I'll come back. Michael and I will be back before you know it.' She tried to look away from the urn on her desk. It kept dragging her eyes back. It felt as if Arthur was listening, or as if she was betraying him by talking in front of him, ignoring him.

'What if you change your mind?'

'About what?' Michael turned over, sighed. She looked back at the urn, tried to ignore it.

'You might change your mind about coming back. Marrying me. You don't even have the ring yet!' The ring had come back from the jewellers, but not much smaller, so they'd sent it back again.

'Of course I want to marry you. I promised.'

'You might change your mind. Associate America with everything bad. But it's been good too. Remember?'

'I promise,' she said. 'I promise I won't. I'll come back and we'll get married. Properly, as we hoped.'

The banks were calling in the loans. She'd had letter after letter. He had borrowed so much against Flapper Foods, forged her signature on documents. She could never pay it back. She thought of Miss Salm and the girls, relying on her, the great opening they'd had in Bergdorf's, their smiling faces. All the orders they had in. They couldn't stop!

'I'm sorry,' said Mr Galss. 'You either sell or they will call on Stoneythorpe. He put that up as well, you see.'

'No. I can't sell the house. My parents!' Rudolf and Verena, Emmeline, with nothing.

'Then it must be the business.'

'If she just goes to the banks, they'll give her nothing,' said Jonathan. 'I'll help you find someone to buy the business, continue it, someone who will give you a fair price.'

'And the women might keep their jobs?'

'Maybe. I can't say. But at least there will be a business. And maybe you can come back to it, one day.'

In the following days, Jonathan hunted for a buyer and arranged meetings. She put her best suit on, pretended to smile as she talked about Flapper Foods to three bankers, a New York steel magnate who wanted a 'little business' for his daughter, and a widow with money to spend. She showed them around the Brooklyn kitchen, introduced them to the staff. The magnate offered the most money, but the widow was close – and she promised Celia she'd keep on Miss Salm and the salesgirls and see what she could do for the rest. The money she gave her was enough for the banks' demands but not much more. She cried when she said goodbye to Miss Salm and the women. She went into Bergdorf's, took one last look at their display and wept again, but hurried away when she saw a man from the store coming to move her along.

'Let's just hope Arthur didn't borrow anything else,' said Mr Galss. 'There's no guarantee this is the end of it.'

'They'll have to write me off as bankrupt.'

'Let's hope so. If they don't, they might look at assets abroad.'

'But I thought selling the business would be enough. I did that to save Stoneythorpe!'

'I'm sure you have. If he hasn't borrowed more. But I confess I am fearful that he might have. A friend of mine was telling me that he thought he had had all the debt requests in for a client – but then more arrived yesterday. If I were you, Miss, I'd encourage your parents to put the house on the market, quick. Then take the money and split it between you or put it in the children's names. They can't get at it that way.'

'And then you can all come and live in America,' said Jonathan, happily. 'Even Emmeline. She and I will try to get along.'

But Celia couldn't hear his joke. She sat back. They were in the dining room at the Plaza, still busy, despite the Crash, low conversations between businessmen. The place still had the chandelier, the fine damask tablecloths, the heavy cutlery. And they were sitting there and telling her that still there might be more ruin. The Florida beaches were covering them in sand. She felt like a shipwrecked person, clinging to a raft, owning nothing.

'Think about it, Miss Witt,' said Mr Galss. 'Persuade your parents to sell.'

Celia, Jonathan and Michael were walking through the park. She knew it was one of their last times. He gave her a bunch of gardenias as they strolled. Men passed them, looking for work.

'A photo?' said a man in a brown hat – and Jonathan said yes. So the little man arranged the three of them, Michael holding her hand, she clutching the gardenias. He pressed down the shutter and preserved them on the steps of the church, outside of time, forever.

PART TWO

TWENTY-ONE

Stoneythorpe, February 1930

'Here is your home,' she said to Michael, as they stepped out of the car. 'We'll meet your grandparents.' *The ones who sent you away.*

Perhaps if Arthur hadn't died, she would have stayed in America. But she had to see them.

On the last day, she had walked around New York telling herself she would come back. And yet still, a part of her body was behaving as if she never would, imprinting the city on her memory, the park, tall buildings, the museum, the lines of men looking for work. She and Arthur had tried to survive and they had not succeeded.

On the boat over, she balanced the urn on the floor of their cabin, propped up by pillows so it wouldn't fall. Jonathan thought she should have put it in her trunk but she would never do that. Trunks could get lost. The first night, she had barely been able to sleep for worrying about it. Michael slept in her arms, Harvey clutched to his chest and the wooden horse under his pillow, stowed together on the lower bunk of the bed. He didn't want to sleep alone. It had pleased her, that he had treasured one horse and Red had another.

In the last few nights, she'd waited for Red, left some sweets stuffed in a crack in the bricks, written to Violet, settled the business with Mr Galss, talked with Jonathan about the wedding and tried not to cry when she was alone.

On the second night, the passage turned rocky and Michael was sick, repeatedly. They sat on the floor outside the bathroom, pressed themselves against the wall of the cabin. She cradled him in her arms, holding him tight, trying to get him to drink water. Sometimes he slept. Then woke. Sometimes she wasn't sure whether he was awake or asleep and she talked to him, stories about home and the days before the war.

Also, she told him lies. 'It was another relative who was staying with us. Aunt Deerhurst.' Blushing for her untruth, the poor woman had already been dead for so long by then. 'She took you away and nobody knew. It was terrible.'

She thought he was asleep. And then he opened his eyes.

'Who is my father?' he asked.

Her blood beat fast in her mind. 'He was a soldier in the war. He died, just after. I wished you could have met him. He was a good man. Kind. He would have loved you so much.' This seemed to satisfy him. She had guessed – and it seemed to be right – that he would mind more about what his father thought about him than what he really was. But still. Soon he'd ask more questions. She held him tight on the cold floor as the ship swayed. She asked him about the Whetstones but he said he didn't want to speak of them. She heard him cry out in the night, begging someone not to do it.

'What will they think of me?' asked Michael, in the car from Dover. Jonathan had given her money, she'd changed it at the port. Still relying on him, another man keeping her afloat. She clutched the urn in her arms.

'They'll adore you, of course. They've been looking for you for so long.' How easy it was to lie to a child. He trusted her to tell the truth.

Jonathan had taken them to the port, brought them up onto the boat, rubbing their hands against the cold. 'You won't forget, will you?' he'd said, clasping her hands. They'd waited a few weeks before leaving – thinking that a passage in January would be too cold for Michael to bear. In the last week, she'd held Jonathan so much.

She'd shaken her head. 'Never. We'll be back as soon as we can.'

She took his money in her purse. They watched him walk down to the quay, the Statue of Liberty framed behind him – and she almost called him to come back.

Celia and Michael walked up to the front door. The trunk was left at the end of the drive, the urn at last tucked safely inside. She held Michael's hand as much to steady her own as to reassure him.

When she'd approached, the house looked like it had been hit by a giant storm, the roof crumbling, and the walls unkempt. The place looked nothing like it once had. The house was covered with ivy, too much of it, Celia saw now. Every spring, in the old days, men would hack back the ivy, because if they didn't it would grow into the hollows between stones, force them out and the house would start, slowly but surely, to fall. No one had touched the ivy in years and bricks had fallen out, some still lying in the front. It had been Rudolf's idea to buy Stoneythorpe. He'd put down his fork in the middle of dinner, when they lived in Hampstead, announced he had seen a house that he was going to buy. Celia had imagined a castle, thanks to the romantic way that Rudolf had spoken of it. The reality, a great heavy pale stone house, two red-brick front wings coming forward, three ornamental curved porches covered with carved stone like lace, high chimneys, grounds either side. Dozens of windows, thirty rooms, but few of them were now used. Celia's favourite room had been the library but it had been locked up because of the damp.

'It's very old,' she said, patting Michael on the shoulder. 'Not all the houses in England look like this.'

A woman who Celia didn't recognise opened the door. She'd told her parents and Emmeline by telegram from Dover that they hoped to arrive in the morning – they were already late. She walked into the parlour, holding Michael tightly by the arm.

The parlour was older, shabbier but otherwise the same: the old yellow-and-blue-striped chairs, cream sofas, pale walls with family portraits, big glass windows opening onto the garden, overgrown now. She paused by a table near the door, then walked forward.

'Here he is, father,' she said, gazing at Rudolf, smaller and older than ever in the straight-backed chair. 'I've brought Michael home.'

Verena gasped. 'Celia! You found him.' Michael held tight to Celia's hand, still clutching his bear.

'I did. I told him we'd all been looking for him. I said you had too.'

Verena and Rudolf were staring at Michael, two china dolls, unable to move. They had lost so much. They were bearing it so bravely.

The door burst open and Lily rushed in. 'Don't run!' Emmeline was shouting. 'Stop!'

'Who are you?' Lily said, eyeing Michael.

'This is your cousin, Lily,' said Celia. 'Michael has come all the way from America to stay with us.'

Lily jumped up to Michael. Celia wanted to reach out for her – her gangly arms and legs, her dark hair, her snub-nosed face – capture the last of her childhood. Adulthood was taking her up, winding its tendrils into her body, inevitable, changing her. Of course it was as it should be, but something in Celia pulled against it. She wanted her to be a child forever and ever – not have to negotiate the adult world, ungenerous, inflexible.

Emmeline looked the same, even in her old grey dress, as if she'd jumped out of a ladies' magazine advertisement for soap, the golden hair curling around her face, the figure that went in and out. Lily had her little nose and pink cheeks, but the rest of her was all Janus, dark hair, pale skin, the contrast that people had admired when she was a child, struck at Celia's heart now she was older. Her niece was so handsome. But part of her was like Celia as she had been when she was young, the thin, stalky bird movements of the legs, the constant look of nervousness.

'You've grown so much, Lily.'

'Adults always say that.' Lily was staring at Michael.

'Well, I don't know about you, but I am going to hug my nephew,' said Emmeline. 'Time for us to get acquainted.' She lifted Michael up in a bear hug.

'Now my turn!' said Lily. She put her arms out and pulled him up. 'Look!' she said, her face red with the effort. 'I can.'

'Now my turn to pick up you,' said Michael, when she had set him down.

Michael reached for Lily and she jumped away. 'You've got to catch me first!' she cried and fled from the room, laughing. Michael turned to look at Celia – and then ran too.

'Well, isn't that nice,' said Emmeline, hands on her hips, looking at the door. 'Poor Lily has been missing Albert – he's just started school. Now she has a friend to play with.'

'Lily is a practically a boy herself,' said Verena.

'Good,' said Emmeline. 'What use is ladylike behaviour? It's a new era now.'

There was a scream outside and then a shout of laughter. A door banged and footsteps skittered off towards the garden.

'Mind the vases!' shouted Emmeline. She turned and flopped into a chair. 'Well, Celia, surprise after surprise. Tell us where you found him. He's a handsome little boy, isn't he?' *Is his face that of his father's?* Celia guessed she was thinking.

Celia sat down on the sofa. 'Honestly? I asked someone to steal his address, then I half begged, half threatened his parents. But that didn't work. Then they lost all their money in the Crash and gave him to me.' She stared hard at her parents with the word 'steal'. It was what you made me do.

Verena's face was pale, crumped. 'I never thought you'd find him. Do you think he will forgive me? Us?' Verena whispered.

'He'll never know. I told him it was Aunt Deerhurst and that's what he believes.'

Celia watched the relief in her mother's face and felt a twinge of anger at it: cowardice. 'It will be our secret.'

'Yes, yes,' nodded Rudolf. 'All water under the bridge now.'

She felt another spark of fury. It was water under the bridge for him. But what if she'd never found Michael, never lied, sent Red to steal, threatened, begged?

'We were lucky he was alive,' she said, angrily. 'I'm sure some of the children sent away like this died. They beat him, mistreated him. You wouldn't believe it. He won't really talk about it.' She kept asking him about it and he said he wanted to forget. And maybe, she thought, perhaps he was forgetting. Perhaps the days with Jonathan, the ice cream parlours, the new country, might be enough to make him forget.

'Two hours with Lily and he'll forget everything,' said Emmeline. 'That child never stops with her imaginary worlds.' And she was right, that was what Celia hoped too, that Lily and all of them could make him forget – and her too, so that every time she looked at her parents, she wouldn't think: *It was your fault.*

Verena smiled. Celia looked at her – and then the portrait of Arthur over the mantelpiece, above her head. And she realised they didn't know. They were smiling at jokes, laughing. Lily was tearing through the house, giggling.

'You don't know,' she said.

'Know what?' asked Rudolf, suddenly seeming to grasp the conversation. 'Are you talking about the Crash? We hear about nothing else. I've been writing to Arthur about it but I haven't heard back. I presume the stock is lowered? I don't doubt the company is strong. Everybody needs to eat meat!'

'Was it awfully dramatic?' asked Emmeline. 'It must have been quite a shock.'

'The company has lost a lot, Papa. I don't know how much. But – didn't you get my letter? And the telegram. Jonathan and Mr Galss wrote too.'

'Who is Mr Galss? And Jonathan? I didn't get any letters or telegrams.'

'I expect she means Jonathan Corrigan,' said Emmeline. 'Is he still desperately in love with you, Celia? Anyway, what do you mean, lost a lot? I thought Arthur was setting up factories in America. *They* can't have collapsed. How much?'

'But I wrote. I sent a telegram. Jonathan said he did, too. I know he did.'

Out of the corner of her eye, she saw Emmeline sit up. 'Saying what? What did the telegram say? What's happened?'

Celia shook her head. She could feel the tears coming. 'I can't.'

'Can't what?' Outside, Lily and Michael were in the garden, screaming and whooping. 'What's happened?'

She looked at Rudolf, Verena, her sister. 'I wrote. They did too.'

'What? You tell us. Now!' Emmeline leant forward, started out of her chair. 'What's happened?'

'It's Arthur. I brought him back with me. He – he died.'

'No,' said Emmeline. 'No. It's not possible. Don't listen to her, Mama. She's just joking. No.'

'He's dead. Almost two months ago. I wanted to bring him back. To bury. They wouldn't let me. I've got an urn instead—' The tears engulfed her. She looked up and Rudolf had wrapped his arms around himself, was rocking back and forth. He was singing to himself, softly, a song she recognised – a German folk song he used to sing to her when she was a little girl. Verena was lying back on her chair, eyes closed, arms shaking.

'How?' said Emmeline. 'Tell us how. You have to! Was he ill? Did he get hit by one of those cars in New York? What happened?'

'He died. He just died.'

'He just died? No one *just dies*.'

Celia shook her head, looked down. Arthur, eyes wild, pulling her towards him, pushing her against the iron of the balcony. 'He threw himself out of the window. He wanted to die.'

Verena slapped her hand on the sofa. 'He didn't. That's a lie. He never would. Tell us the truth.'

The words flashed through her mind. *Louisa*. She pushed them away. 'We – lost a lot of money. In the Crash. Arthur was afraid.'

'He died for money?'

'You – don't understand what it was like. Everyone was afraid. Lots of people were – inviting death. He thought he'd lost everything.'

Emmeline stood up. 'But it's only money. Money's nothing.'

Verena was sitting forward, intently. 'He thought we'd resent him. He thought we'd be angry. That's it, isn't it, Celia? He was ashamed – of what we'd say.'

Celia looked at her mother, sitting on the sofa, the portraits of Arthur and Michael ranged over her head, her face cut over with guilt. Patches of red were rising on her mother's face, her skin flaming up with misery. She could release her – tell her the truth. *It wasn't you. It was because he'd killed Louisa and then lost it all, that's why.* Verena's eyes were filling up with tears. Celia could set her free, tell the truth. But the truth was worse. *You'll have to keep it,* said Louisa's voice in her ear. *Don't tell.*

But why do I have to keep all the secrets? Why me?

Verena was weeping. 'My own son! Why wouldn't he trust me?'

'He did,' Celia said, but too weakly.

Emmeline took three steps towards her. 'Why didn't you stop him? You must have known if he was feeling angry. You should have been helping him.'

'Emmeline,' said Rudolf. But he wasn't warning her strongly, not really. Celia gazed at him. Maybe he even agreed with her.

'What about when it actually happened?' Emmeline went on. 'Were you there? Why didn't you stop him?'

'I tried! I tried to hold him back. But he – you don't know what he was like. He was – terrifying.' *He was going to kill me. He said he killed Louisa.* She couldn't say that. She'd never know it was true. He had lost his reason at the end, nothing was real. She would have to bear the burden of what he had said, never knowing the truth, could not tell them because what would that do but hurt them more?

'Look, Emmeline. I'm sorry. But it wasn't my fault. He was so upset. He couldn't even be happy about Michael.'

'Michael? What did that matter if he was going to do what he did?'

It was her grief speaking, Celia knew, but still.

Celia sat back on the chair. She was engaged to Jonathan. They were getting married. She was supposed to go back. But how could she leave her family, broken, reduced.

'Emmeline,' said Rudolf. 'You're making Celia cry.'

Celia gazed out of the window. Lily and Michael were chasing each other around, rushing back and forth, dashing around a tree. Lily tripped, then Michael, and they were both on the ground, laughing. She watched them look up at the sky, still laughing.

She had done the same herself, as a child, chasing around with Tom, remembered the wonder of staring up at the sky, heart racing. And now Michael – her poor, sad Michael – was there too, laughing, without a care. She knew that if she looked into her heart, it would be a selfish one, so flooded with happiness about Michael that she couldn't agree with the words her parents and Emmeline were saying behind her: he should never have gone to New York, the city killed him and they should have stopped him. She wouldn't agree. New York was where she'd found Michael.

'Celia,' said Verena. She turned around. 'Thank you for coming back. I don't think I could lose another child.'

This was her moment to say *but I'm not back for very long. I'm going to be married to Jonathan and I need to go back to him.* She didn't. She couldn't, not then. She'd tell them later, talk about a big wedding in New York, some good news. She watched Michael, up again, running after Lily. She rested her head against the window, gazing at him. And then she saw herself, running through the gardens, dashing away from Tom. She stared at her son, watching herself racing through the gardens with him.

She watched the others grieve, feeling out of sync with them. They were steps behind, still shocked, when she was growing closer to – if not accepting, being able to say that Arthur was dead. She let them, sat quietly by them until Rudolf went to his study, Verena fled upstairs.

'Is Samuel in Spain?'

Emmeline raised an eyebrow. 'Indeed. Gone to save them from tyranny. He said he'd write. I've told the children he's taking a little holiday.'

'Poor you.'

'He said he wouldn't be long. Who knows? I've written letters. Five so far to the address he gave us. But there's been no answer. Lily has been moping about the house. Albert's at school now and she's been feeling sorry for herself. Michael might just be what she needs to cheer her up.'

'Where is Albert at school?' asked Celia, trying to be polite, distract her mind from screaming at her father. *You send one grandson to school, the other smuggled out and shipped abroad.* 'Does he enjoy it?'

'London. Harrow. He seems happy enough,' Emmeline said. 'I've had a few letters mostly just asking for more sweets to share with the other boys. Samuel probably wouldn't approve. He's learning Latin and all the tools Samuel would say were of the elite. So it's the only advantage of my husband being away. By the time he gets back, it will be too late to move Albert to somewhere else. We only managed to get him in in the middle of term because another boy was ill and had to leave without notice.'

'I'm glad you didn't send Lily to school. So Michael has a friend.'

'That would be too much. Samuel couldn't have them both learning to be cogs in the capitalist wheel. Anyway, Papa can't afford two.'

The children played all evening, protested loudly when they prised them apart to go to bed. Celia put Michael to bed in her room, lay next to him stroking his forehead until he slept. She waited to check he was fast asleep, holding tight to Harvey and his horse. Then she crept away.

That night, when everything was quiet, Celia wandered around the house with her light. The weeds hadn't just been in the garden. There were a few in the corridor near the kitchen, scratching through the stones. The ceiling of the hall was covered in a thick dark mould. The wallpaper was peeling in all the rooms she could open – and there were cobwebs thick with spiders in the corners. She walked up to Michael's room, tried the door. Still locked. She wondered if they'd changed it since her brother died, whether the little wooden planes he'd been so fond of making hung down from the ceilings, fluttering in the cold air on tiny white strings. She walked up to Arthur's room, tried the door. That was open. She slipped through. She hadn't been in Arthur's room for years. It was still as he must have left it when he eloped with Louisa, except the maids had stripped the bed. There was a pile of clothes on the chair that she supposed must have been thrown aside because they couldn't fit into his suitcase.

She knelt up on the bed and touched the shelf full of things, silver ornaments, candles, old books. She didn't recognise any of them, supposed he must have bought them in Paris, little trinkets from market stalls that caught his eye. An old box of chocolates with a few crumbs inside, bloomed with white. She had not realised he was so sentimental. Something about the things hurt her heart – the intimacy of them, collected and then left behind. She held an ornamental box to her, as if by clutching it, Louisa would have never gone with Arthur, didn't fall from the cliff.

She felt the tears on her cheeks. She lay down on Arthur's bed, staring at the cracks in the ceiling, let the tears fall.

'Winter Meats didn't succeed in America and it won't survive here unless something changes.' She was sitting in the parlour with Emmeline, Verena and Rudolf. Michael was outside with Lily, chasing squirrels, probably, dashing through the overgrown grounds. It was a week since Celia had arrived and told them about Arthur. And Winter Meats in Britain was without anyone to run it now. They had the family lawyer who Arthur had appointed before America – Mr Pemberton – but they needed someone in charge.

'You can do it,' Rudolf had said. 'You manage the business. These are different times.'

'I'm not sure I can,' she said. She couldn't do it from America. And besides, even though she knew she could run Winter Meats, she didn't know if she wanted to. Not stacking up figures and going to factories. It was selfish, she knew. For how else were they going to protect the house? She looked at her family and her soul twisted because there was nobody else to help them.

'We might have to sell the house.'

'I won't hear of it,' said Verena. 'Stoneythorpe is our home.'

Celia thought of Mr Galss. Everything she had done to save the house. And yet they might still have to. As he had said, they should sell it now and put the money in trust for the children.

'I think we should consider selling. This is too big for all of us.'

'Never,' said Verena. 'No.'

'Surely you can make us money,' said Emmeline.

'We lost a lot in America,' said Celia. 'We may have to sell.' She didn't want to, wanted to keep the house for Michael forever. He'd been denied it. But if the debts came, they would all be lost.

Her mother gazed at her, pleadingly.

All she could think was, *they sent your child away!* But they were still her parents. They'd lost so much. She couldn't lose any more. Maybe she could look after Winter Meats for a short while. And she could start Flapper Foods here in Britain. She had told them all about her success. She could do it again, in Britain, try again. There were flappers here too, young girls in shops and offices who needed to eat! She thought of herself, busy again, using the recipes, buying the stock, reusing the advertising. But then. She didn't want to stay here. She was supposed to be going back to America to live with Jonathan.

She knew that Mr Galss would say they were wrong. He'd say the roof was full of holes and the walls crumbling. No one wanted to work there. If there were more of Arthur's debts, it could sink them all.

'Please,' said Verena.

Celia tore her eyes away from her mother's. She wanted to throw herself at Verena, tell her that they'd find a way. She'd sold Flapper Foods to protect the house because she couldn't bear it – seeing her old home broken up, her dell where she'd sat as a child, conjured her stories. If they sold it now, they'd have nothing left of Michael and Arthur. And she'd have sold her company for nothing.

'We just need the financial situation to improve,' said Rudolf.

Emmeline put down her teacup, crossly. 'That's not going to happen any time soon.'

'The decision is final,' said Rudolf. 'We're not moving.'

Celia looked at the painting of her brothers on the wall. 'So what do we do?'

'When your mother and I die, you can sell it. Not before. Our graves are waiting in the graveyard. That is where we'll be buried. This is our home.'

'Look,' said Celia, hating every word. 'You could go somewhere much nicer. More modern. Somewhere warm in the winter. You have weeds growing through the cracks in the hall. And there's mould.' She thought of Arthur's room, the silver ornaments on the shelves. They'd have to clear them away, stow them in a box in the loft in a new house. Verena would have to unlock Michael's room and they'd put his wooden aeroplanes into boxes.

'We want to live here,' said Verena. 'We want to die here.' She shook her head. 'Celia, we have you back here. We can all live together.'

'I can't. I have to go back to America. It's Michael's home. You could come with me!'

Her mother simply nodded. 'Our home is here. But of course you can go back and forth.'

Celia tried to hold her gaze. 'No, I have to go back.'

She'd dropped her big news about America, what she had been so afraid to say. But Verena wasn't listening, had barely heard it. Neither was Emmeline, who stamped her foot. 'Don't you care about your grandchildren? What about Lily? Albert can get a job – but what about her? You don't care. What you're saying is that we have to wait until the house is falling down around your ears before you'll move. We have to wait until the roof falls in and then nobody will buy it?'

'We'll find a way,' said Rudolf, placidly. 'Celia will help us.'

TWENTY-TWO

Stoneythorpe, April 1930

England looked no different. But Celia felt she had completely changed, that she was a new person encountering it now, the old one lost like clothes you had disposed of, tried to get back, but realised even if you did, you'd changed too much and you had to be different now.

'You can't go,' said Emmeline. They were out in the garden, tipping back their faces to catch the sun. 'You can't leave me with all this. You need to help us. You can't just go back to America.'

Celia gazed around the overgrown garden, the weeds crawling over the flower beds, a fallen tree splayed across the lawn. She'd been down to her old place, her little dell. She'd thought it wouldn't matter that the rest of the garden was neglected, for her space had always been wild. But she couldn't find the same magic in it. Before, it had always felt as if fairy people had run away just before she arrived. Once, it was her secret place. Now there was something flat about it, dull and old. And it was vulnerable, not safe, could be pulled down at any time and all of her would be left exposed.

'He seems happy enough here to me. Lily loves him. You can barely keep the two of them apart.'

What about Jonathan? she thought, but dared not say. She'd been writing to him, three or four times a week, telling him everything but not what was important. There had been so much to do. Comforting the family, another small funeral in the church for Arthur, burying the urn next to Michael in the graveyard, a reception with Verena's elderly cousins from Dorset. Then the journalists who got wind of the story and remembered about the trial and came down to knock on the windows and say, 'Don't you want to give your side of the story?' They didn't. Although, Celia had to admit, the resulting reports hadn't been too bad. There was a lot of sympathy for America and the businessmen who died. The only problem was that it meant all the British factory suppliers had written to them in a panic and Celia had had to send letters saying everything was fine, proceeding as usual and the losses in America had been minimal, just very distressing.

She had had meetings with Mr Pemberton to go over the accounts. The business was not in a good way, orders were down, there were large loans outstanding and stores had returned a lot of stock.

'Perhaps it was simply that we were in need of leadership,' said Mr Pemberton. 'You can turn Winter Meats around.' She was going to have to do it herself, head it up, visit the factories, talk to the men, make new plans. She agreed, even though her heart was reluctant. She wanted to marry Jonathan. She was *engaged*. She hadn't told the family yet, but since they had barely noticed when she said she had to return to America, she supposed they would ignore that too.

Emmeline tossed her head. 'We need you to run the business.' Every day Celia stayed at Stoneythorpe, she imagined Mr Galss telling her she was wrong to try to prop it up, Jonathan saying the same. The house was full of dust, falling apart. Rudolf and Verena sat in the middle of it, like two statues, resplendent as their temple collapsed around them, thrown open to the burning sun, beating rain. The newspapers said houses were declining in value. They'd get more now than if they waited.

She couldn't tell Emmeline about the possibility of the debts. There was no point worrying her, for perhaps it might not happen. The thought of Michael spending time in her old home was too overwhelming. He deserved it. His childhood here had been taken from him.

'Let's see if the situation improves.' The sun was shining too hard in Celia's eyes. She looked out again. 'No word from Samuel?'

Emmeline shrugged. 'Nothing. Maybe that address doesn't work. I don't know. I presume they'd tell me if he were dead.'

'Dead? Why would he be dead?'

'Who knows? I don't know what he's doing. I'm beginning to think he'll never write back. But I'll keep on sending letters. You never know. Sometimes I feel selfish, because I don't just miss him. I miss our flat in Bedford Square, living in London. I wish I had the money to rent it again. We're just getting along here.' Emmeline cleared her throat. 'What are you going to tell Tom?'

'To tell Tom?'

'About his child. About Michael.'

'What are you talking about?'

'Don't lie, Celia. I'm your sister. I always thought it was him. Well, I believed that lie about the soldier in the beginning. Then I thought better of it. You'd at least make some effort to find the man – or talk about how terrible he was. You didn't do either. And who else would you have given in to than Tom? And now you turn up with this child who has the look of him. I see his sister in his eyes.'

'You guessed.'

'Don't worry, the others haven't. He has the resemblance, but you have to look for it. So are you going to get him to marry you?'

'Never, Emmeline! He's not – he's not. He's not part of it.'

'Of course he is. He's the father. What do you think he's going to say if he hears about it?'

'He won't know.' She hadn't seen him since her terrible words to him around Arthur's trial. And then the time before when she'd told him she'd had a baby – a soldier she'd met one night – and he'd been shocked, disappointed by her. He didn't love her. Never wanted her – so how could he want her son? If she met him with Michael, he might feel obliged to try to love them both. She couldn't bear that.

Emmeline didn't understand. She couldn't. Celia could never tell her the truth, how Tom had stood in a half circle around their brother in 1916 and shot him. She'd thought she could never forgive him. But she knew that what he'd told her was the truth: he'd had no choice. Even if he'd saved Michael on that day, still the authorities would have found him again, put a hood on him, taken him out onto the grass to be shot. Only this time, Tom would be standing next to him.

Celia had to keep the secret. She couldn't tell. It would kill her parents, break Emmeline's spirit. They might even blame Michael for it now, see something of Tom's terrible acts in the child. She couldn't open up that dreadful box, because if she did, all the secrets might be set free and, after all they'd suffered, it would ruin them if they knew the truth about what had happened to her brother: that the army had condemned him as a coward.

There was a scream behind them and Michael and Lily hurtled into view, laughing. 'Get her to give it back!' Michael was shouting.

'It's mine! Finders keepers!'

'What is going on?' demanded Emmeline, turning around. But they were off again, laughing, Lily's skirts flying out behind her. 'Remember! No going to the woods.'

'I've never seen her so happy,' Emmeline said. 'Not since she was a little girl. Certainly not since Samuel left...'

'Why are you always telling them not to go to the woods? I don't think we cared much about them when we were children.'

'We ran wild. You have to be careful nowadays. You never know what's out there. Especially for girls. Well, it may be different for boys. You're far too protective of Michael already. You can't hide him from all the evil in the world, you know.'

'I know! He's seen enough, that's all.'

'So, my question. What if Michael asks about his father?'

'He asked on the boat over and I said he was dead. But maybe when I marry, I'll say he was the father all along.' Jonathan and she together in a big hall full of flowers in New York. In sickness and in health.

'He'll start asking more soon. Everybody wants to know who their father is. Your son's a bright boy. He's going to want to know.' Celia shook her head. 'Look, why were you always moping after Tom in the first place? A servant. What did he promise you?'

'Nothing. He promised me nothing. Anyway, it was all me. He didn't want me, not really. He said I only loved him because of our childhood together – and it wasn't an equal friendship anyway.'

'Well that's probably true. But Celia! Why were you chasing after a servant? Even Jonathan would have been better than that.'

'What's wrong with Jonathan?'

'He's so brash. But Tom? I don't understand it. You were just trying to live your childhood again. It's time to grow up, Celia. If you refuse to tell Tom, find a proper man. Tough with a child in tow, since there aren't many of them to be had, but if you stop being so mopey and put some make-up on, you just might do it.'

'Emmeline. Jonathan has asked me to marry him. I've accepted.'

'You have?'

'He loves me. I love him. Would you come with me to live in New York?' Her sister, so brittle on the outside, soft and afraid under it all.

'Why didn't you say about Jonathan before?'

'I wanted to save up some good news. Please come with me.'

Emmeline tipped her head back to the sun. 'What – America? Of course not. I can't do anything until Samuel gets back. And I doubt he'd want to. Anyway, we couldn't leave Mama and Papa.'

'They could come too.'

'Don't be ludicrous, Celia. They'd never leave here. They're too old. If you go to America, you go alone.'

'I'm not going to look after Winter Meats – I don't think anyone can save it.'

I'm going back to America, she should have said. *I'm going to be married to Jonathan and then I will send back money for you all.* She was about to.

'Please, Celia. You have to help us. I'll look after Michael for you. He and Lily get on like a house on fire.'

She couldn't say it. 'Well, just for a while. And then I have to go back to America.'

TWENTY-THREE

Stoneythorpe, July 1930

Britain was trying to pull itself out of the Crash, that's what every-one said. There was terrible unemployment and British exports were dropping in price. It didn't seem fair – no one in Manchester or Glasgow had invested in Miami apartments or Hawaii hotels. But, still, what shook America shook the world.

Verena and Emmeline closeted themselves away, reading. Verena had the latest Agatha Christie novels sent over from London the minute they were published. She and Emmeline swapped them over. 'She is exactly right on an English village,' said Verena. 'They are cruel places.' Verena loved Hercule Poirot, too, his neatness and precision, said that she thought Miss Christie should write more of him. Most of his success, it seemed to Celia, seemed to be in encouraging people to speak and through them learning the truth. Another royal baby was to be born and Lily said it would be a boy, the future King.

Celia told Rudolph and Verena about the engagement and they begged her to stay, just for a little while until they were on their feet. She wrote to Jonathan that they would soon be on their way, she just had to help her family with business first. He was disappointed but said he understood and she assured him she would not be long. She spent the early summer looking over the papers and taking Michael with her on tours of the country, the factories and Winter Meats properties across the Midlands, North and South East. It had taken her a long time, sorting through the papers with Mr Pemberton, to work out exactly what was what and where everything was. But she thought she understood the business now. She'd listened to managers talk about the products, she'd visited shops, talked to workers. The loans were daunting and the demand was collapsing. It was impossible to keep it alive. All she wanted to do was set up a version of Flapper Foods here in Britain. She had come so close in America – and surely she could do it again, under a different name. She and Michael stayed in hotels, looked at factories, but he yearned so much for Lily and Stoneythorpe that she felt bad taking him away and decided she would go back and send Pemberton to look instead. And the more he loved Stoneythorpe, the more she refused to listen to Mr Galss talking reason in her head and decided she would do anything to keep it.

Rudolf called Celia into his study one day.

'We haven't had much time to talk since you've got back,' he said. 'I miss my little Celia.' She edged in, pained at the sight of him looking so old, bald-headed, his stomach fat, almost like an old round baby in the chair. How could she be his little Celia now, after what she'd seen? Arthur had killed himself in front of her and she could never tell her father the truth.

Rudolf smiled. 'Why don't you come here and sit by me? Tell me how you are, Celia. I miss our talks.'

'I'm very well, Papa.' She thought of him standing up, crying out 'America' on the evening they went to celebrate Arthur's freedom. The night in the Ritz, lifting glasses. They'd drunk to truth and justice.

Hot words flamed in her head. 'Do you not think you were wrong, Father?'

'Wrong?'

'You were wrong to send Michael away. You broke my heart. And now look at how happy he is. Aren't you going to apologise?'

'Celia, Celia, it's all over now.'

'Not for me. I still remember it. I remember having him and waking up and he was gone.'

Rudolf was shifting about, uncomfortably. 'Your mother,' he murmured.

'Not just her. You could have stopped it. You were – what? Trying to save our reputation, such as it was?'

Rudolf nodded. 'It all worked out in the end.'

Celia was seized by fury. 'No it didn't! Anything could have happened. The family didn't love him, mistreated him. Jonathan paid them off – did you know that?'

'Jonathan.' Rudolf smiled. Celia could see her father was desperately clutching at a reed that would pull him out of her hot pool of anger. She looked at him, old, shrunken in the chair, and the idea of him doing something so terrible seemed cruel and impossible. He wasn't a tyrant, he was a little old man. And yet he *had* done wrong, he *had* taken Michael. He smiled at her. 'Jonathan is just who I wanted to talk to you about.'

'We can talk about Jonathan later! Why did you do it? Michael might have died. Your own grandson.'

Rudolf shook his head. 'Verena! Emmeline!'

As if on cue, Verena came through the door, Emmeline too, Lily behind her.

'What's happening?'

Celia swung around. 'We're talking about Michael. Lily, go and find him and play. This is grown-up talk.'

'Oh, *dull*,' sighed Lily, skipped out of the room.

Emmeline hurried over to Rudolf, put her arms around him. 'What's happening?'

'I'm asking Papa why he and Mama did it. Why they sent Michael away.'

Verena was sitting down now, her hand on her forehead, her body still holding a dancer's grace. 'Celia, it was what was right at the time.'

'The family in America hated him. I was just telling Papa. They weren't going to give up Michael for free. They wanted ten thousand dollars. Jonathan got it in a day. Without him, Michael would be – well, I don't want to think.'

'Jonathan gave you the money?' Emmeline was gazing at her. 'He gave you ten thousand dollars? Do we have to repay him?'

Celia shook her head. 'No. I was – am – his fiancée. He knew how much I needed it. And I want to know why they did it. I want them to tell me why!'

She looked away from her sister, at her mother and father. Her father was weeping softly. She hadn't seen him cry since he came back from the war.

'Forgive me,' he croaked, looking upwards, like a small child saying his prayers. 'Forgive me.'

Verena shook her head. 'Celia, you have to believe us. Maybe we were wrong. But it's not easy for girls to raise a baby alone.'

'You love your grandchildren, Albert and Lily. You're spending your last funds sending Albert to school. Why didn't you think you might love Michael, too?'

Rudolf shook his head. 'Let us forget it. When you are married you can have more children.'

'So I must go back to live in America. But I don't want to leave you. Why can't you come too?'

'He could come here.' said Rudolf, brightening. 'This is excellent.'

'He can't,' said Celia. 'His life is there.' But then, a feeling crept up in her. Why not? If Jonathan really loved her, why could he not live here with them?

INTERLUDE

She'd realised as soon as she saw Michael that they would be friends forever.

She'd taken Michael into the garden, this shy boy all the way from America. 'Let me show you somewhere,' she'd said, took him down the garden to the place where Aunt Celia had used to like to sit.

For the first month or so, he'd slept in Aunt Celia's room. And then they'd put him in his own room, one that used to be a box room at the top of the stairs. She'd crept out of her bed, to stand just in the corridor outside, in the shadows where nobody could see her. She'd heard him say, 'I will be fine, Mama. Don't worry!' She'd heard Celia standing outside for half an hour or so. Then her footsteps walking away. Lily waited. Then, when the corridor was silent, she hurried through to the door, pushed it open, gently.

'It's me!' she whispered. 'I came to see if you were all right.'

He gazed at her, eyes wide, over the cover. 'This house is too big,' he whispered back. 'It creaks too much.'

'Oh those are just the pipes. You'll get used to them. I did.'

She sat on the eiderdown. 'I'll stay with you,' she said.

He held her hand in the darkness. 'Our secret,' he said. She held on hard, two sets of fingers, intertwined.

The house became their wonderland. The adults didn't use even half of it. They didn't see a thing. He and Lily found rooms that were supposed to be locked but the locks had broken so you could easily creep in and no one would know you were there. They stole cakes and biscuits from the kitchens and ran upstairs with them, made dens in the sheets on the old broken beds. They imagined they were everything: African explorers, magic men flying to the moon, tigers prowling for prey. They could be everything. They wouldn't be like the adults, hidebound, always talking about the dreariest subjects. 'Let's never have secrets,' she said. 'Let's always tell each other everything.'

Lily told him about her father, always plotting something if he was at home, living in Spain and creating adventures. 'He's so brave,' she said. 'He will do anything for honour.'

They imagined what it must be like for him in Spain – as he hid in trees or behind bushes, worked hard to save the world.

'One day, I'd like to be like him,' said Michael. He wasn't sure that he really did. But Lily adored her father and he wanted her to love him as much too.

She told him how sorry she felt for him. He talked about the Whetstones. But it seemed so far away from him now, almost like a dream, so he felt bad when she cried for him, the little boy locked up in the attic with no supper when he hadn't done his work properly. He found it hard to explain – that child in the attic was a different boy. Mama had rescued him and now this was his life and sometimes he had to remind himself that he hadn't always lived here at Stoneythorpe, holding Lily's hand every night when she crept into his room after Mama had gone. She put her beloved purple cat, made for her by her father, next to his bear Harvey and they were best friends too.

The only place they weren't allowed to go was the woods at the end of the garden. The nearest they were permitted was the dell where Mama had used to sit and imagine fairies when she was a little girl. Mama liked them to go and sit there but they didn't much like it – Lily found it damp and he thought it was too dark. But he told Mama that they loved it and could see fairies there like she could. It was worth the lie to see how happy she became when he said it. Privately, he thought that Mama's childhood must have been very dull if sitting on that wet rock next to a pond choked up with weeds was the highlight.

Sometimes he and Lily sat and talked about the woods, invented what they thought might be in there. There must be something terrible, if they were so forbidden.

They sat through breakfast, just waiting until the moment when Mama or Aunt Emmeline said that they had been there long enough and could leave the table. Then they went off into the garden and they were free. Their minds hurried until they were called in for dinner. And then, at night, the moment that made his heart soar, when Lily came in and held his hand until he slept, slipped out again so that Mama would never know when she came to look in on him before going to bed. Because if he went to sleep holding Lily's hand, then that meant she was in his dreams. They ran together, through his night world, holding hands and laughing.

TWENTY-FOUR

Stoneythorpe, September 1930

Celia wrote to Jonathan to say she was still delayed. They were coming. She promised they were coming. Her parents kept asking – shouldn't you have a ring? What about a wedding? She couldn't answer. She couldn't make sense of her thoughts. She wanted to be married to Jonathan yet living in Stoneythorpe, looking after her family. And she couldn't be two things, two people. She had to choose.

There was always somewhere where the business needed her. Even though it was struggling, she could not think of a way to tell Rudolf. She knew she should be straight: Winter Meats was a business for life under the old King, we live in a different world now. But it was easier to travel to the customers, the suppliers, the factories, than it was to stay at home and speak the truth.

She arrived back early one morning from a tour of department stores from London to Manchester, raced in and ran up to find Michael, not even bothering to change out of her brown suit. He wasn't in his room – and then she tried hers and found him fast asleep in her old bed, trusty Harvey in his arms. She lay down next to him and put her arms around him, listening to him breathe.

She woke up to Emmeline coming into the room. 'I heard you were here,' she said. 'You've come back.'

Celia looked up, still holding Michael who hadn't stirred. 'It's been too long. I thought it was only going to be two weeks. But – there was so much to do.'

'Well, hopefully you made a success of it. Anyway, someone's here to see you.' Celia's heart struck. 'Jonathan's been here for about a week.'

Celia jerked up. 'Jonathan? From America?'

'He's the only one I know. We tried to send a telegram but you never seemed to stay in one place long enough. He says he wanted to see you. Did you ask him to come?'

Celia shook her head. 'I'll come and see him.'

'In that? Don't you think you'd better get changed first?'

Celia looked down. 'I suppose so.'

'There's hardly any hurry. He's been waiting here for nearly a week. I'm sure he could manage another half an hour.'

She shut the door after her. Celia looked down at her son, then changed into one of the skirts and jumpers left in her wardrobe. She hurried downstairs. Jonathan was sitting in the parlour, under the pictures of Arthur and Michael. His hair was longer, his cheeks pink through a new tan on his skin.

He looked up. 'You're back. Your sister said you have no money, that the business here is ruined too. Is that true?'

'No. She doesn't really understand money. Something could be done. But it would take a lot of work. And I'd have to borrow. But I want to do my foods again.'

'Flapper Foods again? In England? I thought you'd given that up.'

'I sold Flapper Foods so we could keep this place. But I could still start it here.'

They were skirting around it, the two of them, two dressed-up dancers circling their way around the subject. It was like a dragon in the middle of the room.

'You've been here a week,' she said.

'It's been so long since I came here. I was nineteen, then. I've been walking around the grounds, remembering. Or trying to. I've been with Michael and Lily for much of it. Your parents, a little.'

She felt hot and flooded with shame. 'I'm sorry,' she began. But he was speaking at the same time. 'I wrote.' They crossed, excused each other. 'You start,' he said.

'No, you.'

He shook his head.

She breathed. 'I've been – busy. The house, the family. Michael. The business.'

Her mind flashed with a picture of the two of them in the speakeasy. She'd told him she loved him. He looked taller and older. Her thoughts were on fire.

He stood up and walked to the window. 'Your father said I should have asked him if I could marry you. Then he said I should move here while you ran the business.'

She nodded. Her heart was striking hard. Everything hurt. 'But you see they're desperate. They need me.'

'Michael seems to think you are staying here forever and ever.'

'Oh. That's just because he likes Lily. I told my family I was leaving.'

'But they want you to stay. Everybody wants you to stay. And you?'

'I was going to come. Michael and I. Just after I'd sorted out the business.' She meant it, the vision of herself booking the passage, standing onboard the ship. She and Michael in New York. But then, there was that other self, with Rudolf and Verena, Emmeline.

'Why can't you come to live here?'

'I'm needed there.'

'Why do you matter more?'

They were silent.

'I've brought the ring,' he said. 'I think they've finally got it right.' He took the box from his pocket, opened it. The ring was there, newly cleaned, sparkling. The diamond looked even bigger out of New York. She tried it on and the ring fitted perfectly but the whole thing was so bright and new, it was America in Stoneythorpe and it made everything around it look old. 'Thank you.'

'It looks perfect,' he said.

'They need me, Jonathan. You can see that. They're chained to this house, the business is falling apart.'

'Yes, but I need you as well. You are going to be my wife.' The word shot through her. 'Mr Galss told you to sell it. He was right. You should. They'd manage.'

And she knew what he was saying was true – she should put it on the market and they would manage, of course they would – and they would do even better if they had him and his money. Giving the money to mend the roof would be nothing to him. She wanted to put her head in her hands. The air was parting and it was tearing her in two.

'Why are you always tied to your family?'

'I'm not.'

'It's always the same. You sacrifice everything for them. When are you going to stop? They can't have your whole life.'

'They don't want my whole life.' But as she said it, she knew it wasn't true. They had done, in the war, Verena wanting her to stay with her. And now, to them she was thirty-one, not married, and needed at home for ever and ever.

'They sent your child away. Now, when you finally find him, they want to play happy families.'

She wouldn't have him without Jonathan's money. Rudolf and Verena wouldn't have had the money, probably wouldn't have given it to her even if they did.

'Please stop.' She gazed up at the picture of Arthur over the mantelpiece.

'I'm sorry, Celia. I didn't mean to hurt you. But I'm your fiancé. And you can't be with me, because of your family.'

'I'm sorry,' she said.

'What are we going to do?' he said. 'You know, I have a ticket for you and Michael. It's here. For next week. We could all go back together.'

She wanted to fall into his arms. It would be so comforting, Jonathan organising the journey, whisking her back to New York, making everything easy. She gazed at him.

'Is that a no? You won't come.'

She dropped her head to the sofa. 'I can in a little while.' She cleared her throat. 'Why don't you come to live here? With us. I just don't think I can get Papa and Mama to leave. They're so old. This is their home.'

'And America is mine.'

Everything was tearing. She couldn't say no. If she did, then that would be the end of it.

'When? Two weeks? A month? When?'

'Six months,' she said. 'Let me help them. Get the business on its feet. Then I'll come. We'll both come.'

He sighed. 'Six months?' he said. 'You promise.'

She nodded. 'I promise.'

'And you'll tell your parents that you'll be coming to New York in six months.'

She nodded. 'I promise. When things have faded here with Arthur. I promise I will.'

'Tell them they're not too old. They'd love New York. After all, what is there for them here?'

The idea entranced her in its simplicity. But it would be too much for Verena and Rudolf, surely. 'I'll ask them.'

'Good.'

He stood up and he was embracing her, kissing the tears on her face. 'I'm so relieved,' he was saying. 'I thought – I thought all sorts of things. But I was wrong. Only a few months and we'll be together. Man and wife. Just like we always wanted to be. I'll get everything ready while you're here. The house – well, I won't choose the decor. That's up to you. But maybe I can choose a summer house for us. How about Long Island? Do you like it there?'

She held herself tight into his body, listening to him talk, pressing her ear against his chest, hearing the movement of his blood.

TWENTY-FIVE

Stoneythorpe, October 1930

Jonathan had done so much for her since he had arrived, talked to her parents, looked over the accounts for Winter Meats, said he would consult Mr Galss about the plans. She'd asked him if he'd seen Violet and he had done that for her too – gone to see her twice and given her money. He agreed with her that her mother could look after herself, preferred to depend on Violet.

'Such an intelligent girl,' he said. 'But she won't leave her mother.' They'd moved house again to somewhere even smaller, cheaper. Violet had a job in a hat factory, came home exhausted, hands stained blue with the dye, coughing from all the chemicals.

'Don't worry,' he said. 'I'll help her find a better job. Something in an office.'

'That's good.'

'How did you girls meet? She won't say.'

'Oh, you know, New York.' So Violet hadn't told him. Perhaps *she* should. If anyone could get Hope back, it would be Jonathan. When she went back to America, she would explain everything to him and they would find Hope.

Celia got up, sighed. 'I'm coming!' she shouted. She'd counted to forty – now she had to try to find Lily and Michael. It was the fifth game of hide and seek they'd played that day.

She walked out into the garden, shielding her eyes from the sun. She pushed through the hedge at the back and into the overgrown garden. The fountain that Verena had put in so long ago was grown over with moss. She walked sideways to pass under the trees. 'Where are you?' she called. Her voice came back to her from the branches of the trees and the walls of the house. She called again. It was as if the garden was completely deserted. She walked up to the flowerpots by the French windows leading out from the parlour, all of them full of weeds. There had been a sundial here when she'd been a child; but somehow the dial had been broken off and there was nothing left but a stone stump. 'Where are you?' she called again. 'You'd better be in the garden. If you've gone into the house, that's not fair!'

She almost felt like the youngest again, wandering around looking for the older ones, left behind as usual. She always failed to find them in hide and seek, felt as if she was rambling around while the others watched from their hiding places, laughed at her. And now, it was the same with her own son and niece.

'You'll never find us!' they had said. 'Go and count.'

'I'll find you!' she cried. Her voice echoed back. A tendril of fear curled around her.

Half an hour later and Celia had searched every place she could think of in the garden and was beginning to feel properly afraid. She'd shouted, turned everywhere she could think of upside down. When her voice echoed back for what felt like the fiftieth time, she seized up her thick skirt and ran to the house.

Ten minutes later, she was out with Emmeline and Jonathan while Verena was searching the house. 'But they can't be in the house,' she was saying. 'They promised me they wouldn't. I worry they are in the woods.'

'Oh, no!' cried Emmeline. 'They'd never go there. Lily promised.'

'I'm sure we'll find them. Did you try here?' Jonathan gestured towards the little pathway under the trees.

'Everywhere.'

'We'll try them all again. Come on.'

And so they did, walking diligently around every tree, every rock, behind all the hedges. Jonathan looked up in the trees as well – which Celia hadn't thought of – but there was still no sign of them.

The dusk was beginning to darken the trees. The garden that

had been for so long her friend, her refuge, was thick with looming shadows, dark monsters.

'If they're not inside, then they have to be outside. Listen, we'll have one final quick search and then I think we need to get search parties from the village.'

Celia gazed at Jonathan, her heart reeling. 'I should have come and got you earlier.' They had been lost for almost an hour. Anything could have happened.

'We'll find them. Wherever they are. Come on, Celia, you need to be strong.' He took her arm and they were rushing to the hedge at the bottom of the garden.

'You looked down there?' he said. 'The place where you used to like to sit?'

'I counted there. They can't be there.'

'We should check, just in case. They could have slipped in after you left.'

Of course! They might have done. She hurtled through the hedge, under the willow and into her dell.

They were there. She was about to scream out for Jonathan – and then she stopped herself. They were curled up next to her favourite stone, fast asleep, wound around each other so she could barely tell where one started and another ended. Her hair across his face. She stared at them and her face began to flame, as if she'd walked into a secret room, staring at something that shouldn't be seen. She tried to tear her eyes away, but she couldn't. It was only two cousins, she told herself, it's nothing! And yet the intertwined bodies on the floor had something in them that made her fear. She ran out of the dell.

'They're in there, Jonathan!'

'Oh, thank God.'

'Run and tell Emmeline they're here. I'll bring them up.' She mustn't let him see them. He walked up and she rushed back to the dell.

'Wake up!' she said, shaking Michael, then Lily.

'Ah,' said Michael, looking up first from Lily's arms where he lay. 'You found us.'

'We've been looking everywhere.' Lily was stirring.

'We like it here,' he sighed. He closed his eyes again.

'No, no! Up you get.' She hauled him up. She was furious – but what could she say? That they hid too well? That they shouldn't go to sleep? She should be happy that they were so close, so eager to be friends. She hauled Lily to her feet, too, biting back words.

'Come on,' she said. 'Let's go back to the house.' They followed her, meekly enough. Emmeline and Verena were relieved, delighted, told Michael and Lily off for scaring them, said they couldn't have any pudding. Then that was that for them, the event was over, put in the scrapbook of memories that didn't matter. The jolting fear in Celia faded – but something remained, a thin, nervous misgiving.

'What do they think about Germany in America?' Rudolf asked Jonathan at the table. 'The press here say that they're creating more industry. Perhaps Germany might be an area to take the meats.' Celia's heart broke over how much Rudolf liked Jonathan, wanted to talk to him. She fiddled with the engagement ring, unfamiliar, heavy.

Celia thought of her last time in Germany – just after the war. Her cousin Johann's body wrecked by Passchendaele, his mind fogged with pain and memories that made him cry out at night. How the neighbours gossiped about Celia and so Heinrich thought it best to leave, and they all travelled to Baden Baden, ostensibly to find a husband for Hilde, really because they wanted Celia to marry Johann. And then her night with Tom, ruining all their plans. Rudolf had said that the Crash had hit them hard, they had even less money, and Johann and Hilde were still unmarried although Hilde had a job assisting in the local school.

'I'm not sure, sir. In fact, I'd hazard a guess that going into Germany now would be nothing short of a disaster. I wouldn't do it.'

'Ah,' said Rudolf. 'What would you do then?'

Jonathan began to talk and Celia saw Rudolf, slow, old, sometimes lost, capturing Jonathan into his net of plans. She watched her father, then looked at her mother. She wasn't speaking, but she too was casting a net, Celia in a white dress, marrying Jonathan, made respectable, rich.

'America might still be an excellent market,' mused Rudolf. 'If we went slowly this time.'

'Oh yes, America,' said Verena. She was weaving, they were both threading the images, Celia surrounded in flowers, a gold ring on her finger.

She knew her parents were holding back, but really they wanted to talk about the wedding, how they would have a ceremony in Stoneythorpe, how Celia might be the beginning of a re-entry into English society: 'My daughter, married to the American millionaire. The Corrigans, do you know them? One of the best families in Connecticut.'

She said nothing, watched Verena smile at Jonathan, attempt to weave a spell of charm, all desire and need.

She looked down at her wine glass, drew her finger through the cut flowers on the side.

'Are you sure you won't come with me?' Jonathan asked the night before he left. He'd been called back to America by his father. The business needed him.

They were in her room, cramped, late at night. She couldn't bear to speak to him in Arthur's room, which he'd been staying in, so she made him sneak over to hers after everyone had gone to sleep.

'I can't now. Just five more months. Let me get this lot on their feet.'

'Of course.'

The words sounded so clear as she said them, real. Cramped in her tiny room, still full of her childhood books, ornaments she'd collected, pink cushions and brass models of horses. 'I promise. Michael longs to go back to America.'

He raised his eyebrow. 'Maybe. Well, anyway. I'll tell my parents to expect you soon. I'll take a house for us.'

'I think they should all come,' she heard herself say. Verena, Rudolf, Emmeline, Mr Janus, Albert and Lily, all together with them in the New York townhouse that Jonathan was going to take. 'I'll persuade them.'

'You will?' His face was disbelieving, shot over with relief.

'Yes. There's nothing for them here. Emmeline might be harder to convince. But if we take her over before Mr Janus comes back – it would be fait accompli. Not even he could resist that. And there's lots of demonstrating to be done in America.'

'But I thought you said they'd never leave.'

'I thought that. But my father – he was so interested in Winter Meats overseas. He's perhaps not as stuck here as I thought. They have to sell this place sooner or later.'

'If you think you could convince them.'

'I can.'

She could, she felt sure she could. It was convincing herself that she couldn't vouch for. But he didn't ask her, and so she didn't have to say – and the words hung, heavy and unspoken in her mind.

'Well, that's wonderful then.'

'Isn't it?' He couldn't see through to her heart and the truth. She wished she couldn't. She didn't want to talk any more. Instead, she put her arms around him and drew him close – and then they were on her bed, her small single bed, falling together, and he was holding her close and whispering something in her ear and his words were growing louder, his mouth hot against her skin and she drew him closer to her and held on.

INTERLUDE

Michael tried hard. Did he remember Stoneythorpe? If he was born here, the place was surely deep in his bones. He walked all around the house, trying to see if his memory caught to a door, a wall, a view and said, yes, you were here. But it did not. It was always remote to him. But then, everything was when he was not with Lily. Even the adults were gauzy and indistinct when he was not with Lily. Only she made everything clear.

He held his bear tight. New York grew fainter, the outlines of the city less straight in his mind. But not his life with the Whetstones. That was painted hard and bright across his eyes, with him late at night, always there. Mama wanted him to forget and his heart sank that he could not, no matter how kind and loving she was to him, how much she bought for him, their house was always there, tormenting him, the beatings, the cruelty, the hatred. So he had to pretend he had forgotten, that it was all behind him now. 'Children forget,' he had heard his mother say to his aunt. He had to act as if those days were over – but at night, he closed his eyes and there was someone beating him again, locking him in the attic, never coming. He crept into Mama's bed and she held him tight.

He would not forget. But the only person he could tell was Lily. He told her – and she listened to all of it. And then, after a while, he didn't want to tell anyone but her – it was the stories she knew, the whole world that was only hers.

There were so many secrets in this house. That's what he hated the most about it. He knew he was lucky to be away from the Whetstones, that Mama had rescued him, and he was safe here. But still. Sometimes he wanted to say: *Why won't you tell me anything? Who was my father?* The adults thought they were playing

African explorers. And they were, some of the time. But more and more they were exploring the house. They wanted to find things. Uncover secrets.

'After all,' said Lily, 'if they won't tell us, we'll have to find out for ourselves.'

Mama said she wanted him to be happy, not think about the past. She'd told him not to talk much about what happened with Arthur because it would only upset everyone. Not that he had much to say since no one had told him what was happening. They wouldn't even let him come to the funeral.

He didn't want to talk. He wanted to ask questions. There was so much he didn't know, years to make up for because he hadn't been here. But Mama said, 'Oh, it's not worth worrying about. Go out and play!' When he asked her about her brother, who he was named after, she just said, 'He died in the war. He was killed going over to fight.' And he knew because of the way she looked up to the side and fiddled with her hands that she wasn't telling him the truth. And sometimes he even thought there was something odd with the story of Great-Aunt Deerhurst giving him away. No one would ever talk about it.

He hated Great-Aunt Deerhurst. It was wicked to say but he did. She had sent him to misery when he could have grown up here, been with Mama and Lily – and Grandpapa, who let him stuff his pipe. He hated her so much that he wanted to ask questions about her too, so he knew exactly who it was he should hate. But no one would tell him.

'We must try to forget about it,' said his mother. 'It was a terrible thing, but it is in the past.'

'Oh, the adults are always lying,' Lily said. She was obsessed with Aunt Louisa, Aunt Deerhurst's daughter, who had been married to Arthur and died. 'We need to find out what really happened to her. No one will *ever* talk about her,' she said. In one of the upstairs rooms – the ones that were supposed to be locked and never were – they'd found a bundle of things that Lily said must have been Louisa's. A photo of a pretty girl with thick fair hair, a small photo of some older people who were maybe her parents. There were two trunks of what looked like clothes. Lily pulled a few dresses out, pushed them back. There was a pile of books on the floor, novels about love that she opened, cast aside. 'Soppy stuff!' she said.

In one of the old rooms, they'd found a pile of newspapers stuffed in a corner. First of all, they'd thought they were just rubbish – and then they'd realised. All of them were about a trial involving Arthur.

'Look at that,' said Lily, sitting back on her heels. 'Amazing. They thought Uncle Arthur killed her.'

Emmeline had told Lily that it had been a terrible accident, that Aunt Louisa had fallen off a cliff. Mama hadn't told him anything at all about Aunt Louisa. He'd asked once and all Mama would say was that she had died just after the war.

'I had no idea,' breathed Lily. They spent hours reading the articles, discussing them.

'There's so much in here about being German,' he said. 'Decline of a noble family.'

'Mama always tells me to say I am entirely English,' said Lily. 'Easier that way.'

For the next few days, they stole bread and biscuits from the kitchen, sneaked it upstairs, and sat over the newspapers, read all the stories. 'It's not our fault,' Lily said again. 'If only they'd tell us.'

After that, she was even more obsessed with Louisa. One time he came up after going down to get cake and found her lying face down on a pile of gowns.

'Lily?'

'I'm trying to be her,' she said. 'I'm trying to feel what it was like to be her.' She paused. 'Mama probably knows exactly where my father is in Spain, but she won't say.'

'Really?'

'Father was always planning things and Mama would never say what. So I think she knows where he is. Maybe Aunt Celia does too.'

They wrote to an address Lily had for Mr Janus – he'd given it to her in secret before he left. They used their pocket money, gave it to Dorrie from the village who came in to clean, to take the letters to the post office and buy stamps. Michael didn't have much to write because he'd never met Mr Janus but he liked to help Lily. She wrote pages and pages to her father, all about the days at Stoneythorpe, how she did miss London, but then Michael had arrived! Michael wondered if he shouldn't really be looking over her shoulder when she wrote about him. But she didn't seem to mind and nothing made him happier than reading those words: *Michael is so much fun! We play explorers. We have found so many things in the house.*

And they had. Secrets. One afternoon, while everybody was at tea, they crept into Grandmama's room. On her bedside table were stacks of murder mysteries that she should have taken back to the library. They looked into her vases and found dead spiders, rusty keys. And a purse filled with hundreds of pounds.

Michael kept one secret from Lily: he was Grandpapa's favourite. In the daytime, sometimes, or after dinner, he'd beckon Michael into his study and then he'd talk to him about his old life in Germany, his boyhood and growing up. Sometimes he'd get out his photograph album and they'd look at all the family photos.

Michael lied to Lily and told her that Grandpapa was just lecturing him about how to run the business one day. That seemed to satisfy her.

But then, he had heard another lie. His mother saying that she would go back to New York to see Jonathan in six months. But those months were passing and there was still no mention of leaving. Not that he wanted to go. He wanted to stay here. But still. Adults said they told the truth and they did not.

Rudolf turned over the pages of the photos.

'We thought your mother might marry Johann,' Grandpapa said. 'But children do what they want to do.'

That made him dizzy. Instead of here, he might be living in Germany, the son of someone called Johann.

'My father is dead,' he said. 'Mama said my father was dead.' He had been a soldier. Sometimes, at night, when he woke up and couldn't sleep, Michael told himself about his father: he'd been a prince, the owner of a chocolate factory, a pilot who flew round and round the world and saw every animal and the pyramids in Egypt.

Rudolf nodded. 'Truly sad.'

But there should be a picture of his father in the photograph album. There should be a photograph of him, next to his mother.

'Don't you have a photograph of him?'

Rudolf shook his head. 'I don't think so. But I am very behind with the book. I haven't even got a photograph of you yet. We should have one done.'

And so they did. Two days later they went into town. Rudolf and Michael stood in front of a man with a black sheet over his head and smiled. He wished Lily was there, just the two of them with their arms around each other. She might have flowers in her hair.

TWENTY-SIX

London, February 1931

'I don't think I can do it,' Celia finally said to Rudolf. 'It's been a year since I got here and the business is still losing money. We need to change.' She told him how she had been laying the foundations for restarting Flapper Foods. She had asked the department-store buyers what they thought – and each one had been delighted by the idea. The fact that she had made the business successful in New York was even more of a selling point.

'Beloved of *New York girls*,' breathed one of the buyers.

Rudolf shook his head. 'We have always been meat,' he said. 'That is our business.'

'Not mine,' she said. 'Mr Galss, Mr Pemberton, they all agree. Winter Meats is dying. If you want to save the house, you must try something else.' And she talked on until he was shrunken and defeated, agreeing, and she hated herself for having to make him face it, the balance sheets covered with minus signs, the stacks of meat nobody wanted to buy, dwindling orders, the loans from the banks. 'I'm sorry.'

She passed the news to Mr Pemberton. 'There is only one problem,' he said, solemnly. He looked at her hand. 'The ring will make people think you are not serious. You will marry, have children and forget about the business. Are you about to marry?'

She couldn't say yes.

'I advise you to remove it.'

That night, she slid the ring off, but she could not bear to remove it altogether so put it on the other hand.

And so she began. She hired a kitchen in town and a Mrs Craigmire, a young widow who had been a restaurant cook before her marriage, eager and energetic, said she had dozens of ideas to try. She went to the banks, talked about the recipes, and watched the men nodding and smiling, just as they had in New York.

'But what will the name be?' they asked. 'You cannot call it Flapper Foods.'

The men were right. She couldn't.

'What about Celia's Kitchen?' said Mrs Craigmire.

That was it! Something home-like. But not Celia. She needed another girl's name. She thought of all the girls she had known, Shep and the others, the girls at Winterbourne – then she thought of Violet! It was clear that all the girls in England dreamt of a New York girl.

'Miss Violet's Kitchen,' she said to Mrs Craigmire.

'Perfect,' the woman replied.

The banks agreed and there was money for her, pots of it, to start again, for advertising, packaging, developing, transport. When Mrs Craigmire had the recipes made up, they sent it to the Winter Meats factory, canned them, tested them.

'I've called the business after Violet,' she wrote to Jonathan. 'Please tell her. I hope she'll like it.'

She went for meetings with London stores – Harrods, Selfridges, Harvey Nichols, Liberty. Once they had delivered the first orders, she would put the ring back on, go to America to Jonathan.

'Come on! We'll be late for the show.'

Celia held Michael's hand tight. Already he was growing up. A month ago, Emmeline had made a decision.

'Those children have been running wild. We will get them a tutor for the mornings – so when we move to town, they're ready for school.'

'Well, I can see the point of that,' Celia said, grudgingly. Actually, she should have thought of it herself. Michael had been so happy at Stoneythorpe that she'd put his education out of her mind. He was quick and intelligent – but she supposed he did need to be taught things: Latin verbs, comprehension, algebra.

She had been remiss, so grateful to have him back that she hadn't wanted to lose a single bit of him, not even to school.

Emmeline had sent to Winchester for some tutors, ones who could cover both a boy's and girl's curriculum. Of course, as she was told, it was quite unorthodox, children of this age should have separate classes. But one tutor was all they could afford.

They hadn't had many applications in the beginning. Emmeline said she supposed all the best teachers were in school these days. They called in the last one. A tall, thin man walked in, youngish, fair haired. He had an unfortunate squint, otherwise you might call him handsome.

'Do sit down,' said Emmeline. She gave the introductions. Mr Brennan said he'd been a schoolmaster in Kent but was desiring more individual contact. 'School is like a factory,' he said, 'turning out children who are all the same.'

'Our children are rather different to the normal,' Celia said. She kept talking and Emmeline chipped in and Mr Brennan smiled and looked at them both, open, honest. He had a blob of darkness on his right eye, as if the pupil had flowed out of its boundaries, a teardrop. Celia looked away.

'We have to give him the position,' Celia said to Emmeline, after he had left the room. 'He's the best.'

Emmeline nodded. 'I like him. He's one of those people you feel like you've known forever as soon as you meet them. But the children should see him before we commit. He almost feels familiar. Lucky us.'

They called down Michael and Lily and introduced him. They watched them talk to him, saw Michael and Lily blossom under his words.

'So it is agreed,' they said. 'You start next week.'

The children had taken to Mr Brennan, working with him every morning. Michael was coming on in his studies, doing particularly well, Mr Brennan said, at mathematics. Sometimes, Celia would walk into the sitting room and Michael was so busy reading that he no longer ran to her. He was already moving away from her, as he should, little by little, going out into the world. She looked back at her own younger self, so fascinated by looking into her own soul, how her parents had only been shadowy figures in the background of her thoughts on the future, hoped that he wouldn't be the same.

'You are lucky children,' Emmeline was saying, stiffly. She disapproved of Celia's idea to take Michael and Lily to London. Albert did have a holiday from school but he had fallen behind with his work so he had had to forfeit it. 'Lucky Samuel's not here,' she added.

'He'd have taken him out ages ago,' Celia said, but without force. Pretending that Mr Janus was coming back seemed to her a ridiculous farce. He was either too ensconced there to ever come home – or he was dead. Otherwise he would have written. She had tried to suggest – gently – that it might be worth thinking of another future. But Emmeline wouldn't listen, even to the most delicate of hints. The minute Celia mentioned Mr Janus, she changed the subject – or turned furious.

'At least my children know who their father is,' she said. 'Don't you think he's got a right to know? You need to tell him. And you need to tell Tom.'

'No! He wouldn't want to know. He – he doesn't want me.'

'But Michael's still his son. You should tell him.'

'No.' Their argument circled, hopeless, resentful.

Even Celia's idea of today's trip had taken some negotiation. She had decided to treat Michael in London – after all, he'd never been. Of course, Lily had to come too. Celia had to plead. 'But Michael won't go without her. Please.'

They were going to see the whole of London: the Changing of the Guard, Big Ben and the Houses of Parliament, and go to Leicester Square to look at the theatres and eat a meal. Celia had it all planned out. They were going to have an enjoyable, pleasant day in London. Like two normal sisters and their children. That was what people did, wasn't it?

'We'll go to London,' Emmeline eventually said angrily to Celia. 'But don't think I think this is a good idea.'

Finally, on a chill February morning, they were on a train up to London, the children excitedly looking out of the window, spotting farm animals in fields, bonfires, the decorated boats in canals running alongside them. Celia looked at them, Lily and Michael, dressed in their best coats, their shoes newly shined. Michael had wet his hair to flatten it and Lily had spent extra time on her plaits. Her son and her niece, so happy together. What more could she want? She had her son. Everything else was small, little things that didn't matter.

Emmeline shook her head and turned to the window.

Then they were in Victoria station and caught up in the swell of crowds, moving forwards. 'Awful crowds,' said Celia, as she always did, but she didn't mean it really, she felt exhilarated by the movement, the rush, and the anonymity. She could be anyone. They headed out and caught a taxi to the Changing of the Guard.

'Will we see the King?' asked Michael.

'Definitely,' she said. 'Look very carefully at the windows. I am sure the King will poke his nose out.'

They watched the Guards, took a bus to the Houses of Parliament and Westminster Abbey.

'Now, time for lunch,' said Celia. 'Then perhaps we might go to a toy shop.' What she really wanted was to visit the department stores in Oxford Street and Knightsbridge and look at the food halls.

'Let's sit the children together,' said Emmeline at a restaurant she had chosen near Green Park. 'Then we can talk.'

Celia nodded. 'Choose what you'd like,' she said to the two of them. She smiled at their faces; they were delighted because they were sitting at their own table, like grown-ups. Michael patted her hand. Her heart wrenched. She would never send him to school, didn't want him to go away, preparing for the world, where his future would matter to him more than she would. Hadn't it been like that for her once, eager to leave her parents behind? She never thought she'd one day be the same, a barrier to escape, a block between the world and the freedom of it, the feeling of lightness in his bones. She'd thought it would be the two of them forever.

'Ice cream, please. I think.' Michael was so polite, it made her proud.

'Chocolate? You just tell the waiter what you want. But choose something proper, some hot food, too.'

He nodded. Soon he wouldn't even want chocolate ice cream and it would be too babyish for him. Everyone said that children as they approached adulthood were horrid, always angry. She couldn't imagine Michael like that. But still, he was growing, his voice was changing. He'd be a man. He'd grow up, make his own life. Without her.

Emmeline was talking about the royal princesses. Celia gazed at the menu. The modern girl, working in London, probably had to come to places like this to eat her supper. With Miss Violet's Kitchen, she'd be able to look after herself – and much nicer and cheaper food too. They just had to get the canning to work.

'Hello Celia.'

She looked up and Tom was standing there. Her heart stopped and she turned away, couldn't look at him, his dark eyes, smooth face, dark brows, the hair just over his forehead. She hadn't seen him since the trial, when they'd argued.

'What are you doing here?'

He didn't answer, looked over at Emmeline. Her sister looked at the ground. Celia looked back at Tom. 'What's happening?'

They both looked away.

'You arranged this.'

Emmeline didn't reply.

'What's going on?'

'Don't make a fuss, Celia,' Emmeline said, quietly. 'We're in a restaurant.'

'I thought you were both expecting me.'

'I lied,' Emmeline said. 'She didn't know.'

Celia turned to Emmeline. 'What are you doing? What have you done?'

'The best thing. Sit down, Tom.'

Celia looked over at the children. They were still gazing at the menu. 'No. Tom, you have to go.'

'Stay,' said Emmeline. 'For half an hour.'

The air stood still. It felt as if there was a battle, the air crossing. They were all holding invisible swords.

'I should go,' said Tom. 'This isn't what I thought it was.'

'What did you think it was?'

'Sit down, Tom.' Emmeline's voice was more urgent.

He looked over at Celia. 'It's been a long time. You look well.'

'Thank you. So do you.'

Tom touched his ear. He'd done the same as a child, a nervous tic. 'How is everyone?' He was still standing.

'Arthur died in America. He fell from a window.'

He nodded. 'I did read. Terrible.'

Of course.

'I wrote to your family. Perhaps they didn't receive it.'

Rudolf hadn't said. She hadn't seen Tom's handwriting. She'd recognise it, out of a million letters, she'd know it.

'How is your company doing?' She cast an eye over to Michael. He was listening to Lily, looking at other people's ice creams.

'Not too bad. 'Now I have moved into the accounts side, there is a lot of business. No company has their accounts up to date. You'd think they would.'

She stared at his hand. No ring – but not all men wore them. He could be married, have two, three children. He probably was. He was thirty-two now, handsome, rich. He could marry anyone. She imagined him in front of a series of numbers, adding and subtracting.

'And what about the rest of your family?'

'They're well.'

She wanted to tell him everything, that the house was falling apart, might have to be sold, that Miss Violet's Kitchen was on the way to success – but perhaps not fast enough to save them all. But she feared he'd say what he'd done before, when she'd poured out her heart, remind her he wasn't their servant any more, that they had separate lives now.

'Do you hear much from your family in Germany?' Tom asked.

Her uncle. Heinrich. His father. 'My father's had a few letters. They don't have much money after the Crash.' That night in Baden Baden, Tom's fury, Heinrich's refusal to see him as his son.

Tom looked at her. 'Does he ask after me?'

'I don't know.' Celia had asked Rudolf about Heinrich, the week before, wondered if he ever wrote about Tom. Rudolf said he didn't. She knew he didn't really write much at all. 'He's old now.'

'I wondered if he'd died, if that was why you invited me here.'

She looked up at him and the restaurant whirled around her and was gone. 'I'm sorry for what I said last time. It was very wrong of me.'

'Last time?'

In front of the British Museum, him telling her she should prepare herself for the worst and so she'd lost her temper, incensed that anyone might not think her brother innocent.

Well, you'd know all about being a murderer. Wouldn't you.

'Oh, the trial. That was so long ago. You were upset about your brother. Only natural.'

He'd practically forgotten it. And it was seared hard on her soul, shouting at him, running from him.

'He was found not guilty, after all,' he said. 'So your faith in him was right.'

She nodded. Arthur danced in front of her, trying to pull her out to the balcony, throwing himself off. *You'd be flying. And then, the moment before you hit the ground, how would that be? You'd see the truth then, wouldn't you?*

'He was in a bad way at the end,' she said. She couldn't say more, not even to Tom.

'Stoneythorpe may have to be sold,' she then said. 'We're trying to persuade Papa. It's in a bad way, almost falling down. I was hoping my business might save it, but I don't know.'

He paused. 'That's a shame. I grew up there,' he said. 'Even if it wasn't always happy.'

'I know.' *Don't start,* she wanted to say. *Don't start telling me how it wasn't ever a friendship and you were just paid to be kind to me. And you never* wanted *to ride with me or hunt for tadpoles or any of it.*

The waiter approached carrying a chair. 'Sir?'

'It doesn't look quite right, standing,' broke in Emmeline. 'You need to sit down.'

'We're going,' said Celia.

'No we're not. He can sit for a minute.'

'The gentleman will have to sit or leave.'

'Just for a moment.' Lily and Michael were still deep in conversation. They wouldn't move, she thought. She couldn't let Tom go, not yet. They would exchange words – and then he'd go and never know. She drank from her tea again. 'How about you?' she managed. 'What about your family?'

'Missy is a nurse now. She's married, living in London. Maggie is married too, in Brighton. Mother lives with her. She's getting old.'

'Everybody's getting old,' said Emmeline. She flashed Tom her wide smile, the one that had worked so well on Sir Hugh and the rest when she was young. She looked beautiful, suddenly. A strange feeling of jealousy touched Celia's heart. She shook it away. She looked down. And when she raised her head, everything had crashed. Michael was at the table. 'Mama,' he said. 'The waiter asked if we wished to order. Can we have ice creams before anything?'

Tom looked at her. 'Mama?'

She flushed. 'Yes. Anything. Off you go.'

Tom stared at him. 'You're Celia's son?'

He nodded. Celia was stabbed with a desire for him to be polite, hold out his hand, impress.

'Go back and sit with Lily,' said Celia. 'No – actually, we should go. We need to go now.'

Tom looked at her as Michael trotted back. 'He's your son. You found him? You said they took him away from you.'

'I found him in America.' She couldn't trust herself to say more. 'We should go.'

'No, we shouldn't,' said Emmeline. 'I'm going to stay. Lily!' she raised her voice. 'Both of you, come over here.'

'That must have been hard. Did the father help? The soldier.'

Celia shook her head.

'Did you tell him?'

'No.'

'Why not? At least for the boy. He should know who his father is.' *I never did*, he didn't need to say.

'I know. But I thought he wouldn't care or want to know. He probably wouldn't.'

'Is he married?'

'Probably.'

'Don't you think you owe it to the child?'

Michael and Lily returned, shyly hanging back. Tom held out his hand. 'Hello, I'm Mr Cotton, but you can call me Tom. It's nice to meet you. What's your name?'

'Michael. It used to be Sebastien. Sometimes I forget which one I am.'

'Let's go to the lavatory, Lily,' said Emmeline.

'I don't want to.'

'I do. You're coming with me.' They stood up, left in a flurry of skirts.

'Oh, I see.' Tom nodded. 'So you used to live in America. How do you find England?'

Celia listened to Michael chattering on about the boat over when he was seasick. *Can't you see?* she wanted to say. *Can't you see what's going on?* Even Emmeline had seen his sister Missy's eyes in Celia's son. Tom was asking Michael how old Lily was and what they liked to play. Michael started talking about hide and seek and chasing frogs.

'Oh yes,' said Tom, smiling. 'Your Mama and I used to do that sort of thing in the garden when we were younger.'

Celia stared at him. It had always been her bringing up the memories – he always tried to push them away. But there he was, conjuring them up again.

Michael smiled and starting talking about Lily again.

'They certainly are very good friends,' said Celia.

'That I can see!' replied Tom.

But can't you see anything else? She gazed at Tom, talking to Michael so kindly. *How can you be so blind?*

Celia was back in Baden Baden, walking down to the lake with Tom, the stolen bottle of wine, telling him she'd had other men, that it didn't matter, feeling his arms around her, wanting to tell him she loved him, pulling him close. *Go on*, she said. *Yes.*

'I like chocolate ice creams too,' said Tom.

Michael said, sadly, 'I love ice creams. But they go too quickly.' She and Hilde had wandered Baden with ice creams, trying to look like girls of good family so that men might come and speak to them. Then they saw Tom. And later he'd pulled her down to him by the lake and she'd suspected, known even, that it wasn't really her, he just wanted a woman, but she had fallen into him and welcomed it and never wanted it to stop.

'Oh dear. Shall we order you another one?'

Michael nodded. Tom called over a waiter, a fat smiling one who was passing.

'Another ice cream, please?'

'How kind of Papa,' said the waiter, jovially. 'Another ice cream for his little boy.'

'He's not my Papa,' said Michael. But the waiter was already ambling off to the next table.

'He's not my ...' Tom had been talking too. Then he trailed off, stared at Michael, then Celia. 'He's ...' He stopped. 'Celia?'

She looked down.

Tom looked at Michael. 'You told me you were nearly nine. What's your birthday?'

Michael grinned happily. 'Well, I never knew that. Not in America. The Whetstones said it didn't matter. But Mama told me 12th April 1922. So I have a birthday now. Next birthday, Lily said she was going to make me a cake and we'll have a proper party. You can come too, if you like.'

'Thank you.' Tom's voice was strangled.

Michael started talking about his party again.

Celia couldn't look up. She knew she had to. She couldn't. Tom would be looking into her eyes.

'Celia,' he said. 'Is that right? 12th April 1922?'

'Yes,' she said, bringing her head up, finally meeting his eyes. 'That was the day he was born.'

More ice cream arrived with the jolly waiter. They all smiled. 'Eat up, sonny,' he said. 'You're a real ice-cream lover, I can tell.'

The waiter walked off. He must be used to it, Celia thought, so many people in restaurants talking over love, war, relationships ending, beginning. He must bring women their food when they were weeping, watch arguments, take away half-cleared plates.

Tom was still looking at her.

'So he was conceived in ... the summer before.'

'Yes.'

'With—'

She shook her head. 'The soldier was a story. I lied.'

'So ...'

'Yes. He's—'

Tom put his head on his hand. 'I – there aren't. How did this happen?'

'What?' asked Michael, happily spooning up chocolate ice cream.

Tom looked at him. Celia's mind felt as if it was crumbling, sparking into flames – *why hadn't she told him? What had she done?* She should have told him the minute she'd come back with Michael, as Emmeline said.

Tom was shaking his head. 'I should have thought. I should have guessed.'

'No.'

'Why didn't you say anything? Why didn't you tell me? Don't you think you should have told me?' The colour was rising in his face now, the anger too. She'd seen this before, in Baden when he lost his temper with Heinrich. 'Why didn't you? What's wrong with you?'

Michael dropped his spoon, his face crossed over with fear. 'Mama? What's happening?'

Celia forced herself to breathe. 'Michael. Go to the door and wait for me. I know you haven't finished your ice cream. I'll get you a cake on the way home.' Michael shook his head. 'Go, please.'

He gulped down more ice cream. 'What about Lily?'

'I'll buy her some more too.'

'Don't worry, Celia. I'll go. They haven't finished.' Tom smiled at the child. 'Go and sit back at your table. Lily will be back in a moment. Take the ice cream with you.'

He picked up the glass dish, nodded obediently. 'Goodbye, sir.'

Tom looked at him, dazed. 'Goodbye. No, not goodbye. I'll see you again.'

'Go to the table, please,' said Celia.

He nodded, confused, headed off back to the table. Emmeline and Lily swished past, sat with him.

Celia wanted to stand up to leave, but Tom seized her hand, hard. 'What's going on? Is he really mine?'

'He's mine.'

'Stop it, Celia. You know what I mean. How could you have kept this from me? How could you? I can't believe this of you. You told me in Paris that he was a soldier's. And you were lying to me all along.'

Her heart was rising. He was still holding her hand, hissing at her. Then her blood rushed and her heart exploded. 'Well, what did you think?' she said, trying to keep her voice down, failing because the sound billowed out at the sides. 'You know what we did. Didn't you ever think there might be a consequence? No! Of course you didn't. Because you're only ever thinking about yourself. How you've been excluded or this or that. Nothing about the rest of us. You never thought that I might need help. You just forgot all about it, carried on nursing your wounds the way you always did. And he was gone for so long, there wasn't a point in telling you. And now I have him back. Well, you never cared before, not for me or anything. Why should you care now?' She was standing now, and the people next to her could probably hear what she was saying. But she didn't care.

'Celia—'

'Don't tell me to calm down. Or whatever you're going to say. Michael's mine. Not yours. You never wondered. You didn't even really want to, that night. I just happened to be there. And it's me who's been wanting him, searching for him all this time. Not you. You probably don't want him either. I bet you've got a wife and a perfect family and this would just be an interruption. Well, I don't care. He and I – we don't need anyone else.'

'I don't have a wife. Or a child. I wanted one. I've always wanted a son.' He held out his hand to the table where Michael sat, looking out at the passers-by on the street.

Suddenly, a terrible vision loomed in Celia's head; Tom wealthy and prepossessing, giving Michael everything she couldn't, expensive schooling, toys, lessons in whatever he wanted. Michael preferring him – because he was glamorous, rich, and lived in London. The pair of them driving off in a new car, leaving her behind.

'You have to go,' she said. 'Please. Please.'

'Celia. He's my son. I need to – understand this.'

'Please go. Or I will. But I don't want to drag him away.'

He stood up. 'If you insist. But will you meet me again, just to talk?'

She nodded. Anything to get rid of him. 'Of course. I'll write.'

'Can I say goodbye to him?'

'Quickly.'

'Thank you. Thank you, Celia.' He walked away, spoke to Michael. She could see him wanting to touch Michael, catch his hand. Emmeline held out her hand and he shook it. Then Tom left and Celia went over, sat there, staring at the dish of melting ice cream.

'Come on,' she said. 'Let's go home.'

'I thought we were eating lunch?' Emmeline looked up. 'They need to eat, Celia. More than ice cream. I'm going to order them some chicken and potatoes. You can wait if you like.'

Celia looked at her sister. 'How could you?'

'Who was that man?' Lily asked.

'It's just someone I used to know. When I was young.'

'Like me and Michael.'

'Yes, like you two.'

'Except you're not really friends with him any more,' broke in Michael. 'Lily and I will be friends forever.'

'Well, you're cousins too, so you'll always be together.'

'Always?'

'That's right. Like me and Emmeline. Always together.' She glowered at her sister.

'I was right. You'll see.'

'I'm going to the lavatory.'

'I'll order you some lunch.'

'Don't.' Celia rushed off to the lavatory, filled the washbasin and plunged her hands in cold water. She doused her face, so it wet her hair, looked at herself in the mirror, eyelashes sodden. She wanted to wash it all away, everything, the last hour, everything. But she couldn't. The past, Tom, was lodged hard under her skin.

That night, there were a pile of figures to read from Winter Meats – still all minuses even though they'd sold five factories – and some from Miss Violet's Kitchen, good but not enough. Celia sat down to write to Jonathan. *I need more time. I know I promised you six months. But I have found there is so much to do. But I will be with you in a year. Give me more time. Please.* She couldn't leave. Everybody was depending on her. She asked him to come to her. *You could come for as long as you like,* she said. If only there were two of her – one to live in America and one to live here. She meant to write to Tom, couldn't.

She walked downstairs to put Jonathan's letter for posting.

'What are you doing there?' Emmeline came around the corner, her hair escaping her bun.

'Leaving my letter. Don't come and talk to me.'

'Oh don't be silly, Celia. It had to be done. I did you a favour. He needs to know.'

'Now he hates me more.'

'He doesn't hate you. He's as moony-eyed over you as you are over him. It's just that neither of you can see it. And it's better that way, if you ask me. But he had to know the truth.'

'Why? Why tell him? You told me I was wrong ever to like him.'

'You were. You are – don't try and pretend you don't still. But you should hear Mr Janus on this. Men can't escape their responsibilities. Certainly not him.'

'You didn't think he might give us *money*? You're not saying *that*?'

Emmeline turned, flushed. 'I just think he needs to know his responsibilities, that's all. Why should we shoulder it all?'

'We? What do you mean – *we*? I am. Who paid for us to go to London? Me!'

'You and Michael living here, with us, eating the food, in the house that is barely standing.'

'I'm running the business! Making it work again! I've been working for it every day! Leave me alone. Go and talk to someone else. Haven't you done enough?' She rushed upstairs, wished she could take Michael and flee from them all.

INTERLUDE

'You can tell me anything,' Mama had said to Michael in New York. They slept together in her room, cuddled up in the middle of her giant bed. Her clothes were thrown on the side and he loved that because the Whetstones had been so tidy. It was one mixed-up friendly monster of clothes and books and papers. Sometimes he perched Harvey the bear on top of it all. Then, he'd felt as if everything of Mama's was his, all shared. None of the 'this is mine and you can never touch it' like at the Whetstones'. At night, when they couldn't sleep, Mama told him everything, all about her childhood and her houses. But now they were back in England and there was nothing but unspoken words.

At first, he and Lily had been secret chasers. Hunters. They chased the secrets through the house. He had thought they were all about the past. But now – it was clear that the secrets weren't stopping. Now they were about the present as well. Jonathan wrote to him sometimes and to Mama and he tried to sound happy. Lily wrote to Mr Janus but he did not write back. If he did, Lily said, they could go to stay with him. For surely life was better there, clearer, more honest, than the net of lies and hypocrisy, small pettiness, untruths, that was Stoneythorpe.

Mr Brennan listened to their secrets. They talked about Spain and he took their letters for them. He told them about other things that the adults did not – the politics of the world, war. Lily listened. And Mr Brennan had ideas. He told Michael to draw. 'You have a talent. That will make sense of the world.'

And he drew and drew but still he had not made sense of things. New York, the past, Lily. And now the other man who'd met them in the restaurant, been so keen to speak to him. Mama and Aunt Emmeline had been so angry with each other on the way home, continued it when they'd got back. Michael had tried to ask about him but Mama said not to worry and Emmeline told him to ask Mama.

'Oh, who knows,' Lily said. 'Some adult thing.' She wanted to lie in Louisa's clothes again, draw them over her face. 'I'll make myself as beautiful as her.'

'You already are. More so.' But she wasn't listening. She didn't seem to want to listen to him at all. When he asked her questions, she shrugged. He begged her to play hide and seek and she told him she'd rather stay inside. She closed her bedroom door and only ever came to see him in his. He tried everything to please her. He even drew a picture of a drawing room for Aunt Emmeline, since she wanted it so much, but Lily snorted at it, said he was giving in to the seduction of *things*.

Then he did something to be ashamed of. One morning, he waited until she'd gone down to breakfast, then he crept into her room. He gazed around it. Pretty things sparkled and danced and caught the light, bracelets and necklaces, beads on a string, pink, green, blue, yellow, cream. He walked to the bedside table, picked up a handful of them, tangled together as if they'd been dozens of skeins of wool. There were some hung on the hooks on the wall, casually, as if she'd thrown them there. The chest of drawers had more of them, bits of bracelets and more beads. He walked over to the window ledge. It was covered in glass animals, three glass fish of different colours, a butterfly, a dog of pure black and a soft purple cat. He ran his finger over them. There must have been twenty of them, beautiful intricate little things. You could have them play and talk to each other, a little world of pretty toys. He picked up one of the blue fish. 'Please can I play with you?' it said to the purple cat. 'Don't leave me out again.' He wanted to take them out, capture the colours in his sketchbooks, but none of the colours he had were sufficiently beautiful.

'What are you doing?' He swung around. Lily was standing there. 'What are you doing in here?'

He stared at her, stammered. 'I meant, I meant to come to

look for you. Then I started looking at these. They're so beautiful. Where did you get them?'

'This is my room! I didn't say you could come in here.'

'I'm sorry.' He was still holding the purple cat in his hand. 'I just—'

'You just thought you'd be nosy, that's it, isn't it?'

'I'm sorry.' She was angry with him, so angry. Her face was red, eyes screwed up. 'I'm so sorry. I was wrong.' She was going to cry. She was going to cry in the middle of her bedroom and it was all his fault.

She sat down. 'Go away. Just go away.'

On Sunday, walking back from church, Lily caught up with him. 'I've decided to forgive you,' she said. 'But you know it was very wrong.'

'I'm sorry,' he said. 'I really am.'

'Don't do it again,' she said.

In return, he had to let her spy all over his room, go through all his things, read some of the letters he wrote in secret to his father.

'Now we are even,' she said. 'And it won't happen again.' It wouldn't. He'd seen how delicate, how breakable their friendship was. It was a glass heart, balanced on a window ledge – he had to watch it, hold it carefully, because if he dropped it again, it would always be lost.

TWENTY-SEVEN

About a month or so after Tom had met Michael in London, Celia had come down to the parlour and Michael was not there. She'd gone to the garden, expecting to see him running around with Lily. She gazed out, smiling. There he was, dashing about as she'd expected. But then her heart lurched. Tom was standing there as Michael showed him his favourite tree, inspecting it, running his hands over it. She threw open the French windows and rushed out into the garden.

'What are you doing here?' she panted, skirt wet from the damp grass.

'Mama!' shouted Michael. 'Look! There's a new spider laying eggs here. Mr Cotton found him.'

'Tom, please.' Celia seized his arm. 'I need to speak to you!'

'It's nice to see you too, Celia.' He was tall in his suit and smart shoes, his hair slicked back, his wide handsome face and her son's eyes looking at her. The scar of a shot wound on his cheek that filled her with pain because it reminded her of her brother.

Michael was happily peering into the tree trunk. She lowered her voice. 'What are you doing here?'

'What do you think? You rushed off so quickly we didn't have time to get acquainted.' He reached out and patted Michael on the head, the movement of his hand searing through Celia's soul. 'I must say he's a very fine young man, Celia. A real credit to you.'

'Mr Cotton bought me a present!' said Michael. 'Look, Mama.'

Celia noticed a large cardboard box at the foot of the tree. Her heart filled with dread. 'What is it?'

Michael took his hand away from the spiders. 'The most amazing thing, you must look.' He knelt down and undid the cardboard lid, reverently, lifted out a gleaming red toy car. He ran his finger over it. Celia didn't know much about cars. She supposed it must be the latest model.

'That looks very expensive,' she said. 'I hope you said thank you.' She heard her own voice, angry, pinched. She couldn't help it.

'He did,' said Tom. 'A very polite thank you.'

Michael held the car up. 'It's the most beautiful thing I've ever seen.' He rushed off, holding it high, making zooming noises.

Celia turned to Tom. 'How could you?'

'Look, Celia, I know I should have asked you first. But I wanted to see him – and I thought you'd say no.'

'So you come here and try to buy him with an expensive toy? Do you often just march into people's homes because you feel like it?'

'If my son is there, yes.'

Anger seized her. 'He's not yours! He's the soldier's. I was just trying to upset you.'

'Anyone can see that's not true.'

'You never cared about us before. Now you do. Why – because you didn't have the son you hoped? So you thought you'd have mine?'

'Celia. Be fair. I didn't even know he existed until two months ago.'

'You didn't think? You didn't think when I said I'd had a son – perhaps that he was yours?'

Tom shook his head. She thought she detected a little shame in it.

'Well, you should have done!'

'I know I should. But you could have told me.'

'And now you're here trying to take him away from me.'

'Celia – please.'

'I searched for him. I thought about him. I found him. You don't know what I had to do. And now you want to come in and get him.' Michael was running up to the French windows. Lily was standing there in a white pinafore. She was waving at him, running towards him, laughing. Michael wouldn't come back for a while now he was with her.

'I just want to get to know him.'

She drew a breath. 'Tell me the truth. If I'd have said to you, when we met, I had your child and he died, would you have been sad?'

'Of course.' But he looked at his feet.

'Would you? Or would you have said, *Let's look to the future. Some things happen and God understands.* And what about if I'd told you that they'd taken him away from me. Would you have tried to help me find him? Or would you say, *It was probably for the best.*'

'Celia. I can't say now what I would have said then. It was nearly ten years ago.'

'So I'm right. You would have thought it was right to give him away. You wouldn't have wanted a tie between us.'

'I don't know.'

'But I kept looking for him. And now I have him and he's handsome and polite and clever – you want some of him. Well, you can't!'

'Celia. Doesn't the past mean anything to you?'

'To me? You're the one who was always saying our friendship meant nothing and we had to forget about it, that you hated us for having been a servant here. You kept pushing me away.'

'I'm sorry. I know I did.'

'And now you want to be best friends again?'

'I wish you'd let me explain. I said we had to move on – well, don't you think so? I didn't want to tie you down, both of us down, to childhood – to promises then that we shouldn't keep.'

She leant her head against the tree. 'You weren't worried about tying me down. You're trying to be kind. You didn't want me.' His tanned face, the handsome flow between eyes and nose and mouth, the face that didn't love her, but still, reached out for her that night in the dark in Baden Baden, by the lake, when all time had seemed to stop.

He looked down.

'And you were angry with me over the whole Heinrich thing. That Rudolf wasn't your father. You hated me because of that.'

'Not *hated*. Celia, these words are all too strong. Why does everything have to be so dramatic?'

'Because it is! It is to me. My childhood friend tells me he doesn't want to see me again. Then I lose my child. And I get him back – and, oh! You have a change of heart.' She was back in Stoneythorpe now, in Emmeline's room and they were all scream-ing at her because the baby was coming. And then he was on her breast and she was holding him close and her heart surged with love for him. She felt sleep overwhelm her – and they said they'd take Michael, just to be sure. She woke up, her breasts hot with pain and Verena said he'd died.

'Celia. I just want to see my son.'

'He's my son. You can't claim him. I can deny it.'

'Celia. Can't we discuss this?'

'He's not a toy. I know what you're like. You're always so curious. You want to know things. You can't just come into our life because you feel like it then go off again. You grew bored with me. What's to say you wouldn't think the same way about him?'

'Of course I wouldn't.'

'How do I know? He's been through so much. I have to protect him. I can't have you jumping in and out.'

'You don't really think I'd do that, do you?'

'How can I tell?'

What she feared was that he'd take Michael away. Michael asking about his father, his words echoing in her mind. And those nights when she'd heard him telling himself stories about who his father was – a prince, the owner of a chocolate factory, the builder of hundreds of houses, the pilot of a round-the-world plane. She'd heard him talking about the same to Lily as well. And now here was a real-life father, who was rich and handsome, despite the faded scars, and came bearing toys. What if he preferred him?

'I wish you'd leave us alone. We were fine without you. We don't need toys.'

He shrugged. 'You win, Celia. I'll give you time. You can let me know when you're ready to see me. Will you walk back with me to the house?'

She nodded. He put his arm through hers, like any gentleman leading a lady, and his hand burnt her arm.

'The house is in a bad way. Needs a lot of repair.'

She looked up and saw it through his eyes, ramshackle back, windows broken, fallen chimneys, tiles missing on the roof, the ivy cutting into the brickwork. The house was splitting, more so every day.

'The foundations are strong. It's been here for years.'

'Don't you think you should sell it?'

'Emmeline and I did want to. But my parents refuse. And I love seeing Michael here,' she said. 'I'm trying to prop it up with the business. But even if I can't, I'm not sure we could sell it. I spoke to an agent and he said no one really wants such a big house; so much work as you say. People want a modern look.'

They continued up to the house.

'Will you let me say goodbye to him before I leave?' They were nearly at the French windows to the parlour.

'Of course. He'd be sorry not to say goodbye to you.' She shouted for Michael and he and Lily came careening out from the side of the house.

'Mr Cotton is going now,' she said, stiffly. 'He's keen to say goodbye before he goes.'

Lily jumped up. 'I like the car you bought Michael. Have you got a present for me?'

He shook his head. 'Maybe next time.' Celia stared at him and he looked away.

'When will you come back?' Michael was asking.

'I have to go away for a while. But as soon as I get back I will come and see you.'

'The minute you get back?'

'The minute.' He avoided Celia's eye.

Michael threw himself at Tom's legs and hugged him hard. 'Thank you for the car.' Then Lily was throwing herself at Tom, too. 'Thanks for Michael's car. Next time bring something for me!'

In a moment, they were both running off again, hurtling towards the trees.

'You certainly had an effect on them,' said Celia. She pushed open the door to the parlour and Verena was standing there.

'Oh! I heard you had a visitor, Celia. I thought it might be—' She broke off. 'Have we met?' She was holding out her hand to Tom, who had taken off his hat. She didn't recognise him, Celia realised. She saw the handsome face, fine clothes – and she had no idea who it was. Celia saw hope shine in her mother's eyes and her heart sank.

'Yes, Mama. Don't you remember? It's Tom Cotton.'

Verena's eyes widened – but you couldn't fault her composure. 'How nice to see you again, Tom,' she said, shaking his hand. Her manner and tone had changed, become less breathless. She was smiling in the distant way that you would to a waiter or a man in a hotel. Celia looked at Tom, and he had seen the change too. He straightened.

'Likewise, Mrs de Witt. I am glad to hear you are still here at Stoneythorpe.'

She smiled. 'Until we die. That is all we ask. Here until we die.'

He nodded. 'I am sure that will come to pass.'

'Mr Cotton has to go now,' said Celia, quickly.

'It's been marvellous to see you again, Mrs de Witt.' He gave another gallant sweep of his hat, replaced it.

Celia propelled Tom out of the room, into the hall. 'Now can you go?' she hissed.

'Why are you being like this?'

'Because I know you. You come in and out of my life. And what if you did the same to Michael, sometimes see him, sometimes not. You admitted it, practically.'

She closed the door against him, leant against it. A fat tear ran down her cheek. She didn't try to brush it away.

She would find a way to keep the house. She would double the efforts of Miss Violet's Kitchen. She would fill department stores with silver-covered jars and boxes. Wherever you looked there would be Miss Violet's Kitchen. Every girl would be eating it. She would support them all, no matter what. She would keep the family together, keep the house, keep them alive. Shops would be full of her glittering jars and cans and boxes, wrapped up like presents, held close by girls on the way home on the omnibus. She would get the business up and running and then be able to go back to Jonathan for a little while, start a new Miss Violet's Kitchen in the US and then come back here. She would save them all.

'And here is the map of the Secondary World,' a voice was saying. Celia was passing the schoolroom when she heard Mr Brennan's voice, booming out. The Secondary World? What did he mean? She stood outside, listening against the door. The voices had dropped and Lily and Michael were talking now. Could she just walk in? She and Emmeline had sat in on a few lessons and it had all gone swimmingly. Lily and Michael seemed so happy that they hadn't needed to enquire. And Michael was clearly learning something – she'd caught him deep in an algebra problem when she'd entered his room a few weeks ago. But what on earth was the Secondary World?

She knocked on the door and entered. Lily, Michael and Mr Brennan looked up – Mr Brennan smiling.

'Welcome,' he said. 'We were just deep in geography.'

Celia couldn't read the children's expressions. Lily looked almost hostile, she thought, Michael was maybe surprised. She seated herself at the back. Mr Brennan was talking about the geography of Europe. He held up his book, listed rivers, mountains, talked about plains and weather differences, oceans and currents. Michael and Lily were scribbling down the information in their exercise books. He quizzed them on what they had learnt and Lily answered more correctly than Michael. It was all entirely normal.

'Thank you,' she said. 'It has been nice to hear the lesson.'

They wished her goodbye. Lily was pleased to see her go, it was clear. Celia walked out, trying to shake off the misgiving.

Seventeen years ago, she'd walked in on Emmeline and Mr Janus reciting from *Romeo and Juliet*, seen nothing then. *Why didn't you know?* Verena asked her. *You were there.* But she didn't know, saw nothing.

And now this? What was a Secondary World? Her mind spooled into magical worlds, second lives, parallel ghostly places, the stuff of stories. She wanted to go there, wherever it was. She wanted to take all of them there, far away from reality, live forever.

PART THREE

TWENTY-EIGHT

Stoneythorpe, March 1933

Two years had gone by and the only way you could see the passage of time was on the children, Michael nearly eleven, Lily fourteen. It was as if Lily was gaining more colour every day, redder lips, black hair, like a Snow White in the midst of the forest. Her beauty blazed so hard that sometimes Celia had to look away, it was too new, scorched you with its ardour and its hope. When they went up to town, men stared at her in a way that infuriated Celia. 'She's only a child!' she wanted to shout. But she could see it in their faces, they didn't see her as a child, but a beautiful thing that had the power to burn them too – unless they seized it and made it their own. But Lily didn't seem to notice. Her thoughts were always elsewhere.

Michael too – he was no longer a boy. Every day, sloughing off the old self, becoming new, galloping towards manhood. She remembered herself being desperate for adulthood, the freedom she thought she'd get, not understanding how cruel the world was. Michael still came to her to be held – but he didn't creep into her bed any more. So if she woke up late at night, she would tiptoe into his room, watch him sleep, pleased that he still held his bear to him, kept the wooden horse under his pillow. She wished she could catch his dreams by holding him – but he lay there, serene and absorbed, far from her.

Jonathan had come over once for Christmas and he had meant to visit again – but his father had died, unexpectedly. He had been absorbed in the death and what had to be done with the house and the business for the past year. Celia had offered to go over but he said she should stay, that they were too occupied. She wrote to him twice a week. But how could she go to America, move Michael again? Emmeline and Lily would never come and her son adored Lily more than anyone.

Jonathan wrote that he'd found Violet a good job in an office. Violet even wrote a small letter to Celia, saying she was flattered that her name was there at the business but glad the flapper didn't look like her! Celia treasured it, every word, kept it in her bureau to read over again.

Miss Violet's Kitchen was flourishing, ever since Celia and Mrs Craigmire perfected the canning. All the Winter Meats canneries were busy producing for Miss Violet's Kitchen. The big shops in London placed endless orders and Celia went up most weeks to check on the displays, in pride of place in the Food Halls of Harrods, Selfridges, Harvey Nichols, even Fortnum and Mason and Liberty too. Department stores all over the country had followed suit – Norwich, Cardiff, Birmingham, Manchester, Edinburgh, Exeter. All the newspapers had run articles about Miss Violet's Kitchen and interviewed Celia about 'The American Girl'. She was grateful to that department-store buyer for giving her the tip, just as she was starting off – everyone wanted to be a New York Girl.

They put advertising in newspapers and magazines and even on the Underground. 'Miss Violet's Kitchen. For the New York Girl in You!' Miss Violet, as created by their artist, was blonde and sassy, smiling out of every poster, holding bags of jars and cans, going home to make a party for all her friends out of jars and cans. 'More time for dancing!' she cried, always smiling, always happy. There had been criticism too – it was said that Celia was feeding this *Refusal of women to be properly feminine.* Because women were there to cook – and if they did not cook, what would happen to civilisation? Some people wrote letters demanding how these young women were ever going to be able to cook for their husbands and children – were they going to give their children food from a can? But others were more afraid – said that Miss Violet's Kitchen meant that women would never get married at all – because surely women got married because they wanted to look after their husbands and a home, and if they didn't dream of this, cooking food in their own kitchen, then *Maybe they would never get married at all.*

'They're all men saying what women should want,' she told journalists, smiling. 'We know what today's woman wants and that's time. We're giving our girl more time. And if she wants to spend it cooking, then she can! We're just giving her the choice.' And they had actually found out that their buyers weren't just women. Men bought Miss Violet's Kitchen, too. They'd even had a few wives who said their husbands preferred it! 'All kinds of people buy our foods,' Celia said. 'We are giving them what they want and making their lives easier – so that they can enjoy a nutritious meal at the end of the working day, without spending three hours preparing it.' The newspapers printed profiles of her, noted as 'The Modern Woman', took photographs of her after a woman had come and painted her with make-up, made her lips red.

Celia bought an office in Winchester and rented the shop below it. She and Mrs Craigmire hired painters and decorators to paint the interior a warm yellow, put in shelves and large glass windows. They filled it with pretty chairs and fine curtains, a neat desk. A sign-painter painted 'Miss Violet's Kitchen' in gold on a wooden sign. They hired three shop assistants from the area, who all looked a little like Miss Violet themselves. It proved so popular that in three months, Celia was looking for a property in London to do the same, found one in Oxford Street. A few companies, including one called Flower Foods, were trying to break into their market but were having no success. Their customers were loyal – and there were more of them all the time.

Celia kept the key for the office and shop in her pocket, always, her treasure. On one day, she felt daring and enquired with an agency about taking a light advertisement in Piccadilly Circus, but they told her that there was a long queue and it tended to go to the more established brands – Coca-Cola, Rowntree, Cadbury. Mr Mars had made a new chocolate bar at his factory in Slough and he had taken the space for nearly six months.

Rudolf said he was proud of Miss Violet's Kitchen – but she knew he was disappointed. She knew he thought that if she'd put the same effort into Winter Meats, she would have made that succeed too. There was no point telling him that the world had changed – it had not changed for him. One day, they would have Miss Violet up in lights in Piccadilly Circus and she would take him to see her and he really would be proud.

Tom had written and she'd written back. He'd come to visit Michael regularly, once or twice a month, but hadn't told the boy or the family the truth. They pretended he was visiting her. 'Why won't you let me tell my son the truth?' he said.

'I need you to prove it,' she said. 'I don't want you going in and out of his life. He has suffered so much.' Her heart swelled with fear that once Tom married and had children of his own, he would forget about Michael and leave them all behind. She saw his visits with confusion in her mind. Michael deserved to know his father and it would be cruel to keep him away. She could not imagine how Jonathan would see it, feared he might view it as disloyalty, so did not tell him.

Every visit made her heart hurt. But Tom was kind and patient, talked to them all, bought Michael and Lily presents. She forced herself to think rationally – it wasn't Tom's fault that he didn't love her. She couldn't resent him for that. Tom had written occasionally to Heinrich, received no response. At least he didn't blame her for that.

'You were right, Celia,' he said one day. 'That night in Baden – I didn't think about it again – not in this way. I didn't think it might have – consequences.'

She remembered Violet's words: *Men do what they want*. Tom wasn't like that.

'I should have done,' he was saying. 'I was so angry about what happened with Heinrich – I didn't think about you.'

'Thank you.' She couldn't think of anything else to say. She'd wanted him to love her, then. Now – he only felt sorry for her, guilty for not having thought. At night, her heart snaked with fear, Tom would marry, set up a rich home and he and his wife would take Michael for himself.

In May, he mentioned to her on a visit that he was engaged, and her face clenched with panic. She didn't ask about the fiancée or the wedding plans, dreaded him telling her.

The children were still working hard for Mr Brennan. Emmeline had been right – he had been an excellent choice for a tutor. Lily was flowering under his close attention, answering comprehension questions, memorising history and geography. Michael was fond of history too, but she was most surprised by his love for art. No one in the family had ever been able to draw – and here was Michael, sketching trees, flowers, the house, the whole family – and then figments of his imagination, fantasy worlds with elves and pixies and fairies. He could spend hours and hours carefully drawing the details of a flower in the garden. Celia admired it, was proudly surprised by it, for she knew nothing of such detail, couldn't train herself to such minute attention, and yet Michael found – showed – a whole world in the varying colours of a single petal of a flower. And it was all thanks to Brennan – Celia would never have noticed, expected it, fostered it.

'He really is very talented,' said Mr Brennan. 'He might want to study art when he is older.'

Rudolf was dubious about art. 'He should be planning for Oxford,' he said crossly. Celia disagreed. Her son had a talent and in the new world, artists could make money too – what about Lowry, his canvases of hundreds of people, so alive that they could walk out of the painting any minute. Michael carried a sketchbook everywhere now, was always drawing – and even when he wasn't, she saw him looking at something – the whorl of wood on the table, her own hand and its interwoven webs of lines, and knew he was thinking of drawing them. Sometimes, she would creep into his room when he wasn't there and look over his sketches. She knew she shouldn't, that although it wasn't looking at a diary, still it was private, but she couldn't help herself. Looking at his drawings, she felt that they gave a pathway to the hidden rooms of his heart. She looked at pictures of Stoneythorpe, the gardens, the flowers – and her soul flowed when she saw he had drawn her, caught unawares and looking the other way, sketched with love. And other pictures too – some of the skyline of New York, the view he must have had from his constricted windows. And then some sketches that she didn't recognise, pure imagination – leaping dragons, monsters, fairy maidens chained to rocks, a fish of flowing, vibrant green passing through transparent water. One particularly elaborate, entrancing picture of a girl fleeing a monster almost had Lily's face. She traced her fingers over the picture. He barely wrote in the book – the odd name of a flower, a place, 'Mama' under her picture. But he had written 'Brennan' a few times, once under the maiden.

'You chose an excellent tutor,' Rudolf often said. 'So good with the children. And so unobtrusive. You would hardly know he was here.' Mr Brennan had his own key, let himself in quietly, walked up the stairs to the classroom where the children were waiting for him. Celia had asked him to stay for dinner, invited his mother, asked if they might like to pay a visit at Christmas, but he was very strict, said no. She supposed he was right – if you got too close to the family, then it would be harder when you had to leave them. That was what they dreaded. The day when Mr Brennan told them that he had got a job in a school – and of course he should because he was such a talented teacher – and he would be leaving them. They gave him a rise, repainted the classroom and bought new desks, offered him extra holiday but he never took it. Celia wondered if he was in love with Emmeline, wanted to be close to her and perhaps that was why he was so complaisant. She watched him – and he did follow Emmeline with his eyes. She pondered saying it, did not. Emmeline might panic and send him away – and Michael was so happy with him. Sometimes, she picked up essays of the children's, left in the schoolroom. Lily had written six pages about the misery of being trapped by your possessions, the cruelty they imposed, how things kept you down and enslaved. She thought of speaking to her about it – but then did not. It was only the natural extremism of being a young person, when it was all or nothing, no half area in the middle.

Just for fun, she asked Michael to draw Miss Violet – and the girl he produced was much better than the one they already had. She was more vibrant, more engaging, less beautiful but that was *better* – more like any pretty girl on the street. The first Miss Violet had had the sort of face that would always be beautiful, get more so when she was forty, fifty, into greater years. Michael's Miss Violet was the girl who was most beautiful in her youth, bright and shiny with hope. You could see the sheen of newness on her, the fresh arrival into the world, knowing little, happy because that was so. And oddly, even though she was blonde and slightly caramel skinned, when Violet had been dark haired and very pale, and although Michael had never seen her, she had a look of the real Violet about her. Something in her eyes that could switch so quickly from merriment to sadness, something searching, looking, even though, perhaps, she wasn't sure what it was.

She gave the first artist a pay-off and Michael's Miss Violet became the girl. She put pictures up of her in the shops, a giant one on a wall in London, smaller ones for posters on the Tube. 'We will get her up in Piccadilly Circus.' She gave Michael and Lily a small payment, to split between them, because otherwise it wouldn't be fair – and Mr Brennan a bonus.

Lily and Michael glittered with the sheen of change, every moment a new spark of electricity passed across them, altering their bodies and their minds. But she and Emmeline had merely lived longer, passed more days, done nothing with them. She could see the fine lines on the face of her sister, the thinning of the skin around the mouth. Her sister's golden hair was greying now, her waist thicker. Still, thought Celia, Emmeline was beautiful, more so, to her.

She found herself wondering about Emmeline's old fiancé, Sir Hugh, horrid anti-German snob – but still, he'd loved her once. She asked after him, and the vicar told her he'd died just after the war, from the Spanish flu. Celia counted the months and realised she'd been in Germany at the time. He said that Emmeline had been to the funeral and Celia wondered at her sister, at how much she didn't know about her.

'Emmeline,' she said one day, while they were washing up the breakfast plates in the kitchen. 'When did you last hear from Samuel?'

Her sister shook her head. 'I'm not talking about this. I told you last time. I can't remember just now.'

'Look, Emmeline, have you had a single letter from him since the first few when he set off?'

'Don't, Celia.'

'He hasn't written to you at all, has he?'

'Twice. At the beginning.'

She held her sister's soapy hand, lowered her voice. 'Emmeline. What if he's not coming back?' She couldn't say the rest. She couldn't say, *What if he's dead?* That would be too cruel. But it was what she thought. Four years gone and so long since she'd had any word from him.

She tried again. 'Emmeline. I know you're loyal. You're a good wife. But he's been gone for four years. Maybe you should start – looking elsewhere.' She restrained herself from mentioning Mr Brennan. He was so much younger – although of course there was the point that he was already fond of Lily.

Emmeline looked up. She was holding a plate in her hand, one of Verena's special breakfast plates. 'Never! I'm waiting for him. He's not dead! He's alive, I know it. And as long as he's alive, I'm his wife!'

She held up the plate. Celia stepped back. *She's going to throw it at me*, she thought. *She's going to.* Emmeline threw it on the floor at her feet and dashed from the room. Celia picked up a broom and began sweeping the bits into a pan.

'There's something I wanted to speak to you about,' Emmeline said, two days later. Had she noticed that Mr Brennan was following her with his eyes? But it wasn't that.

'We need to try and separate Lily and Michael. They're too close.'

'What are you saying? I don't understand.' They were in Verena's bedroom, surrounded by all her tiny bottles and vases. Emmeline had summoned her there, chosen it so no one would hear.

'We have to do something about it,' said Emmeline. 'Don't you see?'

'No. I don't. They're just fond of each other. And it's just a phase,' said Celia. 'It will pass. They'll find other friends, people their own age.'

'It's not a phase. They're completely dependent on each other. It's not healthy.'

'But there's nothing wrong with it.' Celia was gazing at one of the vases, swirled pink and purple. When Celia had been a little girl, Verena had sometimes kept loose change in them so if Celia wanted to buy sweets, sometimes her mother would go over the vases, emptying each one to find the few pennies she needed. Her mother probably kept more there now, she was so busy saying she didn't trust the banks after the Crash. But Celia worried that notes might be getting old and fragile in there, that when they took them out, there would be nothing but tiny pieces of paper, like snowflakes.

'Lily's fourteen. Michael's eleven. They're too old to behave like children. If I could, I'd send her to school like her brother. But Papa couldn't afford her as well. You should send Michael, ask Tom for the money.'

'Never. I'll never send him away.'

'Don't you see how well Albert is doing?' Emmeline was right, Celia had to admit. When Albert came home for the holidays, he was taller, browner, talked about how much he enjoyed school, and so many boys that she couldn't keep track of them all.

'That's different.'

'We have to do something. I think we'll start by saying there's to be no more being together unless there's an adult there too. They can't be alone any more.'

'Come on, Emmeline. They're going to hate that.'

'Celia, you were young once, so was I. Feelings run high. And there's no way back for girls.'

'I don't like what you're implying. Michael loves Lily. She's his cousin. Anyway, he's a child.' She was sitting too close to Emmeline. She could see the red lines in her eyes, the wateriness of the tear ducts. She looked away.

'Don't be naive. They're getting older. You were in love with Tom at thirteen.'

'That's different.' Celia paused. 'Did you know?'

'It was obvious to me. Probably not the rest of them, they're so blind. But that's what I mean. And you carried on mooning after Tom long after you should have done – and now look at you.'

Celia stood up. She walked to the window, clenching her fists, trying to control her feelings. The room felt suffocatingly hot, Emmeline's scent, the plump fatness of Verena's pillows. 'Oh, stop being so self-righteous. They're young. If they want to be together, they should be. It's only friendship.'

'Lily needs other friends.'

She gazed down on the garden, the trees around the sides, the overgrown flower beds, the fountain in the middle, all inspired by Verena's love for Versailles. She couldn't see either of them. 'But they're children.'

'My rules stand.'

'But listen, Emmeline, how about we let them play together after lessons? It's harmless.'

Emmeline shook her head. 'I've made up my mind. She's my daughter. I have to protect her.'

Celia almost hated her then. 'But Michael's had so little in life. So little happiness. This is all he's got. Don't take it away from him.' *Lily didn't need protecting from her cousin!*

'Oh, don't be so melodramatic. I'm not taking anything away from him. They still have each other. It's just – they're coming up to a dangerous time.'

Celia pushed her back against Verena's thick curtain. She wanted to break one of the tiny vases, smash it to the floor. 'They're friends. Nothing more. He's so young. They need each other.'

'Well, you can take whatever view you like, Celia. Fact is, I'm in charge when it comes to Lily and these are my rules for her from now on. I don't care if you agree or not.'

'You're wrong. What if they come to resent us?'

'I don't care. We know we're right.'

Celia ignored her. 'Not me. You. They're your rules.' She grasped her sister's hands. 'Don't do it. Please.'

Emmeline shook her head. 'I have decided. You can't change my mind.'

'I'll stop!' said Celia. 'I'll stop doing all this for the business so we can all live.'

She shrugged. 'Then we'll be poor. I don't care. These are my rules and I don't care whether you agree or not.' She hurried from the room.

INTERLUDE

So often when he couldn't find her, he knew where she'd be: in the room they thought was Louisa's, looking at her dresses.

He wanted to do what they used to do – explore the whole house, find out secrets. But Lily was changing. She wanted to talk about grown-up things. She was fascinated by Louisa. She was convinced she had been killed, and thought that if she looked through her belongings, she would feel closer to her.

'Look,' she said, holding one up, a pale-blue gown embroidered with sequins. 'Isn't it beautiful?'

He nodded, stared at the pile of gowns around her, heaps of pale yellow, green, pink and cream, sparkling bags, high-heeled shoes.

'These are party dresses, for London parties. For a pretty girl.'

He sat down on the broken bed. It was another room that they said was locked, but it wasn't really. Nobody ever checked.

'You're pretty.'

'Not as pretty as Aunt Louisa.'

'Prettier,' he said.

But she wasn't listening, she was looking through the gowns, sorting them, humming to herself. 'Let's never have secrets,' she'd said in the first days. But now there were secrets, not just of the grown-ups, but theirs too. Hers.

Mr Brennan was always talking. After art, Michael liked maths the most, the clean lines of the numbers, how they fitted together and there was always a right answer. Lily preferred composition, would write pages and pages of stories about things he barely understood: people flying through the sky, fish at the bottom of the sea, love stories between handsome men and girls who lived in lonely cottages in the wood, alone and waiting to be rescued.

He didn't know how she imagined such beautiful things. He knew that Mr Brennan was similarly amazed, for he took Lily's book and read it and when they were both supposed to be working on composition or reading or maths, Michael would sometimes look up and there was Mr Brennan, holding Lily's exercise book and gazing at it.

He'd hated Mr Brennan at first because there was less time for playing with Lily. But now, as she was changing, harbouring secrets, he found himself looking forward to their classes. For in the sitting room that they used as their schoolroom in the mornings, Lily was knowable, happy, keen to answer, always smiling. He could predict her, understand her. But then, in the afternoons when they were free together, he felt as if she was slipping away. Even when they were alone in a room together, she wasn't with him. Her mind was in another world.

So he drew. He drew and he drew and he drew, creating lines, systems, shading, focusing on detail. Lines made sense of the world when words only confused it. He drew Miss Violet for Mama and she had been delighted. She said that his picture had reminded her of her old friend, something in the eyes. But he'd never seen the friend – when he'd drawn Miss Violet, he'd been drawing Lily's eyes: sadness, excitement, anticipation and something else, a jumping, always out of reach quality he neither recognised nor understood.

When he went to see Grandpapa and look through the photographs, Lily didn't seem to mind any more. Once, Grandpapa had let him go early because he had a headache. He ran out to look for Lily but he couldn't find her anywhere. Then, when it was just time for supper, she reappeared.

'I've been looking for you!' he said.

She smiled beatifically. 'I went for a walk. Down to the woods.'

One day, while exploring the rooms upstairs, alone because Lily had gone off somewhere and he couldn't find her, Michael looked behind a bed and found a padded box containing two old pistols. They looked like ones from the war. He held it up, touched the rusty trigger and the end. There were bullets in it. You could shoot someone with it. Perhaps the owner already had.

'I found two guns upstairs,' he said to Rudolf, one evening while they were looking at photographs. 'I think they're very old.'

Rudolf shrugged. 'So much old stuff in this house. I never imagine any of it works. And now antique guns. I suppose they belonged to one of the soldiers in the hospital.'

'I think it still works.' His hand on the trigger, curving around it.

'Oh no.' Rudolf smiled. 'Now to these photographs.'

But Michael couldn't forget about it. At night, the gun spun in his mind.

TWENTY-NINE

Stoneythorpe, August 1933

A letter came from America. Celia tore it open. She stared in horror. Mr Galss had been right to suspect that there might be more of Arthur's debts – and she had been wrong to imagine that he would not borrow against Rudolf's name. The solicitor wrote that the bank noted below expected this money paid and the family was liable because Arthur had signed them all under his name. He had used Rudolf as guarantor and they must pay the money. He owed thousands upon thousands. The bank noted that they were willing to waive the interest that had accrued since he took the loan to the date of sending the letter, as they understood that the family may have overlooked the matter. But now, they would request it be repaid as soon as possible.

Celia stared at the letter. She'd never be able to repay them, not even if she got Miss Violet up in Piccadilly Circus and their products in every shop in London.

They would have to put the house on the market. They had to sell. Everything she had been working for. She'd put her marriage on hold, told Jonathan to wait. She'd thrown herself into trying to save the house, for them, for Michael. But now it was lost. However hard she worked, she couldn't beat Arthur's debts. They had to sell. Miss Violet's Kitchen was as nothing, hopeless, empty snow falling on them. The future she had expected, wanted, was broken and she had failed.

Michael heard his mother and grandparents talking. Some money had been lost. Someone had made a mistake. He heard his mother weeping when she told his grandparents. His grandmother screamed.

Stoneythorpe would have to be sold. He didn't want it to be. He didn't want to move again. He had thought he would stay here forever and ever. He wanted to live here with Lily and run through the garden with her.

Aunt Emmeline was trying to hide her tears, he could see. She was practical. He felt sorry for her. And then she said something terrible, a few days later. 'Well, we'll move house and things will have to change,' she said. 'It's time you were separated. We had been thinking about it before this news of selling – but now we're sure. You will go to school, both of you, like Albert. No need for a tutor. School is much better. Celia and I enjoyed school, didn't we?'

Celia shook her head. Emmeline lit up Winterbourne, beautiful, popular, good at games. Whereas she had been shy, out of place, always reading, girls like Eloisa mocking her.

Emmeline started talking about the sitting room she would have in the new house, blue and rosewood. The subject of school was closed. It had been decided.

And so the children saw the future. Everything they had would be over.

'Why are they doing this to us?' he said to Lily.

She gazed past him. 'They must be stopped.'

'I think we should have a party,' Celia had said at the dinner table, one night soon after.

'A what?' Emmeline looked up from her plate.

Celia pushed her dried-out beef to the back of the plate. 'A party. To say goodbye to the house. If we're going to sell it and never come back.' She was growing used to the idea. They could find a new home, put the past behind them. Michael had been taken from her here, Louisa had run away with Arthur. They could go to a new house, a different life.

'We haven't sold it yet,' said Rudolf, 'remember.'

'Well, we will. Only a matter of time. And surely summer would be best for a party. And this way we can celebrate it before we have to move too many things around.' The agent they'd already arranged to come and see their home had expressed concern that the house was too 'cluttered'. Things would have to go into storage. The modern buyer wanted a 'clean' look, apparently. Stoneythorpe was 'too Victorian' – in every way.

'And who on earth would come? We know no one.'

'Celia, what has got into you? You never have parties.'

'I just think we should say goodbye, that's all!' She didn't know what had got into her. The words had sprung into her head. In her heart, though, what she said was true, she wanted to wish goodbye to the house.

'We once had so many parties. When I was a little girl, you were always throwing them.' If they didn't have one final party now, then that would mean that the last party they'd ever thrown had been that disastrous one, just before the war, when no one but Tom and his sister had come, the whole village ignoring them because they were Germans and the enemy.

Celia stopped for breath and then she wasn't in the sitting room at all, but in the garden, just before the war, and they were waiting for the children to come to the party. The table was heavy with cakes, carrot, sponge, one thick with lemon icing. Mr Thompson and Mr Smithson had laid out all the tables and decorated them with bunting and paper stars. And there were games: pin the donkey, blind man's bluff and a box of lucky dip almost as tall as Celia. Jennie and Verena had spent hours wrapping up the presents for it. Celia had been in love with a big wax doll, with blonde hair and blue eyes, a beautiful thing, terribly expensive. Of course, at fifteen, she was too old for dolls, but something in her yearned for it, to be a child of seven and playing with such a beautiful toy. She'd helped, wrapped it carefully, covering its limbs with tissue paper and folding its velvet gown around its legs so that the material wouldn't crease. 'Good girl,' said Rudolf, watching her wrap it. He had bought it in London, carried it all the way home.

For two weeks, the house had been bustling, Rudolf planning, Mrs Bell conjuring pies and jellies, Verena organising the games.

And then they were waiting in the garden, the icing sliding off the cakes in the heat, buns glistening, and Jennie came around the corner.

'There aren't many children, Sir.'

'Oh, I am sure they are on their way! How many do you have now? Ten, twelve?'

Jennie dropped her head. 'Two, Sir.'

It was Tom and his sister, Maggie, only just seven. So Maggie had to be every child, pinning the tail on the donkey, playing blind man's bluff with Smithson. The tables stood to attention, full of food that no one would eat. The heavy icing on the lemon cake began to heat up and collapse in on itself. Maggie, exhausted, her eyes brimming tears for being watched by so many adults, was finally allowed to go home by Rudolf – but before she did, she was sent to dig deep into the lucky dip. Each time she took a present, Jennie shook her head. 'No!' she said. 'That's not the one!' And she did it over and over until the child pulled out a big parcel, wrapped in blue with purple ribbon. Maggie clasped it to her chest.

'Open it,' said Rudolf from the table.

Maggie stared at him.

'The poor thing's a little tired,' ventured Tom.

Rudolf gazed back. And then his voice cracked. 'Please,' he said, desperately. 'Open it, just for me.'

And Maggie, eyes of everybody upon her, carefully tore open the paper and then the tissue and pulled the doll out. She looked at it.

'It's beautiful,' Tom said. 'Say thank you, little one.'

Celia knew she was afraid of it, too grand, too expensive.

'It doesn't matter,' Rudolf said. 'As long as she had it.'

They watched Jennie take Tom and Maggie away. The sky reached down and touched them with its fingers of blue. *Didn't you realise?* it said. *The English don't want you here!*

Jonathan had seen all that, their great humiliation. And yet his increasingly infrequent letters said he still loved her, wanted her to come back, and that he couldn't leave America, his father's business. She was beginning to worry that the outlines of his face were growing fainter to her, something about it indistinct, as if she was looking at him through a window covered in mist, no matter how many times she looked at the photograph of them.

'It's an idea,' said Rudolf, slowly, looking up, breaking into Celia's thoughts. 'What do you think, children? A party?'

Michael and Lily were eating with them, which they didn't always do. They sat silently. It was five months since Emmeline's new decision that they could never be alone and Celia had to admit it was going better than she could have expected. They seemed to have accepted it – and they had begun to lead their lives separately. In the morning, they worked with Mr Brennan, then after lunch, walked separately around the garden. For the rest of the day, they'd read with the adults or rest before dinner. In January, Michael would be going to school with Albert at Harrow. And when they moved, they were going to try to find a school for Lily, just a day school so she could live at home.

'See, I was right.' Emmeline had whispered. 'They're young. They don't care.'

Celia sighed. Perhaps Emmeline had been right. Michael seemed accustomed to it, Lily too. Something within her sank at how he would go to school, make friends, move on to adult life, and forget about her. And it was right. He was almost a man. Children only wanted to be with you all the time when they were very young. It was too late now. She couldn't get those days back. The Whetstones had had them – and hadn't wanted them.

'Children?' prompted Rudolf.

Michael looked up, said. 'We could help.'

'I wish we could have a party!' said Lily. 'It would be wonderful. Imagine. We could make this place look like fairyland. We could put lights in the trees, cover the rooms with flowers. And people could dance in the gardens.'

She was looking upwards. Everybody was staring at her, surprised by her fervour. Celia looked across quickly – and saw Michael gazing at her too, not surprised, but mesmerized. She looked away, just in case Emmeline might see and follow her eyes. Lily was still talking about her plans.

'I just think it would be magical,' Lily said. 'Don't you think?'

'Well, we could certainly try,' said Rudolf, beaming at his grand-daughter.

'It would be nice to say a proper goodbye to the house,' said Verena, slowly.

'There we go, then,' said Celia, before Emmeline could start throwing cold water around. 'We have to have a party. Lily is in charge of the decorations. The rest of us can do the guest list and the food. When shall we do it?'

'September,' said Verena. 'After that it will be too cold.'

'That's a month away,' said Emmeline. 'We can't do a party in a month.'

'Of course we can,' said Rudolf. 'We don't have anything else to do.'

And so they did. The next month was a whirl, of letters and planning and moving furniture and discussing who might come, might not. They planned to have food laid out in the parlour, then outside, under the lights that Lily was talking of for the trees, people would walk and maybe even dance. Mr Brennan was superbly helpful – making lists of food, planning decorations, taking the children into town to buy what was needed. Celia asked him if he'd like to invite his mother, but he declined, said she grew shy at parties. He found them a string quartet, who'd come all the way from Winchester to play.

'This seems like a ridiculous expense,' said Verena. But Emmeline reminded her, when they'd sold the house, they'd have plenty of money – and they had to say goodbye somehow. Emmeline was being practical about the sale and Celia knew she hoped to take up their old flat in London, wait for Mr Janus there. Verena ordered caviar from London, venison, fancy puddings that would have to come down on the train packed up in ice. She shot off invitations to everyone she could think of. Lady Redroad, the old doyenne of the area before the war, was long dead, but Verena invited her son and his wife, who sent a reply saying they would most probably come. Their old servants, Jennie and Mr Smithson, married now and living in Winchester, where Mr Smithson ran a pub, said they'd come – with all five of their children. Rudolf offered to pay Mr Thompson's fare from Scotland, where he lived now – but he said he wasn't strong enough to come. Most of the other servants who'd been with them during the war were dead now.

The school even allowed Albert special dispensation to come – although none of his friends were allowed to accompany him.

'Why don't you invite friends, Celia,' Emmeline said.

'From Winterbourne? I'm not sure I even know where they are.' Nearly twenty years later. She tried to remember them, could conjure up only shadowy forms, shapes against the large windows at the back of the assembly hall. Popular Eloisa who had snubbed her – where would she be now? She tried to run through other friends. The only names she remembered were those of the ambulance girls: Waterton, Fitzhugh. The girls she hadn't really paid much attention to because her heart had been so caught by Shep. She supposed that Waterton, ex-Head Girl, always telling people what to do, constantly ordering, talking about Doing Your Bit, was busy organising church fêtes somewhere, the pillar of the community. She'd once seen mention of Geraldine Fitzhugh's marriage to an Earl, while idly flicking through the pages of *The Times*. Both of them would be far too busy to come.

'I don't think I have any friends,' she said, decidedly. 'I've invited Jonathan. That's enough.'

He had been at the last party, the one that had failed. Now it would be different. And they could go to America, once they had sold the house. They could try again with the American Girl, selling her breads and cakes and pastries and stews to the modern girl in Los Angeles, New York, Detroit.

'Unless you would rather invite Tom?'

'Stop it, Emmeline.'

'Because you can't have both, can you?'

'Emmeline, I said, stop it. I've invited Jonathan. And the rest is none of your business.'

'Of course not. We'll just stand by as you make a mess of things.'

At that, Celia felt her blood rise. 'Me make a mess of things? What about you? You run away, marry Mr Janus – and then we all have to tiptoe around you, let you say whatever you want? Of course, he's off fighting for freedom – saving the world. But he never bothers to write to you and so here you are in the same position as me – still living off your parents – and you're thirty-six! At least I do important work, manage the company.'

She threw out the last words, ran off, up the stairs. There, at her desk, she wrote a telegram to Jonathan, in case he hadn't received the letter in time. *We're leaving the house and we're having a party here. Please come.*

The pencil in her hand twitched, wanted to write to Tom, too. *Come.* She threw it to the floor. She sent the telegram to Jonathan. It might be impossible, difficult to travel at such short notice.

She wrote a letter to Tom after all. He wrote back that he didn't wish to say goodbye to the old house – the place where he'd been a servant. Anyway, he said, he was busy with the wedding. She had to force herself not to think of his fiancée, how pretty and engaging she must be.

Verena had invited people she hadn't seen in years – and even more surprisingly, most said they were coming! Everybody was helping. Even Lily and Michael were busying themselves with carrying things back and forth. For the past few weeks, the men and women from the village had been helping them clean the house, repair a few of the more obvious bits of damage, and now they were decorating the house with flowers. Rudolf had said they must spare no expense, should spend whatever they wanted. It was their party to celebrate the house that had been theirs for so long. They must go out with a bang.

THIRTY

Stoneythorpe, September 1933

Now the party was almost on them, Michael and Lily were laughing and busy, putting up decorations with Mr Brennan directing them, always helpful. Celia's heart pierced at their happiness, the finality of it, before separation, school and more of Emmeline's rules. They had told Mr Brennan that they aimed to send the children to school soon and he had been very polite about it, said it was better for the children to be at school and it had been a privilege to teach them. Celia saw him staring after Emmeline, felt pained for him.

Jonathan's car arrived from London two days before the party. She was amazed he had come all the way to see her. Her heart filled with joy. Life with him had been so simple. She went up to her room beforehand, put on the ring, felt dishonest and as if the ring would expose her, too clean, out of place.

'The place looks transformed,' he said.

'I thought you wouldn't come.'

'Almost like the old days.'

She nodded. 'They've been working at it.' A fear of going to America had filled her heart. What if, now the economy was improving, the Whetstones demanded Michael back? They'd have no rights in Britain, surely. But America? That was different. And even though the house was being sold, something was holding her close to it, as if there were roots going deep, love and history and fear of the future so long and tangled together that she didn't know where one started and another began.

'Michael's been so looking forward to seeing you,' she said. 'He's off somewhere with Lily. I'll go and find him.' Something in her wanted to hurry away, stop him from looking at her. And then Michael and Lily came hurtling through, saw Jonathan and wanted to show him the trees, the decorations, everything they'd done.

Celia kept talking, desperate not to let the silence in. She told him about Miss Violet's Kitchen and its success. He talked about his family and the business in New York. He mentioned that since Violet had taken the job he'd found for her in an office as a bookkeeper, she was earning enough to rent a better flat for her mother and herself.

Celia didn't ask after Hope. She still didn't know if Violet had told Jonathan. It was Violet's secret, not hers to tell. If Jonathan had not mentioned a child, then Violet surely had not got her back, perhaps not even seen her.

Violet was a safe subject, like the house, the business. Anything but the question – when will you come? She wondered, even, if he still wanted her to. Perhaps he had grown weary of waiting, fallen out of love.

Albert came home on the train, excited by time away from school, full of stories about rugby matches and the maths master who told jokes. They all bought new gowns, Rudolf said again how he could justify any expense as it was their last chance. The final party. Celia bought a long red gown in Winchester, covered in sequins, terribly expensive. Emmeline wore a primrose-yellow dress, embroidered in seed pearls over the bust, pearls tumbling down the skirt, like flecks of ice. Mr Brennan would admire her in it! She and Emmeline put up each other's hair. She thought of Arthur saying, *You never had a coming-out ball*. Well, this was it. The end of the house. A few people said they couldn't attend at the last minute – some cousins of Verena's, and Mr Brennan telephoned to say his mother's cold had worsened and needed his attention.

They woke up in the morning to the sun, pasted up the last of the flowers, opened up the door to the delivery of food. And then they were downstairs and the house was full and there was music playing in the sitting room and people dancing and Stoneythorpe was beautiful again, as it should have been for Emmeline's wedding to Sir Hugh, all the parties they would have had if the war had never happened.

People were laughing and talking and moving over to the table. Celia didn't recognise many of them, perhaps she had known them years ago but their faces were blurred now. There were colourful dresses, hair piled high with jewels and ribbons, men in black ties. Smithson asked her to dance and they whirled under the lights, surrounded by the other couples, pink-faced and happy. So happy! Why was everyone so happy? Smithson was explaining about his children. She nodded, smiled. The music came to an end, she breathed, bowed out. She stood on the edges, watching the dancers dive in. Albert was listening to the music, watching the men playing with rapt attention. Michael was talking with Lily in the corner. They both looked so smart, so grown up, it touched her heart. Lily's first grown-up dance, Michael's too. *They are friends, only children. Can't you see?* She thought of the speakeasy she'd been to with Jonathan and then it struck her – he was not there.

Celia walked away, under the lit-up trees to where it was darker. She leant against a tree, enveloped in the blackness. She didn't want to smile, think any more. Here it was quiet, the party noise just background laughter, like something turned down on the wireless. She could hear the night noises of the garden, insects settling, the rustle of mice and voles.

'I suppose you're trying to be alone.' Jonathan's voice.

'No.' He walked towards her. Closer. He held her hand.

'You haven't seemed to want to talk much.' They'd been in the garden together, just before the war, nearly twenty years ago. Little German Fräulein, he'd said, swooped down to her, kissed her. His cigarette lit in the dark. She'd been stunned by it – then the war had begun and other things had crowded it out of her mind.

'Celia. You know it's been four years. We've been engaged for four years. And we've been apart. There's something ridiculous in it.'

'I'm sorry.' The ring was huge, ungainly on her finger, felt wrong and out of place.

'We have a house, a life waiting for us. And your family. They can all come. Now you're selling Stoneythorpe, what's to stop you?'

She couldn't answer. Then she looked up. 'What's that?' She could just make out two figures hurrying down the garden. They were giggling. 'There's someone there!'

Jonathan didn't turn around. 'It's probably just someone playing a game. Someone in love. Like we're supposed to be.'

'But who is it?' The voices, whispered voices, she recognised them. She heard the woman laugh.

'It doesn't matter. Stop trying to change the subject.'

'Don't you think we should go and warn them? It's not really safe around here in the dark, where it's not lit. They might fall.'

'Celia, if they fall we'll hear them. Now, tell me. When I got your letter to come here, I thought, well, this is it. I'm being invited because we're telling everyone. Stoneythorpe is selling and Celia and the rest of them are going to come to America. And I get here and everything's the same. Nothing's changed. So, I've decided. We have to tell them tomorrow. We are going to marry. Move to America. They can come if they like, or not. But we are going.'

The noise had stopped. The couple had clearly run past, right down to the hedge. Or maybe they'd gone back up to the party again. Celia wanted to chase after the couple, say *How do you know you're happy? How do you know you wouldn't rather be running down the garden with someone else? Why him? Why her? How can you be sure?*

'Jonathan. I'm sorry. I just don't know.'

'Don't know what?'

'Whether I can move to America or not.'

She saw his eyes widen in the darkness. 'Oh.'

'It was so right in America. But – well, I'm not sure any more.'

'Why can't we be in America again, then?'

'My life is here. Michael's life is here. I think he wants to stay.'

'You had lives in America.' His eyes were bright, the whites hurt her against the darkness. He lit a cigarette and his face flamed briefly in the darkness.

'I know. But it doesn't seem it now.'

'Are you telling me that you don't want to marry me?'

She tried to look past him. 'No! I do. But – where do we live?' The lights up at the house were glittering. She could hear people laughing, talking.

'You live in America with me. You said you would before.'

'I told you, Jonathan. I just don't know. I can't tell. I wish I did know. I wish I was sure.'

'It sounds to me as if this is it. You don't want to be with me. Do you love me?'

'Yes! Of course I do.' Everything was so confused. 'I do love you. It's not about that. I just don't think I can live in America.'

'You want me to live here, is that it?'

'Yes. But you can't, I know that. But I feel like I belong here. With them. I do love you. But – I love them too.'

'It's not the same sort of love. I want to be your husband.'

'I'm sorry, Jonathan. It's just the way I feel.' The tears were fighting at the back of her eyes.

'We should go away. We haven't. That's what people in love do. Italy or somewhere warm with a beach. Or back to Los Angeles.'

She and Jonathan together in a hotel in Italy, looking out at the sea, admiring the view. Their problems forgotten, drinking wine on the balcony, talking about the future, a long road that gleamed. She could say yes, he'd take her and then she'd be free, happy. Or she could stay here in the tangle of her family's emotions, Tom who didn't want her.

She felt the tears on her face, couldn't say anything.

'Celia, this place drags you down. Your family does. You're not their servant.'

'I have to help them.'

'So you love me but you don't want to be married to me?'

'No! I just don't see – I feel I must stay here. At least to see them into another house.'

'What about me? I wait for your parents to die?'

The blood rushed in her head. 'It's not all my fault! Why can't you come here? Why can't you live here with us?'

'My life is in America.'

'Like mine is here! So why are you blaming me?'

He shook his head. 'You promised me you could live in America.' He turned away.

'No. Don't go. Please.'

He lit another cigarette, his hands bright in the flame. 'I'm going to go back now. I'm not going to stay. I'm going to leave and go back to America. If you don't write to me in a month, I'll consider the engagement off.'

The words seized her breath. She saw the lit end of the cigarette in the dark, heard the sound as he turned and began walking back up the garden. She leant against the tree, wept in the dark, cried for the past, for Arthur, Michael, Louisa and for her own heart that couldn't leave it all behind to be married to Jonathan. She was already regretting it. But then the tangle of family love clutched her, pulled her to the earth and her heart was shattering, breaking into a thousand pieces.

She could have chased after Jonathan then, begged him to come back, and said she didn't know what had come over her. She told herself – if he comes back, I will go with him. If he comes back, helps me to cut these roots away, I will go with him.

He didn't turn around. She watched his shadow walk up to the house. Then she wept again.

After what felt like an hour or so, she couldn't cry any more. Her face felt swollen. She wanted to wash it, lie down. The party sounds had receded. Perhaps she could hurry past them and straight up to her room, without too much questioning. She started to walk back.

Up at the house, the party had quietened. The string quartet had gone and the women from the village were helping Emmeline tidy up the food on the tables. There were people sitting in the parlour, talking. Smithson and Jennie were deep in conversation with Verena. Rudolf wasn't there.

'Oh, there you are,' said Emmeline, straightening up. 'I wondered where you'd got to. Jonathan came through in a hurry, said he had to get back to his hotel. I take it he saw you?'

Celia nodded. 'I think I have a cold. I'm going to bed.'

'Is Lily coming up behind you?'

Celia shook her head. 'I haven't seen her.'

'You haven't seen her? We thought they were with you.'

'Who?'

'Michael and Lily.'

'No. I've been alone. I didn't see anybody.'

'Emmeline, dear, they'll be in the house, somewhere,' said Verena, placatingly. 'They've probably hidden themselves away with some cake.'

'But, Mama, they're not allowed to. They're not allowed to be alone.' Emmeline's colour was rising, her voice frustrated and angry. 'You *know* that.'

'They're probably upstairs asleep,' said Jennie. 'It is late, after all. Albert's in bed. They're probably fast asleep too. Why don't we go and check?'

She heaved herself to her feet. Celia hadn't realised that Jennie was pregnant again. That would be number six. She wanted to ask her *How did you know? Were you quite sure? Didn't you think you might love someone else?*

'No, no, you mustn't go up the stairs. You need to rest,' said Emmeline.

'The exercise is good for me after sitting down all evening. Anyway, no one knows the nooks and crannies in this house better than me. It hasn't changed that much, after all.' She smiled at her husband, squeezed his hand.

'I'll come with you,' said Celia. She walked up with Jennie, asked her questions about the baby, ignored the slow hand clutching around her heart. The sound of two people – young people – giggling in the dark, running to the bottom of the garden. How long ago had that been – two, three hours ago?

They walked to Lily's room. The bed was neatly made. Celia looked in the wardrobe, couldn't be sure if anything was gone. But she knew that things had been taken. Something in her knew that they had.

She turned and ran to Michael's room, burst in through the

door. The bed was made too, the place neater than she'd seen it for a while. She pulled up the bed and looked in the bedside table. Michael's sketch book wasn't there. Her heart froze. She looked at the shelf over his bed. He was gone, Harvey the bear that she'd bought him on the first day in New York. The horse was gone from under the pillow, but the farm was still in a box under the bed. The air was strangely still, as if it had been empty for days, even though she knew it couldn't have been, of course it couldn't. She gazed at the empty room.

'What is it?'

Celia turned to Jennie but couldn't speak. She clutched her throat, tried, still nothing came out. All the times in New York she had been with Michael, turned around and panicked, and he'd been the other side of her all along. The fear that seized her heart in public places, in case they got separated, the relief when they had returned home together. All useless, all pointless. She grasped Jennie's hand.

'Celia, what is it?'

She felt dizzy, dark-headed. Her body was losing itself. She could hear Jennie shouting her name, then Emmeline and another voice she didn't recognise. But it was lost, lost under whispering voices running down the garden, laughter. She clutched for Emmeline's hand but it was too late. She was lost to the darkness.

INTERLUDE

Where had the idea come from? Neither of them could say. Perhaps it had always been there. They'd wanted to run, be free of the adult world of money, cruelty, compromise. One mother endlessly cutting out pictures of sofas and sitting rooms while the other could spend all day putting a bow on a jar. They had to make their lives different. And they had to hurry it up, when the adults started talking about London and schools and separation. They watched the plans for the party in the house. The others were absorbed, discussing guests, food, timings, music, their obsession with the tiny things that showed they'd forgotten about what was really important in the world, if they'd ever known it at all. Their mothers were talking about dresses and table layouts and they despised them for their pettiness. They knew about the important things: love, truth. *Only you understand me.* They'd told each other this, late at night, crept to each other's rooms. *I can't live without you.*

Lily said her family had always been like this, never keeping anything that mattered, forgetting, forcing everybody into their world of keeping to appearances, no matter what cruelty lay underneath. Michael wasn't sure, thought of his own mother and her fight to find him. But now – here she was, trying to separate them too. A big school near London full of boys where he would never see Lily again. Once the house was sold, Lily and he knew, it would be the end of everything. They were in the air and the adults were trying to pull them down to the ground. They had to jump.

At the end of the garden, in the dell, they hid clothes, warm things, a knife they'd taken from the upstairs rooms, money they'd taken from the adults, bits and pieces here and there. Books, his wooden horse, Harvey (Lily said it took up too much space but he insisted), his sketchbook and pencils (again she said they wouldn't be needed and he said he had to take them), things they couldn't leave behind. 'We have to travel light,' they'd agreed. They were going to be free, after all. But he knew that she was packing up the purple cat her father gave her and so many of the pretty things in her room – the stack of bracelets as slippery as ice, the purple cat that he wanted so.

The string quartet were playing loudly, the parlour was flooded with people laughing and talking. They slipped in between the people, no one noticing them. They stepped out into the garden, under the trees covered in lights. Then they smiled at each other and began to run.

THIRTY-ONE

Stoneythorpe, September 1933

'They can't have gone far.' Celia came round on the floor and thought she'd only been gone for a moment or two. Emmeline was standing over her, sorting through Michael's shelves. 'They must have left a note. There's nothing in Lily's room. It must be here.' Verena was talking, Jennie too.

Celia propped herself up, dizzily.

'Oh, you're awake,' said Verena. 'Mr Smithson has gone out with the men to look for them. They must be somewhere near.'

'Yes.' She'd run away once with Tom, barely got as far as the village. But something struck hard in her heart and made her fear that this was more.

'One of your father's friends saw them go out into the garden. That's why we thought they were with you.'

'I think I might have heard them run past. I heard two people, laughing, running. Whispering. It must have been them.'

Emmeline stopped moving things, turned around. 'You heard them?'

'I think so.'

'You *heard* them and you didn't stop them?'

'I didn't realise it was them.'

'What do you mean, you didn't realise it was them?'

'Stop it, Emmeline. You can't blame me. I didn't recognise them. It could have been anybody. Why would I have stopped them?' *They sounded so happy*, she didn't say. *They seemed in love.* 'I might blame you. You told them they were going to be split up even more in London.'

'Oh, that's got nothing to do with it. They've taken my money.

I kept it under my bed. Twenty pounds. I was saving that for the new house. Whose idea would that have been?'

Her sister was always dwelling on those magazines, looking over the ideas for decoration, clipping out the pictures, piles and piles of pictures of sofas and cupboards.

Celia struggled to her feet. 'I'm going to help the others find them. Emmeline, I'd like you to leave Michael's things alone. Go and wreck Lily's room if you must.' She stood up and folded her arms until they left. Then she ran downstairs and out into the garden. The trees were still lit by the fairy lights. She dashed to the bottom, her feet catching on the wet grass, shouted, 'Michael! Lily!' The words came back to her, weaving around the branches, skittering up to the clouds. If only she'd said something to Jonathan, followed the noise; if only they'd both walked out and seen Michael and Lily. She could hear the shouts of the searchers outside the garden, see the flash of torches. She walked back up the garden, through the doors of the parlour and pushed her way out of the front door. There were men from the village, assembling on the drive.

'Lily!' she shouted. 'Michael! Come back! I'm sorry.' She walked down into the group of men, asked for a torch. She was going to walk with them. She was going to keep on until she found them.

Celia opened her compact, checked her face for about the twentieth time since she'd sat down at the café table. She snapped it shut. Tom was now twenty-five minutes late. Perhaps he wasn't coming at all. The waiter was hovering, but there was no point ordering more tea if Tom wasn't going to come. She sighed, gazed out of the window again. She'd written to tell Tom, two days after it happened, after the search parties had been around and around the village and all the villages about, come back, found nothing. No one had seen them. He'd written back saying he'd help if there was 'anything he could do'. She hadn't replied, hoping he wouldn't be needed, that they would come back and it would all be over. Now, a week and a half later, no sign of them, she had written to beg him for help. The police had been all over the house, questioned them all dozens of times, taken clothes and toys as 'evidence', written endless reports.

'We will find them,' said the detective, but his voice trembled when he spoke and Celia knew he was lying. 'They have very little money. Lily's mother's won't last them long. So they'll be back soon.'

The newspapers gave it front pages for the first three days or so. 'Romeo and Juliet', the journalists called them. 'Love Triumphs over all'. There were a few articles about danger and children disobeying their parents – but one columnist said it was the triumph of romance in a cynical world. And if Lily and Michael were in love or Romeo and Juliet – what did that make her and Emmeline? The cruel parents, the wicked elders in the fairy story, forcing their children to do as they wished, not caring for their hearts.

It wasn't that, she wanted to say, looking at the papers. *We thought they were too young. Emmeline did.* So far she had fought herself down, not said to Emmeline, *Why did you do it?* Her sister was suffering, she didn't need Celia telling her what she already knew, that she had been wrong to try to separate them, for it had only pushed them further together. They'd sent Albert back to school, as quickly as possible, hoping he wouldn't read the newspapers. 'Don't worry,' she'd said to him, holding him on Winchester station platform. 'They'll be back in a moment of time!' They'd stuffed his box with biscuits and chocolates. She'd sent a telegram to Jonathan – just in case he'd seen anything at the time. He wrote kindly offering to come back – but said he'd seen nothing of value. She told him to remain, knowing she should send the ring back. The police sent him a list of questions which he returned swiftly – nothing there.

They'd had two viewings of the house, people who were clearly just coming to snoop about the crime. Celia told the agent to wait for a month, until all the gossip had died down.

'Don't you think we ought to bring Albert back from school?' Celia had asked. 'Just for a little while.'

Emmeline shook her head. 'It's better for him to continue. Take his mind off it.'

Celia supposed Emmeline was right. Home was a mess, Verena weeping, Rudolf hiding away in his study. He had taken it badly, worse than she could have expected. Celia heard him crying when she walked past his study door. She knocked, but he wouldn't answer.

Mr Brennan had come to express his sympathies, accompanied by his mother, a small, respectable-looking woman in a brown hat she was too shy to take off. Verena gave him two months' pay.

'Such a tragedy,' he said. 'I only wish I had some clue about what they were thinking, so I could tell the police. But I've racked my brains in our interviews and can't think of a thing.'

He looked so devastated by it, poor man. 'You weren't to know,' Celia said. 'It wasn't your fault. None of us realised.' He looked so very distressed. He'd loved them too, of course, felt just as betrayed that he had not realised they were running away. He was gazing at Emmeline again and Celia's heart dropped for him – no chance of that now. 'School is a factory,' he'd said at his interview, talked with such colour and attention that they knew he was the right one. Emmeline, heartbroken. She'd torn up her magazine pictures of sofas and sitting rooms, thrown them into the bin, confetti with no wedding.

Mr Brennan said the police had asked him about their state of mind. 'I really couldn't think of anything,' he said. 'They seemed perfectly normal. Excited about the party. We were all completely in the dark.' His mother was close to tears, he held her hand tightly. 'If only I'd been there at the party,' he said. 'I might have spotted something going on.'

Mr Brennan was right. They had all been in the dark – Celia most of all. She had been blind, hadn't seen a thing. The children had run past her and she had been too caught up in herself to even recognise the whisper of her own child.

'Hello, Celia.' She looked up into Tom's face. 'I'm sorry I'm late. I was kept at the office.'

'Thank you for coming.' He sat down and she cursed herself

for the electricity that ran through her body. And her vanity, that she'd fussed over her outfit, fretted at her hair, checked her mirror dozens of times.

'Is there any news?' He waved the waiter over. 'Tea please.'

She shook her head. 'They've vanished. It's like they have, at least. We can't find anyone who saw them after they left the garden.'

'No one?'

'We've searched, asked. The police have tried. Nothing.' They'd even all been up to speak to Albert at school – and the police came too. He said that he hadn't heard back from a letter he'd sent Lily. Emmeline was convinced he was telling the truth.

Celia looked back at Tom. 'We've tried everything. No one has any ideas.' She wasn't going to ask about his wedding, the beautiful fiancée, their plans for the future. She was probably sitting with her doting mother at this moment, working out her table plans.

'They must be hiding out in a city. Maybe they're even here.'

'I don't know how we'd ever find them here.'

'No. Maybe not. You don't have any idea why they did it?'

Celia told him about Emmeline's rules, separation, school. She trailed off, thinking of the sketchbooks, the dragon trying to capture the maiden with a face like Lily's. Had they been the dragon, she and Emmeline, trying to take Lily off to school?

'Don't blame yourself. Children have to go to school eventually. I'm sure they'll see the error of their ways and come back. Don't you recall when we ran away?'

His words jolted her. She'd never have imagined he'd remember. When she was seven, he nine, Rudolf had told them that they weren't allowed to go into the village – and so they'd made plans to escape. They'd stolen bread, cheese and knives from the kitchen and packed them up in a basket. She'd taken her journal and they'd both written letters to their families. Celia told Verena and Rudolf that she was going into the world to make her fortune and would come back, richer than King Midas. Tom wrote a letter to his mother but didn't show it to Celia. They took clothes and books and made plans to go to France. They crept down to the woods together in the early morning – and planned to spend the day there. But by late afternoon, they were bored and hungry for tea. Celia had been worrying about Rudolf and Verena being alone and when Tom said he was beginning to think twice, she almost hugged him. When they went back, Verena had just started searching for them.

Celia was about to reach across for Tom's hand. Then she remembered. 'You were whipped.' Tom had been punished for leaving his duties, beaten and locked in the stables overnight.

'That wasn't your father's idea.'

'But he could have stopped it.'

'Yes. He could have.'

Her heart filled. 'That was what you meant when you said the friendship wasn't equal, wasn't it?' They should have kept running. They should have never gone back.

'Listen, let's not talk about that now. Anyway, Celia, they'll find the world outside isn't so easy. Look, there must be some clues. Who was the last person to see them?'

'Me.'

'You?'

'I heard them. I was out in the garden, at night. I heard giggling and someone running past me. Two people. I didn't think anything of it.' *What were you doing there?* He would surely ask it.

'You always did like wandering around in the garden,' he said. 'Look, they clearly wanted to go. You can't force them back.'

'So we just have to wait for them.'

A tear was welling up in her eye, drying her throat. She'd thought that Tom might have a solution, be able to swoop in with his new money and his success and make everything right again.

'There's nothing you can think of? Not to find your son?' She was beginning to beg now.

He looked up at the word, jolted. It was the first time she'd used it. 'Well, I suppose we might try a private detective. You never know. He'd ask you for leads, though. Their thoughts in the run-up to it all.'

'I don't really know.' She felt shame once more. 'We were

planning the party. We were so caught up in it. We didn't really notice them.'

He raised an eyebrow. 'Oh yes, the party.'

'Jonathan came from America. He was asking me questions.' She had to send the ring back to him, even though he hadn't asked. She couldn't go back now. But the ring was so final.

'Oh, him. That was why you were outside. Talking to him. That was why you didn't think twice about people running past. He's always around, isn't he?'

'Look, Tom—'

'Is he going to find the children for you? I suppose you argued? It's always the way. Needed when you need me, otherwise nothing to you. What did you think I was going to be able to do, anyway? Find someone when the police can't?'

'I don't know. I just thought you might have an idea.'

'Well, there's nothing I can think of but a private detective. I suppose you want me to pay for it.'

'No! That wasn't what I meant. Of course not.'

He stood up. 'I'll give you the money. Find a detective and get them back. And when you do – you can tell him who his father is. I've played your game for far too long.'

'I'm sorry.' She tried to catch his hand, even though they were making a scene in the café. People were turning to look.

'I'm going to go now. You can write to me. If I can help. With money or whatever it is you want. I'll send you a cheque. But that's it!'

He hurried out of the café. She paid the bill quickly and followed him – but he had gone.

She walked towards the Underground, to head back to Victoria. She supposed she'd look up a private detective in the newspapers. It was hardly as if there was a street where they all had their offices, like Harley Street for doctors. She ducked down into the dirty staircase for Covent Garden. Something in her dreaded the idea of a private detective, searching over their belongings and asking questions, just like the policemen had. Verena would hate

279

it. And she'd have to explain that she had been outside talking to Jonathan, considering breaking off their future forever.

Still, they had to try. Celia wrote to a Mr Pilsdown who advertised in the back of *The Times*. He had assured her by phone that 'missing persons' was one of his specialities. She promised him one hundred pounds as a retainer and invited him to look at the house. He arrived with a quiet young man whom he sent off to draw a plan of the grounds. She followed Mr Pilsdown as he sorted through Lily's things, Michael's books. He ran his hand over Michael's papers, admired a few sketches that had been left behind. She tried not to let his kind words pierce her heart. He took notes, looked at the windows, and checked the doors. Then they walked out into the garden. She showed him where they had been standing, took them both to the dell where she thought they'd probably planned it – and then to the gap in the hedge at the back where you could cut through to the forest.

'The police searched the forest,' she said. 'They're not there.' She held tight to the photograph of her son, taken by Rudolf at the studio in Mareton. The police had asked for it but she was never letting it go.

'We'll find those two, don't worry,' he said. 'They don't have much money. They can't have gone far.'

And yet. After Mr Pilsdown and his man had left, sent in a cab to the station, she ran upstairs, headed to Verena's bedroom. She burst in, to the chintz and the velvet and vases, dozens and dozens of vases. She started pulling at them, opening them, holding them upside down, tipping out keys and dust and dead flies. She pulled the Wedgwood boxes out, tugged off the lids, cast them aside. She opened the mystery novels, found nothing, flung them aside.

'What are you doing?' Emmeline and Verena stood in the door. Her sister stepped forward. 'Are you trying to wreck the place?'

'Did you have money in here?' Celia asked. Verena stood back. 'You did, didn't you? You had money in here.'

Verena gazed back, her eyes milky.

'Where is it? I know you had money in here. You always said you didn't trust the banks. Did you have money?'

Verena nodded.

'They took it,' said Celia, sitting back on the bed. 'They took the money. How much was it, Mama?'

She wrapped her arms around herself, made herself small. 'I don't know. Six hundred, a thousand. Maybe more.'

'Well, now they'll never come back,' Emmeline said. Her whole body sank. 'They took twenty from me, but they wouldn't have got far. But they stole yours. They could go anywhere.'

'They didn't steal it,' said Verena in the doorway.

'What?'

'I gave it to them.'

Emmeline was staring. 'What do you mean?'

Verena was breathing heavily.

'What do you mean, you gave it to them?' asked Emmeline.

Celia stood up. 'Come on, Mama.' She pushed past Emmeline, put her arm around Verena, and took her to sit on the bed. Her mother's shoulders were shaking.

'I didn't know,' she said. 'They just asked me for money. They said they needed it for something. I didn't know what. I didn't ask. I thought they were going to get something for the party.'

'With so much?' Emmeline kicked the doorway. 'How could you?'

'I wanted to give it to them,' she said. 'I sent Michael away. How could he ever forgive me? Then when he asked me for money – they both asked me for money – I thought, this is something I can do. I can give them the money. What do I need with it?'

Celia tried to make her voice gentle. 'Mama, if you were saving money, wasn't it to be used for their future? For school.'

Verena was weeping now, head in hands. 'They asked for it. I wanted to give it to them. I shouldn't have sent him away.' She was hiccupping as she spoke.

'No, that's true. But, Mama, don't you see? Now you've given them this money, they could be anywhere. They could go to France. Anywhere. We'll never find them now.'

'When were you going to tell us?' said Emmeline. 'When were you going to tell the police?'

'I was afraid you'd blame me.'

'Well, you were right. You were completely right.' Emmeline stormed from the room and they heard her footsteps hurtling down the stairs. Verena burst into another storm of weeping. Celia put out her arms, brought her mother to her, rocked her gently, as if she were the child.

Celia wrote to Jonathan to tell him what had happened. She couldn't go to America now. She could never go. She had to wait here until Michael came back. She took off her ring, wrapped it carefully in paper and put it in the parcel. Her heart broke in two. Rudolf was angry, said he couldn't understand how she couldn't have persuaded Jonathan to live in the house with them, but she hated hearing him talk about Jonathan's money and what that could have done. It had been about love.

This was her life now and she could never leave.

'We'll never find them now.' Emmeline was sitting in Lily's room, holding her pillow.

'I don't know,' said Celia.

'The only hope that the police gave us was that they didn't have much money. Now look.'

'Well, now they'll come back because they love us. Not because they have run out of money.'

'Maybe. But what if they don't think they can come back? What if they're afraid? We need to find them and tell them we want them back. This place is going to be sold, eventually. We won't be here. We shouldn't have ever let them be together at all. You should have sent him off to school first thing.'

'No! You can't blame him. They went together.'

Emmeline snorted. 'It was his idea, I bet. So you find them.'

But Celia didn't know what any of them could do this time. The children had disappeared – two birds flown up into the sky.

INTERLUDE

There was someone there. A person behind them. Michael swung around, looked for Lily. Nothing. The branches lay bare, the ground tangled with moss.

His heart clenched. Someone had got her. She was going to die. He ran forward, his heart smashing in his chest. It was his fault. He shouldn't have turned away. Well, he'd save her. He'd run to her and rescue her. He'd fight off whoever had her. Even if whoever it was had a gun, he'd fight him off.

'Lily!' he shouted. The words echoed back to him, mocking. 'Lily! Where are you?'

A bird fluttered up. The air around him was silent. Someone had her. He was stopping her from crying out.

'Don't be afraid!' he called out, as loud as he could. 'I'm coming to save you.'

And he was. He was a knight, there to save her, strong and true, better and braver than any of the knights in the stories. He didn't need a sword or even a horse. He rushed forward, broke through the branches. 'Don't worry!' he shouted. 'I'm coming!'

But there was nothing. No sign. He ploughed on. He didn't know where he was going. He felt hopeless, exhausted. Lily had the map. He looked around, could see nothing. It was so dark. The cool dread grasped his heart. There could be a murderer in the woods. But Lily was strong! She wouldn't give in. She'd fight back. And she had the weapon in her bag – a knife they'd found in one of the top rooms. He'd wanted to take the old gun, but she'd told him to leave it.

'Lily!' he cried. 'I'm coming.' But it was cold and damp and tiring and the branches snapped back in his face. He needed to sit down. *No!* But the tiredness was threading its way up his body, weighing down on his face and eyes. He sat down on the floor, leaning against a trunk. It was just for a minute, just briefly. He closed his eyes, willing himself not to feel fear, so that when he opened them, the world would be right again.

'We've been looking for you.'

His eyes snapped open. The moonlight darted through the trees above his head, too bright.

'It's you!' he said.

It *was* him. He was standing there. He was standing next to Lily. He had his arm around her. *What was he doing here? Had he followed them?*

'Hello, Michael.' Lily was smiling. 'We've been waiting for you. Now we can begin.'

THIRTY-TWO

Stoneythorpe, February 1934

'People can't just disappear,' said Mr Pilsdown. 'But these two – somehow – they have escaped us.' It was as if they had vanished into thin air. Over the last five months, he had interviewed everybody possible. Mr Brennan was the only one he hadn't spoken to; his mother said that he had gone to look for work in France. She'd given him a forwarding address in Rouen and he'd sent a letter.

'Apart from him, I've spoken to everyone. And I have – I am afraid to admit it – very few leads. It is as if they had help and assistance on the other side. But we know they didn't. So all I can say is that they must have got lucky. And they had that money, of course, which changes things. It's the perfect disappearance.'

Now the publicity about the disappearances had died down, they had begun offering people viewings of the house again – but there hadn't been much interest. The agent was not optimistic. It didn't suit modern tastes, too big, too ramshackle. 'We only need one person to love it,' Celia told herself. She wished they could keep it, so that Michael would come back to it, the only real home he knew. But she knew they couldn't. Arthur's debts were too large. She applied herself to the business. She put up Michael's picture of Miss Violet over department store displays, sent it off to be printed as a poster for the Underground and thought her heart would break. She worked on contracts, machine outputs, and accounts. She tried not to think about anything else. She locked the office at the end of the day, went home, talked to her parents and Emmeline, went to bed. She was working to make them a new life.

To save money, they lived in even fewer rooms. She walked in one day after a day of meetings to find Tom there. Emmeline and Verena were already with him. He was sitting upright, smartly dressed, his silver-topped cane beside him.

'Have you found out anything?'

'I wish I had news,' he said. 'But I came for something else. I had another idea.' He paused.

'Yes?' said Verena.

'You said the children love it here.'

'They do. As we did,' answered Celia.

'They didn't want to move to London.'

None of them answered. Celia waited. He surely hadn't come to them to repeat what they already knew.

'So I thought to myself, perhaps, after all—' he broke off.

Verena sighed, so quiet you'd nearly miss it.

'What is it, Tom?' Celia asked. 'What's your idea?'

He smiled, nervously. 'I thought I could buy Stoneythorpe. I cannot see it sold before we find them. Not if they were running away because you were selling it.'

'What?'

'If the children love it, I could buy it. Then they won't have lost it. They'll know they can come back.'

'Come back?' Celia stared at him. 'You'd buy Stoneythorpe so they could come back? You can't afford it.' Some other woman, Tom's wife, living in Stoneythorpe. Filling it with her children, smiling happily up from the bed as the doctor showed Tom his latest baby. Children dashing around the garden, climbing the trees.

'I can borrow. I've looked into it. It can be done. That is – if you want it to be. It's up to you.'

Celia could feel both her mother and sister looking at her. She tried to avoid their gaze. Emmeline was speaking: 'But how would it work? You buy it, you live here? And what if you're not here when they come back?'

He shook his head. 'I buy it. You live here.'

'We live here?' Not true, thought Celia. He was engaged. His *wife* would want it.

286

He nodded. 'You can pay me a rent if you like. I don't mind. It's not just this. I grew up here. I don't want to see it fall apart. Of course, I would love to come here sometimes. I should be in London, but there are other times. But it will be yours to live in.'

Verena breathed. 'Tom – Mr Cotton. That is such a very generous offer. Let me please discuss it with my husband. I'm sure he'll be delighted.' She spoke slowly, graciously, the tone Celia recognised was for talking with the serious, the dignified, those requiring respect.

'Of course,' he said. 'It would take me a month or so to get the money, anyway. You don't have anyone else who wants to buy it?'

'No! You can't have it, Tom.'

'Celia!' said Verena, as if she had been ten, not over thirty. 'Stop that!'

'But he can't, Mama. He can't come here as if he could buy us. You can't, Tom. It's not fair.'

He stared back at her. 'I'm not trying to buy you, Celia. I only mean the house. I want to keep it in the family. Our—'

'We're all wrong! We think that if we just keep the house, they'll come back? They've gone! We drove them away and it was all our fault. They're not coming back.'

'You don't know that, Celia,' said Emmeline. 'Please calm down. Tom's only trying to help.'

But the white heat had caught Celia and it was firing her. 'I don't need your money!' she said. 'I don't need your money to get Michael back. After all the times you've said you hated this house and you hated your life here, that every moment you spent with me was work you didn't want to do. All the rest of it. And now you want to buy the house. You say you won't live in it with us? It's not true. You'll visit for a little while. Then after you're married, your wife will want us out so you two can live happily ever after here.' What if she were very rich? And it was her money Tom was using to buy their home?

Tom was looking at her. She could see the pain behind his eyes. She kept going. She couldn't stop. She was talking, spewing out the hurt, all of it, the times she had tried to speak before and did not. Emmeline was telling her to stop and Verena, too, but she couldn't, kept forging on.

Tom stood up. 'You don't need to continue, Celia. I understand. You don't want me here, or my help. I was wrong to offer it.' He turned to Verena. 'Thank you for the tea. I'll go now. My car is outside.'

He looked back at Celia. She could say it then, speak, apologise, say she never meant it. The words wouldn't come.

He walked away. She watched him go. Then she ran to the hall, heard his car start. She leant against the wall, put her face against the cool marble.

The time afterwards was terrible. Verena and Emmeline had been angry with her, Rudolf so furious that he could barely speak. 'Our only chance to get it back,' Verena was weeping.

'We can't be dependent on him,' Celia said. 'Don't you see? He's engaged. He'd only buy it and move in here with his wife.'

'Of course we could be,' said Emmeline. 'He offered it. It's our only hope. But you threw it away. And now what – poverty?'

'Well, you go and get it back from him,' Celia said.

'Oh, don't be ridiculous!' Emmeline shouted. 'It was for you. Not for me. He was giving it to you! It's you he wanted.' She stood there, silent, stared at her. 'Well, if you won't take his money, then you need to get it. Make more money from the business. Or find a buyer.'

'And what about you?'

'Someone needs to look after our parents. Anyway, you got us into this mess. You can get us out.'

INTERLUDE

———

Michael opened his eyes. The light burnt his face, swords of it coming from the sky. He had been asleep.

'We've been looking for you,' said Mr Brennan again. He was smiling. He had his arms around Lily.

'Now we can begin,' Lily said, caught Michael's hand to help him up.

And so that's how it started, their story. Mr Brennan – call me Don, he said – had planned it all along, with Lily. Michael hadn't realised it, but of course that's what they'd been doing when he found them talking or when she went off to the woods alone. They were planning. And so Mr Brennan met them there, and took them to a house of another friend who was on holiday in France. They waited there while he went back home and checked for a few days to see that the coast was clear (he said the police wanted to ask him questions but he'd never say anything, ever).

Lily didn't want to talk to Michael, tried to brush him off.

'But I only ran away because I thought I was going to be with you! Just the two of us,' he said. He wondered about all the words they'd said together, that they wanted to be free, different to the adults. Mr Brennan was an adult!

'We are together,' she said, smiling. 'This is the best way. Always together.' She smiled and, like a flower, turned her face to the light.

Mr Brennan said he had somewhere for them all to live, forever. They were going to live in Year Zero. The children of the future.

PART FOUR

THIRTY-THREE

Stoneythorpe, January 1936

Celia was examining the accounts of Miss Violet's Kitchen in the sitting room. The world outside was changing but here at Stoneythorpe, they were not. She had written to Tom but he hadn't replied. Maybe he was married now. She hadn't heard from Jonathan. No one wanted to buy the house. And there had been no clue about Michael and Lily. The police said the file was still open but that they currently had no leads. Mr Pilsdown said that he was stumped. They had disappeared.

She gazed at a new letter. From Mr Crennet, who had taken over from Mr Pemberton, who had just retired to a small house near Devon. She tore it open and read that the agent had found a buyer. A girl's school. The agent said that was what was happening to all the big houses these days. Two thirds of the asking price.

They had had just three viewings over the last year. All three families had declared the house needed too much work.

Celia looked out onto the lawn and imagined the dell razed down to make a hockey pitch, girls playing lacrosse where Verena's fountains had been.

She had to let it happen. She turned to find her father.

'You're making us leave our home,' said Rudolf. Verena had shut herself in her room, weeping. Celia couldn't bear it either and felt cruel. She hated the thought of leaving the graves behind. They had to. Mr Galss wrote often that the banks were asking for the money.

Now, when she looked out onto the lawn, she saw Michael and Lily coming back. Not builders, tearing out the pipes, rewiring, plumbing in modern sinks for dozens of girls, and knocking down the walls to make dormitories. I can't leave you, she whispered to the garden. It had swallowed up Michael and Lily into thin air. One day it would give them back.

INTERLUDE

The New Children. That's what they were called. They'd create a new world, better than the last. They'd take everybody back to the beginning, Don said. This was the vision. Lily believed it, every word. Michael saw her writing it down, to better remember it, surreptitiously. They weren't supposed to write anything down. Because they were going to Year Zero – when they couldn't write. The written word had polluted mankind and the purity of his thought.

They went to a part of London but he didn't know where it was. They travelled across in the car of a man that he'd never met. He didn't introduce himself, they never did, but bundled them both in the back under the blanket and they drove. Michael wanted to leap out somewhere, take Lily with him. But then, Lily would never leave Mr Brennan, so he had to stay with her and make sure she survived. He'd promised that he would look after her.

The home was a tall house in London – a place he didn't know. There were already too many people living there, so many that all he wanted to do was hide. They didn't introduce themselves either, so who knew who they were, they were always different. The adults took the bedrooms and the children slept together in what would have been the sitting room.

Most of the beginning of the new world was going on in Russia, Don explained. They had learnt to live without possessions, all those things that cluttered you up, stopped you seeing what was really important. They were free. No names, no money, no jobs. Nothing that tied down ordinary humans, none of those emotions that activated their petty lives: jealousy, competition, avarice. Don talked about how people were so deluded in everyday life that all they wanted was to earn more, get more than their neighbours. It didn't matter how much it was, it just had to be more.

So Michael understood. All those words that Lily had said to him about being free of possessions. They had been Mr Brennan's first.

Don and the rest said they were free. The problem was that people were so far behind in their country. So you had to be careful, for everywhere were people who wanted to betray them. They were conventional, tied up in their lives of getting and spending, slaves to the men of business and the systems of money, comforted by the baubles that the system gave them. So they had to be always alert to anyone who seemed to be giving up on the group, thinking of leaving. Of course, if you wanted to leave, you could, they were free, freer than anyone else, but if you did, you had to go quickly without infecting others. No one had, as long as Michael had been there. Why would you want to? They had made life perfect.

Don reported to them from the corrupt world: a mother of six collapsing and dying while bathing her baby twins because she was starving; men who hadn't worked in twenty years, no jobs and the government kept men low by giving them relief that wouldn't feed a family. The country was starving and the government kept cutting relief, sitting in their fine dining clubs and expensive country houses. The government did this to keep the people down, because if the working classes were hungry, they wouldn't have the spirit to attack the government. Even when they did march to London, the government sent them away, told the women they should work in domestic service. They wanted the people to be starving, so when they did find a job, they were so desperate that they'd allow themselves to be treated as badly as the employer desired. They were all together, politicians and big business, making money out of misery, determined to keep people low and poor, because if you had working men with nothing to do but make dolls out of wood in the hope of selling them for a few pennies, you could do whatever you liked. And they did.

They needed to pull themselves out of the world of money because some would always have more.

Michael supposed that these were the sort of words Mr Janus had said, before he'd disappeared off to Spain. He knew Lily was thinking about her father because he saw her sit up when there was ever any mention of Spain, listen closely. But she never talked about it with him now.

They were just going to break everything apart and rise from it, the phoenix from the ashes. How they were going to smash everything, though, he didn't know. And people seemed to him to like buying things and watching cinema screens. Mr Brennan stood at the front and talked vaguely about how everybody would join their vision and then the world as they knew it would end, people would no longer be chained to the old ways of money, getting and spending, their false seductions.

Michael, Mr Brennan and Lily took a small room at the back but they weren't supposed to be there much. The whole idea of Year Zero was that they all lived together – Mr Brennan said that they'd pull down the walls if they could because walls were bourgeois and repressive – but they'd started trying to do it and they had realised that the house might fall – they needed all the walls to support the roof. So the idea was that they would *pretend* not to have walls. Thus, the less time they spent in their room the better. They should always be in the communal room, where everybody ate, cared for the babies and children, played, talked, read. Michael dreaded the days. They always seemed to have to explain the rules to him. He'd use a teacup and someone would tell him that he couldn't, he'd used that teacup before and he was wrong. You weren't allowed to use the same thing twice. Then you were almost owning it. And ownership was evil and pulled the whole world down with it. He'd sit and he'd sat in the same place yesterday and had to be moved. His favourite chair was in the far corner, a squashy, old brown one. Sometimes, when everybody was asleep – even though people slept in the communal room – he'd sneak down and sit in the chair. Just to feel as if he owned it. He wasn't going to give up his wooden horse and his bear. Lily still had her purple cat. He'd seen it under her pillow. If they took away his horse, he'd tell on her purple cat. But something told him that she'd be allowed to keep it, no matter what.

Michael said to Lily, 'I don't like this.' He missed Mama, all of the family and particularly Grandpapa, who'd showed him books in his study. He wondered if they could go home. 'Please,' he said to Lily.

'I'm staying.'

'But why do you like it here?'

That was clear enough. Everyone loved Lily. They looked up and smiled when she came into the room. Women patted the seats beside them and asked her to come and speak. The men nodded when she spoke. Mr Brennan was respected too. Michael was wary of him now, wanted to question everything he said. Why was what he said so important? What was the Secondary World? If he wasn't talking to Lily, he was talking to the group, droning on and on about the New World and the future.

There was so much work, too. He and the five other children, three boys, two girls, had to clean the communal room every day, then the kitchen after all the food had been prepared. The women were doing the washing then. They took the two toddlers with them as they cleaned and tidied. Mr Brennan and the other men were out giving speeches, persuading people to join. Lily usually went with him. When they came back, the meals had to be prepared (great vats of stew, always vats of stew), so the afternoon was chopping vegetables, stirring, under the instruction of the women. He sometimes tried to give the younger children lessons in whatever he could remember, even though he'd been told not to. School, too, was an oppressive system. But he could remember less and less, and it wasn't very easy to teach anything without books. After a few months, he'd given up, just let them play their jokes and games. He grew rather fond of Bear, a six-year-old boy who loved pretending to be planes, and Rainbow, a girl of maybe ten who made them all laugh by playing silly tricks, falling over and pretending she was stuck. The adults said laughter was the corrupt world's way of getting them drunk, forcing them to ignore their position of being exploited. But they usually let them laugh for a while, smile too, themselves.

Lily barely spoke to him. She was always too tired when they got back from speaking. At night, she wouldn't go up to sleep until Mr Brennan did, so Michael went early, listened to the shouts from downstairs, waiting for when Lily curled up next to him and he could pretend they were twins. She never did. He held tight to Harvey, his bear, too old for it he knew, not supposed to have it because possessions were a trap, there to distract you from your oppression, form a warm cocoon around you so you didn't realise you were trapped. He felt for the other children, not allowed toys, saw some of them taking carrots or potatoes to bed with them, wanting some type of doll or bear. He carved faces on their potatoes, great smiles, big eyes, thought of names for them. He gave them his tiny horse to play with, made them promise not to say. Then he lent Rainbow his bear. She wanted it desperately, but he couldn't give it to her. 'You know we're not supposed to have things. I'd get in trouble.' He thought of taking Lily's purple cat for them but he looked for it in her things and couldn't find it.

'Why can't I go lecturing too?' he asked.

They told him he was too young.

'Why do we get to keep our room?' Michael wanted to ask, didn't dare because he thought he'd never manage to get to sleep in the communal room. Other people had to move between rooms. But they were always allowed to keep theirs. He supposed that Mr Brennan must be very favoured.

THIRTY-FOUR

Berlin, 1936

The only way to stop the pain was by keeping moving. Celia busied herself with the business, so she didn't have to think about Michael, Lily, Tom, Jonathan. The bankers said she should try Europe. The sale to the girls' school was proceeding and Rudolf and Verena blamed her. She told herself that she was going to Europe for the business so they would have enough to buy a home. But really, she couldn't bear to be there to see it, her parents' misery as they packed their boxes.

She wrote to Tom. 'I am leaving for Germany. I don't know how long I will be. I can't stay any more. The empty house is too much. I can't bear that I have lost Michael again.' She didn't leave an address for him. She didn't want a reply. No one could help her in the dark hole, her pain that Michael might never come back.

She travelled to Paris and Madrid – and now Berlin, researching bringing Miss Violet to Europe. She had talked to department stores on the Champs-Élysées, showed pictures of Miss Violet to groups of young French girls, to see what they thought of her, visited possible factories outside Paris and in Lille and Lyons, as well as visiting some big French farmers. She had stayed in a grand hotel in Paris, looking out at the Place de Concorde, gazed out at the lights of houses where she knew nobody. Men tried to speak to her in the hotel restaurant, waiting in the lobby, on trains. She carried Michael's sketch of Miss Violet, the photographs of the products and the displays in Harrods, her shops in Oxford Street and Winchester. She came from Paris with orders, plans of hiring a salesgirl who spoke French.

When people found she was English, they wanted to talk about the King. The old King George was dead, died late at night in Sandringham and the new King was on the throne, young and glamorous, the Prince of Wales who had been so popular was now Edward VIII. Who would he marry, they all wanted to know. She had to tell them she knew as little about the royals as they did. Most of all, the French talked about war, much more than they did back at home. They feared Germany and invasion. 'Oh no,' she said. 'It won't happen.'

In Berlin she took a room in the hotel there. The city was all building, the new stadium going up, hundreds, thousands of men carrying bricks, climbing ladders, hammering steel. They were making a new road from the stadium to the palace, widening it so great processions could walk down it. They were chopping down the trees along the route, lime trees said to be the heart of Berlin, even though there was protest in the newspapers. The Olympics was coming and that was most important. So much talk in the newspapers about the Chancellor making Germany great again – it was as if no one knew that people in Europe were afraid of him.

She walked into the centre of the city and surveyed the great Wertheim department store, glass roof vaulting high into the sky. She imagined a big display of Miss Violet's Kitchen in the front window.

But the women looked so much more cast down than they had in England or France. They wore grey coats, shapeless hats, heads down as they hurried onto the trams. She wasn't sure if they would even like carefree Miss Violet at all. The men too were sombre – but the women looked so sad. She went to the Haus Vaterland, which housed the biggest café in the world, crammed with tourists and people after a long day's work. Surely they would be happy there. She wandered the Hungarian village inn, the Turkish café (so busy), wished Michael could be there to see the cowboys in the Wild West bar. There was a Rhineland café, surrounded by an artificial river, an hourly storm that showered the people wandering around the pretend countryside with rain. The Rhineland that they had occupied, without permission – it

301

was what they said they wanted. But, despite that, all the fun of Haus Vaterland, still the Germans looked fearful, and refused to speak to her, a foreigner.

One of the bankers she met told her that Hitler had plans for a great new city, Germania, a dome that rose a thousand feet into the sky. The whole place would be rubble, allowing the new Germany to arrive.

There wasn't much interest in Miss Violet's Kitchen. Everyone was being told to buy German. The stores were polite but said that women in Germany wanted to cook for their husbands – that the Chancellor stressed the importance of being a good housewife and tins would not be popular.

'Well, Papa, I tried,' she said to the sky.

She travelled to see Johann, Hilde, Lotte and Heinrich in the Black Forest. Heinrich and Lotte were poorer than before. Hilde was still living at home although assisting with teaching at the local school. Johann was still making windmills out of matchsticks. Her heart tipped. If there was a war, how would they survive? 'You could come to England,' she said, but of course they would not and so they barely heard her when she said it.

'Tom is doing well now,' she wanted to say. 'He's rich.' If only Heinrich had acknowledged him, he could help them. But Lotte would never allow it and not even Hilde asked after him, her half-brother. She ate soup with them in their dark house, heard the news about the Olympics fourth- or fifth-hand from neighbours passing it along. They all shared the new gossip that the lesser newspapers were printing, that the English King was in love with an American – and in early December, it was proved to be true. Edward abdicated. Emmeline's beloved Princesses moved into Buckingham Palace, the little Elizabeth possibly the future Queen. Celia followed the news as avidly as anyone. But underneath it all she worried – that while the newspapers were watching Mrs Simpson, her tiny waist, strings of pearls, the German Chancellor was dreaming of expansion, of making the whole world like the restaurant, each country a captive playground for his imagination.

She wrote to her parents, saying that if they needed her to help with packing up the house, she'd come back. They didn't reply. Emmeline wrote short letters, no detail. She presumed they were busy and she felt guilty for not being there to help with all the movement of the things, years and years of belongings piled up in the rooms.

She followed news about the war in Spain, too, always hoping for sign of Mr Janus. She never said so to Emmeline, but guessed that her sister too was doing the same thing, buying newspapers, looking for hints.

She stayed with her aunt and uncle for far longer than she had expected. Hilde said she was grateful for her company and Lotte thought she brightened Johann. She told Heinrich that her son was Tom's but he refused to listen. Still she took comfort from being with Michael's grandfather, even if he would never admit it. They had celebrated Christmas together and spring drifted into summer. She had been in Germany for almost a year. She hated being away for so long, but Lotte and her cousins needed her. She felt useful, loved even, and even if Michael and Lily were gone, at least she was still helping her family somehow. Back home, the business was doing fine without her.

Eventually, one of the banks called her back to Berlin for a second meeting. They said they had an idea, a property they wished her to review. She arrived back in the city and found it entirely changed in such a short time. There were always military processions now, going back and forth, lines of the Hitler Youth or the League of German Girls or just groups of soldiers, sometimes followed by great black cars containing Nazi Party members and you had to salute. There were loudspeakers along the roads blaring out the words of Hitler and Goebbels about the return of the Empire and the greatness of Germany. She watched the Hitler Youth, marching. If she had been living here, Michael would have been forced to join.

The bank had hoped, it turned out, that she'd buy factories left over from a takeover. When she refused, they tried to sell her other buildings. They said there was no money left in Germany, they needed English money. She smiled, declined, said she would leave. But she stayed for the visit of the now abdicated Edward VIII and Mrs Simpson, gleefully touring a school that would create perfect Aryan boys. She waited in the crowds for their car, saw a tiny blond-haired man in a heavy coat step out with his wife, thin as a bird, held tight to his side as if by a sheen of mesh, and it was, for how could she or he escape, they had to be in love forever and after.

'Where he leads, other English will follow. They will see our greatness,' said the woman next to her. Celia watched the party members curtseying to Wallis, bowing to the Duke. She read the newspapers back at the hotel, Edward saluting outside a mine, visiting Hitler's mountain retreat. Berlin had gone Britain mad – there was a new British café in Haus Vaterland, serving up Yorkshire pudding and Cornish pasties. The radio praised England and the excellent foresight of the Duke. She clutched the photograph of Michael in her pocket and felt filled with fear.

The bank's idea for a property turned out not to be a good one. She would have to bear all the risk. It was time to return home.

In December, she woke up one morning to a knock at her hotel door. The woman said there was an urgent telephone call for her. She scrambled into some clothes, hurried downstairs. She picked up the telephone to hear Emmeline's voice, tinny, distant, the line sounding as if it had a million other breaths on it.

'Celia, you need to come back. They've closed the file. They say Michael and Lily are dead.'

INTERLUDE

Everything was supposed to be shared. Even people. That made Michael sick because it *wasn't true*. They said it, over and over. But over the past few months it had changed. He'd been told to move into the communal room. He lay at the end with the other children, couldn't sleep for all their snuffling and turning. And Mr Brennan and Lily remained in their old room.

Of course, he'd always known that Mr Brennan – Don – preferred Lily to him, right from the start. Perhaps he should have been better at hiding how much he had grown to dislike their old tutor, then maybe they would have invited him out with them. She was seventeen now, more beautiful than ever, her dark hair and bright eyes. It hurt his eyes to look at her.

He'd always known that Mr Brennan liked her.

But he hadn't thought she liked him best *back*.

And they were the children of men. They should like each other equally.

'This isn't how it's supposed to be, Lily,' he said. 'Everything's supposed to be shared.'

She smiled, that perfect beatific smile that she'd turned on him before, at Stoneythorpe, when he'd asked her where she had been. 'We *are* sharing,' she said.

'No, you're not.'

She smiled again. 'Some things are special.'

That night, alone in their room, he took out a pencil he had swiped from the downstairs room. Even that was breaking the rules, because no one was supposed to own anything, no one was supposed to keep anything for themselves. He took it out and he began to draw. He drew a line along the bottom of the wall, where he sat. No one could possibly notice that. They would surely think it just a crack if they even looked at all! The walls in Stoneythorpe had been criss-crossed with cracks, so many that if a giant put his fingers in and pulled, the whole place might come falling down. He carried on tracing the line. Then, when he reached the edge where the line and the pillar met, he began to draw.

THIRTY-FIVE

Stoneythorpe, December 1937

Celia sat in the back seat of the car on her journey from Dover, leaning her head against the window. The glass was hot against her forehead. She kept moving, to capture another piece of cool clear glass, but there was no chance of comfort. Each time, it heated up quickly and everything was on fire again. The flames danced in her thoughts, black and dreadful, seizing her into their furious heart. 'Make it stop,' she said in her mind – and then she realised she had said the words aloud.

How could the police do it? They had made so little effort, it seemed, and then to close the file! To say they had probably died on the road or in the woods, at some point. She couldn't see it – and then she tried to and that was the horror. She knew in her heart that they weren't dead. Michael was still alive. She would know if he was dead. She was sure.

You didn't before, the voice came to her. *Your family said he was dead and you believed them.*

That was different. She knew him now. He was alive.

She took the old route to Stoneythorpe, the one she thought she'd never take again. She'd thought she'd be coming back to another house, a crammed little one in Winchester, maybe. But the message had been clear. Come to Stoneythorpe. She couldn't understand why, how, they were still there. But then, she'd said she'd come back to help and they had never asked her. She'd thought they were perhaps busy, that Emmeline hadn't wanted her to come back.

Emmeline opened the door and paled immediately. Then she flung herself into Celia's arms.

Celia held her close, stroked her back, painfully aware of her slept-in clothes, unwashed hair and body. Emmeline was weeping, incoherent words here and there. 'So awful... All alone... glad you're back.'

'I'm here now,' said Celia, patting her back. Although she wasn't sure how much comfort that could be to her sister. 'Don't worry. Don't cry.' She manoeuvred Emmeline back inside and managed to close the door. Celia stroked her hair. 'I know. I'm here to help you now. I'll do everything.'

Celia didn't ask why they still hadn't moved out – after over two years! – would do it later. She hugged her sister.

'The police are wrong,' she said. 'I know they're alive. Emmeline, it doesn't matter if they close the file. We are still looking, Mr Pilsdown is still looking. We know they're not dead!'

Emmeline was still crying. Celia tried to listen but a wave of tiredness from the journey was sparking, slowly, across her face. She tried to resist it, looked at her sister. The books all said that the Roman statues were probably garish, in their first instance, bright red lips, flaming blue eyes, a child's painting of a face, no light and shade, no subtlety. And then time wore it down and they were more handsome with no colour at all. Emmeline's face was still beautiful, the features regular, small chin, perfect nose. Time had taken all the colour away. And so maybe it wasn't true, that the statues had been less beautiful then, it was just something said to imagine that modern people weren't missing out on anything. She wanted to reach out, trace her sister's face. *Let's go back*, she felt her heart saying. *Let's go back ten, twenty years, when we were still children and we were all together.*

'I'm so sorry you've had to deal with it all,' she said. 'How are our parents?'

'Afraid of war. That's all they talk about. Papa said it was better for Michael to die this way because he'd only die in war.'

'No. I won't hear it!'

Emmeline sat down in one of the alcoves in the hall, the one that had once held a marble statue of Venus. It was gone, broken maybe, shattered into pieces. She leant back against the wall.

'I can hardly talk to them now,' she said. 'They're preoccupied by the news. It started just because you were in Germany and they were interested in the news from there. But then they started to talk about it the whole time, scouring the papers. They bought extra ones for detail.'

Emmeline started talking about Berlin, the Army, the Führer.

'I saw it first-hand,' said Celia. 'It's like a hysteria for him. Well it was. The people seem less willing to salute now but they have no choice. They're afraid of war too.'

'So if they're afraid and we're afraid, then why do it?'

'It won't happen,' Celia said, stoutly. 'We had a war to end all wars. It won't happen again.' But then. Those Hitler Youth wanted to fight. The grandeur of Empire. How could it be gained, they must think, other than through fighting?

Emmeline held out her other hand. It was cold from the marble too. 'Help me,' she said. 'Please help me.'

Emmeline had recovered and they were walking out, towards the garden.

'You will cheer them up,' she said. 'Tell them what it's really like in Germany. You can tell them that there's not going to be a war.'

Celia shook her head. 'I don't know if I really can,' she said. The loudspeakers screaming out the words. The party rallies on the radio. 'I'll try. Why haven't you moved – I thought the school needed to start work on adapting the house?'

'They have had a money problem. Mr Crennet has offered them a discount but still they're not sure. He thinks we might have to drop again.' She turned to Celia. 'How could this all be worth so little?'

Michael and Lily, walking up to the house, looking for them and finding teams of girls playing netball, stern teachers, a secretary saying they had no idea.

*

That night, Rudolf showered her with questions at dinner. He asked her about Germany, the people, Hitler, the economy. 'He hasn't been this animated since you left,' whispered Emmeline, squeezing her hand. 'You're a tonic for him.'

Rudolf grinned expansively. 'I knew my Celia would tell me the truth! You and Tom.'

Celia dropped her fork. She turned to Emmeline. 'Tom?' she whispered.

Emmeline shrugged.

'He came to visit. I wrote to him when the police first mentioned the notion of closing the case. He passed on a few things that the detective had said, nothing useful in any of them. We asked him to stay, two months ago. He comes and goes, he has his own work of course. But he's been a great comfort to Papa.'

Celia felt her blood rising, fury in her throat. 'The fiancée, wife even. Was she staying too?'

'Oh don't start. We asked. He came. We're lonely. I don't care what you think.'

'But—'

'You left us alone!'

'I was going there to help you!'

'He's been so kind!' She grasped Celia's hand. 'You're so lucky.'

'What?'

She lowered her voice, whispered. Rudolf was talking to Verena about the Führer, not hearing.

'You're so lucky that he loves you. I wish he loved me. I've been wrong about him all this time, I'd almost think of offering myself in your place, if I knew for sure that Samuel wasn't coming back, but I doubt he'd take me. It's you he wants.'

Celia looked at her sister's hand. She had to focus on the hand. She stared at it, four fingers, thumb, skin thin over the knuckles. Her heart was beating hard. It was too much. She wanted to tell her to stop.

'He's married. He has a wife. If he's coming, it's just to be kind to us.'

'He's not married. He said it was off.'

'Off?'

'I expect he'll come tomorrow,' said Emmeline. 'He'll be pleased you're back. Now I'm tired. I'm going upstairs.' She stood up and brushed past her, skirts catching. Not a statue, but human, someone real, blood rushing around her, feelings catapulting through her. *I wish he loved me.*

Why shouldn't he? Celia had said she could never love him, grown angry with him, sent him away. So why shouldn't he love Emmeline? He and her, they had none of the history of hurts and divisions, love and hate that Tom and Celia had. Their love could be pure, clean, not tainted by years of cruelties, lack of emotion, resentment. They could start again.

'You have him,' Celia whispered to her sister's back. *Emmeline, you take him.* If she said it out loud, everything would change. And then Michael's father would be always near, Tom could look after all of them. Because Emmeline was surely wrong to say that Tom could never love her. She was beautiful, graceful, *you wanted to protect her.* More fun than Celia, too, witty. Men often loved women and their sisters, didn't they? Celia had read gossip articles about Virginia and Vanessa Bell, exchanging men. In the Bible, weren't men supposed to marry a sister, if their wife was barren? Or something. It had been such a long time since she'd read it.

You have him. Simple words. All she had to say. Tom wanted to marry – and Emmeline was better for him than Celia. Gentler, less angry. If she loved her sister – and she did – she should be able to give him up. Emmeline had lost her husband, lost so much. Surely she deserved this.

Next morning, they were washing up in the kitchen together, after breakfast, when Emmeline heard the front door jangling.

'That must be Tom.'

'He has his own keys?'

Emmeline dried her hands, walked up the stairs, and towards the hall. Celia followed her. They walked through to the parlour and towards the French windows. There was Tom, his back to her. He was standing, smoking. Something in her wanted to run. She wanted to dash back into the house. But Emmeline had hold of her hand now and they were walking forward.

You have him. She couldn't say it.

'Tom,' said Emmeline, her voice too bright. 'Celia is here.' Her sister's voice wasn't normal. It struck hard at Celia's heart. Her sister was in love with Tom. She was in front of her now, saying something to her.

Why hadn't she thought? How long had it been? Was this the reason why she'd never found someone new, rather than Mr Janus, even after his long absence? Surely not, surely that couldn't be so. Emmeline never kept secrets – she would have said something long ago. And yet still, Celia watched her sister, face upturned to gaze at Tom, nodding at what he said. She should say it, give him to her sister. *I don't love him. I never will again. He's yours.* The words wouldn't come. A bird passed low over the trees at the side. It was one Celia didn't recognise – a kite, maybe. It swooped up. The prey it had seen wasn't there.

Tom turned. 'Hello, Celia. I'm so sorry we still haven't found them.' Her heart smashed, hit the floor. A thousand pieces of it flew into the air.

He caught her in his arms. *Like a brother-in-law*, she thought, was that it? A *brother*.

'I'm sure they'll come home eventually,' he said. 'Whatever the police say, I don't believe they're dead.'

'Thank you,' she said, strangled, pressed into his chest. 'Thanks for calling me home.'

He loosened her and she turned her head slightly. Emmeline was standing, just behind them, staring, and the look on her face made Celia's heart break again.

'Emmy—' she began to say. But her sister was walking away and Tom still had his arms around her and she felt as if he was telling the truth, that they would come back and be happy once more. He knew. He must know.

'Emmeline said about your – marriage. I'm sorry.'

He shrugged. 'She found someone else. A richer man. I expect they're married now.'

'Is that you, Tom?' Rudolf called from the dining room. 'Come and talk to us. Celia has brought news from Germany.' And they went in, talked of the cars, the factories, people's desires. She told him that Berlin was always being built, that the people saluted because they had to, talked of the power of the government. Rudolf's eyes were flaming, so bright he might have been feverish. 'The moderate Germans will win out,' she said. 'I feel sure.'

Tom shook his head. 'I don't think so. Something tells me we are on a course for war. Only war can stop it.'

She listened to them talk war, back and forth, her mind flooded with the boys marching.

'How's Albert?'

Emmeline played with her fork. 'Better than he was. Tom and I went to see him last week. He wants to stay at school. It's probably best.' They were eating from Miss Violet's jars, but Rudolf and Verena refused them, wanted a proper meal so Emmeline had cooked up some chicken and cabbage.

Albert had lost his father, sister, cousin, in such a short time. Easier not to think about it. 'I'm sure he's getting a good education,' she said.

'Oh yes,' Tom said. 'I spoke to some of the masters while we were up. They're very pleased with how he's buckling down.'

Celia cleared her throat. 'So what is the news on this money problem of the school? I don't think we should let them be so casual like this. Either they buy or no more.' In her heart, she longed for them not to, to have the place back so Michael could find them once more.

Emmeline looked at Tom. She didn't reply.

'What is it? Did something happen?' Her heart lurched. 'Has the school changed its mind?'

Emmeline was looking at her plate.

'What's happened?'

'It was me,' said Tom. 'I gave the girls' school money to wait.'

'You?'

'I know you didn't want me to buy it. So I won't. But they

were happy to stay the moving in, with a bit of money. Emmeline asked me to come and help with the business while you were on the continent. I thought I might as well do it from here.' He was talking fast. 'Miss Violet's Kitchen is doing well. You could release some of the capital and in a few years even keep the house, I'd say. As long as the country keeps getting richer. Your sister and father knew nothing, though. You took a risk leaving it in their hands.'

She'd wanted to keep the house, for Michael. But not like this. She stared at Emmeline. 'How could you do this? How could you let him?'

Emmeline sighed. 'Celia.'

Tom stood up. 'I was trying to help! And you throw it back in my face.' He flung his napkin down and took himself from the room.

'Look what you've done,' said Emmeline, turning to her.

'How could you let him? You should just have left. You know it. You were wrong to keep hanging around here.'

Emmeline stood up. 'You know nothing! Absolutely nothing!' She rushed from the room as well. Celia sat there, stared at her parents, then got up to go to bed too.

That night she lay in her empty room, unable to sleep. She heard banging doors, the creaks of the corridor outside. One was going to the other's room. They were both lying up there together, talking about her. Probably laughing at her. She shivered, anger and jealousy coursing through her mind.

INTERLUDE

Why did they always have to be together? Micheal didn't understand. What did the two of them have to talk about for all that
time? They were always close together, sitting in the communal
room, deep in conversation. And – even worse – they went up to
the room that had been theirs together, even in the daytime. Yes,
Lily was an adult now, she was eighteen. But why couldn't she
talk to him? No one seemed to stop them. What did they find to
talk about? Why *him*?

At night, he sent his heart up to Stoneythorpe. He sent it flying
to his mother, imagined her receiving it, holding his love tight,
not forgetting him.

He felt so lonely. He missed home, his mother, his grandparents,
all of them. But most of all, he missed Lily. Surely if he just waited
for long enough, she would invite him back again, be his friend
once more.

He had begun to sense that the other people in the house were
talking about Lily and Mr Brennan. He saw them look strangely
at them when they left the room. The women in particular stared
at Lily. When he watched them stare, a hot feeling crept up inside
him, something like fear. He tried to push it down but it came
flooding upwards and filled his mind and the words that it made
weren't clear. He tried to grasp them, but he knew that it was
trying to tell him: *stop. Make it stop.*

It heated his mind, twirled around his eyes, burned his face.
Something bad is happening. And you have to stop it.

But he didn't know how to.

THIRTY-SIX

Stoneythorpe, December 1937

Next morning, they didn't speak about it. None of them mentioned Celia's outburst. They skipped and stepped around it as if it was a giant snowman in the middle of the place. They were polite. Emmeline received a letter from Albert and read it all to them. They had won again at rugby and Mr Stretton was particularly pleased with his latest English composition. The masters suggested he might try for Cambridge.

The newspapers were full of the latest fighter aircraft to be bought by the RAF and the excellent prognoses for Mr Joseph Kennedy, the man who some said might be the next US ambassador to Britain. Something about Mr Kennedy's photograph reminded Celia of Jonathan: handsome, confident that the world and everything it had was open to him. There wasn't much in the newspapers about Germany. They were more concerned with the former King, now living in France, than Germany and the little man she'd seen, lost in his coat in Berlin. Perhaps, she crossed her fingers, perhaps they were right. But she thought of the young men in uniform, lining up and marching through the streets and her mind tipped.

They were going to have a small Christmas, for Albert. They promised each other that they'd eat a proper meal of turkey. But nothing else, no decorations, no tree. Presents only for Albert. She decorated the Miss Violet's Kitchen shops in Winchester and London beautifully, though – a tree covered in little foil-wrapped biscuits and sweets, greenery decked around the walls, beautiful stacks of Christmas puddings and cakes in glowing red and green paper. She wondered about Tom – did he wish he was spending Christmas with the girl he was meant to have married, now buying presents for another, richer man? She sometimes saw clouds pass over his face, supposed it must be pain, was too shy to ask.

Rudolf wouldn't stop talking about the likelihood of war. He was always asking about it. 'The King should be practising shooting,' he said. 'For when the invasion comes.'

'There won't be an invasion,' Celia said.

She had got used to Tom being around on the nights he stayed, maybe three a week, the rest being spent in his home in London. At night, if he was in the house, she found it hard to sleep. One night, when Emmeline had gone to bed and she'd drunk wine at dinner, she found herself telling him about New York and finding Michael, pouring out the whole story about finding his address, and Violet, and conning her way into the Whetstones'.

'Do you think worse of me?' she asked.

He shook his head. 'Of course not. You did what you had to.' He smiled.

'It's astonishing to think they just gave him up to you, after all that time.'

'Yes.'

'For a lot of money. Celia, how could you afford it? Ten thousand dollars. Arthur had to find it for you?'

She blushed. She hadn't told him about Jonathan. She had barely mentioned him at all.

She shook her head.

'Look, Celia, I know you don't want my money, but at least let me give you that. Or half of it. Please.'

Her face flamed. It was like that day with the great new toy car. Tom could buy Michael with his money. It was all so easy for him. Her voice wanted to burst out but she pushed it down. She had taken money from Jonathan, after all.

'No,' she said, trying to be polite. 'There's no need.'

'Please.'

And then the truth was pushing at her heart, welling up like

317

water inside her and she couldn't stop it. 'I didn't pay it. We didn't have it. Jonathan gave me the money.'

'Jonathan?'

'Michael's old university friend. He lives in New York.'

He stared at her. 'Oh, yes, I remember. Big, blond fellow. Always talking.'

'He helped us.'

'You let him buy your son for you?'

She looked away from him. 'I had no choice.' *You were just offering to do the same*, she wanted to say.

'Why would he do it for you? Was he in love with you?'

She blushed. Jonathan with her, running through the streets, his arms around her, asking her to marry him.

'He was, wasn't he? He was in love with you! And so he paid for your child.'

'It wasn't like that.' The scar just under his eye was a brighter red than it had been before.

'Did you tell him he was mine? Or did you try that soldier story on him too.'

She nodded, miserably.

'You lied to both of us. Well—' She saw him clench his fist. He stood up and in three fast steps had slammed out of the room.

She hurried out, passed Rudolf on the stairs. 'Did you see where Tom went?'

He shook his head, grasped her by the arm. 'Tell me again. Why do you think Adolf Hitler is so successful with the German people?'

She answered hurriedly, impatient with his constant questions about Germany, anxious to find Tom.

'But would a war be like the last one?' He looked like a child, then. Waiting for her to reassure him.

'Papa, Germany lost last time. They won't try it again. It's just this madman leading them.' She broke off. 'I'm sorry, Papa. I really must find Tom.'

She dashed into the garden but she couldn't see him. Perhaps she shouldn't chase him at all, he was so angry with her. Well, she reminded herself, what choice had she had? She had to get Michael back. Jonathan had offered. He'd loved her. She'd loved him. And she'd got Michael back. Who was Tom to tell her what to do, how she should have behaved?

'I think we really need to move,' she said to Mr Crennet at their next meeting. The interest was mounting. And Tom had paid the school for six months – but there was only two months of it left to go. He couldn't pay again, she wouldn't ask him. And she feared that that the school would change their minds entirely, find somewhere else for the lacrosse pitches and classrooms.

But the school agreed that the family could remain in it while they prepared for the maintenance work and made it habitable for three hundred girls. They had to pay a tiny rent, which infuriated Rudolf so much he wanted to ring the school and complain, until Celia had convinced him they were lucky. The governors said that they wanted someone living there for security.

There would be six months of work. Then they would have to move out and find somewhere else to live. Stoneythorpe would never be a home again.

They could delay no longer. They would have to find a new place to live. Celia went through the accounts. Once Arthur's debts had been paid, they would barely have enough for a small house in Winchester. Emmeline and Celia walked around Winchester looking at houses to rent. Celia said they were cosy, but Emmeline was angry, said they were tiny, few-bedroom places, poky front rooms, scrubby gardens.

'It's all your fault,' she said. 'Tom could have held them off again.'

'They'd have changed their minds. Anyway, the debts need to be paid. The interest is huge.'

After four days of it, they found a house that was bearable enough, not far from town, a Victorian house on the corner of a road, four bedrooms, and a small garden. The kitchen was in a bad way, but this way they got more space than the others, so they would have to bear it. And they'd still have the money for Albert to go to university, which Rudolf said was vital.

'Although what kind of home poor Albert comes back to, I don't know,' said Verena, sighing.

'Celia needs to help us,' said Emmeline. 'She needs to find a rich husband who can help us. Like Tom or Jonathan.'

'And what I do for the business means nothing?'

'You could never get as much money as a man could give you.'

What followed next was boxes. Boxes and boxes to be packed. Everything else from the house had to be collected together and put aside to be given away or thrown into the rubbish or wrapped up and piled to be stored. Mr Crennet had found a farmer who would give them part of his barn to store their belongings.

'Although why we're storing anything, I don't know,' Emmeline said. 'As if we will ever have a house that can contain them again. All thanks to you. Tom would have let us stay but you wouldn't let him.' Celia ignored her comment, carried on piling things up. They were in the sitting room, wrapping up the ornaments and putting them into boxes. They'd done the same in the war, when they were turning the place into a hospital, so she could pretend that it was only a temporary measure again. Mr Grey and his wife, who'd come from the village to help, took the ornaments from them when they'd wrapped them in newspaper, placed them in a giant cardboard box. After they'd finished with the ornaments, he started rolling up the rugs. Then he stood on a ladder to take down the portraits from the walls: Rudolf, Verena, Michael, Arthur, Emmeline, Celia. Then she thought her heart would break.

After the sitting room was nothing but an empty shell, stains on the walls where portraits had been, furniture covered over and waiting to be taken away, they cleared out the hall, wrapping up the marble statues in the alcoves. Rudolf was packing up the books in his study, Mrs Grey and some others were in the kitchen, wrapping up the cutlery and dinner services. Verena was giving them the saucepans – you hardly needed very many in the new place they would be living. Celia was grateful for Mr Grey, for his calm presence meant that Emmeline couldn't remark too much more about how everything was Celia's fault. The sisters didn't talk, just picked up ornaments and wrapped them up in angry silence.

After that there were the other rooms on the ground floor that had never been used for very much, those that hadn't already been converted into dormitories or classrooms, one full of broken furniture ever since the war, other sitting rooms that had always just been locked, unused. So wasteful, she thought now. Then they went up to the bedrooms.

'I'm not throwing away Michael's things,' said Celia. 'Or Lily's. We need to keep them for when they come back. We need to take them with us to the next house.' They were standing in Michael's room. Celia gazed at his things; the books, the space where the bear that she'd bought him in New York had sat.

'Where are we starting, ladies?' Mr Grey arrived at the door.

'A different room,' said Celia. 'One of the spare ones.' And so up they went to the top floor. They were easy enough, most of them packed high with junk, old beds from the hospital time that were still there. They should have thrown it all out long ago. But perhaps, Celia thought, they had never believed that they would ever leave.

'What are we going to do with it all?' said Emmeline.

Celia imagined it, a giant hole in the ground, full of things no one wanted, things they'd bought, desired once, and then not, snapped tables, old chairs, dolls with no legs. Her mind flitted back to New York, Arthur.

After a while, they climbed up to the loft and started looking through the boxes piled up there. Celia hadn't even been there since she was a child. She opened boxes of her old dolls and Michael's toy planes.

'We can't throw these away,' she said. 'They're our history.'

'Well, where do we put them?' asked Emmeline. 'What's the use of them now? You never missed your old doll before.'

She was right. Celia held up her doll, Magdalena, bought for her when she was seven.

Rudolf had taken her to a department store in London, they'd gone up into the toy section and he'd said she could choose a toy, any one she liked. She'd picked out Magdalena, blue eyes, long brown hair in ringlets, a neat red and green suit, with a matching hat. The pretty saleslady had said she'd made an excellent choice, then started showing them all the other things you could buy for her: a set of gowns, a nightgown, outside coats, rainwear. And a wardrobe made of oak to put them in, a grey dappled horse made of china for Magdalena to ride with a leather saddle and a harness. Rudolf had been filled with bonhomie, charmed by the woman behind the counter, and he said Celia could have the whole lot: clothes, wardrobe, horse. She'd walked out into the street, holding his hand and clutching the box with Magdalena in it, thinking she'd never feel sad again.

The saddle had snapped after a while and the horse had broken when Arthur had thrown it over a chair, pretending it was making a jump. Emmeline had wrecked two of the gowns with scissors and ink, when they'd been playing dressmakers. But Celia had kept Magdalena herself safe, hiding her under her covers in the daytime so the others wouldn't find her, brushing her hair at night, washing her porcelain face with a flannel once a week. And yet, then she'd forgotten about her and someone had packed her up into a box – and Celia had never even missed her apart from when she'd thought briefly about her again after Lily had been born, but then Michael came and she forgot everything.

She held her close. 'She's still a beautiful doll. There must be a child who'd like her.' She could have given her away years ago, to Lily or a child in the village. Instead, she'd kept her stuffed in the bottom of a box in the attic, no use to anyone.

'I shall give her to a child,' said Celia.

'Are you expecting to have another? You've left it a long time.'

Celia ignored her, pulled out the gowns from the box. The moths had got at the velvet dress, it was covered in holes and the lace collar was in tatters. But the raincoat was still wearable, and the nightgown was only a little yellowed. The red and green suit was worn and fraying at the edges.

'That's the sort of thing that needs to go in the bin,' said Emmeline. 'We can't take everything. You can't. The more space we use up of this barn, the more we have to pay.'

But in every box they opened, there were things they wanted. Their old schoolbooks and what even looked like old schoolbooks of Verena's. Emmeline found pairs of knitted baby shoes – which child's, she didn't know – children's outfits, a rocking horse. Some of it could even once have been Rudolf's. Things flowed every-where.

'You know, I think we should just not open these,' said Emmeline, kneeling back, her hands covered in dust. 'If we never wanted them before, then we don't need them now. This is just taking up time.'

Celia wanted to argue. But still. Each box made her feel so sad – for time passed, people gone, days she could never get back. Perhaps there was something to be said for being free of it, all the memories, weighing you down, giving you pain because you could never return.

'We must check each one, surely?' she said. 'We should keep the old toys. Just a few of them.'

Celia gazed at the boxes. Rudolf and Verena had probably started with very little – but now, here it was, boxes and boxes of things, clothes, toys, books, so many of them that you couldn't tell who they'd once belonged to. Some of them were her brother's. The books he said she was too small to read, more of the toy planes that he'd hung from his bedroom ceiling. They were only things, she reminded herself. They didn't signify. It was the person who mattered. It was Michael who was special. But she had to look at a photograph to remind herself of what he looked like. He was gone, not real any more, held forever in 1916. And it didn't matter that thousands of boys had had planes like them. Michael had touched these, loved them. They still carried tiny pieces of his skin.

'Let's keep them all,' she said to Emmeline. 'We have to.'

They carried on through the house. So many doors that she'd thought had been locked simply came open in her hands. She pushed open a door back down on the third floor – and realised that the room had been Louisa's. There were two trunks in the corner. She walked over. Full of gowns, beautiful pale blue, delicate green, primrose.

'I didn't know these were still here,' she said to Emmeline. 'I'd forgotten.' The hotel must have sent them back after Louisa had died and someone put them up here. Carelessly. The gowns were thrown in any which way, tangled and crumpled as if they'd been stored in a hurry. Celia sat down against them, pressed a silk skirt to her cheek. 'How pretty she was.'

Emmeline stalked to the corner. There was a dirty pile of newspapers. Emmeline shook out one. 'It's from the trial. Who kept these?'

Celia moved closer, looked over her shoulder. Those words. She remembered every one. 'Throw them away. I can't bear to see them.'

'Poor Arthur,' said Emmeline.

Celia nodded, didn't trust herself to speak. The air around her broke and she was in New York again, held too tight by Arthur over the balcony. Why did it have to be her? Why was she the one who had to keep all the secrets?

They ate dinner with Rudolf and Verena, hands still covered in dust, no matter how much they cleaned them. Rudolf read the newspapers and listened to the wireless all day, and in the evening, he talked of the war, the soldiers mobilising, the building work in Berlin.

After, Celia and Emmeline bent over the washing up together. 'How long is Tom going to stay?' she asked Emmeline.

'I like having him here.' Emmeline passed her a dishcloth. 'You can dry.'

She dried the dishes, thinking rather than talking. Emmeline passed her another cup. And then there was a great bang, echoing around the house. And another. Emmeline dropped her plate, but they barely noticed it crash on the tiles. Celia rushed out, upstairs, following the sound. It had come from the parlour. Something must have fallen, a painting from the wall smashing onto the floor. But twice? She ran.

THIRTY-SEVEN

Stoneythorpe, December 1937

Tom was barring the parlour door. 'You can't come in,' he said. 'I forbid it.'

'What do you mean?' Celia threw himself at him, felt the warmth of his chest.

'You can't come in. Neither of you. You have to go and phone the doctor.'

'What's happened?'

'Quickly! Tell him to come quickly.'

She stared at him. The door was slightly ajar. She peered past and saw great things she didn't understand come crashing into her mind. Blood. Two bodies. She turned and ran to the telephone.

She was dialling the number for the doctor when she heard someone begin to scream. She tried to talk into the receiver and then she realised it was her.

The hours that followed were dreadful. The ambulance came, a black one because what was the use of colour now? Celia was walking asleep, not thinking because thinking was too terrible. Tom took care of everything – the arrangements, the doctors, the discussions about funerals.

'Where did they get the guns?' she asked. She was begging, asking. 'Where did the guns come from?' She couldn't see because the police were in the room.

'They were old,' Tom said. 'Maybe from the war. I suppose they were here for years. They'd probably forgotten about them.'

Until they tried to find them. Until they went looking.

Outside, in the garden, Celia tried to walk but crouched on the grass, crushed into a ball. She looked up and the sky was falling. A bird was fluttering above, just escaping, but it wouldn't, how could it, the sky would crush it too.

'There you are.' Tom came down to sit beside her and she held him, feeling as if she was drowning.

'He wanted to talk about the war. I told him I had to look for you. If I'd just spent longer talking to him.'

He drew her to him again. 'Don't blame yourself. They were afraid of a war. They were always talking of it.'

When had they decided? When had they thought: there is no turning back?

'What did you see?'

'Sorry?'

'What did you see? You walked into the parlour. You saw them. What did you see? What had they done?'

'I didn't see much, Celia. I just – walked in and I realised what had happened, so I – then I closed the door again. I came out.'

'You didn't go to look at them? How could you be sure they were dead?'

He looked away. 'I was sure.'

She looked up and the bird was still above them, swooping, circling. And then it dipped and flew high into the sky, almost to the clouds. 'Come back,' she shouted. The words echoed back.

'Who?'

'That bird. I wish it would come back.'

She couldn't make him understand. 'Oh, go to Emmeline! She needs you more!' She set off running down the garden, to the dell that was the only place she had left. She ran in under the weeping willow, threw herself onto the rock. 'Please,' she said. 'Please make time stop.'

When she eventually walked back to the house, the sky was beginning to darken. She stood at the door of the sitting room. There were men in there. She couldn't look in, walked to the dining room where the policemen were talking to Emmeline and Tom.

Which chair did they die in? Where did you find them? What she had seen through the door – the splashes of blood, the bodies. The shadow of what she had thought she had seen. The head.

'This is my sister, Celia de Witt,' said Emmeline.

The taller, fatter man with pale blond hair nodded. 'I am Detective Bilkson. This is Sergeant Dill. We are just asking a few questions. What light can you shed on your parents' state of mind, Miss?'

'They were afraid of the war. They didn't want another one.'

'And otherwise?'

'Otherwise. Well. They didn't want to leave here, but I thought they'd become accustomed to it. Ma – I mean Mother – seemed to be quite interested in the idea of living in town.'

'You've been away for some time, I believe.'

She nodded, sat down on a stool.

'And during this period? Did you think they'd changed?'

'I couldn't say. They thought that if I went to Germany, I'd tell them the truth. But I did think that war might come and I told them so. So I made it worse.'

Emmeline broke in. 'Not at all, Detective. It wasn't her fault.'

'I am simply trying to understand Mr and Mrs de Witt's state of mind. I am baffled, I might say. Two people, who seem reasonably content, then choose to die? I'm also baffled at the choice of the weapons. Those guns were antiques. That both fired on time, wielded by such elderly people. All I can say is that they must have been determined, don't you think?'

Emmeline sat upright, her face still. The heat was rising in Celia. She fought it down.

'And as I have told Mrs Janus, it is rare that these double pacts tend to work out. One almost always changes his mind, sometimes both. In the end, I believe humans are like cats. We prefer to drag ourselves off to die alone. And so I ask myself, what happened here?'

The heat was high in her now. She just couldn't stop it. It flooded into her mind and she was the bird over the garden and she just couldn't stop. 'Mr Bilkson. Detective. They were so afraid. War is real for them. They were terrified!'

Emmeline looked up at Celia, eyes wide – with what, Celia couldn't tell: fear, dread? But Celia wasn't stopping. 'Detective Bilkson – you don't understand! It's fine for you and all you English people who were born here to English parents. No one is going to tell you to *go home*! Or call you a traitor! Do you know what happened to us in the last war? That's what happened. We lost all our friends. Emmeline lost her fiancé. Someone wrote 'Go Home!' on our garden. And then it got worse. We were supposed to register with the police, not travel. And they took Papa away to a camp. You know, he didn't even get his own mattress there? They weren't even allowed to keep their own mattress, had to hand that in every morning. They didn't want them to have a single possession, because possessions make you human, feel secure – and they wanted my father and the other men to be always anxious. Do you know how many times we've lied, said we're English, changed our name? People would have killed us if they'd known the truth. And then, when all this might be happening again, you say you *can't understand*?'

'Miss – I do understand.' But she wasn't going to let him speak. Her heart wouldn't stop – although it held back other thoughts: *I've been with real Germans. They're not cruel or evil. They are afraid of war too!* And yet, some welcomed it, or at least those young ones who didn't know what it was. The Hitler Youth marching up and down in Berlin, defying their parents who said: Don't fight. Don't let us have another war.

'It was dreadful for us! Everybody thought we were the enemy. And even after the war, it wasn't much better. I made sure nobody knew I had a German father. I lied. But I saw what happened to those who didn't. Stones thrown at them in the street. Turned away from jobs. You're older than me, Detective Bilkson, I presume. You must have seen them. Desperate German men begging on the streets of London because they were forbidden to leave – they only had two weeks to get out, if you remember, and if they didn't manage then they had nowhere to go – and no one would employ them. They were begging for money. But they didn't always get it. Instead people threw things at them. Old vegetables, eggs, dog mess. And do you know what? I never saw them fight back. They just sat there, took it. That's how we were treated. And we will be again. While people like you are *fine*. I mean, I'm sure you've looked hard at our files. When Louisa died, all the newspapers could write about was how we were evil Germans. Killers! And that was years after the war. But that's how Germans were treated when we were at war, no matter how much we'd given the country. *Our* country. And you think my father could face that again? Or my mother? So you have no idea! You stand here and ask questions and say you are *baffled*? How dare you!'

The air in the room stood still. Celia looked at the detective's face, his stony eyes. She might have gone too far. They might all be arrested.

'It's true,' said Tom. 'Miss Witt is right.'

The sergeant coughed. 'This is a civilised country.'

Celia tried to agree. But she couldn't. The fire was still going, flowing up into her mouth. 'That's what everyone says! Great Britain is a civilised country! But it's not. You're polite and generous in your words and then under it all you are angry and furious and ready to knife anyone. You expect us Germans to sit there and take it. *You are lucky to be safe.* That's what they said to my father in the camp. Safe for what? To be tormented, deprived of everything, treated like an animal in the zoo? And you wonder he dreaded it all happening again?'

'Please calm yourself, Miss de Witt. You're clearly hysterical. I didn't mean to cause such upset. I was simply asking the questions that have to be asked.'

'For what? Other people in the police came to investigate when the children vanished. And they didn't find a thing. Nothing. Then they closed the file. They barely even tried.'

Detective Bilkson stood up. 'Perhaps the Sergeant and I might come back another day. When you have all calmed down.'

The word 'calm' infuriated Celia, but the fire had gone now. It was down, back in her heart, angry, flaming at herself, no one else. Her back ached from sitting on the stool.

'Yes, Detective Bilkson,' said Tom. 'I think that would be an excellent idea.' He stood up to show them out.

Celia jumped up, went to the window, hunted for the bird. It wasn't there.

'Thank you,' said Emmeline behind her. 'You told them the truth.' Celia clutched the old table, held tight to it, the only solid thing she could find.

'There's something you're not telling me,' Celia said, that afternoon in the kitchen, making tea. She looked at Tom. 'What is it?'

He busied himself with the teapot.

'You're not telling me something. You won't meet my eye. I know you.'

'There's nothing. I'm going to take this out.'

And yet there was, she knew there was. He was avoiding her. It was something about her parents. Or perhaps Emmeline. The death had shown him that he really loved her.

'Just tell me!' she said. 'I have to know!'

'There's nothing.' He walked out of the kitchen. She heard him balance the tray as he stepped through the door.

She went upstairs, tried to write to Jonathan. The words came out stiff and slow. How long ago it was that they were going to be married. She could have married him, encouraged Rudolf and Verena to live in America and then they would never have died.

Emmeline came and found her weeping. 'You wanted to sell, though,' she said, standing over her. 'Tom would have helped them for longer.'

'And then what? Arthur's debts get so big that they'd swamp us all. It had to be done.' She looked up at her. 'I knew they were unhappy. I didn't pay enough attention.' It must have been terrible, wandering around the house, everything packed away, sparse, like they were living without permission in an abandoned house. Every day closer to when they'd have to finally go.

Emmeline shook her head, sat down. 'Mama said to me that she'd welcome a smaller house, easier to look after. She was lying!'

The thought of Verena saying that, being brave, looking on the bright side, was almost more than Celia could bear. 'What about the thought of war?' she said. 'It was too much for them. They were too old. Too afraid.'

Emmeline shrugged. 'As that policeman said. How rare it was. He said *They must both really have wanted to do it.*'

'Oh God.' She had no more words.

Rudolf and Verena had been taken to the funeral parlour in Winchester. Celia went to see them. She wanted to touch their faces, hold their hands. But when she went into the dingy Chapel of Rest, she found that she couldn't see their faces. They were both wearing porcelain masks, like soldiers in the war had done. Their hair was wigs, Verena's piled high on her head in a way she would never have arranged it when she was alive.

'Can I touch their hands?' she asked the undertaker.

Rudolf was in his suit, Verena in her blue velvet day dress, both outfits looking old now.

He shook his head. 'We've had to embalm them. You'd find them awfully cold.'

'Please.'

'We find it upsets people more than it comforts.'

'I would be so grateful. I wouldn't tell anyone.'

He relented. 'Just this once. Just between us.'

He pushed a chair in between them and he took one hand of each out of the coffin, laid them in hers. He was right, the hands were cold, almost rubbery. She held them tight, as if she could almost force more blood into them.

She tried to talk to them, think of things to say. But all she could think of to talk about was Germany and what she'd seen there. 'You were right,' she whispered to them. 'The boys of the Hitler Youth marching up and down Berlin, growing older, ready to fight for the Party and the future – and Germany becoming great once more.'

On the way back home, the town gaudy with Christmas decorations, she stopped at a newsstand. Tom had told her not to look at the newspapers, but she had to know. Everyone else would have seen it.

'Do you have any old papers?' she asked the bearded, bored-looking man running the stall. 'From yesterday, the day before.'

He shrugged. 'Shouldn't think so, Miss. I can have a look for you, though. I should send them back, mind. So they will cost you.'

'That's fine.'

'I suppose I'm not busy. You give me a shout if any customers arrive.' He walked off to the back of the shop, came back five or so minutes later with a big bundle of papers. 'Two pounds to you, Miss.'

'One.' They were no use to anybody.

'One and six.'

'Done.'

She spotted the words: German, double suicide. 'Yes, these will do.' She handed over the money and bundled them up in her arm, went to catch a cab home.

Sitting in the back, chugging to Stoneythope, she read the front pages. *The Times* talked about the sadness of the 'senior genera-tion', how they'd seen the world make mistakes and couldn't bear to see it again. Other newspapers talked about 'Germans', the inner heart of cowardice, how Germans had tried so hard to ruin the country once upon a time, might do so again. How they let spies in, tried to poison the wells.

'Here, Miss?' shouted the driver, over his shoulder.

'Just here, thank you.' As she sat up, she gazed uncomprehend-ingly at the sentences on the page, all the old German hatred, every word transported, it seemed to her, from 1914. Nothing had changed. The English had just been pretending all this time. When she'd been speaking to Detective Bilkson, she'd been seized by fury. But every word had been true. It was happening again.

THIRTY-EIGHT

Stoneythorpe, December 1937

When Celia got back, there was a letter on the hall table. From America. She tore it open. She scanned the words.

You know I waited. I hoped you'd change your mind. Even after you returned your ring. But I have found another to marry. I am going to ask her and I feel she will say yes.

Jonathan. A thousand miles away. Marrying someone else. A girl who loved America and would never leave. Her mind swooped with the first time they'd kissed, in the garden she could see from her room. Then in New York, when he came for her, after the dreadful ball, running into the hotel and there he was. Walking back to her room and then there together, holding tight to him as he took her to the bottom of the sea. Thinking about how if she had his baby, it would be a sibling for Michael. Going to the speakeasy, walking through the streets, the drink pounding in her head. Him with Michael, her family. The photo of her, clutching her bunch of flowers.

And now it was nothing. To be forgotten.

The other girl. She wondered about her, hoped she was kind and generous, couldn't help but jealously wonder how pretty she was. Their wedding, perhaps even in one of the hotels they had looked at, flowers, her white dress, smiling faces.

She walked to the window. The garden was empty, overgrown. Full of ghosts. Her parents, Arthur, Michael. Michael and Lily. Now Jonathan.

Wait for me! little girl Celia cried. *Wait!* Hurrying after the older children, trying to join in. And now they'd gone ahead of her again. She was left behind.

She walked out of the room, letter clutched in her hand. Down the stairs, through the hall. Tom was standing at the door, smoking.

'I didn't realise you were back from the Chapel of Rest,' he said. 'How was it?'

'They looked peaceful. Maybe content. They'd arranged Mama's hair.'

He shuffled his feet, looked down. 'So sad.'

'And then I had a letter. From Jonathan.'

'The man who gave you the money?'

She nodded. 'He asked me to marry him. I said I would. I was grateful to him. I thought we could make a life in America. And then I came back here – and I couldn't leave Papa and Mama. And Emmeline.'

'Ah, yes. The family.' He pulled the cigarette to his lips, drew hard.

'I probably shouldn't have said yes.' She was talking too much.

'So you didn't go back.' He pulled at the cigarette again.

His face was furious. She shouldn't be telling him. She told herself to stop talking. She couldn't. Tom kept smoking as she talked on, telling him about Michael and how Jonathan offered them both a new life.

He might not even be listening to her. He might be horrified by her. Talking about loving another man, then agreeing to be engaged without giving it any proper thought. She kept talking.

'And when did you tell him it was over?'

'He came to the party. The one—'

'So you invited him and told him you weren't going to stay with him. Poor chap.'

'I was telling him that when I heard the voices. Michael and Lily, rushing down.

'Ah. You said he was asking you questions.'

She watched the light of his cigarette, faint against the sun. He'd caught her to him in Baden and there had been people

335

smoking in the background. Something within her longed for him to do it now. She shook herself. She had just been writing to Jonathan! And here she was, wishing for Tom to grasp her and hold her.

Her heart struck cold. Was it just because she wanted to take him from Emmeline? Shameful. She should be ashamed.

She looked down. 'It was a terrible thing to do. I was cruel to him.'

Tom dropped his cigarette, crushed it under his heel.

'You're too hard on yourself, Celia. I say he knew what he was getting into. Anyone knows how devoted you are to your family. You would never have stayed in New York.'

She had thought she would, once. She had offered herself to Jonathan in the first place. She got caught up in the idea of living with him in America, happily ever after. But she couldn't go back there, leave her family, and had feared that Michael might be taken from her again. And if he wouldn't come to England – then there was no answer. Love couldn't conquer all.

Tom looked away. His eyes clouded, an odd wry look on his face.

'So I've told you everything now,' she said. 'What about you? Have you told me everything?'

'Well, you're right. Emmeline got a letter. They're not going to sell you the house in Winchester any more. Too much scandal. We have to find another one.'

German. Too German. 'Never mind,' she said. 'I didn't like it much. But there's something else you're not telling me. What is it?'

His face hardened. 'Everything I need to. What do you want to know?'

'The thing you're still hiding from me. I know there's something.'

I am in love with your sister, she waited for him to say. *I love her and I want to marry her.*

'Go on,' she said. 'I wish you'd tell me.'

'There's nothing. Really. Nothing.'

'I know there's something.'

He leant back against the wall. 'How, Celia? How do you *know*?

Do you read minds? Or is it just because you keep so much secret that you think everyone else does too?'

She watched him go. Maybe he didn't even see it himself, that he was in love with Emmeline. It was unconscious. The minute someone told him, it would flower into truth. She imagined herself, the spinster sister, third wheel to Emmeline and Tom on a walking holiday, trotting along with Albert. Then it struck her with a rush of cold water. Emmeline was still young enough to have another child. Or two, three. She, Celia, would be the spinster-aunt nanny for their children, holding their hands on the holiday while Emmeline and Tom strode off happily in front. People around them would think how kind Emmeline and Tom were for taking their unmarriageable sister out.

In the days following, they tried not to talk, prepared for the funeral – which the church had said would have to be delayed until after Christmas. Not that it would be large. Rudolf and Verena hadn't had many friends in the past years and there weren't many relations left.

'I wrote to Heinrich and Lotte when it happened,' Emmeline said. Celia stole a glance at Tom. 'I haven't heard back.'

'I think we should go ahead without them,' said Celia. 'I don't think they could afford to come. And travel is difficult now.'

So there was no one from Germany to come and Verena's family were pretty much all gone, with Louisa, Matthew and Lady Deerhurst all dead.

Celia knelt down in the sitting room, by the bundle of papers. They had gone through everybody.

'So it might be just us, then?' she asked.

'My family will come,' said Tom.

'There will be others,' said Emmeline. 'The church, then back here for sandwiches.'

Celia thought of it, the sparse bare room where Rudolf and Verena had died, filled with people eating sandwiches.

Her heart filled. 'And after that we need to leave this house,' she said. 'I can't bear it so empty. The school can move in, we can leave and they can get the works done without us. We'll find something else.' The idea of the funeral, the empty obeisance, the fact that they were gone and nothing could bring them back. It filled her heart, sparked her body with pain.

Emmeline drew herself up. 'Like what?'

'A house, like the one we looked at before in Winchester. It will be perfectly fine. We need to be out of here, pay all the dues.'

'How can you say that, Celia,' said Tom. 'This was their home.'

'How can *I* say that? It's all right for you! You can go off and get married. But we can't live here any more. I can't! Am I going to spend the rest of my life sitting here, watching you two moon over each other? You can creep around, amuse yourselves with thinking I won't notice. Well, I'm not your spectator. So after the funeral, we all move out. The school gets the house and we make a new life.'

Emmeline and Tom were staring at her. Her sister was flushed, tears glistening in her eyes. Tom's expression she couldn't read.

Celia sat, made breathless by her own anger. One of them could speak.

Finally, Tom shook his head. 'What are you talking about, Celia?'

And that provoked more fury. 'What do you mean, what am I talking about? You go into her room at night! I know you do. I hear you!'

'Celia,' said Emmeline, urgently. 'Please.'

'You two are in love with each other! I've seen the way you look at each other. Her staring after you. I'm the biggest gooseberry in the world around you two lovers!'

'Lovers?' Tom was staring at her. 'Me and Emmeline? But – Celia.' He looked at Emmeline, tears running down her face. 'Celia, this is not—' He stopped.

'Hello,' said a cheerful voice behind them. 'The door was open, so I walked straight in. I thought I might find you here.'

Emmeline turned around. Celia did too, saw a skinny, sunburnt man with shaggy dark hair and a huge beard in a dark, scruffy coat, dirty trousers, boots that had split. And then in what Celia – and all of them – would later say was an almost unbelievable moment, not real, Emmeline tried to stand up, and instead she fainted and crashed to the floor.

INTERLUDE

Often, Michael wondered about the world around him. He wondered about the Prime Minister and the new King and Queen. The Children of the Future said that you should never think of such things, that these people were just put in as circus monkeys, distractions from what was really going on, which was great movements of power and capital, and the only way to escape from it was to ignore them all, altogether.

Most of all, he wondered about war. When he had briefly accompanied a group who were knocking on doors, he'd seen a placard saying news about Germany. Invasion! And in Spain, they were fighting still, but losing now. Uncle Janus might be suffering.

Don said it was all lies, that war was cooked up between the rich, just like they cooked up financial crashes, to keep the poor repressed. If people were always afraid of a crash, they never protested their job. And if they were always afraid of war, then they would never resist the government and always fall behind its efforts to make them all the same, all servants of power, wearing the poppy and talking about the sacrifice of ordinary men, claiming that type of memory had purity and anyone who didn't believe in it was wrong. You wear your poppy and you obey and you say you are *patriotic*.

'But will there be a war?' he'd asked.

Don shrugged. 'They always have wars. That's the only way they can control us. Nothing more effective. Those politicians cook up false fights over land and send us off to fight, telling us it's all about bravery and sacrifice.' Don was right, he understood now that the world worked thus. But, still, how could they stop it?

'But now, will they have one now?'

'Why not? It's fun for them.'

'But my family!' He'd heard so much from them about how cruelly the Germans here had been treated in the last war. Rudolf had been in prison.

'There is no such thing as family, remember,' Don said. 'We are your family.'

'Of course.'

Don raised his eyebrows. 'Don't forget it.'

And yet still, when he lay in the common room, listening to the snuffles and sighs of the others, not able to sleep, he thought of boys his age in Germany. He could guess what they were doing. They were marching with guns, practising, learning how to go to war. Something in him yearned to go too.

THIRTY-NINE

Stoneythorpe, December 1937

'Well, that's a welcome and a half,' the scruffy man said, advancing. 'A modern day *Odyssey*. Get back to my wife, and she faints flat on the floor.'

Celia had rushed to Emmeline, but now she was frozen next to her.

'Samuel?' It was his voice she recognised. And, thinking about it, he was the right height. But nothing else was the same! He was rake-thin and dirty, his beard so huge it obscured half of his face, the rest of it hidden by his straggly hair. And his eyebrows seemed to have expanded too – all of his hair had, while everything else had shrunk. His face – the bits she could see – was scorched red and brown. But staring at him, she picked out the old features, the long nose, sharp eyes, left ear that was prone to pointing out of his hair.

'What are you doing here?' she said. 'We – I – thought you were—'

'I said I'd come back, didn't I? Now, what's this with my wife?' He bent down to pick her up and carried her to the sofa.

'I'll get some water,' Tom said, hurrying out of the room.

Mr Janus patted Emmeline's forehead. 'I suppose it was a bit of a shock to her!'

'I should think so,' said Celia, gathering her feelings. 'She didn't tell me she'd heard from you.'

'She hasn't. No point writing. Post never gets through. And dangerous to know too much anyway.'

'But – Samuel – she thought you were dead.'

He was stroking her forehead. 'Still as beautiful as ever. You haven't changed a bit!'

Tom walked back in with some water. Mr Janus sat Emmeline up and tried to make her drink. 'Still out cold,' he said. 'But the pulse is beating hard. We'll wake her up.'

Celia tried again. 'Samuel. It's been eight years. Couldn't you have told us how you were? We all thought you were dead.'

He stroked Emmeline's forehead some more. 'I bet she knew I wasn't. She had faith.'

Celia felt as if she was hitting, over and over, at a wall that wouldn't move. 'But it's been so long! What if she'd remarried?'

'But she hasn't.' He stopped stroking her forehead as she stirred. 'Has she?'

'No – of course not.' Celia stole a look at Tom, now standing watching from the door. 'But she might have done.'

'Might, might. She knew I'd come back. And here I am. Not that I've been stunned by the welcome here. And what's happened to all the furniture?'

'Celia,' said Tom. 'Let's leave them. Emmeline will be fine.'

He was right. Emmeline would be fine. But she couldn't leave. 'Why are you back? And are you planning to stay?'

'I expect you've seen the news from Spain. War there. We couldn't stop it. Anyway, our movement is more needed here than there. You're facing a great war here, I'm sure, Germany against the world. And we're going to stop it.'

'And how, exactly?' said Tom

'You'll see. Peace always wins. Anyway, little sister Celia, perhaps you might find this weary traveller something to eat or drink. I'll take care of my wife. And what about my two? I take it they're at school?'

Celia froze. 'Albert is away at school. But Lily—'

'She's gone,' said Tom. 'She and Michael – Celia's son – ran away four years ago. We've tried – well, we've tried everything to find them.'

Mr Janus's face dropped. Celia couldn't read it. 'But—'

Her heart broke for him then. 'I'm sorry, Samuel. So sorry.'

'I don't believe it—'

'We still can't.'

His eyes dimmed, the colour somwhow changed. 'I told them—'

'What?' Emmeline, now fully alert, reached out, seized his hand. 'What do you mean? You know something!'

His face was flushed. Celia felt resentment flash across her heart.

He turned away. 'They wrote to me.'

'They wrote to you?'

'Celia,' said Tom. 'Come on. This can wait.'

'No. I want to hear it,' said Emmeline. 'Go on, Samuel. So they wrote to you?'

'They did. Same address all of you had, even though your letters must have been getting lost, theirs got there in the end. They wanted to come out and help with the struggle. They said they'd been learning the history of class struggle with their tutor, which I was pleased you'd ensured. I told them they were far too young, and anyway, it was wrong to run away. I told them not to.'

'Why didn't you tell us?'

'I told them not to. I didn't think they meant it.'

She imagined the tortuous toing and froing of letters, Stoneythorpe to Spain and back. How they must have made sure that the family would never find out, hiding letters. They must have had the help of one of the servants. How could she not have noticed? And how could she not have thought it was where they might go? They had thought they'd known their children, but really they had just lived in the same house, domestic intimacy meant nothing, the closeness of sharing possessions, breathing the same air wasn't really intimacy at all. They'd known nothing. They hadn't seen a thing.

Mr Janus's face was drained and shocked. 'I thought they had a pie in the sky idea. I didn't think they'd actually go. Where do you think they are?'

'We have no idea. We had – have – a private detective who said it was the perfect disappearance. And – the police have closed the file. They said they must be dead.'

'Dead! No! I won't have it!' He rose up, was shouting now. 'I will find them. Lily isn't dead! She can't be. Not my girl!'

Emmeline was holding her hands up to him, telling him it was fine, putting her arms around him.

'Come on, Celia,' said Tom again. 'Let's leave them.'

She turned back, watched Mr Janus stroking Emmeline's hair, like she was Sleeping Beauty, woken after a hundred years. And she thought, to him, she had been that, slumbering through a decade, everything that had happened just a dream, that she could be awoken and they could be happy once more. He would have been right – but Michael and Lily were gone.

FORTY

Stoneythorpe, December 1937

Celia and Tom barely saw Emmeline and Mr Janus again on the day he arrived back. They'd been closeted together. Then Mr Janus had borrowed some clothes from Tom, Emmeline had called for a cab, and they'd gone out together to Winchester.

Celia found herself feeling hope. Samuel had heard from the children. He might be able to think of something – a new lead.

'Don't you mind?' Celia had said to Emmeline, when they had met in the kitchen that night. 'Don't you mind that he was away for so long and never wrote? He wrote to the children.'

Emmeline shrugged. 'He's my husband.'

'We thought he was dead!'

'He's not. He's back. And I agreed *for better, for worse*. I was right to wait.'

'I know. But what if he goes again?'

'He won't. He's needed here. You'll see, Celia. He can stop the war.'

Celia picked up her tea cup. 'You never know.'

And then she almost dropped it when Emmeline turned, grasped her shoulders. 'Don't tell him,' she said, her voice urgent. 'Don't tell him about Tom.'

Celia shook her head. 'I would never.' She lowered her voice. 'And there's nothing to tell. Nothing happened. You were just friends. And I misread things because I was jealous.'

Emmeline nodded, her face bowed. 'Thank you.'

'Really. There's nothing to tell. It was nothing. You were just lonely. Glad to have a friend. And I misread the signs because of my own feelings.'

Emmeline smiled. She drew Celia to her. 'We are lucky,' she said. 'Don't you see? Samuel came back when we really needed him. He came back for us.'

Celia shrugged. But over the following days, her sister was proved right. Mr Janus shaved off his beard and cut his hair, bought new clothes – and then said he was going to *take charge of it*. He picked up the funeral arrangements, wrote letters, spoke to the undertaker. He talked to the police and Mr Pilsdown and wrote notes. He contacted the school to meet Albert and went to Winchester to look for houses, trying to be discreet so that the sellers wouldn't know it was the double-suicide family and not sell to them.

'Who's going to live there?' Celia asked, when he was showing them the plans of a Victorian house, just on the outskirts of the city.

'All of us,' he said. 'Anyone who wants to.'

Celia stole a look at Tom over the table. She couldn't read his face. She hadn't been able to, over the last few days. Whenever he thought no one was looking, she could see his thoughts crossing his face, like it was a kaleidoscope, shapes and emotions changing, restarting, joining together. She couldn't guess at what he was thinking.

She'd told Emmeline half of the truth in the kitchen. She had told her that her suspicions were borne of jealousy. But not of being in love with him. It was true, every word. If she had a kaleidoscope inside her, it had turned so all the colours were merged and her heart was swelling and she was thinking, *Why didn't I see this before?* She was in love with him. She loved him. But she couldn't tell him. She was floating in the sea, far from shore, waving at him. He couldn't see her.

Despite the funeral to come, their Christmas, with turkey and pudding, was pleasant, even a little cheerful at times, thanks to the return of Mr Janus and then Albert back for the holidays. But eventually the day of the funeral was upon them. It was sad and slow, quiet as they had expected in the icy graveyard. People from the village, some of the men from the old Winter Meats office, even the deputy headmistress from the local school, Mr Crennet and the shop assistants from Miss Violet's Kitchen in Winchester. They buried them out in the graveyard next to Michael and Arthur and Louisa. Celia felt guilty for not coming to see the graves of her brothers and cousin more. *I haven't forgotten you*, she said. But she had, in a way. She didn't come out to sit by them, talk to them. It made her feel too sad. She'd stayed in the world of the living.

'There won't be a war,' she had told them. 'I promise.' She had lied and thought that would be enough.

She and Tom did the washing up after the reception, still wearing their black clothes, not troubling themselves to change. She wanted to ask him a dozen things, but didn't know where to start.

Albert had come back from school taller and more handsome than ever. He looked like a man, Celia thought, a grown man she hardly knew. He embraced Mr Janus with restraint.

'I know I've been gone a long time,' he said. 'I'm sorry.'

'I told that to the chaps at school. They'd have teased me if I'd said I hadn't got a father. So I said you were in South America, making our fortune. You're not going to make me leave school, are you?'

Mr Janus shook his head. 'Of course not. Of course I wouldn't. Well, at least—'

Emmeline shook her head at him and he broke off.

'I'm nearly finished. Then I'll go to university.' Albert sat down on the sofa. 'I wish my sister was here. She doesn't even know that Grandpapa is dead. Why can't you just find her?'

'We've tried, dear,' said Emmeline. 'We keep trying.'

He glowered across at Celia. 'She used to like me best. Then Michael came along. She stopped writing to me at school. When she did bother, I knew Mamma had made her. I wasn't as much fun as him, I suppose.'

Emmeline put her arm around him. 'She'll always love her brother.'

He shook his head. 'At first, you all said she'd just wanted to run away for fun, and she'd come back. But it's been four years now. And she's not here. She wouldn't have done that if she were happy, would she? You must have made her unhappy.'

'Albert, please.' Emmeline was weeping. Celia looked at her nephew. How could they not have thought? All those cheerful letters about rugby and school dinners and masters. Under it all, he was furious.

'Albert, you're upsetting your mother,' said Mr Janus.

'Well, you'd know about that! Wandering off to God knows where for years on end and expecting us all to welcome you back? I bet you don't know either. What did she do to send them away?' He turned to Celia. 'Or was it you?'

She shook her head.

'So it was my mother, then. Give me an explanation!'

They couldn't. They couldn't think of anything to say.

INTERLUDE

Lily was screaming. Micheal couldn't bear it. He fought to get into the room, desperate to try to help her, but they wouldn't let him. The women barred it against him. He fought them, hearing her desperate cries.

'She's dying in there,' he said. They wouldn't let him go in. He heard Mr Brennan's voice, the voice of the other men and he begged them. 'Please!' They told the other men to take him downstairs and put him in the communal room.

He was fighting hard against them, when he heard another say, 'Let him stay. He might need to be here.'

'Poor boy,' a woman was saying.

'Poor girl, more like,' said another.

'She knew what she was doing.'

'She never had a chance,' said one of the men.

'So much for being free of the outside world,' said a woman.

They shushed her. A man inside the room was talking.

Lily's screams sounded as if something was tearing her in two. He threw himself at the door, and one of the men pulled him back. He was her cousin. He'd known her for the longest of all. Mr Brennan barely knew her.

'Don't let her die!' he shouted. 'Don't let her die!' His heart pulled up to the sky. *Somebody save us.*

FORTY-ONE

Stoneythorpe, January 1938

Albert blamed all of them – and perhaps he was right to. He wouldn't speak to Tom. And now he was refusing to go back to school until Lily and Michael had been found. Celia found herself staring at his handsome, smooth face. She remembered him begin born, after they'd fought their way out of the Victory celebrations, back to the Savoy, the midwives not realising at first that there was a second child behind him.

'You can't stay here forever,' said Emmeline. 'As you said, your schooling is important.'

'This is more so. I'm going to wait here until we find them!' Celia's heart banged hard in her chest. If there was a war, he would go. Tom, Mr Janus, even Jonathan would all be too old. Albert would go, into the trenches, fight, and shoot to kill.

'Don't go, Albert,' she said.

'What?' he said.

She shook her head. 'Ignore me.'

'I can't,' Tom had said. 'Really, I can't. This isn't the answer.'

But Rudolf and Verena wouldn't listen. They wouldn't be told. 'We need your help.'

He'd tried to avoid them, escaping when he saw one of them coming, hiding behind doors. But they waited for him, pressing, patient.

'We need to be ready,' Rudolf said. 'If they come here, I will go down fighting. Just help us do it. It's insurance for us. Peace of mind.' He held out his fingers, curved with arthritis, bright red and swollen. 'A simple task.'

'I can't,' Tom said again, looking at the old gun. He couldn't touch it. And then because nothing else would dissuade them, he told Rudolf about that day, June 1916, when he had been standing in a half circle with the other soldiers, waiting for the traitor. The officers had brought the traitor out, a black hood over his head. They positioned him in the middle. And then the officer tore the hood off and Tom saw it was Michael.

'Stop, sir,' he'd begged the officer. 'We can't. He's not a traitor.'

'Hold your gun, Cotton.'

'But, sir.'

'He is to be shot. He is a traitor.'

'Please.'

'Hold your gun.'

And he hoped that because he was to the side, Michael wouldn't see him, but of course his fuss meant that Michael turned his head – and saw who it was.

'Raise your guns.'

Michael looked at him and said something. And Tom held up his gun. He could shoot fast and first so that the others didn't get him. He would make sure he didn't suffer.

'Fire!'

He did. He held up his rifle and he fired. But the gun flew out of his control, to the side, and his shots hit Michael's feet. The other men killed him, the bullets raking him, jerking him, burrowing into his soul.

'That was then,' Tom said to Rudolf. 'I tried. I failed. I've not been near a gun since.'

'How long have you kept that confession, Tom?' asked Rudolf. 'Since the war? Nearly twenty years?'

'I told Celia. Jonathan Corrigan told her that Michael was shot. Someone forced him to tell her. And I told her the truth. Then she hated me. But he wasn't a traitor or a coward, but ill. After what he saw, he was ill!'

Tom knew about the raid that Michael had led on the German trenches. They had thought it was just corpses lying there. But they had been playing dead and they shot the regiment. Michael's friend, Wheeler, dying, drowning in his own blood.

Rudolf nodded. 'I knew that the regiment was lying. I thought they'd shot him for being German. And now here we are again. A war coming.'

'Don't you hate me?'

'No, not you. I hate the officers. I always knew they were lying. Verena doesn't know. And poor Celia, carrying it around by herself.'

'She's never forgiven me.'

'I forgive you. So she can too. You can tell her when she gets back.'

'Thank you.' The burden he had carried so long, weighing down his soul. He'd thought it would be a relief when it was taken from him. But something in him felt too light, as if not having it hurt even more. Then he knew. If it didn't hurt any more, then Michael was truly gone.

He had envisaged this confession so many times. It had never occurred to him that Rudolf already knew that the cause of Michael's death had been a lie.

'But you have to help us,' said Rudolf. 'When they invade, I will shoot back. I won't die like a coward.'

Tom looked dubiously at the gun. It was so old, too old surely to work. It was unreliable, could blast back any moment. 'That thing's not safe. At least buy a new one.' It belonged in an antique shop, a relic from the Crimean War.

Rudolf shook his head stubbornly. 'This has always been my gun. All I'm asking you to do is to help load it for me, this and its twin. It's just for insurance. We will fight them!'

'You shouldn't have loaded guns in the house. And they aren't going to invade. No one's going to invade. We're not even going to war.'

'Yes we are. And we're going to be ready this time.'

Tom stared at the wall of Rudolf's study, shadows on it where the family portraits had been. Someone had to save him.

'Please, Tom. You owe us this much. We have the gun. It was in the attic. We just need you to load it. And check it. Then you can forget about it.' *You owe it to us. You shot Michael. You made Celia pregnant.* He thought they didn't know about Celia, but he always felt guilty in front of them. He had done so much to ruin their happiness. And now all they wanted was for him to load the guns.

'Rudolf. I had to kill men in the war. I had to shoot Germans, crawling below me. I saw their faces come towards me and I shot them with my gun. Don't make me do it again.'

Rudolf reached out a gnarly, wrinkled hand. 'But this isn't the same. We are defending ourselves. We are defending us all.'

Tom felt his heart fold in on itself, like paper, and all his resistance was gone, and he said, 'Yes. Yes. I'll do it. Yes.'

And he had loaded it for them and readied the gun and Rudolf had taken it in his hand, very grateful, passed him the other. He'd believed them, how it would be a back-up plan, just in case there was invasion and how they were protecting the family. And then they had turned the guns on themselves. He could not tell Celia. He would never tell her. She and Emmeline worried over how Rudolf had managed to load them with his arthritic hands, concluded he must have forced himself through the pain. When they questioned it, he stayed silent, fearing they could see the truth written on his face.

FORTY-TWO

Stoneythorpe, March 1938

Celia didn't take a car from the station, preferring to walk. She was thinking about jars and Mrs Craigmire's idea about having two different puddings in one jar, when Mr Janus came up behind her.

'You made me jump!'

'Sorry,' he said. 'I wanted to talk to you.'

'Oh?'

'You're always so cool with me because I went away, aren't you?'

A car zipped by, heading towards Mareton. More and more of them, every day. Perhaps they'd buy a car, when the children came home – when, not if. She could drive it. They were still in Stoneythorpe. The girls' school had backed out permanently now, talking about financial concerns, the possibility of an approaching war. But Celia saw it in the bursar's eyes when he had met her with Mr Crennet – it was the double suicide, all the cruel words in the newspapers about Germans.

The wind was still chill. She pulled her coat around her. 'We didn't know where you were. We had no idea. You might have been dead. And the children – they wanted to go.'

'I told them not to.'

'But still they went.'

'Yes. Listen, anyway, I wanted to ask you. About that tutor…'

'Mr Brennan?'

'Did they question him?

'Of course. But nothing.'

'Where is he now?'

'Last time they asked, he'd gone abroad.'

'I bet he had.'

'What do you mean?'

'Tell me, what did he look like?'

'Tall, thin, hook-nosed, respectable, quite ordinary really.' She described him in as much detail as she could. 'And he had an odd thing, a blackish speck, just by the pupil of one eye.'

'A blackish speck in one eye?'

'That's right.' He asked her for more details, how large, which pupil, the rest of his appearance.

'Someone with the same name used to come around a little to our meetings. I didn't think anything of it – but he had the same eye. It sounds like the same man.'

'You mean a man used to come to your meetings and then he became our tutor?'

'It sounds like it. We never thought much of him, to be honest. He brought knives to the meetings. In the end, I asked him to leave. Maybe he wanted revenge.'

'Oh no. A tutor.' The answer was touching her heart. Patterns repeating themselves. 'You don't think?'

'I do. Someone had to have helped them. Who else could it have been?'

Celia felt sick. Her mind spooled back. 'Lily?'

'I suspect so.' She stared at him. He was right. It took a man to know it – a man who had been a tutor before. Who had done the same thing. They had been so blind. And all of it due to Mr Janus. Revenge on him for some petty division about who led what, how to conduct the revolution that would never happen. 'If it wasn't for you! This was all about you?'

'I doubt it. Maybe he fell in love with Lily. She's a pretty girl. You should have—'

'Hired a woman? How dare you say that! You left us alone. It was hard enough to find anyone.'

'Sorry, Celia. You're right.'

She held her hand to her head. She couldn't start arguing with him now. They had to think. 'But Mr Pilsdown, the private investigator, interviewed his mother and said it was all fine!'

'Perhaps he made a mistake. I'm sure she lied for him.'

'You're right. If you'd been here—' She stopped. He might have realised then. But *she* should have done. 'We would never have hired him if you'd been here,' she said, realising. 'We have to go and speak to his mother. Maybe she'll tell us.'

'I agree. I wonder if the only reason he started coming to us so keenly was because he wanted to see Lily.'

'I'm going to get the address. I'll ask Mr Pilsdown. As soon as we have it, we'll go.'

Pilsdown had missed it, they all had, it had taken Mr Janus to show them what had been staring them in the face.

Two days later, Celia and Mr Janus were on a train to Reading to visit Mrs Brennan. They had agreed that if she wasn't in, then they'd wait. They took a taxi from the station, drew up to the neat house, white painted windows, tidy garden, in a row of houses that all looked similar. Celia looked at Mr Janus and realised.

'You can't come,' she said. 'You have to wait.'

'What?'

'Two of us would be too much for her. We don't want to frighten her off. Anyway, if I fail, then you can try. It gives us two chances.'

He nodded. 'I see your point.' He leant forward. 'Drive up to the next road, please. I'll wait for you there.'

'Thank you.'

She stepped out and walked to the house, rang the doorbell. How many places she'd pretended to enter, told lies, the Whetstones', trying to find Michael. And here she was, doing it again. The door opened, chain on, and a woman in a fussy blue dress peered out. Her hair was a dark brown puff around her head. Everything about her, the neat dress, the hair, the garden with pink and blue flowers grown from Dutch bulbs in soldier-like rows, was pushing back the wildness, maintaining order.

'Mrs Brennan?'

'Yes.'

'I'm Celia Witt. I wonder if I could come in.' The woman was closing the door against her. 'You see, I've realised we owe Mr Brennan some money.'

'Money?'

'Yes. Quite a bit.' What terrible lies she was telling now. Although, when she thought of it, Brennan had been owed some salary, two weeks or so. They had forgotten – and he had not chased it. Perhaps that should have made them think.

Mrs Brennan opened the door and Celia continued talking, how sorry she was, how she realised that when she'd looked through the accounts, they owed him three months' salary and no one had given it to him. Mrs Brennan smiled, showed her into the sitting room, and offered her a cup of tea. Celia looked around the spotless sitting room while Mrs Brennan was in the kitchen, china ornaments arranged in perfect rows, sorted by animal type, a carpet that looked like it never bore dust. On her return, Celia talked of how sorry she was, said they must send a cheque immediately.

'Where shall we send it?'

'Oh you can send it here.' Too clever for her.

'You're sure he wouldn't like it for himself.'

Mrs Brennan patted her pristine hair. 'No, no.'

'Of course.' What were they going to do? Bring the cheque down and then have Mr Pilsdown follow her to the post office? Possibly that was the only answer. Celia looked round at a row of rabbits on a shelf, the pink notebook by a letter rack. They circled around each other, cheques, addresses. Celia complimented the house, told her how happy they had been with Mr Brennan's work.

Finally, there seemed no point in more. She stood up. 'Thank you for your hospitality, Mrs Brennan. I shall post over the money.'

Then the woman darted across, seized her hand. 'You haven't come about money, have you?'

'No.' Celia met her eyes and saw tears swelling in them.

'You want your child back.'

'I do. I miss him every day. My sister feels the same.'

'I know. You must do. He was my only one too.' She loosened Celia's hands, sat back down on the sofa. 'You're getting closer to them, aren't you? Promise me something,' she said.

'Anything.' Celia held herself still. Something was coming.

'If I give you the address, swear that you won't go after him, just the children. You'll let him go.'

She shouldn't promise. Every bone in her body was saying that she shouldn't promise. He had committed a crime. But what choice did she have?

'I promise.'

Mrs Brennan turned away, scribbled on a paper from the notebook. 'There!' she said, holding it out. 'You promised.'

'You have my word.'

Celia grasped the paper in her hand, stuffed it into her purse, shook Mrs Brennan's hand, let her show her out. When the front door had closed and she was out with the immaculate hydrangeas, she began to run.

Celia handed Mr Janus the paper, blindly. 'Here it is.' He had been right. How betrayed they had been, how blind. She and Emmeline congratulating themselves on appointing such a marvellous teacher. How they were always praising him. How sad they had been when they had told him he had to leave. He had been so calm, so accepting. Under it all, he had been making plans. Such lies. All the while, he'd been keeping them somewhere, while saying to the police and to the family that he didn't know a thing, blamed himself for not seeing anything earlier.

Mr Janus opened the paper and looked it over. 'East London. They're in east London.'

FORTY-THREE

London, April 1938

They got out of the taxi at Liverpool Street station. Emmeline clutched Mr Janus's arm, Albert next to them.

'Jack the Ripper Tour?' offered a man with a beard, holding a placard proclaiming MURDER!

Tom shook his head.

'They go on tours?' asked Emmeline.

'The grisly nature of the human mind,' said Mr Janus.

'Come on,' said Celia. They looked, she thought, no less out of place than the lost-looking tourists gathering around the Jack the Ripper placard. Women in headscarves hurried past them, looking mockingly, Celia thought. She wished Emmeline hadn't worn her best blue velvet coat. It was a little moth-eaten and threadbare, true, but it still cost more than the money some of these women saw all year. 'I want to look smart to see my daughter,' she'd said.

Celia turned to Mr Janus, who was looking out at the people, sizing them up, no doubt, for membership of his movement. 'Could you lead the way?'

He nodded. 'It's not far.' He stepped forward – and so they set off, not on a Jack the Ripper tour, but a walk to see Michael and Lily, five years on. Celia held Tom's arm through the streets, trying not to look like the fish out of water that she felt. They hadn't sent a letter to Michael and Lily saying that they were coming, fearing that if they did, and they were still where Mr Brennan's mother had said, they might flee.

'Shouldn't we tell them?' Celia had said. 'Rather than bursting in on them.'

Something about it didn't seem quite fair. But in her heart, she knew that she'd do anything to have even a brief meeting, even if the way they'd seized it was wrong. They walked around a corner, to a large pub, busy with other groups of out-of-place-looking tourists, gathered around more Ripper placards: 'INNOCENT WOMEN', 'HORROR'.

'The elites slay thousands of us every year, in the course of their power games,' said Mr Janus, loudly, as they walked around one group. 'And yet we're fascinated by the deaths of just a few.'

'*Ssh.*' Emmeline patted his arm.

It was astonishing to Celia how quickly Emmeline had settled into being Mr Janus's wife once more. Patting each other's arms, laughing, smiling across at him. *He could go again tomorrow*, Celia wanted to scream.

'This way,' said Mr Janus, briskly. 'I expect a war will kill our fascination with domestic murder,' he shouted over his shoulder.

They hurried after him, down narrow streets, hung over with washing lines, a stream of dirty water running down the middle of the road. They turned again, and again, into a side road. 'This is it, I think,' he said. They were in front of a tall house, eighteenth-century like all the others.

'I doubt they're here any more,' said Emmeline, under her breath.

Mr Janus stepped up smartly and knocked on the door.

The door cracked open and a woman's face appeared.

'Go away.'

'We've come for Michael and Lily,' said Mr Janus, moving forward. 'We know they're here.'

There were voices behind her. A baby crying.

The woman pushed the door closed – but Mr Janus was pushing back. 'We know they're here,' he said. 'Let us in.'

'Never!' A man appeared next to the woman and they pushed the door shut.

The group stood there, on the doorstep, looking up at the windows.

'Now what are we going to do?' said Albert.

'Wait them out?' said Celia.

'What, camp on the doorstep? Don't be ridiculous, Celia,' said Emmeline. 'We will have to come back with the police.'

'I won't let you,' said Albert. 'The police will arrest Lily and Michael too.'

'I don't think standing here on the doorstep is going to do much good,' said Mr Janus, dryly. 'And I agree with my son, I don't think we want to get the police involved either. Why don't I see if I have any friends who might be able to help us?'

'What, *them?*' snorted Emmeline. 'They'd make it worse.'

'I don't think we have any choice,' said Tom. 'We have to get in somehow. They won't let us in. And if we don't want to break in or ask the police – then we'll have to use someone else.'

'Give me a few hours. I'll come and find you,' Mr Janus said.

Celia cast a last glance at the windows. They might be up there. They could be looking down on them. She was a few feet away from Michael, possibly. And yet she still couldn't touch him.

'What about if they run?' said Celia. 'Shouldn't one of us wait?'

'I'll wait,' Tom said.

'And when I've got the men, I'll come back,' said Mr Janus. 'You lot – get a taxi back to Liverpool Street. Meet me at the station in four hours. We'll do it at night, so no one sees.'

'What if you don't find anyone?'

'Well, then, we will take men off the street.'

They sat in the station café, looking at scones, barely speaking. Celia worried. They were going to break into someone's home. If they were caught, then what? She and Emmeline arrested for breaking into a house? No one would care if they said they were trying to retrieve their children, they'd still be criminals.

'You can't go,' she said to Emmeline. 'It might be dangerous. What if they fight? We'll get dragged into it. You need to stay.'

'I'm going. It's my daughter. I'm going. You stay if you want to.'

'It could be dangerous, Mama,' said Albert. 'Aunt Celia's right.'

'Well, I will have to face it. I'm not leaving now. Why do you want to go, then?'

'I want to be there, too.' Her mind catapulted with scenes of terror and violence. The people, whoever was in there, fighting against Mr Janus's men. Shooting and knives, perhaps. Mr Janus had said Brennan had been interested in violent insurrection. She imagined him saying he would die for the cause. They could die. The children could die. It could be her last moment with Michael.

'They won't want us there,' said Albert. 'Well, maybe me. The rest of you. You know that. They might do anything to get away from you.'

'Look, stop this,' said Celia, breaking in. 'If we're all going, we have to stand together. We need to be there for them.'

They sat in silence. Pictures, terrible pictures fell across Celia's mind. To stop them, she tried to think of how Michael and Lily would have changed. Five years was so long, almost an unimaginable stretch of time for children. After she had missed so much of his life. More of his life had been away from her than with her. Everything had changed. But all she could see was the old Michael – and his lines were still not quite defined. She couldn't even see him.

At eight o clock, Mr Janus met them at Liverpool Street. 'I have the men,' he said. It was dark, the streets that had before looked bustling, cheerful, were gloomy, made her feel fearful. All the Jack the Ripper tourists had gone, tucked up in their hotel beds, she supposed.

'No one's come out,' said Tom, who'd come to meet them. 'From the front way at least. And it's so built up at the back, I can't see where they'd go.'

'Do you really think this is a good idea?' Celia said to Mr Janus. 'What if it goes wrong?'

'No option.'

'What if they're not there?'

'Well, then you dig deep into that company of yours and pay over some money to keep whoever is living there happy and cover any damage we make when we force the door. And then we start searching all over again.'

She clutched Tom's hand. 'I'm afraid.'

He squeezed her fingers. 'Don't be.'

She held his hand harder. It struck her – they were like any father and mother. Two parents, walking to find their son. She vowed that if she found Michael, she would tell him the truth about his father. There would be no more secrets.

As they were following Mr Janus, a large group of men slid in front of them. They were carrying big pieces of wood, like policemen's truncheons.

They curved around the corner, came to the house. There were lights on upstairs.

'Stand over there.' Mr Janus directed them to a house on the other side of the road. They obeyed, walked over.

The men called out to the windows. 'Let us in.'

'Now, please,' added Mr Janus. 'We know you're in there. We're being nice. Let us in.'

There was no reply.

He turned back to the others. His eyes were glittering. *He's enjoying this*, Celia thought. He was enjoying playing the role.

'So, gentlemen,' he said. And three of them flung themselves against the door and it burst inwards. They rushed in. Celia dashed forward. Tom caught her hand but she shook it off. She ran into a dank, dirty hallway and stumbled over broken wood. The men ahead of her were flinging open doors, shouting out 'Stay clear!' But the rooms were deserted, strewn with things, bits of old clothes, food packets, scraps of paper. 'They've left,' she heard Tom say behind her. 'They've just left. They must have just done it as I came to find you. Only five minutes. I was watching. They must have been watching me too. We're too late.'

Celia couldn't believe it. She hurtled to the top of the stairs, ran through the rooms, threw open the doors. Nothing. No one was there. She threw herself against a wall, sat down, closed her eyes. When she opened them again, the room was still quiet. She looked to the side. There was writing there, something scribbled on the wall, a picture. She looked closely. And then she felt sure. It was Michael's hand. She put out her finger, traced his writing. 'Lily,' he had written. Then her heart flew. 'Mama,' in the same hand. She followed the line he had drawn, across the bottom of the wall, and there was a sketch of a house, some trees, a pool. Her heart dropped. He had drawn the gardens. He had drawn the frontage of Stoneythorpe and the gardens. In secret, in pencil, at the bottom of the wall, where no one could see it, he had drawn the gardens. He had drawn their home.

He missed them. She clutched the photograph she always kept in her pocket. He must still be near. *She would find him.*

PART FIVE

FORTY-FOUR

Winchester, October 1938

It was six months since they had found the house in London – but it was, again, as if the children had vanished. They had given Mr Pilsdown all the information and he had been to London, questioned the neighbours and the shopkeepers and spent days there, simply asking people walking past what they knew of the house. They all said they knew nothing, that the people in the house kept themselves to themselves, that they saw adults, children and younger people but they couldn't distinguish which ones, had always felt it was better not to look too closely. When he asked them why, they had clammed up again.

'They were afraid of something,' he said to Celia. 'I hear this man in charge – Don, I believe – had a lot of power. No one wanted to get on the wrong side of him.'

It filled Celia with pain, that if these people had looked closely, they might have seen Michael and Lily, might have been able to rescue them! But, of course she was wrong, the 'disappearing children' story was years old now and no one remembered it but them. They had taken their information to the police, who had been unhelpful, said the children were over sixteen now and could do as they pleased. Albert had begun at Cambridge, along with his best friend from Harrow. At the school prizegiving, he'd won the prize for maths, but on the way home he'd wept and tried to throw it out of the window. 'Where's Lily?' he said. 'I wanted her to be there.'

Finally, after a lot of asking around, Mr Pilsdown had found that a woman working as a cook in one of the pubs that he had visited had been part of the group, chosen to escape. One of the waiters had let it slip to him by mistake.

'Finally,' said Mr Janus, when Celia was reading the letter. 'That man earns his money!'

The woman hadn't wanted to speak, she'd been shy and un-forthcoming and was particularly determined to be silent about Michael and Lily, said she knew nothing. But after Pilsdown pushed her hard, even threatened her with the police, she admitted that the people in the house had split because there had been a disagreement some time before – on what, she would not say – and Michael and Lily had gone. The people who had not let them in and then escaped when Tom came to meet them were the ones who had stayed. She would not say if the children had left with anyone else and next day when he had gone back to interview her again, she had fled.

'Well,' said Mr Janus. 'It is a start. He must continue. Keep making enquiries. And then perhaps we will get somewhere.'

That was all they could hope for, that he found someone else who had been with the group and who could tell them where Michael and Lily had gone. Celia clung to that – and the drawing of the garden, sketched out faintly on the peeling wall.

For now, however, she sat in her office in Winchester, waiting for Mr Crennet. The shops were busy in Winchester and London, and they'd bought a new one in Manchester. It was as if they couldn't stop expanding. She had ordered some catalogues to look into advertising. It was all very well thinking about the modern woman. You had to reach her as well. She looked at her newspaper as she waited.

Chamberlain had been to Germany, back and forth, first time on a plane. Then, when they were readying for the sirens and the evacuation and the blackout – he came back, talked of 'peace for our time'. The wireless blared it out. Germany wanted the Sudetenland from the Czechs. If the Führer got that, then they wouldn't want anything else. The war was over. It would always be over. Albert and Michael were safe and Rudolf and Verena had died for nothing. For the country was going wild for Chamberlain and what he said outside Downing Street was 'peace with honour'. He was on the Buckingham Palace balcony, waving out to the crowds, the hero. No need for the mobilisation of the army after all. Celia tried to believe it, forget the loudspeakers screaming out, the Nuremburg rallies replayed on the radio. The youth marching up and down, in Berlin, determined on the greatness of the Fatherland.

'He's like an innocent abroad. He thinks they're all British gentlemen,' she said.

'Those Czechs,' said Mr Janus. 'Sacrificed.' He was planning a rally to support them. 'The Czechoslovakian problem, indeed!'

'I've read that people want pieces of his umbrella,' said Albert. 'Like holy relics.'

But there was quiet from Germany. Perhaps Chamberlain had been right. Instead, they had other stories of human misery, thousands of refugees from Spain fleeing over the Pyrenees to France. The paper showed queues of them, hollow-eyed, sick-looking, about to die. If Mr Janus had stayed abroad, he would have been caught up in it, desperate too.

'I have good news,' said Mr Crennet, knocking and entering. 'Well, perhaps good and bad would be the best way to see it.' He was holding a letter.

He closed the door behind him.

'The bad news is that the government seem convinced we will go to war,' he said, sitting down.

She shook her head. 'The newspapers say no. How do you know?'

He held out the letter. 'Well, let us say, the Ministry of Food believes there will be a war. They are researching how to feed the nation in the event of war. I have had a request that we draw up our plans and bid for the contracts. They are predicting that many women will be drawn into the workforce and thus they will need our foods and suggest they are sold at subsidised rates in the factories where they will be making munitions and in the workers' restaurants across the country. They are working on the idea that there may be rationing, so we must be creative in what we make. It will necessitate new recipes.'

Celia took the letter from him and read it. She read through requests for confidentiality, details of what they expected, numbers of cafés, factories, workers' restaurants, instructions about the importance of nutritional value and a high energy yield due to the nature of war jobs.

'I don't believe it. We can't be having a war. Tell me it's not true.'

He shook his head. 'There is nothing we can do to stop it. What we can do is help the country prepare. Feeding the nation is paramount, as we are an island.'

She stared at the letter.

'Miss Witt. It seems clear to me that we are in the best position for this. We have the expertise and are far ahead of any of our rivals. It appears to me that we must do this.'

She gazed past him, to the display of bottles and cans behind. The advertising on the wall. They had wanted to make food for the office girl, the shopgirl. Not the woman making weapons. Not war. But he was right. They could feed everyone quickly and efficiently.

'What will be rationed, do you suppose? Lard, butter, sugar, eggs?'

'I expect so. Meat. We can try to get around it, non-rationed foods, although I doubt they yet know what exactly will be rationed or not. They want us to go in next week to discuss the contract. We will have to make some plans.'

She scribbled on her pad. 'And hope they are not needed because we'll have no war.'

'I believe that it will be inevitable,' he said, glancing at her newspaper. 'Hitler will stop at nothing.'

And he was right. Boys marching in Berlin, saluting. Believing, wanting.

Over the next week, Celia worked every moment she could, scribbling out recipes, used flour and vegetables with only a little cheese and meat to add flavour, make it seem more than it was.

The packaging had to be simple, plain, no bows and ribbons and pictures. They would need more factories and more workers.

On Thursday, at two in the afternoon, she and Mr Crennet travelled to the Ministry of Food. She wore her smarter grey suit, tried to arrange her hair. They sat at the end of a long polished table as dozens of men came in and out, asked them questions, gave numbers, pondered recipes. When Celia and Mr Crennet asked questions – how many women do you think? What about the housewives? What about the male workers? Will you concentrate the workers in parts of the country? – none of them could quite give an answer. They shook their heads and said gently that it was all only speculative.

But how can we give you numbers if you can't give anything to us? Celia wanted to shout, but did not. Instead, she and Mr Crennet smiled and nodded and he said, 'Oh yes, if war is announced, we could be ready to go immediately. We don't need any notice.'

Under the table, he kicked Celia gently. It was impossible! Entirely impossible! She had no idea how they'd do it.

'We'll need to rent properties for the factories and warehouses,' she said to the group of men at the end of the table. 'And we'll need to stock up on supplies. The minute war is announced, everyone will rush to the shops to pile up food.'

'That is a good idea,' allowed the man at the end.

'So we'll need an advance against the contract.'

He drew back. 'I'm afraid that is impossible, Miss Witt. You see, there is no contract unless there is war.'

'Of course! But to do this properly, we need money! And what you're saying is that you can't give it to us until war begins.'

'*If* war begins.'

'So we must recruit staff, rent and set up factories, warehouses, buy in the packaging and stockpile the food. And if there is no war, all that will go to waste.'

'I'm sure you can use them in other ways.'

'Well, I don't know we can.' Mr Crennet was nudging her under the table again. He would say that she was ruling them out by being like this, the Ministry would go to one of their rivals. She didn't care. They needed her.

'Because we don't even know when a war would start, if there was one,' she said. 'We might have to keep the factories and staff on for months. Keep buying stock. It can't be done.'

'I feel sure that someone can do it,' said the man, with dignity. 'Perhaps Flower Foods.'

Celia shook her head. 'I doubt they can either! And are the aircraft manufacturers expected to make planes for free, just in case?' she said.

'I cannot say. Not our area.'

'Oh of course they're not. Well, why should we? You should pay for what you're asking for. If you want things done properly. Otherwise, well, Mr Crennet and I and all the existing girls will do our best – but we can't start moving towards a war effort until you tell us and then it will be too late. There will be chaos.'

Mr Crennet nodded. 'Hunger.'

'An army marches on its stomach.' She leant forward. 'Please,' she had forgotten his name. 'Sir. You plan. We need to plan. We can't do it otherwise.'

One bald man was whispering to the one next to him and the one sitting at the end was writing on a pad. Celia smiled at them. The other side were conferring. She looked at Mr Crennet and they both sat quietly, looked out, waited.

The man at the end spoke: 'Let us consider, please, Miss Witt, Mr Crennet. We shall give this some thought.'

They wished them goodbye and walked out through the heavy door into the sun. 'I think you might have won them,' said Mr Crennet.

He was right. Three days later, they received a letter. Five thousand pounds to do advance planning and hire staff and rent factories. The Ministry would expect reports and they would visit at weekly intervals and expect to see the factories. Spot surprise visits would also be carried out. Any hint that there was a lack of proper budgeting and the project would be terminated. And it all must remain secret. No one must know it was war preparations.

'Etcetera!' said Mr Crennet closing the letter. 'We have success.'

'We have a lot to do,' she said. 'We need to start now. How long do you think it will be?' That was the way she thought now – not if, but when. The earth had shifted under her when they came out of the Ministry and she'd known, without even looking at a newspaper, that the world was turning, the boys were marching in Berlin, that Hitler was planning and the planes would thicken across the sky, trails of men walking across Europe, and France would again look like it had when she'd been there, no grass, all soil, pure war.

'How are we going to tell the workers this isn't about war?' she said. 'They'll guess.'

Mr Crennet shrugged. 'We say it's for an overseas market. And if they ask more, we tell them not to. They'll be grateful to have a job.'

She got back to find a letter from Jonathan. He wrote that he had not told her everything in the last letter. He was married now – and his bride was Violet. They both sent their best wishes.

Celia stared. Violet. 'He's married to *Violet*,' Celia said. She had imagined him marrying some society woman, like one of the girls at the ball. He'd told her he'd visited her, promised to check that she was well. And somehow the visits had turned into love. Violet wearing the too-large engagement ring that she had once worn. Yes, Violet was delicate, beautiful, needed his help. Perhaps he would help her find Hope. She was perfect for him – gentle, kind and she never wanted to be anywhere but America. And although Celia knew it was irrational, she couldn't help feel jealous, of him for loving Violet, of her for rebuffing all attempts at friendship, blaming her for being rich when he was the same, and envious of both of them, for finding a love that seemed, to her, looking in, purer and more simple than anything she could ever have, a gift.

INTERLUDE

Don came up to them after another night of shouting. 'There's no choice,' he said. 'We have to leave. This place is empty, false and corrupt and we should never have come.' Mirabel was crying at night and the others didn't like it. She was just a baby. The whole movement was supposed to be about children. And yet they didn't want one when they had one.

'And they don't want us here,' said Michael, under his breath. No one wanted them. They hated them here. He reached out his finger for the wall. He traced the line he had drawn, but didn't dare follow it round to the picture. If he saw it, he thought, he might begin to cry.

'But what about Mirabel?' said Lily. 'They can't keep her!'

'Of course not,' he said, snappily, waving his hand around. 'She comes too. But we have to leave. This place is a disgrace. We need to travel, find purer, find better. And that's not here. Year Zero can never be in Britain. This place is dry, cruel, materialistic. We deserve better! We must go abroad.'

'But where?' Michael asked. 'Where are we going to go?' His heart tugged at the thought of the other children, Bear and Betty and funny Rainbow, the ones who'd almost become his friends. He didn't want to leave them.

'And what about war?' he said. 'I thought there was supposed to be a war coming.'

'I have an idea,' Don said. He reached down, patted Lily, closely. 'It's what you've always wanted. We will go and find him.'

'Who?' asked Michael. But his heart knew, the words in his heart were growing and he saw from Lily's face that she knew the answer too. 'It's too dangerous,' he said. 'We can't!'

'It won't be dangerous with me,' said Don. 'I will look after you.'

'Don't go,' said Bear and Rainbow, still not understanding the rules – no attachments, no affection, love all a myth to keep them suppressed. He wanted to tell them he'd come back for them but knew he never could. He drew them all in his mind because he wasn't allowed to do it for real, sketched out their lines in his head so he wouldn't forget their eyes, mouth, small bodies. He left his toy horse with Bear and his bear with Rainbow. He begged them to hide them, keep them safe, even knowing as he did so that the adults would find them and take them away.

FORTY-FIVE

London, April 1939

Celia worked around the clock – for now they had to keep their own orders fulfilled and prepare for the Ministry. Mr Crennet found five new factories and staffed them. The first, just outside Nottingham, would make soups. 'Once we get going, we will be making five thousand cans a day,' Celia told Mr Greenwood, the man sent from the Ministry. He nodded, approvingly. 'Good. As soon as possible, please. That's the sort of yield we like.'

She nodded. 'Of course.' She'd been right. The earth was moving under her and the planes were ready, coming, rising. Two, three, six months until they were heavy in the sky like crowds of birds at dusk. Not long.

They set up a pie factory in Leicester, a meat patty factory in Lincoln and the one in Birmingham canned dumplings, cheese, vegetables and meat. The Ministry had decreed that puddings were still important and so they would make chocolate sponge, raisin sponge and shortbread biscuits, all in cans.

And the recipes were easy to change, for when things became short in supply. Take out some mutton, add more potato. Take out some leeks, add more potato. Take out some chicken, add more potato. Chocolate sponge with hardly any chocolate in it, they were probably going to have to use gravy colouring to make it brown. She didn't want to think about what would happen when they had to ration sugar and flour.

And if there was no war? They would go back to how they were, give up the factories, lay off the workers. But she knew it was coming. Mr Greenwood talked so seriously about transport,

stressed the importance of secrecy. And the workers knew too
– they didn't ask. Celia sat in her office and went through the figures, wondered how many people all over the country were going
through figures – trains, aeroplanes, hospitals, guns, medicines,
bandages, deaths. She thought of the boys marching in Germany,
faces looking up to the sun.

'If I could give some advice, Miss Witt,' said Mr Greenwood
on one visit. 'I would suggest a stepped-up advertising campaign.
In our target cities for workers, ideally. We want your name in
the minds of the girls – women – so that they will know you so
well that they won't need to think about food or housekeeping.
All their mind will be on their work.'

'Yes, of course,' she said. No point debating with him.

'Oh good. We also wondered if you might show Miss Violet
doing things.'

'Like making munitions?'

He raised an eyebrow. 'Not quite yet. But just general fixing
things.'

She wanted to laugh, it seemed so prosaic. But why not? The
modern girl shouldn't have to wait for a man.

'How about a wireless. She could fix her own wireless?'

'Excellent. Excellent idea, Miss Witt.'

'I have always wanted to put a girl up in Piccadilly Circus. I
want to see Miss Violet up in the lights! But we have been told
there is a long queue.'

'Oh yes?'

'Perhaps you might consider looking into it?'

'Of course, Miss Witt.'

Three weeks later, a letter came. The agency would have a spot
for Miss Violet at Piccadilly Circus in a matter of weeks. The
price was astronomical, but she didn't care. In May, she, Emmeline and the staff from the shops travelled up to London by
train – and stood at Piccadilly Circus as Miss Violet extended
up above them, ten foot tall, in her best blue suit, holding out a

jar. 'Don't stop to cook! Turn to a can!' Her heart was so swollen with joy.

Perhaps Michael would see it one day, admire it, come back. His drawing displayed to all London.

At night, in Mareton, there were practice runs. Men came to dig trenches, their flashlights and lorry headlights shining into Stoneythorpe's windows as they passed. Across London – apparently, the whole country – they were digging trenches in every park, men pulling up the flowers and piling up the soil to make shelters for them, the thousands of souls in London. Mr Janus, Tom and Albert followed the advice in the leaflet and built a refuge in the back garden, walls of sandbags with corrugated iron they bought in the market.

'We are going to war,' said Celia. 'We shouldn't look for the children. If Michael is with us, they will make him go to war.'

'The authorities will find them eventually,' said Tom. 'Conscription is conscription.'

Mr Janus shook his fist. 'It's all lies. We're serving big business whatever we do. The money men make money from war. I refuse to let it happen.'

'I'll go with you tomorrow,' Celia said. 'I'll go to London and I'll join the march.' And yet maybe peace was impossible, polluted, and indeed not peace if it could only be achieved by sacrificing others. The Youth she'd seen would be eighteen now, old enough to fight, ready to sacrifice everything for the Fatherland. 'Why would Hitler give anything to us? Why would he stop?'

Albert looked at them. 'Adults. You ruin the world. Then you expect us to agree and do what you say.'

'Well, hopefully, you can make it better,' said Celia.

Tom put his arm around her, then Emmeline, pulled them together. 'But war doesn't last. Not forever. We can survive it. We did before.' He clasped them closer. 'We have each other.' Celia felt her heart flood with affection and emotion. They had each other. And one day, they would have the children again.

One day, not long after, Celia arrived back from London and there was a letter for her on the hall table. She didn't recognise the handwriting and, peering at the postmark, saw it was from France. They didn't know anyone in France! She sat down on the chair and pulled it open, dreading it, nothing was good news any more, but she'd have to read it. It was like tugging the plaster off, you had to do it quickly. Handwritten, thin paper. She scanned the words, turned it over. Alicia Waterton. Her heart struck. Her old ambulance girl, Waterton, big and brash and bossing them all around, always telling them that 'mother said we should do our bit', former Head Girl of her smart girls' school.

Dear Celia,

It is years since I saw you and we were together in France. But I saw your picture in the newspaper a few years back when you were launching Miss Violet's Kitchen and I felt very proud of you. I hope you remember me from those days. I will never forget them. I sometimes see word of Fitzhugh in the society pages and I hear from time to time from Grant. I think of how young we all were, and I often think of Shepherd and how we are all living our lives and she has been stopped from this and she will always be young, always convinced, as we were, that we could change the world. I hope you remember us all fondly.

Life did not work out the way I had thought it would for me. I never married and suppose I will not now. I trained as a nurse after the war and lived with Mother while I worked at the hospital in Southampton. After she died, I decided to travel and I am with the Red Cross in the south of France now. We are very busy with the refugees who are coming due to the end of the war in Spain. We have thousands coming through every day and we do our best to cope with them. Many are starving. I do not know where they will go from here. I thought I could never be more tired than I was after a day driving in France, and now I can barely drag myself to bed after a day here. But I am older, I suppose, and feel less hope than I did.

But I did not write to share my troubles. I write because I think that you should come here. I am not entirely sure but I think you should. There is something you should see. I am sorry I cannot be clearer, but please believe me that I am serious and would not write unless I was.

If you come here, there are hotels in town where you could stay. I only have a small room on the camp with no space, otherwise you could stay with me. Please advise me what you would like to do. I am sure you are very busy but I will wait to hear from you.

I am pleased that life has worked out so well for you. I have often thought of you over the years – and as I say, how young we were then.

Yours sincerely,
Alicia Waterton.

Celia sat down and stared at the letter. Waterton. She couldn't imagine her as an older woman, the same age as Celia. In her mind, she was the same age as she had been then, tall and confident, talking endlessly.

Celia had always imagined that she would end up being a rich matron in Surrey or somewhere, happily telling the other mothers what to do, organising the tea rota at church, nursing classes for the Sunday school, harping on about her war work as an ambulance driver. Not in the camps in the south of France, surrounded by all those refugees. The picture Celia had seen in the newspaper, hollow-eyed, desperate women carrying children, men, their faces covered in scars, people who'd lost everything. The Waterton she had imagined talked forever about her children and her garden, not, as she must be, desperately asking for supplies and help, trying to keep people alive. How wrong Celia had been.

She didn't seem to want money, although Celia would send her some anyway. She didn't want Celia to go out and help – and what use would Celia be now anyway?

I am sorry I cannot be clearer.

What could it mean? Celia wracked her brain. If Waterton was ill or dying and wanted to tell her something, surely she would have said? And what could she have to tell her anyway? A secret? Celia felt she had had enough secrets to last a lifetime – but even if Waterton had one, what could it be? Nothing about their lives then could have been changed. She hoped that it wasn't something to do with Shep. Surely the poor girl couldn't blame herself for Shep's death? Maybe she was supposed to take that driving shift and gave it to Shep and felt guilty? She shouldn't! They were on the front line and any of them could have died at any time. But Celia knew how you could grip all the blame to your own heart, hate yourself for still being alive when others were dead.

She had to go. If that was it and poor Waterton had been keeping it to herself all these years – she had to travel there. Now that the expansion of the business was ticking along, she could easily leave it for a week or two if she travelled down to the south of France.

But what if war broke out while she was there? Her heart clutched with fear. She had to go, even more so, if war would break out. Waterton needed to tell her now. She would go, hear the secret, tell Waterton it wasn't her fault and get back as quickly as possible. Poor Waterton faced death every day. The least she could do was to get on a train to France.

Over the next week, Celia met Mr Crennet, organised the business, told Emmeline and Mr Janus.

'I should come with you,' Mr Janus said. 'You don't know what it's like down there.'

'No!' Emmeline cried. Celia looked from her sister to her brother-in-law – and knew. Emmeline thought that if her husband went to France, he would never come back.

'I will be fine,' she said. 'Really. I'm not going for long.' She tried to sound more confident than she felt. 'The town will be full of Red Cross people anyway. It will be perfectly safe.'

'They're starving there,' said Mr Janus, flatly. 'They'll kill you for what you have. They'll murder you for your shoes.'

'No, they won't. Anyway, I have to go. She needs me.'

'I've read there's cholera,' said Emmeline. 'You haven't seen her for twenty years. Over twenty years. Why are you doing this?'

Part of her thought the same. Why did she always have to be the one to keep the secrets. Why her? But she had to go. She wrote to Waterton, saying she was on her way. It might be that the letter arrived after her. She had to move fast.

FORTY-SIX

Perpignan, France, May 1939

Celia travelled across the Channel on a choppy ferry that made her sick, caught the train to Paris, and then to Perpignan. As she grew closer, the train started to fill up with nurses, Red Cross people, government workers. When she got out into a station bustling with people, nurses, men shouting in Spanish, she had no idea where to go. She walked to the main square, glad that she had a small bag. The town would be a perfectly ordinary pretty enough small French town – bakery, butcher's shop, toy shop – if it wasn't for all the soldiers walking around, policemen on every corner. Both hotels she tried were full – and then they directed her to a woman who lived two streets back from the main square, who had a spare room.

Celia walked over, knocked on the door and the woman showed her up a narrow staircase to a small room furnished in dark wood, a tiny bed with a pink bedspread, narrow window, clean enough. The woman said no breakfast, no meals, no visitors, and Celia nodded and paid over the money, extortionate but so it had to be if the town was full. She took off her hat, washed her face with the jug of water the woman brought up and headed back out into the square. She would go to a restaurant for something to eat and then tomorrow she would get out to the camps. She was beginning to wonder if she shouldn't have waited at Stoneythorpe for Waterton's reply. But she told herself that she'd find her. The Red Cross headquarters, wherever they were, would be able to direct her.

Three hours later, she was back in her room, ready to sleep. She'd eaten roast chicken and vegetables and started talking to two lady charity workers from Paris. They told her that the volunteers in the camps were rushed off their feet, distributing food and blankets, milk for the children, trying to get the supplies to the children first, the male volunteers attempting to stop the fights that broke out when the food arrived. They said everybody was exhausted, but even worse, couldn't see an end to the situation.

'Where are these people going to go?' one said to her. 'They have nowhere. They're all going to die here. And the world doesn't care.'

She lay in bed reminding herself of those words.

Next morning, Celia found a man who'd drive her out to the Red Cross headquarters, near one of the main camps. She queued up there and found that Waterton was in the Fifth Division camp. Celia left a note with the woman at the desk, staring at the piles of paper to the woman's side, worrying it would never reach Waterton. She turned away, left the queue of nurses and volunteers and soldiers.

She walked back to the village, rather than take a car again, talked to a journalist in the café for a while, walked back to her room and tried to sketch out some ideas for Miss Violet's Kitchen, if there wasn't a war. But her heart wasn't in it and she went back out again, sat in the town square with her notebook in her lap, watching the soldiers passing back and forth, the old men playing boules.

She went back to her house and a large blonde woman in a nurse's coat was waiting by the front door. She knew it was Waterton, from the set of the head on the shoulders, confident, in charge. That hadn't changed, no matter what else had. Celia walked up to her and touched her shoulder and the woman turned and flung herself into her arms. 'You came!' Waterton said. 'I didn't think you would!'

'I had to,' said Celia, muffled into her shoulder, but the woman couldn't hear her. Her shoulders were shaking and she was crying silent tears.

Waterton said she had three hours off as she'd volunteered to take the night shift and they went back to the roast chicken café, Waterton exclaiming about how she thought Celia would never come and how she hadn't changed a bit. 'Mother would be so thrilled to see it!' she said. 'We always kept up with Miss Violet's Kitchen!' She said that her mother cut out every mention in the magazines, had even travelled up to the shop in London for a birthday treat.

Celia felt ashamed for barely giving a thought to Waterton over the years. She called her Celia throughout and Celia struggled to address her as Alicia, gave up and omitted to use her name.

Waterton talked of her work in the camp – the unimaginable squalor, the poverty, the hopelessness, families separated, how disease spread like wildfire and all the children were malnourished. There was cholera, of course, but she and the other nurses in her section were particularly exercised by a measles epidemic that was circulating around the children.

'If they were better fed, we'd have more of a chance,' she said.

Celia offered the money she'd brought, said there was more to come, and Waterton was grateful, said all money had to go via HQ and she would take it in tomorrow. But, still, Celia thought, she was no closer to understanding the letter. Waterton looked exhausted, purple rings under her eyes and grey shadows on her cheeks, but she didn't look like she was *dying* (although who could tell these days?), and although she was keen to talk to Celia about the camps, none of it seemed very specific. Celia could have been any friend from home, a fellow nurse or charity worker even.

But Waterton hadn't just asked her to come all the way because she needed a friend. There had to be something.

'I often think of us, like you said,' Celia ventured when Waterton paused. 'We were all so young, out in France. We had no idea what was really happening. Looking back, I'm almost surprised more of us didn't die than just Shep.'

'Poor Shepherd,' said Waterton, shaking her head. 'So tragic.'

'It was no one's fault, you know,' Celia said carefully. 'Any one of us could have died driving along those roads. She was just very unlucky.' She thought of herself, desperately holding Shep, screaming up to the moon to save her and could hardly credit that she was talking of Shep so casually, eating lunch in a café in France. But she had to say this. No one was to blame.

'Oh no, I agree,' said Waterton. 'Of course, I feel the guilt of the survivor. You must too. But you mustn't blame yourself!'

'No,' said Celia, baffled. What on earth, then, did Waterton want?

Celia gave up, turned her attention back to her chicken. But then Waterton began to speak.

'I can't remember how many sisters you had,' she said. 'Was it two?'

'I have one. Two brothers. One died while I was in France. Near the Somme. The other in America, not long after the Crash.'

'Oh yes,' she said. 'I remember the news. And do they have children?'

Celia talked about Lily and Albert, Euan who died. She said that Albert was at school.'

'And Lily?'

'She ran away. We don't know where she is.'

Waterton nodded. 'How terrible for you all. And she is how old now?'

'She is nearly twenty. An adult. We can't always be chasing her. But still. We thought she was happy with us.'

'Did she run away alone?'

Celia looked at the table. 'No. With my son.'

'You had a son?'

And then Celia was talking about Michael and she couldn't stop. She spoke about how he was born, how he'd been taken from her, how she'd found him, told Waterton everything, said the father had been a friend, because Waterton would never meet Tom, so what did it matter.

Waterton nodded solemnly. 'I am glad you had a child, Celia. I suppose now I never will. Do you have a picture of him?'

Celia took out the picture, at least five years old now, and talked about his good looks, how much she loved him. It was comforting to be able to talk about him, to someone who wasn't going to get upset, like Emmeline – and really she had no one else to talk to. She didn't have a friend.

They talked about Stoneythorpe and selling it and Rudolf and Verena's death, and Waterton shook her head over it all. Then they talked about Waterton's mother and her decline into forgetfulness, the work Waterton did at the hospital. She talked of two near engagements with doctors, neither quite worked out.

'Time goes so quickly,' she said.

Celia nodded. 'I don't think I realised.'

Waterton agreed. 'I should be getting back soon,' she said. 'I'd like you to come with me.'

FORTY-SEVEN

Perpignan, France, May 1939

Celia paid for the meal and then accompanied Waterton on the Red Cross bus taking nurses and soldiers from the town to the camps. They settled together on a back seat and Celia looked out of the window as they left the town behind, moved into farmland, ploughed fields, cows grazing and strings of washing near the farmhouses.

They turned a corner and she could see dozens of low buildings, all surrounded by a tall fence of barbed wire, soldiers patrolling the perimeters. There was a gathering of men and women, sitting on the ground, in worn clothes, calling out to the bus as they passed.

'Who are they?'

'They think their children are here. Or husbands, or wives or parents. But they aren't – the HQ has checked the names. We can't let them in because they'd take anyone they could find.'

'What, they'd take any child?'

'Yes. They want to believe it's theirs. Anything rather than thinking theirs is dead.'

But Celia understood. She remembered learning about sheep from one of their farmers – that they were such keen mothers that if a lamb was orphaned, you could douse it in the smell of another existing lamb and its mother would believe it was hers. She craned back to look, her heart breaking for them.

The bus drove through a checkpoint of soldiers and Waterton signed her in at a small office. She stopped at a wooden door, unlocked it with a key from her waist. 'I have a veil here. Put it over your hair, and under. That's right. There are so many germs around, we ask all visitors to wear them to try to stay healthy.'

Celia wrapped the dark-blue veil tightly around her face, not entirely sure how it worked against germs but supposing something must have to.

'I forgot, have you had measles?' Waterton asked.

'When I was a baby, I think.'

'Good. You can't get it again.'

There were low cement blocks with wooden roofs. Celia walked past one and it was full of women, sitting on beds, nursing babies, talking, sleeping, all of them dressed raggedly, hair unarranged. A lot of them looked sick, coughing, sweating. Cholera, she supposed.

Waterton put her head in. 'I thought they were here. They're usually here.'

'Who?' Celia asked, but Waterton was walking on, nodding to the other nurses as she passed them.

'They must be queueing up,' she was mumbling. Celia hurried to catch up with her, sweeping her skirt out of mud and the rats hurtling about. It was even more awful than she expected, worse than her time during the war. Women slumped against the walls, throwing up, rubbish piled everywhere, flies, cries and moans from inside the buildings. She scrambled to keep up with Waterton. Ahead of them was a long line of older children and teenagers, queueing up near a table serving out food. 'That's it!' said Waterton, and seized Celia's hand. 'Come!'

They passed along the line, up to the servery. Two ladies wrapped in blue veils were passing out bowls of soup to the children, who were queueing up politely. Some of them held the hands of toddlers, siblings, others were carrying babies. They were ragged and dirty and very thin.

'These poor children,' said Celia, walking past them.

'Yes,' said Waterton. 'God knows what they've seen. Some of them are probably even adults but we don't know and neither do they, so why question?'

They came to the front of the queue and the volunteers greeted Waterton, respectfully.

'This is my friend, Miss Witt,' Waterton said. 'She and I might assist you with the queue, if we may.'

'Of course,' said the taller lady volunteer, looking curiously at Celia. 'Perhaps you might like to pass me and Mrs Craig the bowls, Miss Witt.'

Celia nodded and stood behind the stack of wooden bowls, passing one to the tall woman and one to Mrs Craig. They filled them up with soup and passed them forward. Waterton stood at the other side of the table, surveying the line.

The first was a black-eyed girl holding the hand of a small boy. She took a bowl of soup for herself, then loosened his hand to take one for him, put his hand on her skirt, clenching his fingers around the material. She murmured a quiet '*Gracias*', poked the child to do the same. Celia kept on working, staring into the faces of the children, willing herself to tell them apart, remember them, so they weren't just numbers, yet another part of the crowd of human misery.

Waterton patted a boy with russet hair on the shoulder, as he came forward. 'You're bowl monitor, with Jane and Marco, yes?' He looked blank and Mrs Craig started speaking in fast Spanish. 'Make sure you bring them all back,' said Waterton. He nodded.

'They want to keep them,' said Waterton, turning to Celia. 'Not to sell them. They just want to have something they can say is theirs.' Celia thought of her father and what he'd said about not having a mattress at the internment camp in the war. Because having things made you human. Her heart flooded as she looked at the children, so desperate for a possession that they'd keep a dirty soup bowl.

'Come on, children!' said Waterton. '*Vamanos!*'

Celia handed another bowl to Mrs Craig, looked at the child waiting for it. And then her heart crumbled. Two steps behind him was a boy, seventeen or so. He was looking at her. She stared again, clutched Mrs Craig. 'Are you quite well, Miss Witt?' She heard the woman's voice, her sensible, English voice speaking to her but she couldn't understand. Nothing was sensible. Behind him there was a girl, holding a baby and when she saw the baby,

Celia threw her arms around Mrs Craig, trying to hold on. 'Please!' she said. The boy was gazing at her.

'Mama?' he said. 'Mama?'

And Mrs Craig wasn't enough, her pillowy waist couldn't hold Celia and she was falling to the ground.

Celia woke up, lying on a bed in what looked like the nurses' station. She opened her eyes and looked up at a nurse she didn't recognise. 'I'll get Sister,' the woman said, and Celia lay back, clutching the corners of the bed. She heard brisk steps coming towards the bed, the rustle of a uniform skirt and knew it was Waterton.

'I am so sorry!' Waterton was saying, moving forwards to sit on the bed. 'I really am so sorry! I gave you such a shock.'

Celia sat up. 'Michael!' He had looked so different, so thin. His hair was so long that you could barely see his face. Lily's had been almost waist length, so matted.

'Where are they? I must go to them!'

Waterton touched her shoulder. 'No, no. Do lie back. You've had a shock. They're not going anywhere. As you observed, Celia, they can't get out of here. I didn't know, you see. I thought, but I didn't know. And I didn't want to give you false hope. It is your son, isn't it?'

'It is.' Celia could hardly believe she was hearing the words. 'And it looked like Lily with him.' Her head was spinning, circling, lost. 'But how did you know?' And then, her mind turned. *Mother cuts out anything to do with Miss Violet's Kitchen.* All the questions that she had asked her at lunch about her family had just been—'You suspected. You knew they had disappeared.'

'It was all over the papers. I remembered the photographs. And then I came here and there were two children of sixteen or so, although they wouldn't say how old they were, clearly weren't Spanish, the nurses thought, so they sent me over to speak to them. They wouldn't say much. But I felt he was your son.'

'How?'

She smiled. 'He looks like you. But I wasn't sure. And he

wouldn't talk much – and she wouldn't talk at all. So I asked you here. I thought I'd put you together and you'd both know if you were mother and son. If you did not, you did not.'

'But we might not have recognised each other! Time has changed us!'

'Not that much.'

And Celia knew, then, why Waterton hadn't told her the truth, wrote to say *I cannot be clearer*. The women outside the camps willing to take any child, believing a baby was theirs because they were so desperate to have them. If the boy had merely looked a little like Michael but not been him, perhaps she too would have lied to herself, to everybody, said he was hers.

'I can't believe you recognised them.'

'Well, as I said, he looks like you. So does she, a little. And I remembered you from when you were about the same age, so possibly I saw it more. And there was something—'

'Something?'

Waterton shook her head. 'Never mind. Just – I don't know. A feeling.'

Celia looked at her. 'A feeling?' Something not being said. But Waterton shook her head and she thought best not to pursue it. She had them back, after all, and that was all that mattered.

'Is Mr Brennan with them?'

'Who? No. They came alone.'

'Let me see them, please.'

'You must be ready. The children here have been through much pain and sorrow. Few of them will talk.'

'They were in England for a long time. We think we just missed them. Just!'

'Let us go.'

'Well, Lily must be reasonably well if she is helping other women look after their babies,' Celia said, swinging her legs over the side.

'Oh,' said Waterton. 'But that is not another woman's baby. We believe that the little girl is hers.'

Celia held her heart. She didn't understand. She couldn't

394

understand. Lily had a baby? It couldn't be the case. She was a child. She couldn't have a child herself! The whole world was upside down. She gripped the wall but Waterton took her arm. 'Come,' she said. It was too much – but she had to be like Waterton, practical, no emotion. The children needed her. And she followed her, into a room that she said was the recreation room. Celia saw them in the corner, Michael and Lily and the baby and her heart was filled with air and light and she was running, hurtling towards them and then finally, finally they were in front of her and she was falling on them, gathering them in her arms.

'We've missed you so much,' she said. 'I thought I'd never find you again. They told me you were dead.'

Michael was holding tight to her, Lily too. 'You came to save us!' he said. 'I knew you'd come.'

FORTY-EIGHT

Perpignan, June 1939

After that, it was a flurry of passports and discussions and visas and interviews and nothing was as easy as Celia had expected. 'He's my son!' she wanted to say. 'And she is my niece! They have to come with me!' But it wasn't so easy, of course, and she had to sit for hours in HQ and have discussions with different women and men from the Red Cross and men from the army. The baby was particularly difficult, because even though Lily had arrived with her and said she was hers, she had no papers, no birth certificate, no name other than Mirabel, and Lily said she did not know her exact date of birth and would only say she was born in the city. The days dragged on, to the camp and back. Celia begged the Red Cross people – what if they caught the measles? What if Mirabel caught cholera? But things had to be done properly, they said. The children had travelled on false papers and even those were long since lost. Celia railed at the bureaucracy of it all. There were hundreds of children waiting to go, everything had to be done in order. So she watched them get thinner and thinner – and Lily had terrible lice in her hair – and Mirabel cried and cried.

She was only allowed to see the children for an hour a day in a cold room near the nurse's station. She told them that Mr Janus was back and well and keen to see them. She tried to tell them how happy she was to see them again, how she thought she'd lost Michael all over again, how she would listen to anything, that they should say why they had left and she would make sure it never happened again. But she didn't want to push too hard, make them feel guilty for leaving. They had suffered so much.

'We hoped to help in Spain,' said Michael. 'That's why we came. But the war was nearly over.'

'It was very brave of you,' she said, hoping that if she did so, they might talk about why they had, where Brennan was, but they did not. 'It must have been hard travelling here with a baby.'

Michael nodded. 'She was always crying. We tried to hide her but then she cried more.'

'Did Lily have him in London?'

He stared away. 'We're not supposed to talk about London.'

'Who said that?'

He shook his head.

'It was Mr Brennan, wasn't it? He took you?'

He shook his head. 'Don't ask me, Mama. Please.'

She told them about Stoneythorpe and that Verena and Rudolf were dead (although not how they died, that was too much for now). She meant to tell them that they'd probably have to sell the house soon, if they could find another buyer. She wanted to hold them both and never let them go, told herself that she had the rest of her life with them now and she shouldn't hurry them. She held tight to baby Mirabel, when Lily would let her hold her.

Waterton said that they guessed the baby was about seven months old, but they couldn't be sure. It must be that – if they were right about that house in east London – she had been born there. Perhaps that had been what prompted them to go, some kind of division. Who was the father? Michael looked after the baby, held her, fed her with the bottle of milk and always watched over her, but the father? Surely it couldn't be her son.

Celia asked Lily about the baby's name, hoping it would give some sort of clue.

'She was named after a doll I saw in London. Near the flat. Mama took me. I wanted it then but it was too expensive.'

'I'm sorry,' she said, to both of them. 'Whatever we did that drove you both away, I'm sorry. I wish you'd stayed and talked to us. We could have found an answer.'

Michael looked at the floor. 'You wanted to part us. You were going to send us to school.'

'We'll never separate you again. I promise.' She said it with certainty, but still. What on earth Emmeline would say when she arrived home with them – and a baby? She would blame Michael, be angrier with him than ever.

'I can't talk to them,' she said to Waterton. 'Not really.'

'You will get there in the end,' said Waterton. She had been in trouble with HQ for setting up the scene at the soup line, but she'd shrugged it off. 'They've suffered a lot. They need to trust you again.'

'You're right.'

'I'm always right.' Waterton grinned and Celia saw a hint of the girl she remembered – bossy, always taking charge.

'I just don't know how to thank you. You guessed. You knew just by looking at him.'

Waterton took her hand. 'Not entirely. Come and see.' She held her hand and Celia followed her. They walked between the accommodation blocks and through to the one where the children slept. Celia hadn't been allowed to see it – volunteers weren't allowed, let alone ones that had caused chaos in the soup queue. There were children in bed, ones too ill to come out. Waterton led Celia to the back of the neat row of beds. 'This is your son's bed,' she said. 'I noticed something. I should have reported him. Although I have no idea where he found a pencil from!' She pointed down to the floor and Celia crouched down. She looked at the wall. There was the same pencil line she'd seen before. Then a house.

'It looked like Stoneythorpe to me,' said Waterton. 'I always remembered the pictures in the papers of it, thought it would be nice to live somewhere so big and old. Why do you think they left in the first place? Why run away from a house like yours?'

Celia traced the line with her finger, couldn't answer because the truth was that they had run away from them, not the house.

The problems with the paperwork dragged on. In the end, Waterton suggested she hire a notaire from the town – and she went to a Monsieur Grenouille, who bustled in with papers and discussions and hurried everything up, for the price of hundreds of francs.

She sent a telegram to Stoneythorpe, and Mr Janus wrote back saying he'd come, but she told him that by the time he arrived, they'd be leaving.

And finally, she had them, three children with nothing more than their camp-issue clothes – and she had to stop herself from trying to touch them and hold them all the time, so afraid was she of losing them again.

'Thank you,' she said to Waterton – Alicia. 'I don't know how to thank you.'

'It's my job,' said Waterton, briskly. 'If only I could do it for all these children.' But her voice was trembling and there was a tear in her eye.

'Will you come back to England soon?' said Celia. 'It's dangerous here. What if – if – there is a war?'

Wateron shrugged. 'There is always war. I haven't died yet.'

'Come back to England.'

'What is there for me there? You have your family. You have your child and your niece – and the baby. And the business. But there is nothing for me. I belong here.'

Celia nodded. 'Will you write to me? Tell me how you are?'

'And you. I want to hear how the children are settling in.' She clasped Celia's hand. 'Be patient with them. Take them at their own pace.' Celia hugged Waterton hard, not wanting to let her go.

They caught a taxi straight to the café where they fell on plates of steak and potatoes, followed by custard pudding. Waterton had told her not to let them eat too much initially, but she couldn't help it. They were starving. Her child, her niece and Mirabel had been starving!

Michael stared at his plate. 'It doesn't seem fair that we are free to eat this and all the others have to stay behind.'

'I'm sure that people who know them will come and get them,' said Celia, lamely, because she knew it wasn't true, they were depending on Waterton and people like her to help them because there was no-one else. 'I'm sure there are a lot of French families who would take them in.' This was surely true. But the politicians wanted them kept together, cooped up because they saw them as a threat.

After they had eaten, she swept them to the station. She didn't want to stay in a hotel, wanted to get them away as fast as she could, before the visa types popped up with another problem. On the way, they all fussed over Mirabel, whether she was too hot, too cold, wanted feeding. Lily was so quiet, held her baby and the soft purple cat she wouldn't let go of. Celia found herself longing that someone else was there, that Mr Janus had come, and he could talk to their children, where she could not.

They clambered onto the train, took a compartment and Mirabel cried then fell asleep. Michael leant his head against the window, watching the countryside flashing past. He'd told her that he thought they'd been in the camp for three months.

She couldn't help it. The question she was supposed to be suppressing burst out. 'Why didn't you tell them who you were? I would have come to get you.'

He shook his head. 'We – Lily – thought *he* would come and get us. We were waiting.'

'When did *he* leave you?'

Michael shook his head, leant against the window again.

FORTY-NINE

Stoneythorpe, July 1939

They travelled through the night, stayed one night in Paris, then journeyed on to Calais, took the ferry and then they would go on to Stoneythorpe. Michael talked off and on but Lily would only really talk about Mirabel, wanting to discuss her feeding, sleeping, how she responded to stories. Celia said she was putting on weight rapidly – which was true. She seemed the healthiest of all of them. One night, when Michael was asleep, she asked Lily about the birth.

'Did you have a doctor helping you?'

Lily shook her head. 'We don't need doctors. That's what he said. They try and poison us with their medicine so we'll always be slaves.'

'Oh. Who said this?'

Lily shook her head but Celia knew it was Brennan. She had to remember her promise to his mother. Not to do anything. Not to tell the police. Although she had no idea where he was and Lily wasn't going to say.

'Did Mr Brennan go with you to Spain?'

Lily's eyes flickered and Celia knew she was right.

'Did he die?'

Lily shook her head. And then she said they had all travelled abroad to help the fight. But Mirabel was always crying and nothing seemed to go right so he took them to the camp, said he would come back for them.

She waited, didn't want to ask. The train rushed on.

'I knew he wasn't coming back. He didn't love us anymore. I could tell.'

'I'm sure he still did love you,' she said, weakly, only wanting Lily not to hurt. They would never have come with Celia, if they thought he was coming for them.

'How could he leave us there?' Lily turned to her and she was weeping. Celia took her in her arms. They carried on, through the night.

Tom came to meet them at Dover. He said that he'd waited to receive every boat until he found them. Emmeline had said in a letter to the hotel he was still staying with them, dividing his time between Stoneythorpe and London. They all depended on him.

'I thought you might need some help,' he said.

'I do.' She felt a rush of gratitude to him. She hated how awkward she was with them, with Lily in particular.

'We'll drive back to Stoneythorpe,' he said. 'I imagine you've had enough trains.'

They all nodded. He held them all, lifted Mirabel into the sky.

'Whose is the baby?' he said, as they were driving back, the three in the back, asleep.

'Lily's. And I don't know. Emmeline – I know what she'll say.'

'Ignore her. I should have come with you to France.'

He was right. 'I wish you had. It's too awful there. The people are suffering so much.'

'Well, that's just the beginning if there's a war. Although if you ask me, they can't go to war again.

'I don't know. Maybe.' She knew what she'd seen. The Führer wasn't going to stop, all his desires were bound up in wanting land. So either they let him take every country he wanted – or they took him to war. And Michael would be old enough to go.

'You think they were with Brennan?' he whispered. 'What if he and his types come for her?'

'He left them, lying that he'd come back. But Lily knows he won't and even if he did – how could they forgive him, deserting them.'

Celia saw Lily's eyes fluttering. She looked out of the dark window, then fell asleep again.

When they finally arrived, Tom carried Lily and the baby upstairs, then Michael. Emmeline stood there at the door, watching.

'Should we wake them up to let them eat?' said Celia. 'Just Mirabel, maybe.' She took the warm bundle from Lily's arms and down to the kitchen. Emmeline took her noiselessly, fed her with a cup because there was no bottle. 'I'll do it!' she said. 'How would you know?' She rocked her to sleep and took her back upstairs to Lily.

Celia sat by Mr Janus and Tom in the sitting room. She was too tired to think, even to speak. Emmeline stormed in.

'How could you?' she said. 'It's all your fault.'

'Emmeline?'

She was framed against the hearth, a fire goddess, furious, aflame.

'What's he done to her? What has your son done to her?'

'I—'

'I knew it. Do you know, I knew it all along? I knew he was a bad sort. You got him from nowhere. He came from nowhere. And what kind of behaviour did he learn? Now we see! She was good before he came. She was perfect. And he came and ruined her – and now look at her. She's a child. And he's ruined her.'

'Emmeline—' Tom held out his hand.

'Oh, don't you start. He gets his corruption from you! You did it to Celia, all those years ago, and now your son is carrying on the tradition of ruining innocent girls.'

'I wanted Tom to, Emmeline,' said Celia. 'I did.'

But that made her even more furious, stamping her foot.

'Emmeline,' said Mr Janus. They had almost forgotten he was there. 'You'll wake everyone up. They'll hear.'

Celia levelled her gaze. 'Emmeline, you ran away with your tutor. Now Lily has done the same.'

Emmeline leapt forward, Mr Janus holding her back. 'She's right, you know.'

'Look,' said Tom. 'We don't know what's happened. Let's leave them to tell us, shall we?'

'I know what's happened. Michael dragged her off so he could do what he wanted to her. He was bad news.'

'It was Brennan. You know that.'

Mr Janus stood up. 'Let's discuss this tomorrow. We'll leave it until the morning.'

Celia sat on the sofa, listening to them walk upstairs, then the sounds of them walking around, over her head in their room. She lay back on the sofa.

Tom soothed her. 'Don't listen to what she says. She's just upset, that's all.'

'But what if she's right?'

'That's Brennan's child. She just can't admit it.'

That night, Celia woke up, her heart pumping hard. Her mind was running wild, overheated. She wanted to reach out and touch him. She ran to Michael's room, then Lily's. They were all there. She knocked on Tom's door, walked in. The fear bulged in her heart, ran riot. She couldn't help it. She reached down, shook Tom awake. 'I can't sleep. You were right. Someone might come for them.'

He opened his eyes. 'How would anyone know they were here? It's much more likely, if you ask me, that the pair of them will try to run away again.'

'They wouldn't!'

'Celia, let's get some sleep. Nothing is going to happen tonight.'

But she couldn't. She heard creaks and bangs, saw shadows passing the windows, but when she looked up, there was nothing there.

Next day, she told Lily and Michael how Rudolf and Verena had died. 'They killed themselves.' They both wept. Then Lily began to talk, words and words spooling out of her, nothing about the present but memories of Rudolf and Verena. They asked Celia questions and she told them every detail she could – although she realised as she did so that some of them were beginning to slip away from her. She told them about the funeral home, how peaceful they were.

'It was because you were selling the house,' said Lily, flatly. She was still clutching the purple cat, wouldn't let it go, held it as tightly as she held Mirabel.

Celia shook her head. 'Yes, a little. But they were afraid of war, most of all.'

'I would have looked after them!' said Michael. 'Why didn't they wait for us?'

The guilt on his face pained her heart. 'It wasn't your fault. It was the war.'

They still needed to sell the house. As Tom said, it would be impossible to sell if there was a war. But Celia knew the children wanted to stay. It was the only security they had. They'd lost everything else. How could they take them to a place in Winchester they'd never seen before?

'We need the money,' she said, forcing herself. 'Let's ask Mr Crennet to try the girls' school again. Offer them even more money off.'

'I'll try,' said Tom. 'The market is changing.'

Celia looked at all the boxes, everything they had loved packed away, and her heart sank. Emmeline and Tom were right. They should take what they could get. The children were back with them and that was all that mattered.

Lily was often silent. They were all looking, she thought, for those small moments when Lily began to talk and they thought that she was coming back to them. She would give them a little. And then she would stop, close off, and they did not know how to reach her again.

They agreed not to ask them questions, decided to share between them what they heard, judged that they would hear eventually. Celia thought Lily and Michael had mellowed, become pleased to see them, but then sometimes they closed off again and you couldn't talk to them. Lily wandered round the parlour, crying over her grandparents. They all took turns to hold Mirabel. Lily and Michael said very little. But sometimes, Celia turned a corner and heard them speaking to each other, whispering words she couldn't catch.

Albert came down from university and Celia's heart broke to see how distant he felt from his sister. He was trying to talk to them, just as they did, and none of them could get through.

Mr Janus spent most days out, meeting up with his anti-war society friends. Albert had gone to some of the meetings with him. She was grateful for Tom, always there with them.

Sometimes, Lily woke in the middle of the night, screaming, and Celia ran to her but got there and the door was barred. Lily said to her – and Emmeline who was usually there too – that she didn't need help, she had just had a bad dream. Celia bought Michael a sketchpad and pencils but he didn't seem to want to draw. 'Why not draw Mirabel?' she said. 'So we don't forget how she looked.' He shook his head.

The days passed. Celia sometimes looked out of the window, thought she saw a shadow. But then she looked again and it was gone. Nothing there. She was scaring herself, seeing things behind the trees.

She and her sister skated around each other, angry, resentful.

'Don't,' said Tom. 'Don't tell Emmeline what you're thinking. Honesty is overrated. Don't. It won't do any good to say it. I promise. Don't.'

'I'll try.'

And she did, she really did. She tried not to say it. She talked of different subjects, the baby's feeds, how there surely wouldn't be a war. Hitler would see sense – who would want to wreck the peace that had brought them so much?

'Try harder,' said Tom.

And then, in a small disagreement about how warm to make the baby's bottle, it all came. The leaves cleared away from the spring and it bubbled up and wouldn't stop.

'How do you know it was his idea to run away?' Celia cried.

'How do you know it wasn't her? She wanted to be with Brennan, not us, and Michael was her cover!'

The harsh words flowed and Tom came into the kitchen and Emmeline had slapped Celia and she was standing there, hand on face, outraged.

'Stop that!' he said, pulling them apart. Celia held tight to his hand, breathless and ashamed. 'You have to accept what they are now.'

'We should never have found them,' said Celia, breathing hard. 'With the war. We need to go. If we went to America, they wouldn't have to fight.'

'I'm not going to America. Or letting you take my grandchild. You can go alone.' Emmeline spat out her words, stalked out of the room, her hair awry.

Lily was talking more and Tom said Michael had told him a few things – Celia tried hard not to be jealous. Tom said Michael had told him a little about the house, said it was called Year Zero and they'd had many ideas. 'Sounds harmless enough,' said Tom. 'In the ideas at least.'

Celia nodded. 'You're probably right. I suppose at least we must be glad that someone took them in. Until. Well.' She looked at the floor. 'I don't suppose he is talking about that?'

He nodded. 'Michael won't say much. He won't talk. I think he is protecting her. Keeping her secrets.'

Celia was tossing, turning, couldn't sleep. Images flashed through her mind. Nothing would settle. She turned onto her side, tried to sleep again. Still the house creaked and banged around her. And then she sat up. Footsteps, passing her room. She waited, crept to the door. There was nothing. She thought she'd heard footsteps before, Emmeline going to find Tom. She'd been imagining it. But this was *real*. Someone was out there. She pulled a cardigan around herself, pushed on slippers, padded quietly out of her door, trying not to creak as she stepped.

She walked along the corridor and could hear nothing. Perhaps she had imagined it. Then she heard a tiny, muffled cry. The baby! She hurried forwards, down the stairs.

She looked down. There in the hallway, two figures, shadowed, bent close together. One was holding a baby. A woman. It was Lily. It had to be.

Celia stood there, watching. Was she with Michael? It didn't look like him – too tall. And it surely wasn't Tom. What were they *doing*? The baby was wrapped tightly, so it didn't cry, she supposed. They were deep in conversation, heads bent together. The man put his arm on her waist.

'I don't know,' the girl was saying.

He took her hand. She walked forward. The baby was whimpering.

Celia took a step and it creaked out. Lily looked up – and the man with her turned and she saw it was Mr Brennan. She hurtled down towards them and Lily screamed and Celia stopped halfway down.

'You're coming!' Brenan shouted at Lily.

Celia stood still, watched. Lily looked up at her – then at him. Celia could see – she was wavering. 'Stay with us, Lily,' she said. Lily looked at her and the baby, took a step away from Brennan.

'Don't you dare,' he shouted at her. Then he called up towards Celia. 'I'm taking both of them. They're mine.' He pulled the baby out of Lily's arms. Lily screamed again, pitched herself towards him and he caught her.

Celia threw herself down the rest of the stairs. 'Stop!' she shouted. And then she was running towards them and Brennan was dashing towards the door and suddenly there were more of them, Tom, Mr Janus, Emmeline, and Emmeline had Lily and the baby was crying and Tom was running after Brennan. Lily was screaming, weeping.

'I'll get her back!' he was shouting. 'I'll come for her!'

The men ran out into the darkness.

Lily was clutching at Emmeline. 'Don't call the police! Don't! I'll never speak to you again if you do.'

Celia ran past them, out of their great front door onto the drive.

It was so dark, she could see nothing. Men were shouting but she couldn't make out where they were. Then she heard a cry. She bent down. A child's cry. A baby. Her eyes adjusted and she saw it in the gloom. Mirabel's blanket! She reached down and there was the child. She picked her up and cradled her in her arms. She felt the child's warmth, held her close as the men's running feet were further and further away.

'I lost him.' Tom came in to the parlour, breathless. 'I lost him. Samuel is still going but I think Brennan's gone. I think he was hiding somewhere.'

Lily was holding the baby. 'Please don't call the police.'

'Give us one reason why not?'

'We have to,' Celia said. 'He was trying to take you away. And your child.'

'But I wanted to go. He needs me.'

'No, he doesn't.' Celia's heart turned, sickly. Patterns repeating themselves. 'He was the one you went with, wasn't he? We always thought that you and Michael ran away together. But it wasn't about you and Michael, was it? It was about you and him. You ran away with him.' They had given him no thought at all, the pale, shy man who'd done the teaching, poor, schoolmasterly, shy. They had ignored him. What revenge he had taken!

'We wanted to run away!'

Emmeline looked at her. 'He's the father of your baby. He took you and you were just a child.'

'Stop it! It's not true. You're making it low, when it was—'

'What – love?'

'More than that! We were being free, making a new society, we were going to be different from all of you, stuck in your world of money and spending and bills and how you say – men do this and women do that. You are all so cruel and rigid! You make people sit in these horrible holes that have nothing to do with the truth of their souls, nothing! You torment people. We could be free, men and women, loving and living together. All of us.' She clutched Mirabel close.

'He wanted to be free of your parents, I'd say,' said Tom. 'Men will say anythi—' Celia glared at him, cut him off.

'Maybe he's right,' Celia said. 'But couldn't you have stayed and tried to change us?' Although when she said it, she knew how foolish it sounded.

'He said he'd come back for us,' said Lily. 'And he did.'

'But how did he find you here?'

'He was looking for us,' she said, proudly, heart swelling. 'He loved us. He really did. He looked for us in the camps. In ours, there were people we'd known and they told him we'd come back to England.'

Celia shook her head. 'When did he start persuading you to run away?' And then she knew. When she had come into the room and he was showing them a picture of the world. The Secondary World. She'd heard the word freedom and he had stopped talking. Why had she not realised? She had seen nothing in Brennan's pale eyes, his maps, his quiet voice. And all the time his mind had been full of plans.

'Why Michael? Why did he have to come too?' She was aware she sounded petulant, couldn't help it. Why couldn't they just have left him behind? Why if they needed each other, did they have to have him as well?

'Because he needed to be free too! We couldn't leave him to your world. Oppressive, Brennan said.'

Tom raised an eyebrow. 'Was bringing Michael Mr Brennan's idea?'

'Mine. But of course he wanted him! We were friends.'

'Of course.'

Lily held the baby to her. Mirabel was asleep now.

'What have you done?' Celia heard herself saying, knowing she shouldn't say it. 'Didn't you think we'd miss you? Didn't you think your mother would be weeping every night, your father desperate? Didn't you think of me? I searched everywhere for Michael – and then I lost him again.'

Lily looked up at her, clear-eyed. Of course she didn't. Why would she? She was young, confident that the world was there to serve her, she didn't need to hold on to things, grasp hard to people like adults did. Family were just pulling you down, when you could go out and be free.

'I presume he had sent you a letter or something. Thrown stones at your window. Got you to come down. Or were you in contact for longer?'

She nodded, her hair over her face.

'You've been meeting him.' The creaks on the floorboards. The shadows from the windows. This time she had actually been right.

She saw a tear on Lily's face.

'And tonight was your chance to go.'

The tear dropped onto the baby's cheek.

'But you didn't. Why didn't you?'

She looked up at Celia. 'It's – different. He loves me. I know he loves me.' Tom snorted and Emmeline shushed him. 'But I have her, now, Mirabel. And I can't let her go. In the house, she'd be owned by everyone. You don't have parents. You don't have children. You share. I don't want to share her. I want her for me.' Celia looked at the baby's sleeping face, the tiny cheeks and the pale eyelashes. They had to do better with her.

'You share?' said Tom. 'Did you share each other too?'

'People always ask that sort of thing. It wasn't the point.' Lily laid Mirabel down. 'You all treat me like a child! I'm not a child. Mr Brennan saw that! Why can't you! I'm just as grown as the rest of you!'

Tom walked towards them. 'Look, Lily—'

The door opened and Michael was there, standing in his pyjamas. 'What's happening?' He looked at Lily. 'What's going on?'

'Brennan came back for her,' said Emmeline. 'And Mirabel. Samuel is trying to find him but we think we've lost him.'

Michael took a step towards Lily. 'And you were going to go? Without me?' She didn't reply. He looked around.

Emmeline shrugged. 'Without all of us.'

'But he abandoned us. We had nothing! He just left us in the mountains. We might have starved.'

'We didn't.'

'Only because the Red Cross found us! Why is he coming back for you now? I can guess. He wants money. Just like all the money we took for him last time. Does he want money?'

She shook her head.

'That's why you asked me where the key to Mama's office was. He's made you take her money.'

Celia felt in her pocket for her office key. Missing. There had been two thousand pounds in there.

'Is this true?'

Lily looked away.

It couldn't be true! Celia put her hand out to her son. 'Don't get upset, Michael. We don't know what happened.' But Michael wasn't listening. He was rushing forward, coming towards Lily, trying to grasp her. Tom threw himself between them, held them apart.

'You've always hated him!' she cried. 'I thought we were going away together! We'd come for you later!'

'He's always lying to you! Stay with me,' Michael was saying. 'Please stay with me.' Celia, gazing at him, knew he'd love Lily more than he ever did her, his own mother, no matter what, and knew she had been the same to her own parents, wanting to leave. How had she ever thought they would be different? She watched the anguish cross his face as he looked at Lily and knew he was flying from her, sure as if he were up in the clouds. She watched him soar, couldn't wave goodbye.

Celia went to check and a thousand pounds had gone. She forced herself not to say anything to Lily, let her father do it. She had been controlled by Brennan and too young. Too loyal. Emmeline refused to speak to her.

'Aren't you going to apologise?' Celia said to Emmeline. 'For everything you said about Michael?' Her sister's realisation, on that night, that Michael was only the cover. It should be enough, she knew – but still.

'Lily was perfect before he came. Your bad blood.'

'Mine?' She almost flew at her sister. But they had lost too much. They couldn't lose each other as well. She ran from the room instead.

Celia rushed outside, sat on the grass with her face in her knees. A fine mesh of moonlight lay over the flowers, the spiral of the clematis, the dancing whorls of the roses. She felt a coolness pass over her.

'You must be cold out here.'

She looked up at Tom. 'You told me not to say it.'

'Well, you were always going to. Perhaps things will be better now you have. You're not wrong, though. Whatever happened, it's not as simple as Lily says.'

'He was clever. And Lily too. They were in love, or at least she was. Trying to do anything to be together.'

In love. As she had been once. How pure it was.

They sat. She watched the dew glimmer on the grass.

'Would you come to America with us?' The words just came out.

Tom coughed, surprised. 'If there's a war?'

'Yes. I can't bear to see Michael fight. And I want to tell him the truth about you. If you agree.'

'Of course. But why America? Anywhere would do, wouldn't it? Is it because you want to be with *him*?'

'Who?'

'Jonathan.'

She shook her head. 'No. He's married now, anyway.' He and Violet. Happily ever after. 'Just America – it's young. Different.'

She couldn't leave the business, though. The Ministry needed her. She could send Michael on his own. Apart from him again. Her heart was torn.

They fell silent.

He stood for a while, looking over her. It was almost as if he had forgotten she was there. 'I should tell him the truth,' she said. 'About you. He needs to know.'

Tom nodded. 'But maybe we should wait. I can wait. He's had so many shocks.'

'I will tell him.'

'There will be war. It's inevitable.'

'But if there is to be a war, we should seize moments, shouldn't we? It might be our last chance.'

He was staring past her. She couldn't see his eyes, couldn't guess at his meaning.

'It's true,' she said, carefully.

He nodded. 'The future. What do you think about the future?'

'I don't know. I might join Mr Janus's anti-war protest. And even Mr Brennan wasn't wrong with those words Michael said he said about war. It's so hopeless.'

'Just before Mr Janus arrived, you were talking. All those things you said about Emmeline. You thought that Emmeline and I were in love with each other.'

'I did. I'm ashamed of it now. You just seemed so close.'

'I can't see how you ever thought that.'

Jealous. I was jealous!

Tom said, 'I was trying to help your sister. And your family. That's all. There wasn't anything else to it. Because I was doing it for you.'

'What?'

'Everything I was doing for your family. Emmeline, your parents, the house. It was only for you.'

She looked up at him. 'For me?'

'All of it. For you. For when you came back. When you sent me that letter saying you were going to Germany, I realised. I hurried to Stoneythorpe but you'd already gone.'

She breathed, thought. 'What were you going to say?'

'I was going to tell you not to go. I was going to say – you can't. When you said you could be gone for a long time, that you didn't know how long. That's when I realised. I had to stop you. All this time, I thought you were here. And when you were about to go – I thought that anything could happen. You could meet someone else there, fall in love with him. And get married. You wouldn't return.'

'You thought that?'

'Your letter was very final.' And he was right, it had been final. She had written it saying to herself: *This must be the last time.* She was going to forget about him, put him out of her mind. That's what she'd told herself. And instead it had done the opposite. He had come to find her.

She felt laughter bubbling up in her throat. 'We're always out of sync,' she said. 'Never in time.'

'What do you mean?'

And then everything that had happened made her feel grand and bold and the words came pouring out. 'Because every time I am in love with you, you're not in love with me. And back and forth! You love me, I don't love you. Over and over.'

She saw his face crumble. 'So that's what you're saying. You don't love me. I thought – when you were so angry about Emmeline. That there was—'

'No! No! That wasn't what I meant. Not at all! You know what I mean. Always at the wrong time.'

He crouched down to face her. 'Well, what about now? Is this the right time?'

The emotion sweeping her was so strong that she could hardly think. She almost wanted to push him away, it was so heavy, bearing her over. *This will be how it is*, a voice whispered, the air around it rushing as if she was holding a shell to her ear. *This emotion. You'll have to carry it every day.* The tide was battering her in the sea, pulling her forwards. She could let it – or she could run away, opt for what she knew. Safety.

She looked up, turned towards it. 'Yes,' she said. 'Yes, it's the right time.' The wave pulled her in.

Jonathan sent a letter inviting her and anybody who was with her to come to America to safety. He said that New York was the same and wrote about how safe America was. He said Violet sent her love. He wrote that they would all be welcome. He would care for them. Her heart cracked at his generosity. They discussed it – but really, how could they go? It scared Lily to go to town, let alone go to America. She wrote back, thanking him, saying they couldn't go – it would be too much for Lily, they must take it slowly. She said that she had Tom now, and Lily had a child.

Tom put his arm around her in the daytime, they stayed downstairs after everyone had gone at night. He held her tight and she tried to forget the others who were always with her, Jonathan, Arthur, Michael, Louisa, Shep, her parents. They surged back into her mind, but sometimes it was free, a blank page just for him and so she had to hope and cling to that, tell herself that eventually that would become more clear space to be filled up with love, the loss wound underground, always there but not at the front. She loved him, he loved her. That was enough.

The gas masks were issued in July to all of them. They went to the church hall in the next village and stood in a queue to be fitted by two weary volunteers. Even Mirabel had a mask in a canvas covering that tied around her legs like a nappy, made her look a bit as if she was diving under the water. They read the leaflet and practised putting them on, pulling the masks over their heads and tightening the straps. It felt hot and suffocating, smelled of disinfectant. When you breathed in, the mask stuck to your face and made you sick. Lily thrust hers off, refused to wear it and pulled it off the baby.

'Don't force her,' said Tom.

The leaflet said to keep them with them at all times, but that seemed too much so they debated keeping them in the cellar – but thought that would be too far away if the real gas came. So they stacked them in a pile in the sitting room corner.

Celia took Michael to her. 'I have to tell you about your father,' she said.

'It's Tom, isn't it?'

'You knew?'

'I guessed. Anyway, I look like him. Why didn't you want me to know?'

'I thought there had been enough change,' she said, carefully. When had he guessed? She had been trying to protect him. Instead she had only added to the lies.

'I'm sorry.'

'It doesn't matter. Can I go and see him now?'

'Of course.' She heard him thundering downstairs and to the dining room, where Tom was looking over some figures. She heard laughter and shouts. He was happy.

That night, Michael and Lily stayed up late, and after supper – Tom said they needed a break from Miss Violet's jars and asked Mrs Code from the village to bring up some pudding and they ate sponge and custard after the chicken – Lily brought the baby down to sleep in the parlour and Tom put some records on the gramophone. Mr Janus was out at a meeting but they supposed he wouldn't mind missing it, if it were only a small celebration.

They listened to the music. Fly away with me. Celia smiled, looked across at Michael, but he was gazing at Lily.

'We should dance,' said Tom. And so they did – he put his arms around her and they began, whirling around the room. She felt his hand against her back, leant into him. Emmeline was smiling, dancing with Mr Janus in her mind, and Michael and Lily were dancing too. And their arms were around each other and they were smiling and even though there would be a war, surely even now, whatever Mr Chamberlain said, and they had lost so much, they still had each other and there was music and they could dance. She looked through the window and the stars glimmered through the cloud.

FIFTY

Stoneythorpe, August 1939

Celia was rushing from bedrooms, opening the doors, shouting. The air around was hot, the stones under her feet were burning and the sky was on fire too. The log was in front of the back room and it was burning.

She started to panic, ran back and straight into Tom. 'We can't get out,' she said. 'Emmeline?' She'd run back for her.

'She's out. I helped her,' he said. 'It's just us.'

The heat was all around her. 'We can't get out,' she said again. The panic was flaming her chest.

'We can,' he said. 'Lucky you have your clothes on.' She started to tell him she'd been walking outside but he wasn't listening. And then he was tearing at her gown so she could put it over her mouth and seized her hand and he was pulling her up the stairs. The flames were burning at her feet and she couldn't breathe. She had taken Lily out and rushed back for Emmeline – but Tom had come back for her. Everything was on fire.

He was pulling her up the staircase. 'You need to jump,' he said. 'Then maybe we can go back another way. I don't know. But you need to jump.'

He pulled her to the upstairs window, by the top of the staircase.

She stared out. The whole place was flaming. 'I can't.' The house was on fire. The flames were coming high towards her. She looked down and all of it was burning. The house, their home, the place they had given so much to.

'I can't,' she said. 'I can't leave it.' Jumping. She couldn't do it. Arthur had jumped. Louisa had fallen. She couldn't do it too.

418

He grasped her, hard. 'What are you talking about? Come on! There is no time to lose!'

'I can't.' Something in her was dragging her down. They'd have nothing. She'd have nothing. They would have to start all over again. She didn't know whether she could do it. The moment was so violent, so absolute.

'You have to, Celia,' he said. 'You have to.' And as he was saying it, she knew he was right. She had to make a new life. She had to do it for Michael and Lily and baby Mirabel – and maybe for Tom, too. She held his hand and clambered onto the window ledge. She heard people shouting '*Jump!*' below her. She thrust herself from the window and saw below her Michael, Lily, Mirabel, Emmeline and Mr Janus. She fell out towards them. She felt as if she was flying.

She landed with a smash on the ground, even though they'd tried to catch her. Her whole body felt broken. The hot air burned her skin. Michael was standing over her.

'Are you hurt?'

'No.' Everything hurt. 'How's Tom?'

'He's fine. Don't get up. Wait for the doctor.'

But she had to. She couldn't just lie there. 'Help me up.' Michael pulled her up and it didn't hurt to stand. Just ahead of her, Tom was standing too. She leant against them, Tom and Michael, watched the house in flames. Lily stood there with the baby, a little apart from them but nearly together. For a moment, Celia thought she saw a figure at the window. A man, Brennan. But then she blinked and the window was empty of all but flames.

The fire danced forward, ate it all. The flames that you couldn't stop, not if it was your house, not if it was the whole of Europe, consumed by a new flame of anger and war. She watched it fall. Michael held her hand. Tom's arm around her. She held tight to their hands. In the morning the sun would rise again.

EPILOGUE

Everybody had gone to bed. Celia sat in the parlour. The house was quiet. And yet it wasn't. There were a hundred, thousand voices, speaking all the time. She could hear them, always. Her mind could never be free because they were always talking. No one would buy Stoneythorpe due to the war and so the voices would never let go. She could spend the rest of her life trying to keep it up, please all those voices who made her keep their secrets. And then Michael and Lily would have to do the same. Their children again, always attempting to shore up the place – and for what? It was only a house. She had given so much to trying to keep it. She couldn't let her children live like that, chained to bricks and mortar. And with war, everything would be lost, and big houses would be blights, taking up space that could be better used for everyone. Her heart tore for her love of it, her childhood, her parents. They had to live free of the shadows.

She couldn't do it. It would be a crime. But then...

She was the only one who could do it. Set them all free.

She found one of Tom's cigarettes, lit it. It reminded her of Red, running across the rooves of New York, always free. She held it up to the sky. The idea flooded around her. How they could never let go of it, however hard they tried. The insurance.

It was an act of love. It would set her free, set them all free. She stood up, walked to the window. She held the cigarette to the thick gold curtain at the window. A bright flame came and began dancing, like a tiny genie jumping up the curtain.

'But what are you doing?' cried the house. 'I did so much for you!'

She turned away, looked towards the sky. When she turned back to the curtain, there were a thousand genies, all dancing, gambolling across the thick gold. They made the world new. They would set them free, forever, so they could stop looking back. The genies danced further, tore on through the room. She watched them for a while. Then she turned to run upstairs to the bedrooms. 'There's a fire!' she shouted. 'Fire! Everyone! Run!' Michael, Lily, Mirabel. Tom, Emmeline, Mr Janus, they would all come running out. She'd done it now. No turning back.

The fire was behind her, burning it all down, and they would rush into the light. The world circled around them, all of it thrown into the air now, but it was their own, what they had made of it, how they would go on. And they would go on, whatever came, even if it was war. They had a new way now. The voices of everybody from the past, talking all at once, all the people who had come to the house, been a part of their lives, over all of the years. They could hear them now. They were walking beside her. The stars burned the darkness into a thousand pieces.

AFTERWORD

I heard the Witts in my mind for years. Fragments of Celia and the others came to me at odd times, their voices, their thoughts, even though I did not then know what I was hearing. The fragments grew more numerous, joined together and I finally began writing about them in 2010, fascinated by the lives of the Anglo-Germans in Britain, numerous when the war broke out, but forgotten in the rush to declare good/bad. I always knew I would take them to the moment of when the unimaginable happened once more, the thing that everything had been directed towards stopping: total war returning once more. At school, I learned the Treaty of Versailles off by heart for A level, the names of those countries that were given self-determination, and that, along with the huge reparations, would protect the world against the resumption of the horror of war. Kept low and poor, territorially and financially reduced, Germany would never fight again.

The opposite was true, of course. The Great Depression raked the world with its cruelties, yet none so much as Germany, where bad governance and crippling payments thrust the country into economic despair – and the febrile climate of resentment and fear that created the ideal conditions for the rise of Adolf Hitler and the evils of the party.

The Second World War saw the great sacrifice of humanity from across the world, some of which has often been obscured in the familiar narratives of the Second World War – the Empire soldiers who fought so bravely and were promised so much, the soldiers of Russia who arguably drove the outcome of the war. The Home Front saw great suffering, as those left behind tried to continue living amongst the loss and uncertainty. The photographs of the time are incredibly moving: a girl comforting her doll in the ruins of her home, children attempting to play in rubble and broken furniture. The human sprit fighting through in the midst of despair and loss.

Celia and her family see their world and everything around them change. Europe and America are broken and remade, altered forever, new forms coming from what was torn apart. The Edwardian security, the belief when Victoria died that her fondness for marrying her children into European families would protect against war, was broken apart. The Empire as they knew it would crumble, as countries fought rightly for independence.

Life for Anglo-Germans grew harsh again in the war. Once more they were reviled, mistrusted, hated. Celia and her family have to find a way through once more – but that is another story!

I am grateful to the archivists at the Imperial War Museum, the British Library, the Metropolitan Archives and the archives across the country that I used for this book, to look at letters, diaries and other books and records that told me so much about the period. The words that I have read have coursed through my mind, woven through my dreams, been everything for me so at times I was not living now but then.

It has been an incredible privilege to work on the Witts for so much of my life, a period in which my life has changed in ways I could not imagine too! I had wanted to write on the period ever since I saw the trenches in Flanders, on a primary school trip, unable to imagine then and now how men managed to live and fight in such tiny spaces, for years. And the more I read and researched, the more I realised how the First World War shaped lives and feelings for years to come – there was no cut-off point. I have learnt so much from the letters and diaries that I have read in archives and record offices across the country. The Witts are fiction – but every word they say is based on the reality of people in the past, who kept fighting and hoping, even after the war was over.

When I was a child, I made a time machine out of the box that the washing machine had arrived in and decorated it with foil. I put my brother in there and pretended to him it was a time machine. Now I make time machines out of words – thank you for coming in it with me.

I am very grateful to my editors: Clare Hey, who has edited this book so brilliantly and given so much sensitive thought and heart to the family and their story, and to Gen Pegg for being such a superb guide and inspiration and making raw words much better – thanks for everything! My first editors, Jemima Forrester and Jon Wood, were a guiding inspiration and were so generous and gave so very much to the book, when it at times seemed an overwhelming mass of emotion and history.

Thank you to Orion for their wonderful support, to Katie Espiner and David Shelley, Harriet Bourton and my brilliant publicists Gaby Wood, Sam Eades and Virginia Wollstonecraft who were always helping the book and did so much. They were always there for me and the books – and I am so grateful. It is very kind of you! And thank you to Gillian and everyone at Gollancz for making life fun! Thank you to Simon Spanton, who has so many brilliant ideas. I am very grateful to my wonderful agents, Robert Kirby and Ariella Feiner in London and Zoe Pagnamenta in New York, who are always there for me, agents and friends. And to Sue, Sue, Helen and all at Knight Ayton, who are very supportive and friends full of kindness. Most of all to Marcus and Persephone who have to live with me in a different time...

And thanks most of all to my readers, who have given me their time, sent me their thoughts and messages, written and reviewed online, and come to my events – I am so grateful and lucky to have shared some of your lives and I truly could do none of it without you. Thank you.